FLOWER GIRL

A NOVEL

MERIDA JOHNS

Coffee Cup Press

FIRST EDITION

Cover Design by Ruth Miller

Published by Coffee Cup Press

ISBN 978-1-7332790-2-4

Typesetting services by BOOKOW.COM

To All Flower Girls

Acknowledgments

No acknowledgment is sufficient to express my gratitude once again to my husband, Russell, for his loving support, insight, and confirmation of the worthiness of this effort.

My appreciation to my sisters, nieces, close friends, and critique group of women authors whose encouragement drowned out any inner critic that might dare to lurk in the shadows and threaten the completion of the work.

Thank you to my many friends who have followed the creation of this story via social media and whose expectations have kept me accountable for completing this work.

Special thanks to Denise Marie, Janet, Lisa, Marian, Megan, Sue, and Carol, the best cheerleading and beta reader group an author could have.

Finally, sincere thanks to Diane Donovan whose prepublication critique validated the worthiness of tackling the topic of emotional abuse. Many thanks to Kim Bookless, copyeditor, Pat Hertel, proofreader, and Ruth Miller, book cover designer. All of these professionals have helped me make Flower Girl come alive.

Epigraph

"The road is as long and as thrilling as you make it.

Go slow, and the ride is short and boring.

But go fast, and the trip is expansive and enthralling.

Some may say this is life in the fast lane—

I think this is life in the best lane."

Suzanna Jordan - Flower Girl

Prologue

Five o'clock in the morning. A waterfall of worries washes over me, but one remains, one I cannot ignore, one that means my life or death—Do I have the courage to stop this nightmare?

I make out muffled voices and hasty footsteps fading away in the distance. My crisis, already old news, is cataloged on a forgotten document. I am abandoned and left alone with my fear.

I roll to my side and dangle my legs off the bed, gravity pulling my slender five-foot-five body toward the floor. My feet hit the cold cement and rebel—screaming and cramping in pain. My insides shake, and my body wobbles. My eyes blur, and my hands reach out to find the bed. I steady myself and count under my breath, "One, two, three . . ." The agonizing muscle spasms start to fade.

My world plays in slow motion. My eyes drift across the brackish-beige walls, swamp-green curtain, stainless steel instruments, and electronic gadgets—my stomach knots, my heart falls, my mouth goes dry. Helplessness hits me like an animal in a snare.

I spot my possessions, swathed in clear plastic, in the chair in the corner of the room. I hobble over, open, and poke through the bag—a Victoria's Secret midnight-blue lace bra, a red OSU T-shirt, a pair of Gloria Vanderbilt stretch denim jeans, a Coach purse, and white Reeboks. I loosen the ties of the rumpled steel-gray gown and let the garment slip off and land at my feet. To dress in fancy lingerie is absurd, so I toss the bra on the chair and throw on the shirt and jeans.

I stare down at my sneakers and stop. My husband is in my head—I glimpse his squinting eyes and hear his haunting disapproval. "Quit wiggling your feet over the counters of your damn shoes, Suzanna. You'll ruin them!" I shake my head, clench my jaw, and disobey.

I have no strength to bend over and tie the shoelaces. Jonathan would have a nasty comment about this too. I ignore the imagined criticism. My eyes close in victory. *Cherish every step. Each is a grand slam toward deliverance.*

My fingers run through my disheveled hair soaked in sweat. My muscles relax, my brain fog lifts, and the ache behind my forehead fades.

I pull back the curtain circling the bed and grimace—the overhead lights jar me. I pump myself up. *One, two, three, go.* I take off.

I shuffle through the corridor between the beds bordering the room and reach the doorway to the waiting area. If people are here, I am unaware of them. My eyes fix on the escape at the end of the room— the pulsating red exit sign. The floor-to-ceiling doors open, allowing my aching body to limp toward daybreak. The heavy morning breeze hits my face, and the sickening, aseptic scent covering me blows away. I clutch my heart and silently sob. *Thank God I'm alive.*

The joy vaporizes into the humid air. *The war has only begun.* I summon my courage and console myself. *I've gotten this far. I can make it! I can live my truth.*

I gaze up above the horizon and catch sight of my North Star—five points shimmering in the dawn and guiding me toward my purpose. *But before I can help others be their best, I must be my best.*

Outside the sterile walls of a hospital emergency room, I hold my own. I put a stake in the ground. I swear the fight to flee my abuser's snare, save my life, and follow the guidance of my North Star is worth the effort.

Part I

Chapter 1

FLOWER GIRL

I view my life as an open highway crisscrossing the countryside of my beloved home state. Like the scenic and undulating Ohio hill country, there are ups and downs. The challenges are tricky, but their unpredictable nature sustains my interest in seeing what's around the next curve. When things get too risky, off-ramps take me on interludes where I can explore, discover, frolic, and rest. On these forays, I'm playful and skip and run with open arms as a child. I laugh, and I am as free as the breeze whisking over the Buckeye State prairie grass. As soon as my curiosity is satisfied, on-ramps return me to the highway. There, I accelerate to speeds that boost my desire to consume more and more miles of uncharted territory as fast as I can. My philosophy of life: The road is as long and as thrilling as you make it. Go slow, and the ride is short and boring. Go fast, and the trip is expansive and enthralling. Some may say this is life in the fast lane—I think this is life in the best lane.

* * *

Cow Town—that's what some called Ohio's capital. But I always rejected the disparaging moniker of the city where I was born on the first full day of spring, March 21, 1958. To me, Columbus was a perfect place to grow up with a smaller-town charm and residents with Midwest values—integrity, grit, common sense, independence, and self-sufficiency—the kind of principles I'd like to call mine.

Immigrant South Side neighborhoods were falling into decline when I was born. The manufacturing plants were moving overseas, blue-collar laborers were losing their jobs, and white-collar industries and workers were taking their place. The center of everything was The Ohio State University, a city within a city, with a student population rising to twenty-five thousand students.

I grew up in Upper Arlington, an upper-middle-class suburb of Columbus. The village's geographical peculiarity formed three boundaries of the prestigious Scioto Country Club. Hence, the area got the nickname *the Country Club District*. In 1950, my parents, Lillian and Robert Jordan, moved to this affluent address after purchasing a 1930s two-story center hall home with a steel-blue clapboard exterior dolled up with dark blue shutters. The house was what one imagines might exist in a Midwestern upwardly mobile community —a storybook neighborhood of tree-lined streets with sidewalks and well-groomed front lawns and manicured gardens. With three thousand square feet and five bedrooms, the home had more space than my parents' soon-to-be family of four would need. Given my father's budding law career, the house was an indicator of the family's rising social status as much as a place of residence.

Jack arrived soon after my mother and father bought their home. My brother grew to be every parent's dream: socially adept and outgoing, academically accomplished, and athletically talented. From a practical standpoint, the eight-year age difference between Jack and me made each of us only children. We didn't have to share the same friends, teachers, or milestones such as high school awards, graduations, and proms. We basked in our own limelight, and therefore, we weren't rivals. This happy circumstance allowed us to view each other through admiring eyes—for me, Jack was my shining knight, and for him, I was his little darling.

My brother was clean-cut for a teenager during the Beatles era— no long hair or funky clothes. His twinkling, impish dark chocolate-brown eyes and thick, wavy jet-black hair complemented his sculpted features. The sports memorabilia and trophies decorating his room made me believe my handsome brother did the most exciting things.

He was the quarterback on his high school's football team, and given my hometown's focus on the sport, this achievement was a big deal. Jack was also a star member of the baseball and track teams, and how he meshed this athleticism with a healthy social life and achieved the highest honor roll status amazed me.

I ogled my brother's bulky letterman sweater. I loved running my fingers over the tight weave of the raised letters and high school insignia —I considered myself the garment's custodian. Jack drove me into a bad temper the day he gave the prized jersey to his girlfriend Clare. I didn't like the perky, blond-haired cheerleader, who I thought was a phony. Most times, when she visited our home, we acted out a secret battle scene for Jack's attention. When my brother teased me, which he often did, Clare would pucker her lips behind Jack's back and glare at me, signaling to me who was in charge. I'd respond by giving her snake eyes.

"Why did you give the sweater away?" I asked Jack, hands on my hips, tapping my right foot.

My brother bit his lip. "Um . . . because that's what boys give to their girlfriends."

"Well, I thought boys gave their girlfriends kisses, not their clothes!"

Jack raised an eyebrow and grinned. "Just wait. When you're sixteen, a boy will give you kisses *and* his sweater too."

"Yes, but it won't be your sweater," I said through clenched teeth. I turned, hiding a smirk, and stomped toward my room. In my eight-year-old mind, I left Jack standing with his hands on his hips and tapping his foot.

One evening during our family dinner, my brother shared another baffling decision—going steady with Clare! The announcement made my glass of milk slip from my hand, and four pairs of horrified eyes looked on while the white liquid flowed across the tabletop and crashed like a waterfall over the edge to the floor. My misadventure suspended my parents' reaction to Jack's announcement while my mother helped me clean up my mess.

Afterward, with a crinkled forehead and a lawyer stare, my father said, "Jack, better mind your Ps and Qs."

The remark made me wonder out loud, "What's Ps and Qs, Jack?"

I never got an answer since my mother followed with another confounding statement, "No home runs!" Her comment seemed crystal clear to my sibling but left me perplexed. After the exchange, Jack resembled a scolded puppy and excused himself before my mother placed the dessert on the table.

Besides giving up the letterman sweater and going steady, the act that tested the limit of my forgiveness was when Jack gave Clare another prized possession—his high school ring. For me, this was a betrayal of sacred trust, and I put the blame on my sibling's cagey girlfriend. My stomach turned sick when I saw Clare wearing the ring that she had smothered in cotton-candy-pink angora yarn to fit her finger. To alleviate my gastric upset, I turned away, wrinkled my nose, and stuck out my tongue. My mother was too wise to act out like me when she caught Clare's pouty behavior, but it was clear from the look she gave me she disliked Jack's girlfriend too.

Though the event involved Clare, one of my happiest recollections was Jack's senior prom night. My brother was enchanting as he descended the staircase wearing a white dinner jacket and a royal smile. Jack's charisma aside, the fresh flower corsage he had gotten for Clare vied for my attention. After the florist delivered the bouquet in the morning, I tiptoed into the kitchen every half hour, opened the refrigerator door, and gaped at the white orchid beauty lying on a shelf at my eye level. I imagined the sparkling flakes of glitter on the flower's delicate petals were dancing fairy princesses, and I fell to sleep that night thinking no one else but Jack could fill the role of Prince Charming.

My emotions vacillated between happiness and depression when my brother received an acceptance letter from Georgetown University. I was glad Jack would be attending a college that he and my parents talked about in glowing terms as having produced United States presidents, supreme court justices, and scholars with strange names like Rhodes, Truman, and Fulbright. Because my starry-eyed parents had grand plans for Jack, I outwardly celebrated with my family, although my heart ached inside.

At ten years old, I believed my best chum was abandoning me by running off to Washington, DC. *What will I do when Jack is gone? Who is going to tease me? Who is going to give me shoulder punches? Who is going to tell me how special I am?* My mother and father were supportive and loving parents, but no one in my young eyes was comparable to Jack as a cheerleader in raising my spirits. My brother and I had a sibling bond that kept me grounded. When I was sad, Jack told me silly jokes. If I felt plain and unattractive, Jack said I was exceptional and fetching. When I failed to get straight A's, Jack boosted my confidence.

"Grades aren't everything; what matters is what you learn."

I pursed my lips and frowned. "Don't grades show how smart you are?"

Jack put his arm around me. "Nope. Grades are an arbitrary measure. Lots of kids who get top grades are dumber than bricks with no horse sense. What matters more than grades are the choices you make, good and bad, and what you learn from them."

"Pretty heavy," I said, pretending to get the message.

Jack laughed and patted my head. "Just remember. You'll understand when you most need it."

My brother was right. Years later, I got the meaning.

I admired and trusted Jack. During my preteen and teen years, I considered him perfect on every quality society measures an upstanding person. Even though he was at college a thousand miles from home, our bond never faltered. Jack answered my letters, sent mementos, and mailed me funny greeting cards with cartoons and jokes. By the end of my brother's college days, I had plastered one wall of my room with a collage I made out of these Hallmark keepsakes.

I'm a believer in the saying, "What goes around comes around." In a letter to Jack, I wrote I was going steady with a boy named Gary. My brother responded to the point. "You better mind your Ps and Qs with that guy. Remember, no home runs!" Unlike years earlier, I now understood the meaning of those words. I laughed to myself as I folded the letter. *Just third base for you, Gary!*

By the time I graduated from college, Jack was a lawyer working in environmental law with a preeminent firm in Columbus. He was married, though thankfully not to Clare. His wife, Lorna, an attorney too, focused on social justice and worked as a public defender. What a dream sister-in-law. The first time we met, she made me the centerpiece, asking me questions about myself. "Jack says you are a great dancer. What do you like best about dancing? Where did you learn to dance? What made you want to be a dancer? Who is your favorite dancer?" Lorna listened to my responses and gained my trust and confidence. In a matter of minutes, I was spilling out secrets and emotions that went past my passion for dancing—crushes on guys, breakups with boyfriends, struggles with college classes . . .

I was cute and wholesome as a youngster but not a conformist like Jack. Straddling the baby boomer and X generations, I preferred the 1960s counterculture to the 1970s pop culture. I liked stretching the rules, but when I strayed too far, my mother would say, "Suzanna, you were born a decade too late to be a flower child. Straighten up!" I was uncertain how to interpret the command, except I tried hard to have excellent posture.

Unlike the real flower children of my brother's era, my understanding of the seminal events of the era came more from book learning. Different social and political contexts colored our worlds. A five-year-old when the assassination of John Kennedy occurred and a ten-year-old when the assassinations of Martin Luther King and Bobby Kennedy took place, my perspectives were different than Jack's. After reaching my teenage years, I was more concerned with the devastation of Midwest tornados than preparing for a nuclear attack.

Jack obtained educational deferments and avoided military service. Therefore, the Vietnam War was on the periphery of my vision. I was fifteen when the war ended, and afterward, the military transitioned to volunteer service in 1974. Thus, I had no personal association with the draft or the terror or devastating impact the baby boomer war had on many service members and families.

Still, at sixteen, the significance of the Watergate scandal and the crimes President Nixon and his band of crooked men directed did not elude me. Sunday dinner conversations with my family centered on Watergate and taught me firsthand about the legal and constitutional implications and tactics these powerful men orchestrated. My family's discussions influenced my beliefs for governmental transparency, separation of powers, and freedom of speech as lynchpins in protecting our democracy. Dad was fond of quoting Thomas Jefferson during this period. "Eternal vigilance is the price of liberty," he'd say. Later in my life, those words would give me the courage to fight for my freedom when my life hung by a thread.

I'm not sure when I evolved into the *Flower Girl*. My mother's haranguing and comparison, no doubt, prompted my father and Jack to anoint me with the pet name. My imitation of the favorite rock songs Jack listened to may have influenced the nickname's selection too. Often my parents and brother found me impersonating rock singers and pantomiming their guitar strumming and strange stage moves. At those times, my mother issued her familiar refrain, "Suzanna, you were born a decade too late to be a flower child. Straighten up!"

I adored the Beatles. And the sounds of the Kinks, the Doors, and Creedence Clearwater Revival pulsating from the record player in Jack's bedroom mesmerized me. I'd slip into my brother's room when he wasn't home and fantasize I was a spy and examine the album covers of these artists. I was sure the psychedelic colors and intricate ink designs held hidden meanings. I pictured these as portals to places of provocative fantasy—places where I wanted to go. However, it was a Zombies' cover—the sunflower dancing in a breeze—not the band's creepy name that caught and held my attention.

The flower girl image accelerated during my primary grade school years when I started collecting blossoms from our neighbors' gardens. I thought, *If I'm a flower child, I need flowers!* Between spring and autumn, I'd gather my bounty and create necklaces and head wreaths and cheerfully wear these everywhere. Doubtless, this is when I first cultivated my awareness of nature's beauty. Though the neighborhood was devoid of colorful sunflowers, my head spun from the synchronicity of the soft hues splashing against the stirring sunny shades. The mixture of refined and rough textures and the merger of pungent perfumes transported me to a fairyland. Years later, my appreciation of beauty would be a healing balm that helped me reclaim faith in myself.

My inner flower child bloomed in two ways. The first was my decision when I was ten years old to address my parents by their first names. "Why are you calling me by my first name?" my mother asked when I first called her Lillian.

"Because that's your name. Robert calls you Lillian. So does everyone."

"That's not altogether correct. What about Jack?" my mother asked.

I cast my eyes aside. I had boxed myself in. I searched for an argument. "I don't want to be like Jack."

"But you want to be like everyone else?"

I squinted my eyes into slivers, giving myself time to find a rebuttal. "I won't be *exactly* like everyone else. All the other kids call their mother Mommy or Mom."

Lillian shrugged. "Well, have it your way," she said, ending the discussion. Lillian wasn't one to waste time on what she considered petty arguments.

Defying my mother's college choice for me was another matter. She fought for having it her way. I wanted to attend the university I cherished—The Ohio State University. Lillian, though, was determined I go to a school I classified as a "girly snob" college in the East. My mother disapproved of me using such derogatory language to label women's colleges promoting education equal to men's. In retrospect, my judgmental attitude was juvenile, if not sexist.

In an attempt to influence me, Lillian put brochures from women's schools on the dining room table for me to see. Each time, I scoffed and resisted her suggestion harder. She, in turn, responded with disappointment and frustration. "Honestly, I would have given anything if my parents had these aspirations for me and the money to make them come true." Lillian's pleas found deaf ears.

By my junior year in high school, Dad had switched from practicing the law to teaching it. He was now a tenured professor at my favorite university's law school. I used Dad's position to my advantage in cheeky counters to my mother's pleas. "I don't understand what the problem is with OSU. After all, Dad's a professor there. OSU is good enough for him; it should be okay for me."

My mother would throw me a stern, cocked eyebrow glare, signaling I must be brain dead. Lillian never had an argument that convinced me why it was all right for my father to work at OSU, but it wasn't acceptable for me to be a student there. "That's a horse of a different color," she would always say. Unlike the comment, "No home runs," the explanation of this remark never became clear.

I don't blame my mother for wanting the best for me. She believed a prestigious Eastern women's college would bolster my resume and introduce me to an unparalleled social and professional network. Given her background, those views were understandable. Lillian's roots were in a working-class immigrant community. Her parents' highest expectations for their daughter were graduating from high school and marrying a man with a steady union job at a local factory. In her circle, the view of a woman's proper position was as a homemaker, period, end of story.

After Lillian finished high school, it took gumption to ignore her family's jibes. "There goes the old maid," her father said as she trudged to waitressing jobs in the evenings and on weekends to pay for business school classes. "How are you going to meet a man when your head is always in those books?" her uncle said. My mother, though, persisted and focused her attention on a career as a legal secretary. Whenever Jack or I felt overwhelmed and lost our self-assurance, Lillian would tell us, "Buck up! Keep your sights on the prize. Show up all the naysayers."

After completing secretarial college, Lillian landed a position at a downtown Columbus law firm. Her education paid off, handing her freedom few women in her era and economic level experienced. As far back as I remember, Lillian told Jack and me she wanted the same for us. "I got my education and my own apartment, provided for myself, and charted my own course. I made my choices, took risks, and accepted responsibility for my actions. I expect nothing less of the two of you."

A few years after starting her position, the firm hired a handsome young attorney and World War II veteran named Robert Jordan. Dad loved to relive the first day he laid eyes on Lillian. On Saturdays over breakfast, he regaled us with the juicy details while our mother rolled her eyes as she filled our orange juice glasses. His story never varied: "It was nine o'clock in the morning when I arrived, all spruced up for my interview, and a young paralegal passed me in the corridor who caught my eye. I did a double take. She had the beauty, grace, and all the accoutrements of Rhonda Fleming but with raven-black, not red, hair."

After Robert told his tale, Lillian reported her version. "And the first time I walked by your father in the hallway, my head whipped around for a second view! My heart did a flip because I thought I had seen Randolph Scott." Then, Lillian would throw her head back and laugh. "He was the man of my dreams, and the minute I set eyes on him, I wanted to melt in his arms."

Dad was Midwest through and through. He grew up in the up-per-middle-class neighborhood my parents would later call home. The practice of law is a cornerstone of our family. My paternal grandfather, an attorney in Columbus, was one of the early founders of Upper Arlington. Dad was in college when War II and the draft interrupted his education and path to a law career. After the war, he completed his studies at Georgetown University and returned to Columbus to follow his dream of making a positive difference for people. Dad often said to my brother and me, "I want to do good because I've seen what the bad and the ugly do to the world." He never explained the bad and the ugly, but I always believed his horrific war experiences solidified his desire to help others.

Robert was older than most junior associates with the practice, and his maturity impressed my mother. Lillian often confessed to Jack and me how smitten she was with Dad's dapper appearance and his presence.

"Your Dad's good-looking face broadcasted his character," Lillian said. "He was reliable and trustworthy and practiced those virtues every day. When Robert made a promise, he kept it. If he thought someone wasn't living up to the ethical code, he let them know it. He was the most self-possessed and kindest man I had ever met."

Without knowing it, my mother had set a bar for me; I dreamt of having the same experience when I would find my dream guy and marry him.

During the war, my father was a paratrooper, one of the Screaming Eagles, serving in the distinguished 101st Airborne. He lived through some of the war's largest and bloodiest battles. On D-Day, he parachuted into Normandy near Utah Beach. Later, he fought in the Netherlands. The Battle of the Bulge followed, where, surrounded by German troops at Bastogne, his unit refused to surrender. Dad's unspoken rule was to never speak about the horrors of his war experience. But he shocked Lillian and me and broke it on Wednesday, June 5, 1974, the thirtieth anniversary of the Normandy Invasion.

The three of us were sitting together watching an evening newscast about the Allied invasion on D-Day. The room had a strained quiet, thick and cold like an iceberg, as Walter Cronkite narrated the details of that fateful day. My mother unconsciously rubbed her hands together and glanced at my father, whose glazed eyes locked onto the television coverage as if he had crossed into a different time dimension. Without warning, what Robert said sent chills down my backbone. His jaw tight, eyes frosty, he uttered, "In Belgium, I hid in a canal full of water for two days; the Germans were above me the whole time. I vowed they would never take me alive."

My mother and I turned to each other, and our eyes welled with tears. I understood my father's meaning and what he had planned to do. My heart twisted into a painful knot as it became clear why Dad kept the terrors of war to himself and why he said he had seen the bad and the ugly.

Lillian was a self-made woman, and I've always respected her spunk in the choices she made to shape her future. Besides loving my mother, my father admired her political astuteness and knowledge of the law even though she had never gone to law school. With a sparkle in his eye, Robert often reminded Jack and me, "Your mother could navigate office politics, not me. She saved my bacon many times, knowing where to get information or with whom I should talk." After the compliment, he'd give my mother a squeeze, and she'd respond by giving him a smile and planting a kiss on his lips. It was clear to my brother and me that sparks still flew between Robert and Lillian.

I was proud to be my mother's daughter and have her daring. Lillian had laid down a road map for rebellion, and I intended to follow it. Opposing her wishes to attend an Eastern college was one of our major standoffs. For me, this was out of the question. The Midwest was my choice, and I was sticking with it. When my mother and I got into our spats over the issue, my dad gave me a wink, signaling, "Stick to your guns, Flower Girl."

The Buckeye bug infected me. There wasn't anything better than spending Saturday afternoons in the fall at a Big Ten football game or cheering on the school's basketball team in the winter months. Academics were secondary to me. Like a bee to a flower, the traditions lured me to the school. What could compete with the Men's Glee Club harmony singing Carmen Ohio as they strolled across the Quad the evening before a game? What could be more stirring than hailing the marching band parading into the horseshoe stadium performing Script Ohio and playing the Buckeye Battle Cry?

Had I known my career choice at the time, I could have argued with Lillian that OSU ranked as the top university in the nation in my chosen academic discipline. Like many high school seniors, I didn't have a clue about my strengths, much less have a vision of my future or my vocation. This, without warning, would change within a few weeks after my enrollment at OSU.

Chapter 2

GROUNDWORK

Psychology has so many theories of human development, it makes my head spin: psychosocial learning, social learning, cognitive, and ecological systems theories, to name a few. Putting these aside, I've come to believe the foundation on which we build our lives arises from the people with whom we associate and our experiences—events, environment, cultural traditions —in our early years. I call this groundwork. I love the word because I'm a flower child at heart. I take pleasure in thinking that while my blossoms are delicate and my branches are willowy, I am not fragile. My roots are deep. This is my groundwork, anchoring me and giving me what I need to live and grow.

* * *

For the most part, I can say my high school years were ordinary and lackluster. Jack shined as bright as a quasar, but I was a dimmer star when it came to academics and extracurricular activities. While I was content in being a straight "B" student, an occasional "A" did spike the straight line on my academic record. Nonetheless, my musical talent, creativity, and appreciation of nature's beauty compensated for what I lacked in grades.

Dance—tap, jazz, and ballet—was my calling, and when I was ten years old, I increased my determination to perfect my skill. That year at Christmas, my parents took Jack and me to New York City. Among the extraordinary places we toured, one stood out above the others: the

Radio City Christmas Spectacular. After seeing the dazzling fantasy and the dancers' breathtaking precision and sparkling costumes, dance became one of my passions. To become a Rockette, I convinced myself all I needed was a height of five foot six inches and skill.

To satisfy my hunger for the art form, every musical produced by my school listed "Suzanna Jordan" in the program as a dance chorus member. I loved the energy of the choreography, and when I danced, the world around me evaporated, leaving me in a glorious present where nothing else mattered. To say dancing made me as high as an untethered balloon would be an understatement, and unlike consuming alcohol, the afterglow left me exhilarated with no hangover.

Beyond excelling in dance, my singing voice met my high school choir's standards and matched my dance talent. To add to my repertoire, my piano accomplishments put me at an acceptable middle-skill level, and to showcase my ability, I performed Mozart's *Sonata in C* in my last recital when I was fifteen years old.

I had a circle of supportive friends with similar interests in dance, theater, and music and two best girlfriends—Melanie and Ellen. We were classmates from kindergarten through twelfth grade and as tight as sewn seams. Mel was the best dancer in our group, and in my opinion, her skill could have won her a place on the Rockette team given her five-foot-eight-inch stature. Ellen was a committed musician who played first chair violin in high school and performed in summer community orchestras throughout college.

Besides hanging out together at school, the three of us lived within a block of each other and joined the same Brownie and Girl Scout troops. Each year during scout cookie sales, we made the neighborhood rounds solo to see who could sell more cookie boxes. Melanie always bested Ellen and me, but her success never deterred the two of us from trying to unseat her the following year. So inseparable, our fellow students tagged us as the Three Musketeers, and we assumed the title with honor.

We never missed celebrating our birthdays together, anxious to be part of each other's commemoration and ensure we gave the most wanted gift. Little Lady or Tussy Budding Beauty toilet water spray, soap bars, or bubble bath salts graced the gift table in the early days. Later, books about valiant young women from series like Nancy Drew or Donna Parker captured our curiosity. Those stories stimulated our imagination and prompted each of us to write a series of mysteries. During overnighters in our preteen years, we entertained ourselves until the wee hours of the morning with contrived plots and storylines we thought must become bestsellers. As we got older, we advanced from reading young adult mystery books to romance novels. By the end of ninth grade, we relegated our efforts of being the next successful teen mystery novelists to, at best, the back of a desk drawer but more often to the trash can.

I was a typical teenage girl with emotional ups and downs involving, one way or another, the opposite gender. There were crushes on boys that turned my stomach to mush. In general, these daydreams and romantic fantasies evolved into nothing, and reality slapped me down. At other times, my infatuations developed into puppy-love romances, and I became devastated when the inevitable breakups occurred.

Each time someone asked Mel, Ellen, or me out for a date, we rejoiced together. When our teenage flings fizzled, which seemed to be quite often, we consoled one another. The three of us acted our age, tittering about sex, necking, petting, and sharing secrets about lovemaking we got from popular women's magazines like *Cosmopolitan* and romance stories. We giggled over our most intimate moments with boys, and Mel and Ellen didn't hesitate to describe the details when they first did *it*. I, though, was evasive about the *it* moment. Listening to my girlfriends' tales about fumbling boys who lacked panache, having my *first moment* with an inexperienced teenage boy was not on the top of my list.

Jack's forecast I would get kisses in my senior year and receive a letterman's sweater came true, albeit a year later than his prediction. Gary was my steady boyfriend who outclassed everyone in our social group in the new disco craze, but his interests extended beyond fancy dance steps. His devotion to the outdoors and experience in rustic camping and canoeing on lakes as far away as Minnesota separated him from the typical Midwest suburban young male.

Gary was blond and blue-eyed with Nordic sexiness, and his six-foot-two height contrasted to my lesser stature of five foot five. We made an odd-looking couple and laughed at our prom picture, thinking the difference in our heights turned us into Mutt and Jeff in the cartoon strip. Beyond the attraction to each other by teenaged hormones, we were indeed friends. If it hadn't been for Gary's patience and persistence in tutoring me, I'd never have made it through chemistry class or the second course in algebra.

Gary heightened my knowledge about nature and the appreciation of the natural world's beauty that went beyond my preteen flower pilfering stage. Gary used to tell me, "Suzanna, noticing and appreciating nature is the groundwork for knowing and respecting yourself." His theory about this connection eluded me, but my obtuseness did not prevent me from enjoying outings in nature's wonderland with this handsome hunk as a guide. The two of us went on day hikes into the Ohio hill country with woodlands, creeks, waterfalls, giant rocks, and caves to explore. And the showstopping flowers—stunning bright orange butterfly weed, violet blue-eyed grass, purple coneflowers, and grass pink orchids—made me dizzy. It was only Gary's gentle reminder holding in check my flower pinching addiction—picking the pulsating blooms would leave less for creatures that relied on them for their habitat. "You're right. It would be the same as stealing from someone's home," I would reply, and my boyfriend would smile back at me.

The ancient Hopewell and other Native American artifacts, like the massive Serpent Mound effigy and burial mound, left us in awe whenever we visited. Closer to home, the Jeffers Mound in Worthington sat smack dab in the middle of a small modern subdivision a block up from the Olentangy River. Gary would drive on the circular road at a snail's pace around the mound, and chills formed on my arms. I never got over being so close to a Hopewell ceremonial spot used almost two thousand years earlier. I swore their spirits and ritual vibrations still survived.

But stargazing with Gary overtook my soul. While other teens might spend their dates necking in the back seats of cars, Gary took me to amazing dark-sky sites instead. There he'd set up his telescope, and along with other amateur and professional astronomers, we'd amuse ourselves looking for shooting stars and other astrological phenomena. What could be more romantic than cuddling in the out-of-doors with a good-looking young man, his muscular arms around you, and kissing him in between gazing at nature's magnificent light show? For me, these were my *it* moments.

At the end of our senior year, Gary went to the Naval Academy in Annapolis, and I got a job as an assistant counselor at a music and dance summer camp two hours from home. I studied at the center during my high school summers, and now the institute staff considered my talent and ability sufficient to help with elementary-aged students' dance training. Landing the position affirmed to me persistence and hard work paid off. Moreover, the job meant I could help young people. Dance and musical theater had boosted my self-belief, and my greatest desire was to spread the same feeling like fairy dust on everyone else.

Melanie and Ellen had not caught the OSU infection, so after finishing high school, they went out of state to college while I stayed in Columbus to attend the college of my dreams. For reasons unknown to me, my girlfriends enrolled at women's colleges. Mel chose one in South Bend, Indiana, with easy access to the boys at Notre Dame, although she was not without competition since the paragon of football had gone co-ed a few years before. Ellen chose an obscure women's college in Michigan. I suppose, given her musical ability, the small liberal arts college made sense. Since neither of my pals' schools was far from Columbus, we often got together during long weekends and holidays and continued sharing our deepest secrets about our romances and indecision about our careers and future steps.

Gary and I remained friends during our college years, but our geographical distance did not bode well for sustaining a permanent romantic relationship. We kept in touch through occasional letters to each other during the first two years of college. Over time, the intensity of our shared experience diminished as we dated and established relationships with others. Our separation would have made me miserable had I not met Craig, who, like a dancing ray of sunshine, crossed my path and guided me in an unexpected direction.

Chapter 3

LIVE YOUR TRUTH

T uesday, September 21, 1976. It is the first day of my college career at The Ohio State University. With a hint of autumn spotting the trees, the morning is sunny and crisp as I step on campus. My stomach is performing cartwheels, and my smile doesn't reach my eyes. Like in the movie Jaws, *the university swallows me up with the other sixty thousand student body members. I am alone and uncertain. I am as overwhelmed as a goldfish in an ocean. To summon my courage, I remind myself I have walked these university paths many times when visiting my father at his office in the law school. Though many of the nooks and crannies of the seventeen-hundred-acre school grounds are familiar, the palms of my hands are clammy as I approach Mount Hall for my first class.*

* * *

It was a brutal betrayal. My first OSU college class was in Mount Hall, not in one of the revered, Romanesque stone and brick structures where decades of secrets and student emotions dwelled—places projecting power and shouting tradition like Orton, Bricker, and Campbell Halls. The grimy-gray concrete and cigarette-brown brick building's architectural design fit a 1970s custodial facility. The expressionless exterior matched the structure's function as an intake, induction, and training center for university newbies and housed University College. Beyond its facade, what bummed me out more was Mount Hall's location across the Olentangy River and a mile from the heartbeat of student life—the Oval. I wanted to act out, have a tantrum of a two-year-old for the bait and switch. *I dreamed of more!*

I slumped through the double glass doors and stepped into a sterile corridor. An acid taste filled my mouth. Instead of calming, musty scents from the wainscoted walls of the Oval's old buildings, I choked on the stench of disinfectant. *Carbolic acid! Lysol! Bleach!*

I yearned to walk the timeless terrazzo and wooden floors where ages of professorial wisdom and tradition-loving students had trodden. I longed to sit under a canopy of trees that shaded students in 1920s Gatsby-style dress; young scholars in 1930s double-breasted jackets, saddle-shoes, and bulky sweaters; coeds in 1950s poodle skirts . . . I wanted their companionship.

As I hoofed the hallway, I dissolved into the soulless surroundings —a statue amidst students aimlessly pushing past me. *They are as flummoxed as I am.* I found the door to my first class, opened it, and entered. My heart sank to my feet—a gargantuan amphitheater confronted me. The sound of Lillian's voice pounded in my ears, and my stomach turned as sour as the scent of bleach in the hallway. "Attend a smaller college, and you'll stand out. Go to a Big Ten, and you'll be lost in the shuffle." *Oh shit! Was Lillian right?*

I sighed and walked up the most inconspicuous aisle—the one closest to the wall. After selecting the tenth row from the front of the room, I scooted a quarter of the way in and took a seat. I turned my head from side to side. The auditorium was half-filled, and I sat like an island to myself as lonely as a three-year-old on her first day at preschool.

An industrial style clock in the front of the room counted down the minutes to the start of class. More bewildered-looking students entered and hustled to the vacant seats. Soon, I felt body heat near me: two girls sat a few seats away to my left, a couple of students sat in the row below me. Behind, students chattered, and from time to time, a guy with a husky voice, squirming to get comfortable, kicked the back of my seat. I glanced at the clock again. Three minutes until starting time. I reread the class description: *University Survey Education 100.17: Academic requirements and organization of the University, nature of scholarly study, characteristics of successful college students . . .*

"Hey there. I'm Craig. And y'all are?"

I jerked my head up to my right. A handsome face and a pair of friendly eyes whose color matched a dark nutmeg-colored mop of curly, short-cropped hair greeted me. I stared, tongue-tied, at the young man.

He repeated the greeting in a baritone voice.

I did one more seven-second eyeball scan and liked him, despite his hair color. Ever since Tommy Braden bit me on my arm when I was four years old, I was averse to any male with a tinge of red hair. What made me ignore my hair bias wasn't this stranger's broad smile, suntanned honey-colored skin, or rugged presence. It was something I couldn't pinpoint—a magnetism that drew me in when he sat down beside me.

"Um, I'm Suzanna," I said, my body liquifying.

"I see we have a similar interest—a career in teaching."

I frowned. "How do you know that?"

"This *is* the survey class in education, isn't it?"

I rolled my eyes at myself. "Yeah, it is," I said, my composure blown. "I'm crazy about music, dance, and theater."

His brows furrowed. "If that's true, why are you selectin' this class and not one in the performin' arts?"

Boxed in. That was stupid! "To be honest, I haven't decided on a major. But my mother thinks education is a perfect fallback career for a girl." *What an idiot! What a horrible truth to reveal to a stranger.*

My row mate's pursed smile and steady gaze made my neck prickle like a cactus. As the professor walked into the room and to the podium, Craig smiled, leaned over, and whispered, "After class, Suzanna, we need to talk about your career choice."

I scribbled notes in my three-tabbed, ruled notebook, trying to focus on concepts alien to me. It was hopeless to concentrate since I kept sneaking side glances at the cute guy sitting next to me. As I adjusted and readjusted myself in my seat, I struggled to categorize him. He wore a light blue, button-down collar shirt with sleeves rolled up to his elbows, revealing suntanned muscular arms. A white T-shirt peeked out from underneath the shirt top, and as my eyes rolled across his chest, I saw his pecs stressed its buttons. His jeans were tired-looking —washed-out denim that had seen better days. His scruffy-looking work boots tagged him as different from the average freshman guy at OSU who wore Converse or Eastlands. Put all together, Craig was more country than suburban, and his heavy stubble made his appearance more grown-up than the other male students sitting around me. I figured he might be twenty-four or so.

As I tuned out the lecture, I contemplated the virtues of the puzzling stranger. A huggable man was my type, and, at first glance, this Craig fellow fit in that category. I still hadn't had a real *it* moment with any of my boyfriends. *Perhaps he's a little too old for me. On the other hand, . . . he'd be more experienced in sex.* Given these periodic assessments, my notebook resembled scribbles more than detailed lecture notes. The object of my attention, on the other hand, seemed to capture every aspect of the professor's presentation. The idea I might get him to share his notes with me crossed my mind.

* * *

Craig loaded his notebook into a military-style canvas backpack and slung it over his shoulder when class ended. I eyed the strange rucksack —another clue he didn't fit the mold of the usual freshman.

"Hey Suzanna, I've got a break before my next class starts. If you're free, how about gettin' a cup of coffee?" Before I replied, my tablet and class books were in Craig's hands. "I can at least walk you out and carry these for you."

I crinkled my forehead and added in a grin. "All righty. I'd love you to be my Sherpa."

His smile lit his face as if I had given him a Christmas present. We scooted along the row of empty seats to the aisle and out of the classroom. I walked out of the building with my hulking, six-foot-tall new friend, and as we rode the OSU bus to the Student Union, making small talk, a swarm of butterflies landed in my stomach like in junior high days, and an equal number of questions whined in my head. *Who is this guy? What's his story? Why is he interested in little ol' me?*

After we entered the center, I froze in place, looking across the mass of humanity buzzing like a beehive. Although I had visited the university many times with Robert, this was my first visit to the Union. Just as I blurted, "This place is crazy," Craig pulled me from the line of fire of two straggly-haired, frantic-looking dudes making a beeline toward the exit and who missed running me down by inches.

"Almost a hit and run there, Suzanna. Got to be careful of the dazed-out drivers here," Craig said.

Unfazed by the chaos, my new buddy found an empty table in the eating area in no time. The Union had a storied history dating back to the early 1900s. Since then, there had been several iterations of the building, including at one time separate ones for men and women. The current building had the beginnings of a run-down appearance, something mid-century buildings tend to succumb to. Even so, it was vibrant, with students scurrying everywhere, making use of the massive ballrooms, eating areas, meeting rooms, bowling alley, and pool tables.

After Craig commandeered our table, he bought cups of steaming coffee and donuts for both of us. "Got to have dunkin' donuts with coffee," he said, handing me my drink and the calorie-laden delight.

As I hugged my cup and toyed with my donut, Craig sat down across from me and eased out a smile. "Tell me why dance and theater turn you on."

Incredible! He's remembered. I was silent and cast my eyes downward. Why did I find it so challenging to respond to the simple question of why something made me happy? The silence didn't bother Craig, but it made my heart palpitate. *You are an idiot*, my inner critic chided me for the second time within two hours. Craig's continued calmness filtered through me and allowed me to assess what made dance vital to me.

I smiled, and my eyes grew. "I'm alive when I'm dancing. I'm on fire when I perform on the stage. I don't worry about anything. I'm in a make-believe world—a balloon floating in the sky."

He angled his head. "Is that so?"

There it was again—the silence—but Craig's eyes continued the conversation, challenging me like a therapist to uncover the truth.

I fidgeted in my seat. "Um, I'm not in therapy."

"Nice to know, but I didn't ask if you were," he said and leaned in toward me.

Two could play his game. I looked into my new friend's hypnotic eyes and mimicked his clipped sentence and silence. "Really?"

Craig's hand came down on the table so hard my coffee took a dive over the edge of the cup. He threw back his head and laughed, giving me an excellent view of a set of perfect and aligned teeth, no silver fillings anywhere. His revelry was infectious, and I joined in, giggling.

He lounged in his seat, winding his boots around the legs of his chair. "No kiddin'. I want to find out what feeds your desire and makes you float like a balloon."

"Weird! No one has asked me that. And I'm not sure I've ever thought about it. Isn't it enough it makes me happy?"

Craig took a long sip of coffee. His eyes, visible over the brim of his cup, penetrated me. "Hmm," he grunted.

Once more, the curious silence hung in the air. It ruffled me; I wanted a quick answer.

But Craig sucked in the calm. He put his forearms on the table, stared into the coffee cup between his hands, and unconsciously turned it. Then he raised his head and smiled a little and shrugged his shoulders.

"I think we need to understand what's motivatin' our likes and dislikes. So we find what makes us tick. If we don't figure out why things push our buttons . . . well, we end up gettin' pulled every which way. We're unfilled. Without direction, we never achieve our full potential movin' through life."

I couldn't wrap myself around the philosophy lesson but wasn't going to acknowledge my ignorance. "That's kind of heavy, Craig."

He smiled back. Heavy didn't seem to bother Craig, but it bothered me, and he wasn't off the hook. "Okay, why isn't happiness enough?"

He shifted back in his chair, continuing to turn his cup. "You want to hear the long or abbreviated story?"

I checked my watch. "How about the one taking ten minutes?"

His eyes had a childish sparkle. "You got it! Well, you've probably guessed I'm older than the average bear around here. I started college at a two-year school in southern Ohio, near where I grew up. You might have caught the twang I have too."

I shrugged. In fact, how could I not have detected it? Like, who else says "hey" instead of hi, "y'all" for you, and leaves off the "g" on every word in the English language ending in that letter? In the end, Craig's handsome features and easygoing manner overruled any implicit bias I might have had about the accent.

"Anyway, I messed around, didn't study a lick, and ended up bombin' out of school. Next, Uncle Sam comes a-callin' and drafts me. A year ago, I got back from Nam. Bein' over there screwed with my head, and one day I said, 'Craig, you got to pull your shit together and figure out what makes you tick.'"

My eyes shot to attention hearing the poop word and, synchronizing with my expression, Craig half smiled. Swear words were in my vocabulary, launched at will on Jack but never used with new acquaintances. What floored me more was the word "Nam." My family or friends didn't talk much about Vietnam, and I did not know anyone who served there.

"The ten-minute story is I was at loose ends for a while. I traipsed around the country like a vagabond, livin' in my car for several months. I camped and hiked alone on the trails in a bunch of national parks. The solitude taught me I needed to understand myself. I must appreciate my strengths, understand my motivations, and follow my values if my life was goin' to mean a damn thing. Without havin' self-understandin' as a foundation, I would be navigatin' through life, like before the war, without a compass. I'd never find my North Star and live my truth."

He hesitated, and though I didn't fully understand this "living your truth" thing, the weight of the moment made my shoulders fall.

"Suzanna, what the army showed me is life is too precious to squander by bein' aimless and not livin' your truth."

My lips rubbed together on autopilot. My intuition told me my new sidekick's revelation was profound, although I didn't comprehend most of it. I looked aside, unable to meet his eyes.

"Gee, Craig, I never thought that deep about my life." I zoned out, letting my mind wander in rhythm with the background noise of student voices, and stared at Craig, still confused. "I don't get this North

Star stuff you're talking about. Kinda sounds like a hippie thing," I said.

Craig bent over, laughing. After he righted himself, he held up both of his arms and said, "Do I look like a freakin' hippie?"

"Are you evading my question?" I asked.

"I could say ditto for you but . . . okay. North Star. The axis of the earth points almost directly north to the real North Star. Unlike other stars, the North Star doesn't rise or set; it stays in the same position. That's why sailors use it to navigate—it's an anchor, a landmark that doesn't change."

The wheels in my head turned, remembering my stargazing nights with Gary. "Yes! The North Star is part of the Little Dipper."

"Exactly. So metaphorically, when I say I'm followin' my North Star, I mean I'm headin' to a specific destination, to a purposeful direction. It means I know what's significant to me. It means the North Star is guidin' me in livin' my truth."

My life reeled in front of me like a movie projector out of control. I had no clue about my North Star. "All of a sudden, I am rudderless."

A faint smile danced across Craig's face. "That's the point of college, Suzanna. This is a time to explore and connect with yourself and to grow and mature as a human bein'."

I nodded, still confused, not understanding the bulk of what he had said. I covered my cluelessness and barked his words back to him. "In the end, what did you discover about yourself, Craig? Did you find your purpose and live your truth?"

He eyed the wall clock. "I gotta buzz to get to class. Same time and the same seat on Thursday, and I'll tell you all about it."

Our morning coffee ended as it had started—on C note—anticlimactic, smooth, in the middle. We walked out of the Union together and went in separate directions to our next classes.

* * *

For the next two days, this city within a city—a university with its own transportation system, police force, eating places, socializing spots, and housing—was overwhelming. Besides multistory classroom buildings and miles of sidewalks and paths, the campus included massive hospitals and medical clinics that, for some reason, I never realized were there. Although I lost my bearings much of the time trying to locate my classrooms, the atmosphere was exhilarating, packed with swarms of people hanging out on the Oval, at Mirror Lake, and in front of buildings. Just as I had imagined college at a Big Ten should be.

Unlike my pals Mel and Ellen, I did not have to adjust to new living arrangements. Living at home with my parents gave me continuity in my personal life. Familiar things were at my fingertips: my own television and phone, a bedroom to myself, snacks from the refrigerator whenever I wanted, and a mother and father with whom I could share the highs, lows, fears, and anticipations of my new role as a college student.

"How was the first day? I want to hear all about it," Robert said when I flopped down in my chair for dinner.

"Terrific! Except for that terrible Mount Hall."

"What's wrong with Mount Hall?" Lillian asked.

"Your prediction was right! Little fish in a super big pond," I said.

Lillian shook her head and shrugged. "We all make our choices. You'll face the consequences and do fine if you learn from the experience."

That was the last discussion Lillian and I had about my OSU choice.

* * *

Thursday morning arrived, and I found myself once more facing an antiseptic-smelling corridor and a bland classroom. Since Tuesday, I hadn't given Craig more than a glancing thought. He was super cute, but there were thousands of girls at OSU. Why would he catch up with me at our next class? What about me would interest him? *Don't plan on it, Suzanna*, my inner critic warned.

I was a few minutes early, and walking through the hallway, familiar pings of anxiety bounced in my gut, guessing if Craig would or would not keep his promise. I stepped into the classroom and debated whether I should sit in the same place I had sat two days earlier. A little demon knocked around in my head and dispensed contradictory advice. *Bottom line, Suzanna, if he's not already here, you don't want to appear too eager by waiting for him, do you? What kind of message are you sending him? Still, do you want him to think you're stuck up? After all, he did carry your books, buy coffee, and walk you to class! Hey, isn't it juvenile to believe you owe him something?*

I pushed back on the bullying voice and considered what Craig had said about living your truth. I groaned to myself. *What is my truth?* I flipped my hand and whisked away the pesky intimidator on my shoulder as if it were a piece of lint. *Why should I make choices on scores of what-ifs? What if he thinks this about me or that about me? I like him. That is my truth.*

With my inner critic checked, I walked up the side aisle of the lecture hall and stopped at the tenth row. I scooted across to the seat I occupied on the first day of class and fell into the vacant space. Within a minute, a shoulder tap startled me, and I turned to my right. There was Craig's broad smile greeting me. My heartbeat quickened.

"Sorry to give you a scare. I came in through the back door," he said, sitting next to me and unloading his crazy-looking backpack on the floor.

He gave me an elbow nudge. "Suzanna! Seein' you has made my day."

Living my truth made mine, too, handsome.

my ange

Chapter 4

MON ANGE

*M*y homework in French class is to compile a list of ten idioms. The professor has assigned each student a beginning word, and mine is "mon." I love the exercise! Finding these everyday expressions makes learning French more fun—plus, they are easy for me to remember.

I flip through the idiom dictionary and search for the ones I like the best: mon coeur, mon trésor, mon bonheur . . . I laugh at mon gros and mon petit monster, my fat one and my little monster. These are no match for the one hooking me—mon ange, my angel.

I write it over and over again in my notebook like a giddy teenager scrawling her boyfriend's name—mon ange, mon ange, mon ange. I've never thought about having a guardian angel, but if there ever were one for me, it is the man who has glided into my life as gentle as if he were on an angel's wings—the man who is showing me how to find my North Star and to live my truth. It is a perfect term of endearment for Craig.

* * *

Craig and I settled into a routine. Each session of our survey class, we sat together and afterward took the OSU bus to the Union for our standard coffee date. If anyone was at *our* cafeteria table when we arrived, Craig commandeered it with a polite request asking them to move. He assured the squatters we needed this table to commemorate an earlier or an upcoming celebration. His imaginary excuses varied. Sometimes it was a surprise engagement proposal to me. At other times, it was a birthday celebration or a fictional anniversary. His smile and white lie never failed him. When Craig did this, I changed his pet name from Mon Ange to *Mon Petit Voleur*—my little thief. He ate up both nicknames, and whenever I used either one, he would grin and say, "Now, I *know* I'm special!"

Between sips of coffee, we interspersed talking about thought-provoking matters with teasing and flirting. Giving me an up and down scan and referencing the local country music hit *Franklin County Woman*, Craig might ask, "How's my Franklin County princess today?"

"Still looking for a Franklin County prince," I'd reply. Then both of us laughed like middle school students.

As days turned into weeks and months, we joked about our coffee dates that modeled an old couple's routine. Craig called us Beauty and the Old Fart—me being Beauty, of course, and he the Old Fart because of our eight-year age difference. We teased each other mercilessly over our local slang and accents. He threw me wisecracks about how many times I said, "All righty," and I joked with him about leavin' off the g's in his gerunds. We were comfortable in our skins and with each other. At first, I pondered why Craig had latched on to me. *What's his agenda? After all, he's twenty-six, and I'm eighteen.* Later, it became clear Craig truly believed the stuff about living your truth.

"I'm curious," Craig said on our second coffee date. "You've had forty-eight hours to think about it. Why do dance and musical theater make you tick?"

He sat in a lazy-style half-lounging position, an elbow resting on the table. When I didn't answer, he swiveled toward me, coffee cup in hand.

Gosh, he's handsome. How come I didn't notice those cute crinkles on the side of his eyes when he smiles?

I shook myself from my daydream. I was having none of his friendly interrogations even if I thought his facial delivery was beyond charming. "Oh no, Craig! You owe me first," I said. "You promised, the next time we had coffee, you'd tell me about your North Star. Are you a man who keeps his promises . . . or not?"

The crinkles dissipated as his eyelids lifted. He sealed his lips and didn't respond. This was what I came to call the "Craig silence."

He slapped his thigh, looked squarely at me, and grinned. "Hot damn! I've got me a feisty little filly makin' me honest," he said, exaggerating his southern Ohio twang.

"And you have no idea what feisty looks like if you don't keep your promise."

He readjusted himself in his seat, crossed one leg over the other, and folded his arms across his chest. He gave me another Craig silence. His pause this time was uncertain rather than introspective. His eyes lowered and roamed the tabletop, hunting for words.

I ended the search. "You finished last time with traipsing around the country for several months living like a vagabond in your car, camping in the woods, and hiking on trails. What were you looking for?"

He raised his eyes to mine, and his forehead lined with creases. He uncrossed his legs. Under the table, I squeezed my hands together. I said nothing. Silence hung between us like a wall. *Had I pressed him too much? No, he opened this door for a reason.*

He cleared his throat and stared into his coffee. "At first, I was unfocused. I didn't know what I was lookin' for. The military beat me up. My body and soul ached from the emotional and physical stress. When my mother wasn't feelin' well, she'd say she felt like an old wet rag. As a kid, I never understood what she meant. As a twenty-three-year-old going on fifty, I got it. I felt dirty, tattered, useless, weak. Believe me, Suzanna, shootin' people and seein' your buddies killed right next to you isn't what the movies crack it up to be. There's no freakin' romance in any of it."

The silence returned, and a wave of sympathy washed over me. He struggled to meet my eyes. I swallowed hard. From the few stories Robert told us of the war, I presumed he had killed men when he was a soldier, but he was secretive when it came to details. This was more than I bargained for, but I asked for it. I tipped my head to signal Craig to go on.

"Anyway, I had lost all connection with life. I had no hope. I drank and smoked pot a lot to try and stop the nightmares. Deep inside, though, I knew actin' like this wasn't goin' to make me happy. To get on track, to feel better, I needed to understand who I was and where I wanted to go. I ended up thinkin' the best place to start was to go back to the basics—give myself space and peace and try to let nature help me free my tangled heart."

My memory bell rang. *What was it Gary always said? Noticing and appreciating nature is the groundwork for knowing and respecting yourself?*

"My high school boyfriend was an outdoor fanatic," I said. "He told me I could know myself by knowing nature. I never understood how distinguishing between species of birds, trees, or insects would tell me about myself."

After the words fell out, I felt immature, foolish, and petty that I allowed my past to overtake me. The guy was spilling his guts out, and I driveled.

Craig rocked the orange-colored plastic cafeteria chair. His lips contracted. His eyes wandered the ceiling then examined me.

I shifted in my seat. My heart burned. *What does he think of me?*

He squeezed his coffee cup tighter. If he had pivoted to another topic, I would not have blamed him. But he didn't.

"Suzanna, you're right. Identifyin' and memorizin' every woodland species isn't going to tell you about yourself. I'm guessin' what your friend meant is that being open to new things, askin' questions about them, and not jumpin' to conclusions gives you the practice to look into yourself in the same way too." He let those ideas percolate.

I glanced down and chewed on my thumbnail. The meaning didn't bubble through my brain cells.

"Here's an example. Close your eyes."

I frowned and hesitated.

He reached over and placed my hand in his. "No. Come on. Trust me."

I let my eyelids fall.

"Okay, imagine we're hikin' through the woods. Not an ordinary forest, but a spectacular one like the redwoods hugging the Pacific Ocean coast." The fullness of Craig's deep voice kidnapped me. The muscles in my shoulders eased.

Craig squeezed my hand. "Careful now," he said. "Let me help you cross the creek. Don't be afraid. I have you." He was silent, and I concentrated on my steps until I was safely across.

"We're on the other side of the brook now. Our eyes wander from side to side. We are amazed. The largest trees in the world surround us. We stretch our necks. We get dizzy trying to see treetops climbing more than three hundred feet above us. We accept the forest canopy's height and thickness as something our eyes can't penetrate. We refuse to be frustrated or discouraged. Instead, we embrace nature's way. The scent of pine circles us. The tree branches intertwine in an intricate network over us. Dapples of sunlight on the ground hint there is a sky above."

I absorbed those thoughts.

Craig's clasp tightened. The respite was over, and he continued.

"We turn our interest to the small trail in front of us and see the path curving among the gigantic Redwoods. The trees' circumferences are so huge it takes sixteen six-foot-tall men, lyin' end to end, to encircle one of them. 'Imagine that,' we say! Our curiosity overtakes us. We keep askin' questions. 'Where do these trees come from? How old are they? Why are they so massive?'"

My mind is consumed by my surroundings. I reach out. I run my fingers over the rustic bark, poking them into the crevices. I hug the tree closest to me—it is a giant.

I realized Craig had stopped the story. My eyes tried to open, and he pressed my hand again. I knew it was safe to stay in my newfound dream world a little longer. I stretched my arms out and twirled around, and round and round. I was dancing!

Craig leaned in close, and the breeze of his breath moved across my face as he whispered, "We continue on the trail . . . What will we see next?"

We meandered farther into the woods. Dense pockets of ferns carpeted the woodland floor as far as we could see. Between these patches, grasses and ground-hugging flora flourished. They created blankets of contrasting textures and green hues that even a color wheel couldn't show us. Our curiosity got the best of us. *Who decides what real estate each of these plants gets? How do they survive in such dark surroundings? Is this all peace and harmony, or is it conflict and rivalry among the species?*

Tucked amidst the giants, we came across smaller hemlock trees, frosted in intricate patchwork designs of lichens and moss. We wondered, *Do they live in symbiotic harmony with their hosts? Or does their beauty hide their harm?"*

I heard Craig sigh, and I hoped my lesson wasn't ending. I took a deep breath, and I was relieved when he continued.

"Look over there, Suzanna, at the sun's needle-piercin' rays that dance like fairies and streak our pathway. We wonder if there are such things as woodland pixies. We feast on the sight. Our lungs take in the damp air. We are grateful for the moment."

Craig halted, and the silence shrouded us. A minute later, he liberated us in hushed tones.

"We move on and see a swamp. Our eyes are shocked. We judge this quagmire as out of place surrounded by the woodland beauty. The water is dark and murky. Green ink blankets much of it. The air is stale and putrid. We recoil. We want to turn our backs, run from it. Instead, we quash our response. We ask ourselves, 'Why should we form an opinion of the swamp so fast? Why does this place suppress our curiosity?' We accept the challenge and study the swamp. We open our minds, resist our first impressions, and ask, 'What is the purpose of these murky waters? Would it be beautiful if we sized it up differently?'" Craig halted and gave my hand a gentle tug.

I raised my eyes, and Craig's comforting smile welcomed me.

"Any ideas, Suzanna?"

My thoughts bumped back and forth like pool balls. I got the concrete stuff. Like swamps are essential for the ecology of a place, and there's a symbiotic relationship among plants. It was the symbolism I couldn't nail.

"I'm not connecting the dots," I said.

Craig didn't let me off the hook. As I would learn, he didn't dish out opinions. Instead, he made you work for the little gems, asking question after question. More often, what you came up with were not his views but yours. He set the table and let you put the food on your own plate. That day, he pushed me to dig for my answers from our make-believe nature hike. He served up the smorgasbord, but I had to make sense of our pretend adventure.

"The forest is sort of a symbol for my life. To understand my life and its purpose, I have to take, like, a metaphorical walk through it. We find our purpose by looking for it within ourselves."

All I got from Craig was another mini nod.

He was a taskmaster—worse than Lillian. "How do I do that? How do I look within me to find my purpose?"

"How did you do it on our little forest walk?"

"I guess I asked a bunch of questions . . . like you're doing now."

He smiled and did another mini nod. "And?"

"And asking why and figuring out how things relate to each other. I guess the biggie was not jumping to conclusions and prejudging the swamp . . ."

It took time until I made sense of our nature walk. Then, *bam*! The light bulb lit to 300 watts. I had to dig deeper into the forest, assume the role of one of its inhabitants. I decided to be the thing I prejudged as something putrid and ask the questions.

What does the swamp give to the woods?

What strengths does it have?

How does it find its place with others in the forest?

When it came down to it, understanding your purpose was knowing your value and strengths and using curiosity to figure out the best way to use them. My little journey taught me not to prejudge others or even myself. I decided having some compassion for yourself and others goes a lot further in making you happy than indifference or hate.

I was puzzled, though, about how Craig had meandered on his own forest trip. "How did you find your calling?" I asked.

"Well, I started askin' myself some hard questions. Like, 'What are your values, Craig? What are you good at doin'? What do you like doin'?' The one head-scratcher that got me thinkin' hard was, 'What do you want to be written in your obituary?' That one kinda shook me up."

I leaned back in my chair and showed Craig a half-smile of doubt.

"No, seriously! Did I want the obit to say, *Craig Fitzgerald: A son-of-a-bitch who blamed everyone for his problems and screwed up his life.*? Or did I want it to say, *Craig Fitzgerald: A brave son-of-a-bitch who acted on his convictions and helped people and treated them fairly.*"?

I let those nuggets sink in and nodded ten-degrees.

"After answerin' what I wanted my obit to say, it seemed pretty clear to me what my purpose was—helpin' people. Before I could help anyone, I needed to get my shit together figurin' out how I could best do that."

He didn't have to add the one-sentence summation, but I was glad he did. I walked away, realizing I had to ask myself some difficult questions, write an obituary, and get my shit together. What made it perfect—like an extra dash of sprinkles on top of a chocolate soda—was seeing purpose in action—I now got why Craig was hanging out with me. It was about helping others, and I was a prime suspect.

* * *

We didn't frequent the High Street student hangouts or go to football games together, or exchange whimsical Christmas gifts during the fall quarter. Instead, class sessions and coffee dates twice a week made up our relationship. The quarter ended the way it had begun for us—as coffee buddies. The defining outcome of our friendship during those short weeks was that I gained clarity about my purpose and future. My coffee buddy was patient, coaching and prodding me to ask the discerning questions to get to the root of my motivation for dance and theater. His insistence I identify five key strengths to fit my North Star's points forced me to peer deep within myself and get straight what the North Star business was all about.

"Suzanna, your North Star has to have five points," he would say.

In a muddle trying to find my truth, I'd challenge him. "Why?"

"Because stars have five points, not three or four," he would say. "If you want your star to shine bright enough to guide you, Suzanna, you must work out what makes you tick. You can't get on the happy road without a five-pointed star."

After weeks of Craig's good-natured badgering, I landed on my five points. Appreciation of beauty and creativity were easy to figure out as the underpinnings for my affinity to the performing arts. After that, it got more challenging.

As I thought about how I enjoyed and excelled in discovering new ways of doing things in the past, whether it was dancing, preparing food, tramping in the outdoors with Gary, or studying, curiosity appeared as my third point of light. In fact, the way I arrived at Craig's pet name, Mon Ange, was due to my inquisitiveness in exploring idioms for the assignment in my French class.

I worked to pin down the final two points. While Craig and I drank coffee, we tossed ideas between us, trying to come up with the "elusive two," as Craig called them.

Craig cheered me on. "I found the last ones are the toughest, Suzanna. Durin' and after the war, I learned perseverance, pushin' forward, was critical in gettin' myself together. I couldn't succeed by givin' up."

* * *

It was November 6 on a Saturday afternoon with Jack at an OSU football game when my star's fourth point materialized. The answer I struggled to find dawned on me as easy as melting a popsicle in the summer. The frenzied fans in the stadium riveted their attention on another play that would crush Illinois. My brother and I gripped each other's arms in anticipation. In that instant, my connection with Jack opened a window revealing that love—valuing close relationships—was a pillar of my life. *Study your behaviors and be curious*, Craig had told me.

I had locked down my star's four points, but the fifth one still evaded me. One day, Craig challenged me. "Okay, Suzanna, put your strengths of creativity and curiosity into action. How can you find the fifth point in your star?"

I batted around a few ideas. "Let's see. I could make a list of things I like to do."

"Hmm," Craig groaned and gave me some Craig silence before asking, "What would the list tell you, other than havin' an inventory of things you like to do?"

"I need to go deeper and analyze what's below the things I like to do, just like I did for dancing and music. I need to figure out the motivation," I said.

Craig gave me a thumbs-up.

I tried once more. "I could take some kind of test. The counselors here have tests that show you what you do well at."

My coffee buddy leaned forward. "What do you reckon about that?"

I shrugged. Midterm exams loomed in my mind. "I'm tested out."

"Is that a cover-up or a reason?"

"Probably a cover-up."

Craig let my response dangle in a thirty-second pause. "What were your finest moments, Suzanna?"

I rolled my eyes.

"You know, stuff you did that was so extraordinary that the memory of it sticks in your mind like glue."

Silence on my part. Silence on Craig's part.

Craig stacked on another question. "What did you do that was so unique that other people remember it too?"

"What are you trying to do? Confuse me?" I asked.

"Okay, how about this. If you had to defend your life by answerin' why the heck you're here on this earth, what would you say?"

Defend my life! That was something I could sink my teeth in. It struck more than a chord; it was a symphony. I mulled over Craig's question for over a week. Hidden within his explanation, I found a clue: What do others remember as my best moments? I asked Jack to list some of my best moments. I wrote to Melanie and Ellen and quizzed them too.

Jack said, "That's easy, Flower Girl. It's the little bouquets you used to leave for me on my desk in my room at home."

Dumbfounded, I asked, "Something as small and insignificant as giving you flowers? Jack, why?"

"It isn't the size of the gift, Suzanna. What is important is the mean-ing behind it. You gave me the most precious thing you had to share at the time. It made me happy you thought of me for no reason at all. I still have all those bouquets—all dried out, of course."

Jack's confession shocked me, and my eyes watered as I hugged my prince of a brother.

Melanie responded with an unexpected reply too. "Hey, sweetie, that's easy," she wrote. "The time you stayed up all night with me when I found out Larry was two-timing me. I'll never forget how you lis-tened and hugged me. You didn't rag on me and tell me I was a fool. You didn't tell me what I should do. You listened to me and fixed me hot chocolate."

Isn't this something every friend would do? I asked myself.

And Ellen also had an answer. "Suzanna, you always treat people as if they matter. You do stuff for people others overlook. I remember the day we went shopping for our prom dresses, and I was in a hurry to leave the store to go to the parking lot. I turned back, and you weren't behind me. No, you went out of your way and held open the door and helped a mother with her baby stroller. You know, stuff like that."

No, I hadn't noticed stuff like that. That's just me.

* * *

It was at our final coffee date before the Christmas break when Craig helped me put words to the elusive fifth point. Sitting to the side of me, he said, "I want to give you a gift, Suzanna."

"What?" I stretched to see his military backpack canvas bag behind him.

"Nope, the gift ain't there, Suzanna."

I wrinkled my nose in disappointment. "You're in your grandpa pose. You're going to tell me a story again. All you need is a pipe."

He gave me a generous grin. "Yep! Grandpa Craig," he said. He slipped his hand into his deer-colored army jacket, eyes as mysterious as jeweled amber, removed a folded paper, and handed it to me. Leaning in close, he whispered, "Open it."

The sweetness of his breath crossed my face, and its warmth made me off-balance and gushy. I sucked on my lower lip and reached for the creased piece of paper. I stared at the sheet in my hand. What a strange gift. It was folded in quarters, and after I opened it halfway, I glanced up at Craig. What was he up to? His eyes registered my confusion, but his grin teased me. To find out the secret in my hand, I had to go all the way.

I took in a deep breath and opened the last fold. When I set eyes on the contents, I cast a smile as wide as the OSU campus. I opened my arms and floated into my coffee buddy's outstretched ones in an embrace that went beyond a hot romance. It was a hug of friendship whose heat satisfied me as much as lying in the sunshine cast through a winter's window. My North Star was complete.

The paper I clutched had a detailed five-point star drawn on it in hues of purple, orange, green, and gold. Handwritten in calligraphy on each point was one of my strengths—appreciation of beauty, creativity, curiosity, love, and kindness. But it was the last point Craig added that held my eyes. Kindness: being considerate and helping others was my core and how I would defend my life. This is what Jack, Melanie, and Ellen had said too. It was time I recognized it in myself.

* * *

My friendship with Craig picked up again after the Christmas holidays. During winter quarter 1977, we resumed our familiar "old couple" routine: coffee and donuts in the Student Union after our course in career development. To attend this class in Arps Hall, a circa 1926 brick building with all the hallmarks of OSU tradition, was a fantasy come true. I loved it all: wooden desks marred and scratched from decades of student use, blackboards that were black and not green, hallways with musty smells, and small classrooms. This was the college experience of my dreams.

Like thousands of fellow students, my compass wasn't set to true north yet, and I hoped this new course would help me get my bearing. Despite knowing my strengths, I still struggled to find my life's purpose and anchor my direction. Where was the one fixed point that would give me continuity no matter what challenges confronted me?

Within the flurry of campus life, I connected with former friends from high school and made new ones. Parties, keggers, and OSU basketball games kept me in the swim of social life, and light romances gave me some thrills. I was having fun, but it was only skin deep. I yearned for something of substance—the inspiration and motivation poets and philosophers wrote about. Friedrich Nietzsche bounced around in my head: "He who has a why to live for can bear almost any how." *What is the why?* my curious voice asked.

* * *

Spring quarter arrived, and although Craig and I weren't classmates, we met once a week for coffee and donuts in the Student Union. Craig had found his purpose long before me and was on a fast track to finishing his degree. His roots were in a poverty-stricken area of rural America, and he wanted to devote his life to helping young people from poor areas like his fulfill their potential. His eye was on a career teaching secondary school in Appalachia. His star's five points suited his mission. His military service wasn't a secret, though I had to pry from him his war distinctions. But his bravery went beyond physical to moral courage. He was committed to doing the right things, giving voice to his values, and acting on his principles, even if these were unpopular.

During one of our coffee dates, he put his conviction on center stage when he slid a copy of his hometown newspaper in front of me, opened to the editorial section. I scanned the written opinions of the locals and found what Craig intended me to see.

Dear Editor:

Ohio is facing one of the biggest environmental challenges in the country. Air so dirty it plagues our cities and forces people to use headlights driving in the daytime. In rural areas, it is our waterways! Acid drainage from active and abandoned mines poison the water sources used for our farm animals and drinking. We didn't have to have a government report tell us there are 233 miles of continuously polluted streams in our Hocking River, with another 141 miles intermittently contaminated. No, we didn't have to have outsiders come and tell us because we've known this for decades—we've seen it, breathed it, and drunk it for years.

The coal companies quiet us by putting fear in us. They tell us that environmental regulations will threaten our jobs and crush the low-cost electric industry here in Ohio. What nonsense! Look at what happened to Hendrysburg! The whole town disappeared as the companies kept buying up the land to strip-mine. Your homes, much less your jobs and lives, aren't safe with these people.

When will we stop believing the propaganda spewed by a coal industry that doesn't care about us? Shouldn't we demand that the coal industry think more of us than their profits? Isn't the minimum we deserve from their greed clean water to drink and air to breathe? When will we wise up and demand justice for ourselves and our children?

Craig Fitzgerald

Finished reading, my eyes widened. "Gosh, Craig. What's this about? I thought you liked to be a silent agitator."

"Yep, you're right. I don't like to draw attention to myself. Don't want or need all the hassles."

"So why this? Why now?"

"Because I was damned pissed off at these companies. Their strip minin' is layin' waste to thousands of acres of our beautiful land and hills. Sure, we got a bill for strip-minin' passed in '72, and what benefit have we seen of it? These greedy bastards have held it up in court for years."

Given where Craig grew up, his opinion was radical and might be dangerous for him. Because of my brother's environmental law work, I knew Ohio's coal production had ebbs and flows. In the early 1900s, the area was one of the largest coal producers in the United States. The boom changed after World War I when a dramatic slump in production turned company towns into ghost towns. With newer methods of surface mining perfected, coal production increased after World War II. By 1970, the area's coal production reached an all-time annual high, giving the region an economic shot. But the coal industry said government rules and regulations on pollutant sources were a death blow to the industry and the workforce. Many of Craig's neighbors and his family were not sympathetic to his views supporting clean air and reducing fossil fuel use. In fact, expressing these could be downright dangerous.

"You were pissed. But this isn't like you."

"A learnin' lesson, I guess. Sometimes, Suzanna, we must move out of our comfort zone and stand up for what is right."

That episode solidified my opinion of Craig Fitzgerald. Besides bravery, he had a strong sense of justice and fairness. He thought people should not prejudge others by their circumstances. "Snap decisions make poor decisions," he often told me—and then, with a broad toothy grin, he'd add, "unless, of course, you're runnin' away from a saber-toothed tiger."

Craig's other strengths were evident as he encouraged me to identify my strong points. He was creative and playful in challenging me to go deeper into understanding myself. And his broad perspective in looking at situations helped me make sense of the world. The combination of these was inspiring, but what astonished me most was his gratitude. Bad things had happened to Craig during the Vietnam War, but he also had an uncanny awareness of the awesome stuff in life. Unbeknownst to me at the time, his strength of gratitude would be the shining light I needed to lead me out of some very dark times ahead.

* * *

The following months of college rolled on, and Craig wrapped up his education in record time. Referring to his studies, he often said, "Suzanna, I'm goin' faster than a stock car to the finish line." He got approval to increase his course load and crammed six courses into a quarter. A year and a half after we had met, Craig graduated at the end of the spring quarter in 1978. He accepted a teaching position in a small, central school in rural New York State in one of Appalachia's poorest counties. Craig was following his North Star.

During this time, I gave up on the idea that a romantic relationship would develop between us. For one thing, Craig consumed himself with studies; he spent eighteen hours a day, seven days a week on homework, writing papers, and completing projects. Besides time, another obstacle for him, but not for me, was the difference between our ages.

"Suzanna, if I asked you out on a date, I'd get arrested for robbin' the cradle," he joked.

And I'd reply, "I'm a big baby, and I doubt you'd be detained for theft."

With a brush of his hand, he'd whisk off my statement. There was more, though. Craig said he had psychological and emotional issues caused by the war to work through. "These are enough burdens for me to handle. I'm not going to ask someone else to assume them too."

My age and lack of worldly experience made me dubious about his assertion. Then one day in late spring 1978, an event annihilated these doubts. We walked together along High Street, a busy thoroughfare with bumper-to-bumper traffic that borders one side of the OSU campus. That day, students jammed the sidewalks as they headed to fast-food eating places, bars, and off-campus hangouts. While Craig and I shuffled shoulder to shoulder among the noonday throng, a car zoomed past and backfired—*bam, bam!* Craig reacted—instantaneous and violent. He was having a flashback.

My arms were pulled from the back, and I was brought down face forward to the ground. My head landed hard on the cement. The force inside my skull exploded like a pressure cooker. Craig lay on top of me. His massive body crushed me, and my ribs compressed. It was almost impossible to breathe. The fall skinned both of my legs, and blood spurted on the sidewalk from the wound on my chin. Fellow students walking near us stopped and stared. "Hey, dude, what the hell! You on some kind of trip?" one said.

Craig's hands shook as he held a white handkerchief to my face to stem the bleeding. His eyes clouded, and his voice wavered. "Oh God, Suzanna. I'm so, so sorry. We've got to get you to the student health center."

He lifted me up, and while we walked to the clinic, he apologized over and over for reenacting a role from "his other life."

"Craig, I understand. I understand. Don't worry," I stuttered. Uncontrolled tears streaked down my cheeks, and the sidewalk was a pool of mush under my unsteady feet.

After the doctor cleaned my wounds, administered a tetanus shot, and applied adhesive skin closures to my chin wound, we spent the rest of the day sitting along the grassy banks of the Olentangy River near campus. Craig wrestled with talking about the horrors of the war and his flashbacks. Death, blood, despair, and loss were seeded deep within him. He spoke in disjointed passages about machine gun fire ripping apart soldiers standing beside him, but for some inexplicable reason, missing him. Crushing heat, torrential rains, wanton violence, and holding shredded buddies as they died took an immeasurable toll. "Not a day goes by . . . It is like tryin' to assemble broken pottery but lackin' all the pieces."

There were long periods of silence. I listened and didn't utter one word.

* * *

Craig's graduation day arrived, and I attended the ceremony and clapped and cheered with his relatives and friends when he received his degree—the first Fitzgerald to complete a college education. Afterward, Jack and I drove to Craig's family home in the Hocking Hills for an outdoor barbeque party his relatives threw for him. During the time I had known Craig, he never let on he had musical talent, so it stunned me when he was the star attraction in the impromptu band that formed at his graduation celebration.

"Petit voleur," I admonished him in French after he finished playing the first song. He replied with an impish smile.

It turned out Craig was a master at the fiddle, guitar, and banjo. When he played "Soldier's Joy" and sidled up to me, the crowd around us evaporated. His eyes locked on mine while his smile and his bow danced synchronously. Later, the sounds of "When Bidden to the Wake or Fair" wafted through the summer breeze and made me float like the summer clouds. Then, Craig blew me away.

"This next song is for an amazin' girl from Franklin County who says "All righty" a lot, who gets me, and who is *my* Franklin County princess."

I melted as Craig belted out "Franklin County Woman" and changed the lyrics from red-haired to brown-haired woman.

Before Jack and I left, Craig came bounding over and asked my brother, "Can I steal Suzanna for a minute?" Jack frowned, checked his watch, winked, and shot back, "I'm not sure about the stealing part, but, sure, you can have her for sixty seconds—but I'm timing you!"

Craig grabbed my hand and whisked me a few hundred feet away to a small grove of trees. Standing under the canopy of leaves, he turned, faced me, and swallowed me in his eyes. "You'll always be a star in my life, Suzanna," he whispered as he placed a soft, pink cloth pouch into my hand.

My eyes shot open. *A gift?* I was speechless.

"Go ahead, take a peek," he said.

My body pulsated like waves on an ocean shore. I lingered undoing the silk ties. Inside, there was a five-point white gold star pendant. I shut my eyes. Craig's lips were on mine, giving me the kiss I had wanted since the day we met. For one glorious moment, the platonic seal broke under our overpowering emotions of love and gratitude. We lived in the moment, knowing it would have to last us a lifetime.

"You know my demons, Suzanna," he said.

"I do, Mon Ange."

His gift extinguished my hesitance in giving him what I had brought. I slipped my free hand into my jeans pocket, retrieved a small article wrapped in scarlet and gray paper, and placed it into his hand.

"We never give each other gifts, Suzanna."
"Yes, Mon Ange. But today, we both broke that unwritten rule."

* * *

By the time Craig graduated, I had sorted my life path, set on funneling my energy into a career in university student affairs. I had been at loose ends, tentative, and without purpose when I entered college. I wanted to change that for other students—I wanted to help them know and use what was best in them and support them in finding their direction and fulfilling their potential.

Craig and I stayed in touch, sending periodic letters. I told Craig his passion for following his North Star propelled my enthusiasm toward a master's degree in educational counseling. While Craig formed "the math department" in a central school with two hundred students, grades kindergarten through twelve, I accelerated my studies. I had my diploma by the end of August 1982, along with a position as an assistant academic counselor in the School of Allied Medicine at my favorite university—The Ohio State University.

On my graduation day, the sweetest gift I received was Craig cheering me as I received my graduate degree and celebrating the accomplishment with my family and friends at a blowout party thrown by Lillian and Robert.

Chapter 5

JONATHAN

*Wednesday afternoon, October 6, 1982. Dr. Walker, head of the Uti-
lization Review Committee at the university hospital, is scheduled to
lecture to a group of young resident physicians on the ins and outs of following Medicare rules. Today, I am escorting students enrolled in our bachelor's
program in medical record administration to the conference room to listen to
his presentation. It is close quarters in the small space, and I intend to leave
after the students find their seats. But as I prepare to go, the senior physician
catches me off guard.*

"Why don't you stay, too, Suzanna?"

*What do you say to a physician who also happens to be an old friend of
your father's?*

*"Thank you for the invitation," I say and slide into the last empty chair.
I look across the room and catch the eye and a wink from one of the young
doctors. What a suave, bad boy!*

* * *

I glimpsed the physician from across the room eyeballing me during
the lecture. I gave him a quick glance, and his friendly grin and second
wink succeeded in upping my bullshit-guy radar that pinged earlier.
Nevertheless, I allowed my lips to curve up before turning my attention
to absorbing the intricacies of the medical necessity of care according
to government regulations.

Two days later, I sat at my desk in my office, stewing over adjust-
ing student course schedules, when I had a weird sense someone was

watching me. I glanced up. My mouth fell open. Arms folded across his chest, the flirty resident from Dr. Walker's lecture leaned against my office door. His ogling sent a chill down my spine. I was speechless. *How long has he been there?*

The handsome physician walked in and greeted me as if we were longtime friends. "Hey, just dropping by to say hello." He came closer and stood over me.

I raised my head and stared at him. "Can I help you with something?"

"Well, that depends."

The stranger glued his eyes on me and welcomed himself to the chair on the other side of my desk.

I shifted in my seat and frowned. "Depends on what?"

"Depends if you're free on Saturday night to go out."

"Who's asking?"

His lips curled suggestively. "A handsome guy I know named Jonathan Spencer."

My sixth sense soared, suspecting the secretive visitor smiled with a sexy grin at every woman. His self-assured slouch, sharp clothing, and stylishly shaggy sandy-blond hair shouted sophistication, but there was something suspicious about him. Could this smarty-pants take as good as he gave?

"What's wrong with Jonathan Spencer that he can't ask for a date himself?"

The stranger's smile sank, and a strained silence smothered the air. Slapping his hands on the desk, he stood, and as his eyes scrutinized me, I imagined myself as a sitting duck. "I'll tell Spencer what you said."

Then he turned and walked out of my office, and the door slammed behind him.

My face turned hot. My inner critic screamed, *Exactly what you deserve, being glib.* Then another voice sounded a warning: *Beware of a person who doesn't appreciate humor.*

* * *

The enigma who entered my life, Jonathan Herbert Spencer III, landed at The Ohio State University with a grudge planted on his shoulder— his first medical school preference, Case Western Reserve, had rejected him. As I would soon discover, Jonathan was a superb coverup artist, so his friends and family never suspected OSU wasn't his dream choice; he played the game close to the vest, insecurity overriding veracity. I learned the truth during one of his drunken tirades when he told me Case Western was the first of five universities to respond to his application to medical school. When he received the Dear John letter, he had a snappy retort ready for his inquisitive mother. "Thank God, Case wasn't my first choice. If they had accepted me, I'd sure be in a dilemma deciding if I should take their offer or wait on my dream appointment." The next day an acceptance letter arrived from Ohio's flagship university, and Jonathan acted the part well. Head over heels, he proclaimed his number one choice was always the Buckeyes. "I mean, what's grad school without a top-ranking football team?" he said to his pals.

Jonathan grew up in a rural town in northern Illinois that hugged the Wisconsin border. He was the fourth generation of his family from the small community and the only child of Jonathan Spencer II and Marianne Spencer. Although the Spencers were a generation short of being original settlers, that did not stop them, or Jonathan, from portraying their lineage as founding members of McHenry county.

Jonathan liked to brag to me about his father's enviable academic pedigree—Yale Law School. Apologetically, though, he explained that obtaining The Ivy League credentials did not shake Spencer II from the rolling prairie land. After graduation and admission to the Illinois Bar, Jonathan's father, who everyone called Bud, put out his shingle in private law practice in the town where he had grown up. The first time I met Bud, I was struck by his dry sense of humor, so unlike his progeny. I learned he had a passion for jazz and the performing arts, balanced out by his love of fishing in the Badger State lakes. But above all, Jonathan said the locals respected Bud for his integrity and lifelong commitment to civic duty and charitable work, something else unlike his offspring.

Jonathan's mother was homegrown, too, a student and cheerleader of the local high school. Unlike many women in her community, though, Marianne graduated from college—a small women's liberal arts institution of higher learning. She had delicate features, blue eyes, and blond hair, and there was no doubt Jonathan got his striking looks from her. Marianne was more reserved than Bud but, like him, adored live theater, music, and dance productions. She belonged to the local fine arts association, was a member of the resident company of the city's theater players, and volunteered at the community hospital. Marianne told me that Jonathan's desire to go into medicine sprang from her hospital volunteer stories, which I thought was unlikely but made for interesting conversation. Besides these activities, Marianne liked to talk about her close-knit group of girlfriends and their predominant pastimes—card parties, afternoon teas, book clubs, and museum and theater trips to Chicago.

Jonathan attended the same high school as his parents, and his letterman's sweater testified to his sports accomplishments. Looking through his yearbook, it was hard to escape noticing he had racked up achievements most teenagers envy: student body president, prom king, National Honor Society member, football quarterback, and all-around jock. Even in high school, Jonathan had a car fetish and drove a snazzy midnight-blue Firebird, a gift from his father and mother in his high school junior year.

The familiarity and advantages of being a big fish in a smaller pond appealed to Jonathan, so he chose a small private college close to home in Wisconsin for his undergraduate education. There, he excelled in academics but sports of a different nature: pool, tennis, golf, and girls. Good-looking, jocular, and armed with a jazzy car and money to spare, he bragged girls sought him out, and he played the field until he fell for a young woman who matched his glamour and status. I've surmised that's when the trouble began that knocked Jonathan Herbert Spencer III off his high horse, exposed his insecurity, and nurtured his narcissism.

It always mystified me why, after graduating from college, Jonathan chose a medical school outside his home state instead of one of the

Big Ten universities in Illinois, like Northwestern or the University of Illinois. There was a mystery concerning his reluctance to return to Illinois I could never put my finger on. Craig's rural roots stayed with him, making him want to use his talents to help create better opportunities for the people like himself. In contrast, Jonathan wanted to flee his birthplace and had no inclination to share his fortunate advantage with his childhood community. "What a backwater place, and I'm glad to be free of it," he'd often say after receiving a letter or phone call from his parents or an old-time friend. It saddened me to hear his disdain. It was as if he were trying to convince himself his boyhood home was worthless. At those times, I wondered what ended his relationship with his youth. What was the trigger that shut off his connection with himself?

Chapter 6

SETTING THE SNARE

*I*t's two weeks after the young doctor's ill-fated attempt to ask me for a date. *He arrives unannounced and, just as before, leans against my open office door with his arms folded across his chest and peers at me with a shit-eating grin plastered across his face. I look up, and though his eyes have a friendly and disarming twinkle, his presence isn't amusing me. What are we—in grade school? I turn back to the papers on my desk and continue with my work. Perhaps he will leave.*

What I haven't learned is that Jonathan has perseverance. Where others weigh or restrain their course of action with prudence, that virtue is not in Jonathan's repertoire. Yet, no matter the degree of risk or the obstacles in his path, he finishes what he starts and gets his prize.

He doesn't move from the doorway.

"Yes? . . . Are you on another errand for that friend of yours?" I ask, keeping my eyes on the papers in front of me.

* * *

Jonathan considered my words an invitation to enter my office.

"No way! Learned my lesson. This time, I'm here for myself."

He fell into the chair on the other side of my desk.

I straightened in my seat. "And who are you?"

"A smart aleck who is asking a good-looking gal named Suzanna out for a date."

I cocked my head. "For sure, you need to get a better pickup line. I should swish you out of here . . . but you've raised my counselor's curiosity."

He bared a gorgeous set of teeth in a dimpled smile, lounged back, and rapped his fingers on my desktop. "Well counselor, is this going to be twenty questions? You know, like: What are you concerned about? What motivates you? What's difficult for you?" he asked.

"Let's start with something simple. What is your name?"

He paused and readjusted himself in his seat. "Jonathan Herbert Spencer, the third."

This time, his voice was unprovocative and sincere. It took me by surprise, coming from someone I thought was more flippant than forthcoming. When he spoke, it was as if he were pulling aside a curtain, allowing me a peek into the man in front of me. I studied him and realized his eyes were a smoky blue, not the ocean blue I had thought when we first met. His thick blondish hair was on the longer side, styled and silky, and swept back except for a few stray strands sliding across his forehead. He had an unquestionable movie-star presence.

"The third? Tell me about that."

"A long story, three generations, in fact! I'm named after my father, who was named after his father." Observing my nod, he added with a shrug, "Yeah, you would have figured that out."

I smiled and let the silence drift for a couple of seconds. "And what else?"

"I see this is going to be twenty questions after all," he said and repaid me with the silent treatment.

I didn't respond. Craig had shown me the power of silence.

He gave in. "Okay. I was born and raised in a small village in northern Illinois. It has all the trappings of America's hometown: patriotic celebrations, mom-and-pop shops dotting an old-fashioned downtown square, family restaurants serving homemade meatloaf on Thursday evenings, church bells ringing on Sunday mornings, an old-time movie theater, an Ace hardware, and an A&P grocery."

"Sounds quaint."

"Charming. We call it charming. The first settlers were from Vermont. I suppose you can say old-fashioned conservative New England values form the core of the townsfolk. To be sure, one of those is a reluctance to change."

A note of cynicism?

"How so?" I asked. "The unwillingness to change."

He shrugged, wrinkled his lips, and sprawled more in the chair. "When I complain to my dad how stodgy everyone is, he quotes Samuel Eliot Morison, the historian. 'Jonathan, wine of 1656 still gives bouquet and flavor to what is drawn today. Preserving the old ways is not always bad.'"

What was going on here? His tone was bitter, perhaps hostile. My intuition said an internal struggle festered inside the good-looking man sitting with me. Was it a clash between deference and defiance? A conflict between past and present? Through symbols, words, rewards, and punishments, our culture tells us what things are important in life, how we must act, and what we should believe and value. The counselor in me pondered, *What are the traditions Jonathan is defying? What is he fleeing from?*

My frown prompted Jonathan to create air circles with his right index finger directed toward his head. "I see the psychology wheels turning in your mind. Why don't we continue this therapy session over drinks and dinner sometime?"

"Going out with a client goes against ethical principles."

"Right! I like people who follow a code of ethics." He leaned forward and halfway across the desk and said in a stage whisper, "But, counselor, I am not your client, and you are not my therapist."

I leaned back in my chair. I fingered the white gold star pendant I wore, buying time. The handsome man and hypnotic voice overpowered the alarm bells ringing bad news, and despite the warning, I jumped in the dangerous game. "Sometime?" I asked.

"Let's make sometime Saturday evening. Dinner at the old inn in Worthington and later, one of the dance joints on High Street."

I loved the restaurant choice—a place dating back to the mid-1800s. Quiet, quaint, and romantic. "The Inn sounds great. Dance places near campus not so much."

He knitted his brows together. "You don't like to dance?"

I burst out laughing. "Your intelligence gathering could be improved. I love to dance; it is one of my passions. The place is the problem, not the dancing. Don't want to mix it up with the students I advise."

He drew himself closer, his chest over the desk. "I am intrigued! If dancing is one of your passions, it makes me wonder what others you have."

I interpreted his remark as a witty quip and that he might have a sense of humor, after all. "My passions are for me to know and for you, right now, not to."

He slapped his palm on the top of my desk. "Fair enough, Suzanna," he said and slid the notepad on my desk in front of me.

I hesitated and then took the pad.

"If I'm going to pick you up, I'll need an address. And a phone number would help too."

The scratching of my pen across the paper commandeered the room. After I finished, I pushed the information back to my visitor.

He smiled, tore off the sheet, folded it, and placed it in his jacket pocket, his eyes never leaving mine. Once the pin had burst the balloon and released the tension, Jonathan beguiled me with tales about the 4H animals he had in junior high school: goats Shirley and Faye and sheep Goldie and Olivia. Had I misjudged him? Anyone who loved goats and sheep couldn't be a jackass and surely deserved a second chance. Apart from barnyard animals, he shared stories of teen hijinks of TP-ing homes, playing hooky, and drag racing on rural country roads in his Firebird. "As a racer, there weren't many better than me," he said.

Beyond his teenage escapades, it was details about his father that heightened his energy.

"Dad is a charmer. Everyone calls him Bud, and the locals refer to him as 'our simple country lawyer.' Only a fool will let his easy way

belie his intellect and uncanny ability to size up any person or situation
. . . I wish I had both of those traits."

Jonathan told me how the war interrupted Bud's college education
and detailed his dad's pro bono work for the underprivileged, civic service on school boards and nonprofit organizations, and his internship
with the United Nations during college. Our fathers' similarities softened my skepticism about this handsome man and made me more at
ease. *An apple doesn't fall far from the tree. This is true about Jack and
Robert. Why shouldn't it be the same for Jonathan and Bud?*

A buzz from the emergency room on Jonathan's pager cut our visit
and his storytelling short.

"Duty calls," he said. This time when he left my office, he gave me
a sexy smile and a mock salute. "See you Saturday, Suzanna."

After he had gone, I had a different perspective about the suave
young doctor. He wasn't cheeky but charming, and he revealed a vulnerability I liked. How many times had I made a snap judgment about
someone for it to turn out wrong? What was it Craig always said?
"Snap decisions make poor decisions." My new interest in Jonathan,
though, would prove to be my vulnerability.

* * *

I was twenty-four and flying high for a lot of reasons. I had my master's
degree and a full-time position as assistant director of academic affairs
in hand. With a steady revenue stream, I moved out of my parents'
home and rented my own place at the beginning of September 1982. I
had a grand housewarming party over Labor Day weekend to celebrate,
and my guests oohed and aahed over my digs in an area called the Bluffs
near downtown Worthington.

"Suzanna, this is immense! What are you going to do with all this
space?" Lillian asked when she scoped out my duplex.

"Tons of parties, of course," Jack smart-mouthed. I gave my brother
a sharp elbow in his side. "Well, just stating the obvious," he joked.

Lillian waved her hand. "Jack, straighten up," she said.

I turned and winked at Jack. "Some things never change," he said.

Our mother gave us the evil eye, shook her head, and continued examining every corner of my sixteen-hundred-square-foot palace. To be honest, when I rented the place, the same thought as my mother's had crossed my mind: *What am I going to do with a two-bedroom, two-bath duplex with a fireplace, finished basement, and garage?* But the rent was a deal I couldn't resist. And besides, the locals considered the area upper-crust, and my neighbors who occupied the other half of the duplex had a calico cat named Pumpkin whose friendliness sealed the deal.

* * *

I awoke to a crisp Midwestern morning with the sun creeping through the gaps between my bedroom curtains and dancing across the carpet. It was Saturday, October 23, 1982. Lying in bed, I stretched to my full length, settled back, and thought about the evening ahead with the twenty-eight-year-old emergency room resident. *Should I have been so quick to say yes to his invitation? On the upside, he's cute; on the downside, he's puzzling.* Afterward, I chuckled and whispered to myself, "But I do know his employer. I think I'm safe."

Jonathan arrived right at six thirty. When I opened the front door, what I saw took my breath away. My date stood on the stoop with an exquisite bouquet of peach and yellow roses in his hand. No guy had ever shown up on a first date with flowers. I hoped my dropped mouth and pink flush didn't reveal my shock.

Beyond the unexpected gift, the man standing in front of me was as drop-dead gorgeous as the flowers he handed me. I always had seen Jonathan from a sitting position. Now, standing beside him, I realized he was tall—over six feet, perhaps six foot one—with a lean and toned body. While he didn't measure up to Craig, whose rugged stature set the bar for all my dates during my college years, Jonathan's presence put him in a league of his own. His dress was casual but smart—a black pullover, tan slacks, and a dark blue sport coat. Loafers without socks and a gold chain bracelet around his wrist completed his ensemble. The entire package screamed expensive.

I was hip myself, decked out in a designer black wool wiggle-cut dress. The frock had cap sleeves and a rounded neck with a lone button at the nape that formed the top of a sweetheart opening in the back. I wore classic black suede pumps trimmed in silver, and I accessorized with my simple star pendant and a pair of delicate dangling earrings of the same color.

Jonathan smiled as he offered me the flowers and rolled his eyes over me. "Wow! Are you hot!"

My smile dissolved into a schoolmarm's look. I recognized the implicit bias of a vulgar term that turns a woman into a utility. I wasn't going to let the comment pass. "I'm not an oven! Besides needing a different pickup line, you ought to work on your compliments too."

My date drew back six inches. *He doesn't have a clue what I am saying. Why create tension at the start of the evening?*

"Hey, no problem," I said as I brought the bouquet in my hand to my face to breathe in its scent. I could tell an artisan had designed the arrangement of Juliet and Campanella roses mixed with succulents and berries and a dash of deep-blue lavender. Its fragrance was as exquisite as its beauty. "The flowers are lovely and a thoughtful touch. In fact, you must be psychic," I said.

His smoky eyes narrowed. "What do you mean?"

"Bringing me this elegant bouquet. How did you find out my brother and father call me Flower Girl?"

His eyes brightened, and his face grew a warm smile. "I'm happy you like them . . . It could be a psychic phenomenon or simply smart intelligence gathering. Doesn't matter. I've discovered more about you than you might think."

As I led Jonathan into my home, an inner voice warned, *Touché, but a little creepy.*

"Hey, cool place," he said after he strolled through the entry into the living room and scanned my home's surroundings.

"Yeah, I like it. The place has lots of room, the neighborhood is about fifteen minutes from work, and I have terrific neighbors."

"Love the fireplace. Terrific for cozying up to on an autumn night," he said, locking his eyes on me with a slight smile and then glancing away.

Get your mind out of the gutter, Suzanna. It's an innocent observation. He's not suggesting he wants to spend the night.

To be on the safe side, I lobbed back a retort. "Oh, yes! I totally agree, especially with a cat named Pumpkin."

"You have a cat?"

"Well, not exactly. Pumpkin is a gigantic, twenty-pound, yellow-striped feline from next door. We made friends the minute I moved in. He shows up most evenings for a cuddle. He also knows I'm a sucker for handing out kitty treats."

"Is Pumpkin my strongest competition?"

"Okay, doctor, you're fishing, and this trout ain't biting. Come with me to the kitchen and keep me company while I arrange these gorgeous flowers in a vase."

* * *

After I closed and locked the door, Jonathan slid his hand into mine and held it. We stood on the front steps, owning the moment. The evening props could not have been better if designed for a romance play on a theatrical stage. The brisk night air put my senses on edge, the bright sky blanketed us in a shower of diamonds, and the scent of smoke drifting on the breeze from neighborhood fireplaces soothed me.

I raised my head and scanned the evening's offerings. "Stunning."

"Indeed, it is," Jonathan said, looking down at me and giving my hand a squeeze.

He escorted me to his car and opened the passenger door of an older model car. Given Jonathan's trendy dress and haircut, not to mention his high school Firebird, I wasn't surprised he owned a Super Cobra Mustang, even if it was a decade old. Later, Jonathan would let me know what a status symbol and collectible the car was.

We arrived at Worthington Town Green, and Jonathan found a parking spot about a block away from our destination in front of an early 1800s vintage home. I got out of the low-slung vehicle and halted, looking at the clapboard home. "Do you think we'll see any ghosts tonight?" I said out loud.

Jonathan peered at me. "What do you mean? First, you think I'm a psychic, and now you are asking about ghosts?"

I shrugged.

"What's with the ghost thing?"

I laughed it off. "Oh, nothing much," I said as we stayed standing in front of the house.

"Whenever someone says 'Noting much,' I am suspicious. Are you a ghost whisperer?"

I gave him a wink. "All righty, I'll tell you the story."

He took my hand, and we started walking.

"One time, after shopping at the Worthington Square, I passed by this house while the owner was working in the garden. I love flowers, and the beds were impeccable, with a mixture of annuals and perennials that drew butterflies and bees. So I talked with her about her eye-catching plot. And then . . ." *He'll think I'm blazing nuts if I tell him the rest!*

"Go on. Forget the damn flowers. What about the ghosts?" he asked as we continued strolling toward the restaurant.

"All righty. While we were talking, the word 'ghost' popped into my mind, and I asked her, 'Does your home have any ghosts?' I thought the owner's eyes were going to pop from her head. 'How on earth did you know that?' she asked."

From the corner of his eye, Jonathan stared at me, brow raised. "And *how* did you know?"

"It was something I just felt."

Jonathan stopped walking, turned, eyes focused on me. "Well, did she say anything more? Anything specific about the ghost?"

"Yes, she did. Let's not stand here in the cold and go into it. Perhaps, over a glass of wine?"

We strolled for another half block, and the old inn came into sight. The building, dressed in twinkling white lights from top to bottom, appeared like a thousand pixies had descended on it. My head whirled like a giddy teenager on her first date. *I'm entering a fairytale with a handsome knight at my side.*

Inside, the inn was as magical. A comforting musty smell greeted us, flickering flames replaced sparking lights, and a rich mahogany wainscotting covered the walls like in the old buildings at OSU. As we walked across the dining room floor, the dark, broad wooden planks strained and creaked, showing their age and releasing the energy and secrets of generations past.

A reserved table by a crackling fire in an intimate part of the restaurant waited for us. The quivering light from a single candle on the tabletop danced across white linen, pewter silverware, and shimmering crystal water and wine glasses, creating a seductive romantic spell.

"You do like fireplaces!" I said as Jonathan helped me remove my coat, and I slipped into my chair.

"I do, indeed," he said, sitting down across from me. "Fireplaces bring back great memories from when I was a kid. During subzero winter evenings, I sat in front of a blazing fire reading mystery books with our black Lab, Sparky, next to me."

He waited, smiled, and sucked me into his mesmeric gaze. "I hope this fire will kindle pleasurable memories for many years to come."

I swallowed hard. I stared, locked in his hypnotic eyes, and the words, "I hope so too," tumbled from my mouth.

After the server poured the wine, Jonathan pressed me. "Come on and spill the beans. There's more to it. The ghost thing."

His smirk told me he was a doubter, and I kicked myself for mentioning the subject earlier. I kept the tale to the essentials. "Late in the evening, near ten o'clock, the current residents hear footsteps descending from the front staircase. Then, they stop for a second or two, and afterward, the front door opens and slams shut.

"That's it?"

I tilted my head. "That isn't enough? You don't think your staircase groaning with invisible footsteps and your front door opening and closing on its own isn't *a little* spooky?"

Jonathan took a sip of his wine. When he finished, he raised his brows, and his eyes tested me. "What are your feelings about this old inn? Are there ghosts running around here?"

"There are stories about the ghosts here. But you asked me about my feelings, not a secondhand tale." *Playing with this skeptic might be fun.* I lowered my eyes, took in several deep breaths, and a calm wave of energy rushed over me. I didn't want to return to the real world, but I opened my eyelids anyway. I studied Jonathan and leaned closer toward him. "There *are* phantoms here . . . nothing to worry about."

"Rather anticlimactic, but good to know, I guess . . . What raises my interest more than ghosts is why you touched that pendant around your neck when you were channeling the spirits here? The necklace caught my eye the other day. Some type of magic charm? From someone special?" The question hung in the air, begging for an explanation.

My hand went instinctively to my neck. *He doesn't miss much!*

"It was a gift from a friend—a friend who helped me find my purpose in life."

"That sounds consequential. Who is he?" Jonathan asked with raised eyebrows over eyes that had gone dead.

I felt a blush of anger climb my neck. *Besides better pickup lines and compliments, he needs to dial down his sarcasm.* I leaned back and sipped my wine without taking my eyes from his. *Should I ignore or respond?* I gave him the Craig pause and let my gaze wander beyond him into nothingness.

My silence melted the young physician's self-assuredness. "I didn't mean to come off rude or cocky. I'm interested, that's all."

I placed my glass on the table. "I'm glad you asked about Craig. He opened my eyes to appreciating my value and learning to live my truth. Because of him, I decided to become an academic counselor."

Jonathan listened as I explained how the necklace celebrated my strengths of appreciation of beauty, creativity, curiosity, love, and kindness. My date's memory was as sharp as the proverbial elephant, possibly due to his medical training, because without prompting, he probed me with questions about my five points.

"What do you appreciate about beauty? What is beauty, anyway?"

"Why is creativity important to you?"

"What do you mean by love?"

"Give me an example of your curiosity."

"Tell me about a time when you were kind."

His interest quelled concerns I had a few weeks earlier about his bad-boy persona. Now, I responded thoughtfully to his queries, interspersed with lighthearted puns that made us both laugh afterward. My flower girl stories of pinching the neighbors' blooms amused him, and he asked for more details about each event, questioning whether this continued to be a predilection.

"God forbid, Suzanna, I hope you don't have a passion for pirating other things, too, like the silverware here," he said.

"Nope, only flower beds are in danger of being raided," I assured him.

I realized, though, the conversation was all about me. It would be fruitless if I didn't understand any more about Jonathan at the end of the evening than I did at its beginning.

"And who was complaining about twenty questions the other day in my office?" I asked just before the dessert arrived.

"Point taken," Jonathan said as the waiter served the crème brûlée. "Go ahead and shoot, but I'll give you no more than twenty."

I started with the ones I thought would be easy. "Why did you choose to become a physician?"

"Because I wanted to help people."

"Why did you select emergency medicine for a specialization?"

"The fast pace turned me on—lots of chaos, full of surprises. Plus, shift work gives me control of my schedule. Terrific pay, too, helps."

"You said you liked books. Which ones are your favorites?"

"Crime mostly. Stuff like *The Day of the Jackal* and *Red Dragon*."

But whenever I strayed into follow-up questions that probed beneath the superficial layers—such as, "What do you mean by wanting to help people?" or "What do you like about the chaos of the ER?"—Jonathan found it difficult to express himself. Although liking crime stories isn't a red flag about someone's personality, in retrospect, delving into his affinity for the genre may have given me a heads-up about his sadistic inclinations, providing I would have listened.

Unlike Gary, Jack, Craig, Mel, or Ellen, who could share the meaning behind the words they used to describe their reasoning, likes, and dislikes, Jonathan could not go more than skin-deep in his explanations. His answer to my question, "What's important to you?" brought me up short.

He reached across the table and took my hand and held it. He stared into the embers of the fire. "No one has ever asked me that question. I don't have an answer."

He turned his eyes toward mine and brought my hand to his lips, laying the gentlest of kisses on it. "I'm going to think about that. Whenever I figure out the answer, I'll tell you."

Ignoring his inability to answer my questions was something that would come back to haunt me.

* * *

Jonathan's fun side went off like a rocket after we finished dinner. Remembering I loved dancing, he chose a more adult venue than the High Street haunts as a finale to our evening. Driving to the nightspot, I observed Jonathan's identity meld with his Mustang. When I threw twenty questions at him about the vehicle, the man sitting in the bucket seat next to me had no difficulty supplying answers. He knew tidbits about its origin—introduced at the 1964 World's Fair—and its name —first pitched after the WWII Mustang fighter plane but then for commercial reasons named for the mustang horse.

Jonathan relished the car's stereotype of power and masculinity. "I am hyped and in control when I rev its engine and make its wheels squeal."

And, of course, the name Mustang communicated wildness, passion, and recklessness. "The car is my body armor. Sort of like a Romulan cloaking device," he quipped. "It provides an advantage in surprise attacks."

Those remarks should have clued me into Jonathan's sinister side, but his fun-loving Dr. Jekyll concealed his Mr. Hyde. Jonathan was an attentive date and a fabulous dance partner, surprising me with his ballroom steps and disco ability. I would be blind to miss the gawking females who had their eyes glued to the most attractive male body in the place. And Jonathan wasn't oblivious to the stares I got from the guys in the room.

"I see I'm going to have to keep the predators at bay tonight," he said. "I'm up for the challenge."

The Swing is one of my favorite dances, and Jonathan did not disappoint in spinning me across the dance floor. We laughed and teased that we were acting out a mating dance as we wiggled our hips, shimmied our torsos, and bumped our sides. But the slow music left me breathless. When we danced to Eric Clapton's "Wonderful Tonight," Jonathan sang the lyrics in my ear while holding me tight. His warm breath floated across my neck and sent tingles through me to my toes. His massaging touch made me surrender to my impulses. I lost perspective. *Perhaps spending the night in front of my fireplace wouldn't be so bad, after all.*

Lost in my emotions, I didn't realize the snare had been set.

Chapter 7

GIVE AND TAKE

The deception may have started in the beginning—at Dr. Walker's presentation when Jonathan and I first acknowledged each other with teasing grins. Or, perhaps, it was during Jonathan's first or second visit to my office when I straddled the roles between a professional and an ingenue. It could have been when he presented me with the fragrant bouquet of delicate roses and, sensing my appreciation of beauty, took advantage of the flower girl in me. In any case, knowing the start of the ruse is not as important as understanding that, over time, deceit strengthens and builds on itself. It continues until it culminates in destruction. Unveiling the pretense is not sufficient to end its damage. The way to stop the devastation and salvage the remains is to eradicate the deception.

* * *

White heat and a whirlwind of whimsy defined the fall and holiday season. Jonathan's residency schedule left him little free time, but we maximized it. His erratic timetable dictated more takeout Chinese than fancy restaurant cuisine. Cuddling, necking, and more in front of my fireplace during the long nights solidified our bond. I rejoiced in accepting the challenge of caring for an enigmatic soul whose loose ends I wanted to help tie. In reality, I understood little about myself and my motives and those of the man I thought I was trying to save.

Our second evening together, we sat on the floor facing the fireplace of my home, and Jonathan gave me pointers on the proper positioning of logs in the hearth as he placed the seasoned wood in a log cabin configuration for the fourth time. Afterward, he added kindling and struck a match.

"What do you think?" he asked, standing back admiring his work.

I nodded and took a sip of the Grand Marnier from my snifter.

Scooting back, he put his arm around my shoulder. "What's the real story with your North Star and this Craig fellow? Is he in your life now?"

The out-of-the-blue question blew like a siren. I bit my upper lip. "Are you jealous?"

"Do I look like a guy who has to be jealous? I just want to know where I stand."

I tamped down the warning. I nodded. I didn't want to play games —I'd give him what he wanted, what any guy deserved.

"Craig is a war veteran who went through stuff neither of us can comprehend. The experience—the killing, blood, senseless destruction —left him broken with psychological and emotional injuries. I was with him during one of his flashbacks. After seeing its effects, it isn't something I would wish on anyone. With tenacity, he reconnected with himself, found his meaning in life, and started to live his truth."

"And?"

I probed Jonathan's eyes. I thought a light flickered in them as if he were struggling to make sense of what I had said. How could I begin to describe my relationship with Craig? How could I explain the heartbreak of a love I knew could never be fulfilled?

"He's a friend who helped me turn my life in the right direction— find my strengths and apply them. This necklace, my North Star, is a metaphor for these."

"And?"

"And what?"

"Where is Craig now?"

"He's doing what makes him happy. He teaches high school in one of the poorest counties in Appalachia." I wavered, knowing that wasn't what Jonathan wanted to hear. "We stay in touch, once in a while, through letters, but we are not now or ever were lovers."

The admission sounded like an apology. *Apologizing! Apologizing for what?* My face muscles stiffened in annoyance with Jonathan and me —Jonathan for pressing me and me for caving to his demand.

Jonathan saw my expression, looked away, and stared at the quivering flames, looking lost. "Suzanna, I'm asking these questions because I've been hurt in the past. I was deceived, and I don't want to go through that pain again."

His admission knocked me off my balance. It also made me vulnerable, wanting to fix the hurt, sacrifice myself, and reclaim justice for him. "I'm sorry you were betrayed and hurt. Trust is the foundation of a relationship. I will always be honest with you . . ." And then, for an unexplained reason, I added, "As I hope you will be with me."

Jonathan reached over and lightly ran his finger across the front of my neck and rested it on the pendant.

"You know, Suzanna, metaphors are effective tools. They create meaning and often help express reality. I use them sometimes to explain things to my patients. And I encourage them to use metaphors to tell me about themselves. The simple question 'What does that feel like?' and getting an answer gives me clues in figuring out what's happening with a patient."

"You mean like if someone says he feels like an old wet rag?"

"Exactly!" he said. "Such a description can tell me plenty. I'd ask the patient for more detail, but my instinct would be he is tired, lethargic, or perhaps depressed."

Moving closer to Jonathan with the fireplace embers warming my face, I gave him a tender kiss on the mouth and afterward said, "You are a genius, Jonathan Spencer."

He pulled me tight and brushed his lips on the side of my face, whispering, "I love you so much, Suzanna."

Though Jonathan had skirted a commitment of honesty to me, the warning buzzer started to grow fainter as my kindness went into overdrive and hoped to be the one who could help this man find himself.

* * *

My parents and brother were curious about "Dr. Kildare," as Lillian referred to Jonathan. As Thanksgiving approached, they pressed me to introduce him. My family believed I had a revolving door of suitors, which was correct to a certain extent. I had had lots of boyfriends, but none had replaced the unique place Craig had held in my heart.

"Craig's a pretty high bar to jump over," my dad told me several times. "He's been through plenty. It may be best to leave this relationship in the friendship category." If anyone understood Craig's hesitation to be in a permanent relationship, it was Robert, who was battle-scarred himself.

I agreed with my father's assessment, but it was difficult not to measure all my relationships against the bond I had with Craig. We had never made love, but our intimacy was profound, and I did not want to accept a lifelong physical relationship with someone else without the same degree of companionship I had with Craig.

Since Jonathan was a regular overnight visitor to my home—something unusual for me—his appearance on the scene intrigued my relatives.

Lillian uncovered our relationship one Sunday when she came for lunch at my house. "Hmm. Two toothbrushes?" she asked after visiting my master bathroom. Her eyes narrowed, and then she smiled.

Thanksgiving Day was the scheduled "reveal," as Jack jokingly called Jonathan's first meeting with the family. When my new guy-pal arrived, he was an immediate hit with Lillian, handing her an attractively designed flower bouquet that was as beautiful as the one he had given me on our first date. Lillian oohed and aahed over each petal in the arrangement while Robert and Jack gave Jonathan their lawyer eyeball treatment. I winked at Jack, and he threw me a stare beneath a wrinkled forehead. He had barely gotten started sizing up Jonathan.

The dinner gathering went off without a hitch. Lillian prepared a gourmet meal, and the table setting would have challenged a five-star restaurant. Jonathan impressed my family to the degree any boyfriend of mine could. He showed a range of positive emotions on a continuum from humor to seriousness. His listening and questioning skills, honed by his medical training, were impressive, although not matching the family's two legal eagles. It didn't hurt that Jonathan's father was an attorney, albeit just a "simple country lawyer." This turn of phrase made my brother and dad howl.

"Whenever someone tells me he is a simple country lawyer, I get worried," Robert told Jonathan.

After our meal, my parents, Jonathan, and Jack's wife, Lorna, continued the party in the living room while Jack and I did our traditional KP duty. In my preteen years, I was a pesky little sister, more in the way than helping my big brother. As I grew older, though, the two of us became a well-oiled team who could clean up the kitchen in lickety-split time.

"Soooo?" I asked, giving Jack a nudge on the shoulder.

"So what?"

I took the dish towel and snapped it across my brother's backside. "Jack, come off it! You know what I mean."

"What am I? A clairvoyant, now?"

"Oh, cut it out, dumb ass," I said.

Jack sighed and turned back to the kitchen sink to rinse the dishes. This was a sure sign my brother wasn't ready to give my boyfriend his complete approval.

"He's got some pluses. I mean, he's good-looking with an athletic build, although he can't come close to *me* in either of those categories."

"Okay, any other observations beyond the obvious?"

"Yeah, he comes across as okay."

"Hey, I'm pulling teeth here. What's up with that?"

"Okay. The guy is educated. He has some witty comebacks. He's observant and listens and carries on a decent conversation . . ."

"And?" I asked as I placed the last of the glasses in the dishwasher.

"Well, he is very attentive to the ladies."

"And what the heck does that mean?"

Jack turned and faced me, hands wet and water dripping from them on the floor. "I'm uncertain, Flower Girl. He has all the right packaging . . . But he raised my lawyer's bullshit antenna. Dad's went up too. There's a lot of fluff there and no substance. Something in those eyes is masking an insincerity, or perhaps it's insecurity. Hell, I don't think he likes women."

I stood motionless. "What are you talking about? Like he's gay?"

"No, no, that's not it. I'm picking up an underlying contempt or bitterness."

"Jack, you're not making sense. Two minutes ago, you said Jonathan is attentive to the ladies!"

"Yeah, that's the point, Flower Girl. He's too attentive. You've got to watch out for people like that." My brother's frown and tightened jaw gave me a chill.

"I hate the expression, *people like that*," I said under my breath as Jack left the kitchen to join the others.

This was the one time I became hostile toward Jack. I would have been in a better place had I heeded his instincts.

* * *

The day after Thanksgiving, my mother and I hit the Kingsdale Mall for our annual holiday shopping spree. Instead of fighting a horde of anxious and bumper-to-bumper patrons at the downtown department store, we preferred the more intimate and less stressed atmosphere of "our own Lazarus" in Upper Arlington. There, we rode the escalator to the top floor, conducting surveillance for sales and best buys, before working our way down to ground level and meandering through each department in the multilevel store. Laden down a few hours later with our bags of goodies from Lazarus, we tossed them in the car trunk and afterward set out to scout our favorite shops along the mall patio. The highlight, though, was a leisurely lunch at a little bistro, where we filled the time with girl talk.

Lillian wasn't an attorney, but she had lawyer instincts. She could cross-examine equal to my father or Jack, and today she was in fighting form.

"Okay, Suzanna, I'm going to give you the third degree," my mother said after we ordered lunch.

We both laughed at Lillian's code for friendly interrogation, but I knew my mother would have the upper hand. During my rebellious teenage years, Lillian and I were often at each other's throats. Things changed once I turned eighteen and passed the threshold into what Lillian considered my adult stage, and without reservation, she gave up the role of a control matron. She became my confidante; I shared my worries, frustrations, hopes, and joys and often sought her perspectives before I made decisions.

"He's a cutie," Lillian said. "I mean, like, positively sexy. If I were a few years younger, you might have competition," she teased. "What's the deal with Jonathan? Do you think this is the one?" she asked. One of the qualities I admire in my mother is her frankness—Lillian always lays her cards on the table. Now, she sought an earnest discussion about my new boyfriend.

"We've just dated for a month," I said.

Lillian frowned and squinted her eyes. I got her message. She was ready to foil any sorry attempt to steer her off track. "One month with regular overnighters. If you're bedding down with a guy that often, something is happening," she said without embarrassment.

Lillian and I had had the "sex before marriage" talk at the end of my junior year in high school. Without a doubt, it was one of the most freeing conversations of my life. My mother handed me two gifts during that chat: one was autonomy, the other responsibility.

"Other parents might be more conservative than I am on this issue," she had said. "Bottom line—my belief is if you are old enough to vote, fight in a war, or serve on a jury, you damn well can make your own choices about sex."

When Lillian stepped up on her soapbox, there was no stopping her. "I have no problem with you having sex, but two things must be met. One, it is your free choice, not coerced or forced on you. Two, you protect yourself from STDs and getting pregnant. You meet those criteria and I'm fine with it, married or not." This was how Lillian acknowledged my adult status, but it also came with an understanding that I had responsibilities to fill.

"I take it he's good in bed," Lillian said as a statement more than a question. She didn't wait for my response. "You know my thinking on the subject. If the romance isn't going well in the bedroom, nothing else is going well either. That's the lowest bar though." She stopped, and her blue eyes drilled right through me.

"What about his values, his likes, his hobbies, and what he wants in life?"

I sat silent. Could I list these? Even Jonathan couldn't articulate his purpose.

Lillian reached over and patted my hand.

"Honey, if those things don't mesh with yours, being terrific in the sack isn't going to be enough for a fulfilling relationship."

I squirmed in my seat. Jack's shocking suggestion the previous evening about a lot of fluff and no substance niggled at me. I thought about my short relationship with Jonathan, and I didn't recall anything to alert me he had contempt for me or any other woman; Jack was way off base. Now, my mother was shooting me hard-hitting questions, and I was surprised to find myself mentally pushing back.

"Well? Tell me. What makes Jonathan tick?" Lillian pressed.

I fiddled with the food on my plate, trying to recall what Jonathan said about his vision, hopes, or dreams. "He wants to help people. He likes helping people."

"Yeah, I got that last night," Lillian said. "Superficial hogwash! What's the motivation?"

"Motivation?"

"Yeah. A guy can help people because he makes money off it. Or because he likes the limelight or gets folk's approval. On the other hand, maybe it's because he believes in justice, generosity, or wanting to see other people have a prosperous life."

I didn't speak but instead mulled over what Lillian had said.

"And what does he think about you? Does he respect you and your values and what you want in life?"

I averted my eyes, refusing to look either Lillian or reality in the face.

"Sweetheart, I'm not telling you anything new. After all, you *are* the counselor."

My mother's comments felt like an observation, not a sermon. Did I know anything at all about Jonathan? Had I gotten too wrapped up in the excitement he tossed out like a web?

"I love you," I said and held Lillian's hand. "You are the best counselor sitting at this table."

* * *

With our shopping spree finished, I took Lillian home ladened with a half-dozen overflowing shopping bags. On the drive back to my place, my mother's last question at lunch haunted me. Lillian didn't mean the clichéd saying, "Will he respect you in the morning?" No, for my mother, the word meant sympathetic regard for me as a resourceful and creative person who has value in and of myself. Her query eerily harmonized with my brother's observation. As much as I wanted to avoid facing an awkward conversation with Jonathan, the question Lillian posed required answering. My mind pushed to justify and rationalize my reluctance to go toe-to-toe with Jonathan on the subject. *Shouldn't that type of discussion happen organically? Shouldn't I know he already believes I am resourceful and creative and have worth and value?*

* * *

Since purchasing their home, my mother and father held what they called a reunion on Christmas eve. It included our immediate and extended family of aunts, uncles, cousins, and friends and neighbors. The event was on the top of everyone's list of holiday parties, and each year Lillian outdid the preparations of the previous year. Two giant Christmas trees, decorated in different themes, welcomed visitors as they entered the lofty foyer of my parents' home. Catered hot and cold appetizers appeased our guests' appetites, hot cider and eggnog —spiked and plain—quenched everyone's thirsts, and live music and traditional caroling heightened the evening celebrations.

To Lillian's dismay, Robert and Jack strained the local electrical utility's capacity with an outdoor holiday show every year. Two years earlier, she put her foot down on the household males' extravagance. "No more carnival show! Lights only, no moving Santas, singing snowmen, or anything having to do with beasts of burden or resembling chipmunks, caribou, or deer," Lillian ordered. I always believed that secretly Robert and Jack were relieved to have a narrower focus.

The Sunday after Thanksgiving, Jonathan and I had an early breakfast at a small café in downtown Worthington. He had just finished the night shift at the ER, and we were catching some "debrief" time before he went home to crash in bed. Wound up like a chatterbox, my holiday spirit was spilling over as I told Jonathan about every aspect of the upcoming holiday mega-party my parents were planning.

"I hope you'll be getting the evening off. The celebration wouldn't be much fun without you there," I said.

Jonathan's smile drained from his face.

"Oh, no! Are you working the night shift?" I asked.

"No, it's not that, Suzanna. It's that we had Thanksgiving with your family. I want to start our own holiday traditions. I want you to myself."

"Starting our own traditions?" I said, my conscious mind rejecting to record the part about wanting me to himself.

Jonathan put down his coffee and held my hand. "Our first Christmas Eve together will be a singular memory for both of us all our lives, Bunny," he whispered, adding a mysterious smile.

Jonathan's wish to not partake in my family's traditional festivities had never entered my mind. I silently kicked around what he said—making our own traditions—trying to find a mediation.

"How about a little give-and-take?" I asked.

With a closed-mouth smile and the flick of a raised eyebrow over a steady gaze, Jonathan sexually charmed and disarmed me. "I'm all for give-and-take. Exactly what did you have in mind?" he asked.

He tilted his head and left his locked eyes on me. He leaned in, reached beneath the table, and pressed his fingers along the inside of my leg. My body shuddered, subjecting me to his capture.

I lowered my eyes. "Jonathan Spencer, you are impossible and manipulative," I said.

He threw back his head and laughed. "It's working!"

I fell for his Svengali ruse. "Since you like to give and take, what do you have to give?" I asked.

His hand inched higher. "I want nothing more than to have you all to myself on Christmas Eve. You know, dinner, wine, and entwined in front of the fireplace searching for your, um . . ." He grinned like an elf.

I put my hand over his and stopped the private war between us under the café table.

"You still haven't answered my question. What do you have to give?"

"Hmm," he groaned, embarrassingly loud. "I'll give you a sandwich."

"A sandwich?" I loosened my grip on his hand, and he took advantage.

"Unfair," I said, retightening my hold.

He stared ahead, his jaw set. "What time is the party?"

"It starts at eight o'clock and winds up about one in the morning."

"Here's the give, the inside of a sandwich."

Jonathan removed his hand from under the table, and taking both hands, he made bookends on the tabletop. Raising his left hand, he said, "This is the beginning of the evening." He directed his eyes to his right hand. "This is the end." He paused and stared at me.

"So?" I asked with jacked-up brows.

"The space in between is what I'm giving your family. I get the ends of the sandwich."

Chapter 8

CAPTIVATION

A shadow crosses my face when I think about the fall and holiday season in 1982. At the time, I wanted to believe that Jonathan and I were on the same wavelength: having fun, enjoying each other, and sharing affection. On reflection, I see the operative words are "wanted to." What we want to believe is true often turns out to be the opposite.

* * *

Monday, December 20, and I still had no idea about Jonathan's plans for our Christmas eve tradition. That evening over takeout dinner, I prodded him. "Give me some clue about what we will be doing, so I'll know what to wear."

He grinned. "How about nothing?"

"Stop it!"

"Bunny, you always look spectacular."

"That's not good enough," I said.

He stuffed the last of an egg roll into his mouth and made me wait for an answer while he finished eating it.

"Okay, I'll give in."

He steadied his chin on the back of his hand and grinned with his eyes. "Envision formal and fancy. Envision romantic and expensive. Envision looking like the flower princess you are."

He bent forward, nuzzled my neck, and murmured, "And afterward, envision nothing at all."

I giggled and slapped his shoulder. "There's a whole lot of envisioning in your plans."

His prolonged look, followed by a passionate kiss, didn't answer my question. Instead, it held me hostage and hoping there would be a whole lot more than envisioning happening on Christmas Eve.

* * *

Friday, December 24. The big day had arrived. I woke midmorning, stretched, and hugged my pillow, relishing the idle time—no commitments, no demands, and no concessions to intrude on the intimacy of those first morning moments. Though ER docs were supposed to have a structured schedule, Jonathan's had been irregular, and we had spent almost a week apart. We agreed to be an exclusive couple, but we hadn't committed to joint living arrangements. Jonathan kept a one-bedroom apartment and had invited me many times to stay overnight. The thought of keeping two closets of clothes and sets of personal items was not on my wish list. Since Jonathan's personal and clothing needs —shirt, tie, slacks, resident's white coat, shaver, toothbrush—were less than mine, it made sense for him to stay at my place.

Jonathan had refused to tell me where we would be spending Christmas Eve. "It will spoil the surprise," he said. Nagging thoughts ate away at my enthusiasm for the evening. This was Jonathan's plan, not ours. He may have meant well, but it was controlling. Was infatuation robbing me of my autonomy? Why wasn't I more assertive in voicing my preferences in the tradition-making? As fast as these concerns surfaced, I stifled them. After all, I did get a compromise from him to attend my parents' annual holiday party. Isn't that what relationships are? Compromises?

My assumption was our celebration would include dinner at an upscale restaurant, so I shook the pessimistic thoughts from my head, scurried out of bed, and unzipped the garment bag in my closet. I scanned the forest-green hourglass satin sheath—the sweetheart neckline and short puffed sleeves with triangular slits were a nice touch. The color was a perfect match with the hue on my winter color wheel. Its simplicity and rich material were classy and meshed with my black velveteen pumps and dangling white gold earrings.

Standing back and checking out the new evening dress, I fingered the pendant hanging around my neck. A rush of nostalgia transported me to thoughts of Craig. Since the day I received the keepsake, I had worn it. If my confidence needed boosting, a light stroke of my fingers across the star's five points reminded me of my strengths and value. When my mood needed uplifting, a gentle grasp of the memento warmed my heart. If my courage could use jacking up, rubbing my North Star gave me guidance.

Now, I thought back on Jonathan's remarks the previous week and second-guessed myself. Was my unconscious toying with the necklace so noticeable?

"Why are you doing that, Suzanna?" Jonathan had asked.

"Doing what?"

"Rubbing that pathetic star as if you were trying to make a genie appear."

His tone made me jump. "Perhaps one will," I sassed.

Silence. He looked at me like an abandoned puppy.

"Please, Bunny. When you caress that thing . . . it is as if someone else is at the center of your attention. Like I'm unwanted."

My subconscious registered the warning, but I overrode my caution and tried to subdue Jonathan's insecurity.

"It is a habit and nothing more, Jonathan. It helps me remember who I am. It is nothing to do with anyone else. It is like a good luck charm, a talisman."

Jonathan's stare went from victim to glassy-eyed.

"Why do you believe a necklace can replace you?" I asked.

There was another long silence. "The necklace is not the issue. What it represents is the problem."

"Represents? You don't like that it represents me?"

Jonathan's jaw clenched. "It *is* a gift from another man."

I took a deep breath and held it.

"You haven't let Craig go, have you? Christ, that thing is around your neck even when we make love. How do you think that makes me feel?"

I stopped myself from yelling back at him. That would escalate the situation—make him madder. I controlled my emotions and tried to see his perspective.

"You're right, Jonathan. Someone significant in my life gave me the necklace. I can understand how you might interpret Craig's relationship as romantic. I told you before what we had was a friendship. Craig appeared when I needed guidance in finding my purpose. He helped put me in touch with my core, my values, and my direction. The pendant is a symbol of me, not of Craig."

Jonathan's face turned burgundy. His breathing became heavy. My counselor's eyes spotted his struggle to make sense of what I had told him. I waited. I hoped my explanation would assuage his fears.

"I sort of get it. But, Bunny, you need to understand I've never had that kind of relationship with anyone."

He wrung his hands. His mouth twitched.

"I admit it. I'm jealous. What's bugging me is not whether you had a romance with Craig but that you had an emotionally intimate friendship. I could handle it if you had sex with him—no big deal. This is different. This is worse. He is like a soulmate or something."

What type of wounded person was under that handsome exterior? I lowered my eyes and saw his clenched fists. How could I help him? How could I fix this?

"I can't wipe away my life history. I can't delete the people from my memory who have helped me: my parents, Jack, Melanie, Ellen, Craig, Gary, and others. Each of them makes up the fabric I am. The physical gifts—a necklace, a record album, a book, a teddy bear, or a bracelet—I keep to remind myself what each has given me. If I took any of these away, I'd be ripping my fabric to pieces."

Jonathan didn't speak. His silence overwhelmed me with guilt.

"What is making this difficult for you?" I whispered.

"I'm sorting it out, Bunny. Figuring out if I can ever be happy." He squeezed my hand, his gaze still resting on my necklace.

"How can I help you with this?"

His lips smiled but his eyes did not. "Don't get all psychoanalytic on me. How about not touching that thing all the time?"

"I will try to do that," I said, pushing a metaphorical key into a lock and turning it.

"Remember, Jonathan, you are weaving a part of my fabric. You are as important in my life as everyone who has gone before."

"But I want to be *the most* important," he said as he leaned in and kissed my cheek.

* * *

Recalling the conversation as I dressed for Christmas Eve dinner, I fiddled with the clasp on the silver chain around my neck, trying to remove my star pendant. I stopped. Removing the necklace would not end Jonathan's jealousy. It would camouflage it. I promised Jonathan I would try to stop touching my North Star, not remove it. Stripping away the symbol of my strengths to appease his insecurity denied me and my autonomy. I had a choice! It stayed on.

* * *

"The Refectory. That's where I'm taking you," Jonathan said as we got into his car. "By the way, you look spectacular." Then he leaned over and kissed my lips and made me melt.

Jonathan knew the trendy Columbus restaurant, turned sleek eating establishment from an old monastery dining hall, oozed romance and would push my pleasure buttons. Its wood-beamed ceilings created an intimate space crafted for a dreamy evening. Impeccably positioned fine china, crystal stemware, and silver cutlery on starched white linen cloths enhanced each table with flickering candlelight.

As the host seated us, my eyes focused on the wood-burning fireplace next to our cozy table for two. "Are fireplaces to be one of our traditions?"

Jonathan reached across the table and held my hand. "You have lit a fire in my heart that will never be extinguished."

His eyes searched mine across the candle's flickering flame for a like response, targeting my soft spot, my kindness, my wish to make him happy.

I squeezed his hand. "Me too," I whispered as if I were a ventriloquist's partner.

Presented in artistic displays, our dinner fare challenged the most experienced cuisine artist's expertise. We savored exotic delicacies from the tarte Lyonnaise appetizer through the Bavarian pear pastry for dessert. As we sipped glasses bubbling with champaign, we shared our dreams for the future: mine to work toward a doctorate in psychology and his to find a position in academic medicine. As the evening moved on, it was clear Jonathan's vision included making our relationship permanent.

"No girl has challenged me to think about a grander scheme in life," Jonathan said. "Women date me because . . . well, let's be frank, because of my looks and financial prospects. I can tell they like the idea of status more than they like me. You are different, Bunny. You're not shallow. You bring meaning to my life."

His statement startled and saddened me. *How does someone with so much going for him have such low self-esteem?* My limited background in psychology didn't supply an answer, but his remark confirmed why he opposed my star pendant. *With these feelings, no wonder he is jealous of my friendship with Craig.* My compassion urged me to understand.

"What makes you believe other women didn't appreciate you for yourself?" I asked.

He chuckled. "Experience."

"Experience? What kind of experience?"

"The experience of letting my guard down, opening myself up to someone, and finding out later what keeps them coming back is the status of my MD degree. A way of using me to lure someone else. You know, making another guy jealous by dating me. A way of catching a bigger fish."

My heart froze. What was the real story here? What's pushed him to these conclusions? Jonathan had all the privileges one could hope for:

family status, physical attractiveness, excellent education, and promising career. Still, he lacked the keystone of confidence—knowing who he is.

I reached across the table for his well-formed and strong hands—hands I relished as he caressed my body during our lovemaking. I cupped these in mine, stroking the smooth skin underneath my fingertips.

"Several weeks ago, I asked you what is important to you, Jonathan, and—"

"Yes, and I told you I would be thinking about that. I'm still thinking."

I accepted his response; pressing further was fruitless. It was hard to understand how a person who had chosen medicine as a career could struggle with self-meaning, who could not answer that question. Was it because he didn't know the answer? Or was it that he didn't want to admit what it was?

As we drained our last flutes of champaign, Jonathan reached into his pocket. He pulled out a small box whose wrapping I recognized right away as Tiffany's robin's-egg blue.

My heart hopscotched, half expecting a marriage proposal. The prospect frightened me but looking at the parcel, I realized it was bigger than a ring case. I threw Jonathan a girlish smile and let my curiosity take the driver's seat.

He slid the wrapped gift my way. "I couldn't let our first Christmas Eve pass without giving my girl something extraordinary."

"Shall I open it now? Before Christmas?"

He nodded his response and added, "Another tradition in the making."

Over the years, Lillian received many gifts from Robert wrapped in this iconic packaging. The jewelry maker was a favorite of Jack's, who splurged on the engagement ring he gave to Lorna. I untied the familiar silk ribbon that had graced my father's gifts to my mother but had never adorned any I had received. I took my time, unwrapping the shiny paper encasing the small parcel in my hand. I pulled out a smoky-gray box that fit across my palm and gazed at it.

MERIDA JOHNS

"Go ahead," he said.

I opened the spring-loaded lid. I shuddered when I viewed the contents, and regret eclipsed my delight. The expensive necklace with a torpedo pearl and three blue sapphires glistened in the candlelight. But this gift came with strings attached—ones a puppeteer controlled.

"It is beautiful, Jonathan. It is more than beautiful; it is exquisite," I said in a hushed tone.

"Wear it, and you will make me the happiest man in the world," he whispered.

Should I do what he wanted? I had a choice. I hesitated . . . he studied me. I reached for the fastener behind my neck, complying with the puppeteer's pull. My eyes cast down, I removed my North Star and laid it on the table. Jonathan lifted my hands to his lips. He kissed my fingers as if this were a ritual, his seal approving my actions. He removed the pearl and sapphire bobble from its box, got up, and walked to the back of my chair. An anchor of weight and coldness choked me as Jonathan positioned the necklace on me. The clasp shut, and I closed my eyes. Jonathan stroked his smooth fingertips along the sides of my neck, and I raised my right hand and began fingering the new jewels. My blood ran cold. He had sprung the snare. I made the easy choice, but . . .

* * *

We arrived at my parent's home, where the Christmas celebrations had been in high gear for over two hours. Jonathan slowed his Mustang beast to a crawl, gawking at the dazzling light display on the front lawn.

"You were right. It is amazing, but hell, the closet parking spot is a block away."

I jabbed my date on the shoulder. "Should have gotten here earlier," I said and got a shrug in return.

If the outside decorations impressed Jonathan, the holiday wonderland greeting us when we entered the house awed him. "Holy crap," he said under his breath. An enormous floor-to-ceiling Christmas tree, themed with angels and white lights, consumed most of the foyer. Just beyond, the staircase railing, decorated with magnolia leaves, boughs of evergreens, bows, pinecones, and glass balls dusted in sparkling gold, enhanced the elegant vibe.

The family room buzzed with revelers chatting in front of a massive fir tree decked with ornaments and lights that appeared as if they had sprung from the 1920s. Sweet sounds from the string quartet in the dining room swirled throughout the house like a magical carpet of sensuous vibrations. Jonathan nodded at me, and I smiled back. I was happy we could share the "sandwich" experience.

* * *

I didn't think myself inexperienced in the bedroom, considering my sexual experimentation equal to any 1980s twenty-something woman —that is until lovemaking with Jonathan on our first Christmas Eve together. His bedroom technique had always been above par. But that night, he opened a secret door leading me down a path of psychedelic colors and erotic sensations and taking me to a state of sexual arousal I had never experienced. I wept after our lovemaking, and with my body still convulsing, Jonathan placed himself atop of me. Using the chain of my Christmas gift as a trail marker, he planted the gentlest of kisses first along one side of my neck and then the other, culminating with a caress of the pearl and sapphire bobble. I had allowed Jonathan's sexual prowess to mesmerize me. I was his captive.

I awoke Christmas morning to discover the passionate sex the previous evening wasn't a fluke. Given Jonathan's magic potion once, I welcomed it again, and like a child given chocolate, I consumed it in decadent delight.

After we made love, Jonathan brushed his hands across my naked back and smothered my spine from bottom to top in kisses before whispering in my ear, "Hey, Bunny, there is one more surprise to add to our Christmas tradition.

I smiled and turned my head toward him. "Really? What could be better than what I just had?"

He laughed and planted another kiss on my lips. "Get dressed! A suitcase is packed for you and in the car. Grab your makeup, and we'll be ready to go."

My smile dissipated, and my thoughts struggled through a fog. Packed suitcase for me? What about Christmas dinner with my parents? The bookends of the sandwich he promised? Where were we going, and why were we leaving at six thirty in the morning?

I turned over and roused myself. "Go where?"

Jonathan taunted me as if he were a playful four-year-old. "It's a surprise, Bunny."

I regained my senses. I wasn't going to tolerate bamboozling by a preschooler. "I'm not moving from this bed until you give me specifics."

Jonathan frowned and scrunched his shoulders. "Okay, one clue."

The silence built.

"We're boarding a plane in two hours."

I lay immobile. "A plane? We can't be going away in two hours. We have plans to join my family for Christmas dinner."

Jonathan's eyes turned steel-gray and as sharp as swords. Throwing off the bedcovers, he got up. His earlier playfulness changed into acidity. "We spent Thanksgiving and Christmas Eve with your parents. I gave you the damn sandwich."

But he hadn't given me both ends of the sandwich. I looked at him, eyes widening and mouth dropping, incapable of finding my voice.

"How can you, on Christmas Day, reject my surprise gift for you? I'm taking you to meet my parents. I told my folks all about you. I promised I'd bring you home for the holiday. They will be devastated if we don't show up."

I stared into the room that had turned as cold as ice. *What the hell?*

Jonathan's emotions fluctuated like a weathervane. He turned to me, tears forming in his eyes. In a muted voice, he dove into an apology. "Look, Bunny, maybe I should have told you. No, I should have said something, but I wanted it to be a . . . I'm sorry. I'm sorry," he said.

I took a deep breath, but it couldn't cover the sound in my ears of my racing heartbeats.

Jonathan sat down on the bed, his back toward me and his head in his hands. "This is a mess. I don't recall you mentioning dinner with your folks."

I told him several times, but I also remembered he never said yes, and he never said no.

He shook his head with a disparaging snarl. "I thought we'd agreed the Christmas Eve party with them was enough. I made these blasted plans and promises to my parents. Shit! I'm sorry, Bunny. Forget it. I'll fly home. You can go to be with your parents."

I reached up and placed my fingers on the top of Jonathan's shoulder, and he responded, putting his hand over mine. I was torn between anger and confusion. Had I not made our Christmas plans explicit? Hadn't I confirmed this with him? Was I to blame?

My compassion swelled as Jonathan's shoulders sagged and his emotions teetered. I allowed self-doubt to rule, believing in the sincerity of my lover's remorsefulness and questioning my fairness. After all, we did spend Christmas Eve with my family.

We were on the plane to Chicago two hours later to join Jonathan's parents for a lavish Christmas getaway and celebration.

Chapter 9

TROUBLING WATERS

*O*ur *Christmas celebration in Chicago is an epic event. The Drake Hotel rivals those I visited with my family during our yuletide escapes to New York City. While the theater and music scenes can't match the Big Apple, the view of an ice-covered Lake Michigan from my guest room window and the wind tunnels on the thoroughfares off the Magnificent Mile live up to Chicago's two monikers: The City by the Lake and the Windy City. Marianne is stiff. Her embrace is cold, and her smile wavers as she examines me. I should expect this since I am challenging her place as the first lady in Jonathan's heart. Bud measures up to his old country lawyer reputation, but underneath his easygoing façade, he is anything but old or country. His smile is expansive, his eyes are piercing, and his hug feels as if a teddy bear is smothering me in comfort. I can hear Mel's practical sense of humor:* Jeeze, Suzanna, forget Jonathan. Bud's the catch.

* * *

The canceled Christmas dinner baffled Lillian and Robert. When I phoned my mother, I took the blame for the sudden switch in plans. I told her we'd be skipping the holiday feast because I screwed up the communications with Jonathan. I heard the doubt in Lillian's voice when she asked me the simple question, "Is this what you want?" The words reminded me of one of her recitations to Jack and me about adulthood. "You have choices in life. You make the decisions and either reap the good or bad consequences of your actions."

I stayed silent, resistant to acknowledging this was not what I wanted. My mother challenged the truth of my charade, even as I was unwilling to admit it.

"Suzanna, if this is what you choose, we won't argue with it. If this is going to be a permanent relationship, then we must be happy sharing you."

Lillian had substituted the word "choose" for "want." She didn't coax me to change my choice or chastise me for it. Instead, she concluded the conversation by covering me with virtual kisses and urging me to live it up in the Midwestern metropolis. I hung up the receiver and had tears in my eyes. *That's Lillian, realistic and recognizing when to let go. I wish I had her courage.*

My mother allowed me the freedom to make my own choice and enjoy or suffer the consequences, but Jack was not so inclined. He called me at the Drake Hotel the day after Christmas and couched his cross-examination in clowning.

"Okay, Suzanna, tell me how much you missed your favorite brother and KP duty yesterday."

"Jack, of course, I missed you."

"I didn't ask if you did. That's assumed, Flower Girl."

"I missed you a bunch."

"How big a bunch?"

Although five hundred miles separated us, my intuition told me my brother saw me shaking my head and rolling my eyes. "You are impossible. I missed you as much as a billion flowers."

He chuckled. Then, in a lowered voice, he asked, "Are you alone now?"

"You don't have to whisper. Yes, I'm alone. What's the big secret?"

We continued teasing each other about bugged rooms and imaginary unknowns until Jack, always the lawyer with a straightforward statement, extracted from me why I changed my Christmas plans on a dime. "Tell me what happened," he said, and I revealed more to him than I was ready to confess to myself—I had let Jonathan manipulate me. Unlike my mother, Jack offered an opinion, and his advice haunted me throughout the coming year.

"Suzanna, a healthy relationship is a partnership. I don't have a hell of a lot of experience, but what I do know is that partnerships are based on trust, fairness, truthfulness, and acting in ways that show other people matter."

My brother presented his case before the jury of one. He left it to me to decide for or against an acquittal of Jonathan's behavior. As I put the phone receiver down, Jonathan returned to our room with a smiley face and handed me a bountiful bouquet from the Drake Hotel florist. Then, he gave me a tender kiss on my lips to match it.

* * *

Five months after our first date, Jonathan and I got engaged on Valentine's Day. My fiancé dazzled me with a dinner at a posh, intimate restaurant in German Village and sealed the deal with a mammoth yellow diamond mounted in platinum.

"Look at that, Bunny. The rock is bigger than what your brother gave Lorna."

His comment ripped the sizzle from the evening and left me hollow. During the few occasions Jonathan and I were together with my brother and his wife, I caught my boyfriend's eyes locking on Lorna's ring.

"Some chunk of change on Lorna's finger," he'd say when we left them. Then he'd turn to me with his sassy smile, wink, and say, "But you, Bunny, deserve better and bigger than that."

Slapping his shoulder, I'd say, "I'm not in a pissing contest with my sister-in-law." That would end the bantering, except for one time when Jonathan's response cut my heart.

"No, but it doesn't mean I'm not in one with Jack."

"Why would you be in competition with Jack?" I asked.

"Because Jack is perfect, and I . . . Skip it."

When Jonathan compared himself with my brother and came up short, my belief grew stronger that I could quash Jonathan's demons and increase his feeling of worthiness through my compassion and love. In my quest, I smothered Jonathan with more affection and ignored the danger signals.

On my engagement evening, I refused to see what was true—it would always be about Jonathan.

* * *

After our engagement, Jonathan convinced me the sooner we tied the knot, the better.

"Why wait, Bunny, when we are in love? Throw caution to the wind and do it."

His enthusiasm was irresistible. I jumped on his bandwagon, and we picked March 19 for our wedding day. To say my family and friends were not as wowed was an understatement.

Mel met me for lunch the Saturday after I received my diamond ring. I couldn't wait to share my news with her and ask her to be my maid of honor.

"You're not PG, are you?" she asked.

"Stop it!" I said. "He's a physician, for God's sake, and I'm a counselor. I think we know how to take precautions."

"Well then, we need a heart-to-heart."

Armed with a degree in journalism, Mel, like me, had landed her first professional job in the fall of 1982. Her outgoing personality was perfect as a reporter for a small Cincinnati suburban weekly newspaper. Since moving to the Queen City, she'd become an enthusiastic fan of the Cincinnati Reds, a lover of Cincinnati chili and the Double Dog Dare, and a Playhouse in the Park devotee. Even with all the city's pluses, I often joked with Mel she traded our beloved Columbus "Cow Town" for "Porkopolis."

"Knock off this crazy talk!" Mel said. Unlike Lillian, Mel had no hesitation in offering advice. "He's damn cute, but too many hang-ups for me. I mean, just the car he drives is a tip-off of his boatload of insecurities."

"Mel, you're not the one who is marrying him."

"Got that right! But I am the one whose shoulder you'll be crying on when things go sideways."

"That's my Mel. Frank and to the point. Where is your optimism?"

"Forget about optimism. I'm talking about realism. I'm sorry, but I don't get positive vibes from the guy. I've seen a change in you since you've met him—a change I don't like."

My jaw dropped, and I pulled back. "What do you mean?"

"Before you met him, you were lighthearted and hopeful. I don't see that fun-loving girl now." Mel stopped, bit her lip, and fought to find her words. "I didn't say something at the time, but better later than never at all."

I stopped eating, and my worried eyes met those of my friend.

"What are you trying to say, Mel?"

She closed her eyes. My palms got moist. She sighed and looked up at the café ceiling before turning to me. "It was when you and Jonathan went out to dinner and dancing with Bill and me that bells started ringing. I didn't like the criticisms Jonathan snuck in—the slight jabs directed toward you that he wrapped in humor or sarcasm. Like he was joking, but perhaps not so much. Then there was . . ."

Her comments about Jonathan's sarcasm washed over my head. "Was what?" I asked.

Mel slowly shook her head. "Nothing. It's nothing," she said and waved her hand. "Even Bill noticed the snide comments. He said, 'I think the guy has a hang-up about women. I don't think he respects them much.'"

The blood drained from my face. This was what Jack told me too. The problem, I convinced myself, was that people didn't see in Jonathan what I did.

"I admit he's not perfect. He's got his complexes, but who doesn't?"

"Complexes?" Mel pressed.

I swallowed and squeezed my hands. "Mel, I don't know what happened to Jonathan, but somewhere he lost his self-esteem. It may have occurred when Case Western didn't admit him to med school or when some woman jilted him in college. Perhaps it's because he can't measure up to his father or another impossible image.

Mel shook her head back and forth. "My observation is there is something deeper going on with him. Murkier than being denied admission to a college or blown off by some chick—you can't believe those things could knock a guy like Jonathan down."

I lowered my eyes.

"I think he's dangerous," Mel said.

I choked on my water. "Dangerous?"

"Oh, I don't mean taking out a gun dangerous. I mean dishing out a whole lot of heartbreak—diminishing and controlling people."

I heard Mel, but I wasn't listening. I wanted her to see my perspective. "I admit there are some insecurity issues, but I can correct those by giving him love and support. I can help him."

Mel's sigh sounded like a roar. "Tigers don't change their stripes. Leopards don't lose their spots."

"Mel, if I believed that, I would never have chosen the career I have. People can and do change."

Mel reached over and patted my hand. "Yes, they can change but only if they want to, dear."

* * *

Robert, Lillian, and Jack never entertained the thought of a shotgun wedding. Their concern coincided with Mel's, wondering whether Jonathan was as great a catch as he claimed himself to be. Never a wallflower, Jack launched a full-court press on my impending marriage.

"Hey, Flower Girl, how about lunch today?" my brother asked me on the phone the Friday after I got engaged. "Mom says you have a whole lot of rhinestone on your finger."

"Not jealous, are you?" As soon as the words left my mouth, I kicked myself. Jesus, I sounded like Jonathan!

"Jealous of what?"

"Nothing, Jack. Yeah, let's do lunch. Chinese place on Lane Avenue?"

I arrived a little before Jack at the cozy eating spot tucked among the unique shops of the neighborhood shopping center near the OSU campus. I slid into a quiet booth at the side of the restaurant, ordered some green tea, and took a breath, preparing for my defense in what I guessed would be a Jack Jordan mini interrogation. *He's really a great guy. Yeah, he's got a few oddities, but look who's talking. You're off base; he loves women . . .* Bam! A voice knocked me out of my mock preparation.

"Holy crap! Mom was right. What did Jonathan do? Rob a bank to pay for that?" Jack asked as he sat down and eyed my ring.

I put out my hand. "Like it?"

"Yeah, I like the ring, but I'm not sure about the boyfriend."

I stared my brother down. "You wouldn't be happy with anyone, would you, Jack?"

Jack acquiesced with a pantomime of a sword cutting through the air. "Touché."

We ordered and ate lunch, and my brother let the subject drop until the fortune cookies arrived.

Jack cracked his cookie, read the comment, and started laughing. "You know what this says, Flower Girl?"

"No, I don't. I have a guess, though, that *my* fortune says I will in five seconds!"

My brother gave me a smile and handed me the slip of paper. *Present your best ideas to an eager and welcoming audience.* I looked to the ceiling, laughed. "You planted that, didn't you!" I said, wagging my finger at Jack.

Jack had the grin of a Cheshire cat pasted across his face.

"I don't dish out conspiracies, but to be honest, I think Jonathan is trouble. How much time have you spent with the dude? A few months? And you're willing to commit to the next fifty years with him?"

"Well, I could say the same for you. You have spent less time with him than me, and you're passing judgment."

Jack responded with a quip familiar to both of us. "That's a horse of a different color. I'm not committing the rest of my life to him. What's the rush to get married all about?"

I shuffled my feet under the table, and I avoided my brother's lawyer eyes. He had nailed me. I took a sip of the hot tea, and Jack waited.

"Okay, Jonathan has a few quirks. But beneath these, he is a decent human being who helps people every day. He's devoted to his work and skilled at it too."

"And that's it? Enough to pledge your life to him forever? Come on, counselor. You can do better than that."

I took a deep breath, threw my head back, and roamed the ceiling with my eyes.

Jack waited—my brother was terrific at waiting, although his silence was different than Craig's. Craig gave silence as a gift for reflection; Jack used it to give people enough rope to hang themselves.

"I love him, Jack. I love him and want to help him. If it means sacrificing a little of myself to reach that goal, I'm ready to take the risk."

"There are pros and cons to sacrifice in a relationship."

Now, I stalled. I had no idea where to take the conversation, but Jack did.

"There must be a balance, a give-and-take. Too much self-sacrifice, and it's easy to slide into the con side before you know it."

Jack reached over and held my hand. "I'm your brother, and I'll always be here if you need help. I want you to know I love you. If he's what you choose, Flower Girl, yours is the final word."

Jack paid the bill, and as he left, he stopped, bent down, and kissed my forehead. I poured myself another cup of tea, and as I drank it, Jack's words hung in the air.

This is what I choose, but is it what I want?

* * *

Lillian avoided advising anyone—well, at least not directly. Instead, she used questions as her magic potion to challenge people to be honest about their underlying motives. When she asked me, "Do you think he's the right fit for you? Does he complement you?" thoughts of Craig's gentle prodding came to my mind, but I was afraid to dig deep and find my truth.

Since Craig had graduated from OSU, we had seen each other once —at my graduation for my master's degree. Before our separation, I never realized his way with the written word. His letters were gifts of wisdom and beauty, and after reading them, it was as if an angelic cloud wrapped me in love and kindness. Soon after I started dating Jonathan, I wrote to Craig and told him about my new boyfriend. It was as if Craig were an intuitive, someone who could foretell the future. His final words in that letter to me were, "Suzanna, is this a man who loves you enough to give you the independence to live your truth?"

My ego prevented me from acknowledging the facts. I believed there was something worthwhile in Jonathan, and I could alleviate the obstacles to his fulfillment. It wasn't long after I was married, though, when a caution light flickered with a broadcast that nothing could change the lethal side of Jonathan's infectious enthusiasm. *Were Mel's and my family's fears justified?*

*   *   *

Early in our relationship, Jonathan stopped using my first name and started calling me Bunny. In the beginning, I thought it was a cute endearment—Who wouldn't want to be associated with a sweet, huggable, and lovable baby rabbit? My view was undermined, though, as I woke one morning on our honeymoon when Jonathan kissed me on my neck and muttered, "Bunny, you are my beautiful prey."

Groggy, I thought I had misheard. I turned and faced him. "Honey, what did you say?"

"Nothing more than whispering how beautiful you are."

I smiled, refusing to believe what passed his lips a minute earlier.

We started our new life together at the dreamy Hotel del Coronado across the bay from San Diego. When Jonathan was playful, solicitous, and passionate, it was the fantasy honeymoon all brides imagine. At other times, though, Jonathan's behavior made me jumpy. He needed continual validation, and if it wasn't forthcoming, he was argumentative and threw disappointed glances at me for presumed infractions. Over dinner on my birthday evening in the elegant Crown Room, his mood turned bizarre.

"Bunny, are there any ghosts here tonight?"

Since our first date, Jonathan had teased me about my supposed psychic abilities. I smiled at him, ready to play his game. I closed my eyes, tuned into the energy of the room, and let my imagination drift wherever it wanted. I opened my eyes, wiggled my nose, and gave Jonathan a wink.

"I guess there's energy here. After all, an old place like this harbors a lot of secrets."

"Secrets?"

"Sure, you know—nefarious political deals, romantic rendezvous, glorious honeymoons, and perhaps a witch or two."

"Really?"

"Look above at the chandeliers, Jonathan. Don't you think they have an otherworld character? After all, the author of the Wizard of Oz designed them."

"I think I knew that. What interests me more is learning whether you are a wicked witch or a good one."

"How about a bit of both?" I said with a coy smile.

The historic Victorian beachfront resort's grandeur galvanized me when we arrived. The massive five-story white building with a red roof and turrets was the most immense wooden structure I had ever seen—multiples of the size of the enormous wooden barns that dotted the Midwest where I grew up. In the lobby, the rich regal blood-red and gold carpet, immense wooden pillars, and flickering lights from the crystal chandelier and wall sconces transported me to a bygone era of haute couture, sophistication, and staid class society. A cocoon of muffled tranquility engulfed me as well as sounding my paranormal detector. There was a sadness underlying the place's warm beauty. As I raised my head and scanned the exquisite wood ceiling two stories overhead, a waft of air crossed my face as faint as a butterfly's breeze.

Ghosts. They are here.

Knowing that the author who created the fantastical Emerald City designed the glimmering fixtures overhead in the dining room where we sat gave me a slight chill.

Jonathan reached over and tapped my hand, a mischievous smile plastered across his face. "Speaking of wicked, I was reading about one of the resident ghosts here. They call her the beautiful stranger. It didn't end well for her."

Eavesdropping on a couple of tourists earlier in the hotel gift shop, I overheard the story of Kate Morgan. She was a beautiful young woman who arrived alone and checked in at the hotel on November 24, 1892. Five days later, the staff discovered her body on an outside staircase—dead from a gunshot wound to the head. The coroner ruled her death a suicide, but many believed a more sinister cause explained her demise. The look on my husband's face told me he was prepared to dish up all the salacious details.

"Yes, I would say that killing herself wasn't a good end. I can't decide what makes me sadder, the way she died or the suffering that brought her to it."

"Did you consider her suffering might have been self-inflicted?" Jonathan asked.

"Would it make a difference? I mean, don't you believe that someone's pain or sadness, whether voluntarily imposed or not, calls for empathy?"

"Before deciding if people are worthy of your concern, I think you have to consider whether they contributed to their own problems."

My brows knitted together, and my shoulders slumped from heaviness.

Jonathan stirred the olive in his martini. "You know, in medical school, I learned about the doctrine of contributory negligence. Are you familiar with that, Suzanna?"

"I do come from a family of attorneys. Yeah, I've overheard Robert and Jack mention it. I think it means an injured person who contributes to their own injury cannot collect damages from the individual or company causing the injury."

"You're spot on, Bunny. In the ER, I have faced similar situations."

"Really?" I expected a lengthy discourse showcasing Jonathan was headed my way.

"Yeah. Let's say I ask a patient if she is allergic to a specific medication. She knows she has an allergy, but she doesn't disclose it to me. I go ahead and prescribe the medication, and it ends up harming or killing her. Am I responsible for that result? Should I be sorry for what happened?"

"Because you're not responsible for something, does that mean you shouldn't have sorrow for the person involved?"

"There you go with all the psychobabble," Jonathan said, turning away from me. "I can't afford to have those feelings. If I did, I'd flame out in no time."

I took a sip of my margarita and ignored my husband's put-down. I decided that arguing over a legal theory and whether empathy was a critical competency for a physician, to use Jonathan's phrase, *would not end well*. I did what I knew would calm the puppeteer.

"Let's dispense with the legal and psychological mumbo-jumbo and concentrate on your good looks and what comes after dinner," I said.

Jonathan shot me his bad-boy grin and then rubbed his hand along the inner edge of my thigh. "I knew there was a reason I married you," he said.

I was sadly disappointed thinking a discussion about the sordid rumors about Kate Morgan had ended. Later that evening, as we cuddled and made out on the balcony of our room to rhythmic sounds of the Pacific Ocean waves, Jonathan resurrected the tale.

"For some reason, I can't shake the story of Kate Morgan," he said. How does a wife ever come to cheating on her husband? What do you think, Bunny?" Jonathan asked as he kissed and nuzzled the side of my face.

"Let's let Kate Morgan's spirit rest. Whatever happened a hundred years ago has nothing to do with us," I whispered.

"One thing is sure—I would never forgive such a transgression. I wouldn't let it rest. Like Kate Morgan's husband, I would get retribution."

"What do you mean? What retribution?"

Jonathan answered with narrow and cold eyes.

My heart tumbled, and I wondered, *Who have you married, Suzanna?*

* * *

Had I the courage to admit my marriage was a mistake, I would have scurried away from my husband. Devoid of such fortitude, I held on to the fantasy I could be Jonathan's savior and love him out of his insecurities and anxieties. I had enough psychology background to understand this was impossible, but the gaslighting by both of us was well underway.

Chapter 10

RIDING THE WAVES

I am swimming against a current. Rather than making headway following my North Star, I am overwhelmed—burned-out by Jonathan's disapproval, his mood swings, and his need for approval. I'm exhausted from walking on eggshells, apologizing for myself, and compromising my own values and needs. My life's purpose is falling farther and farther from my reach.

* * *

Our job responsibilities consumed more than half of the time during our first months of marriage and left little opportunity for us to be together. My academic counselor's position went beyond regular working day hours. As the new member of our student affairs team, I got the duties more seasoned members preferred not to do. One of these was attending career days within the state and beyond. These trips required long drives or plane rides tacked on to a six- to eight-hour event. Consequently, each month I spent several nights away from home.

Three months after we married, Jonathan began his final year of residency. I respected he had twelve- to sixteen-hour-long days loaded with stresses I couldn't begin to imagine. My husband described his work life as a roller-coaster ride, and his attempt to separate the emotional weight of his job from its effects on him was not a winning strategy.

One morning after an overnight shift, Jonathan came into the kitchen while I finished my morning coffee. I knew something was up since this broke with his usual routine of saying hello when he came home and going straight to the bedroom to sleep.

His pinched expression was a mixture of annoyance and agitation. He grabbed a cup of coffee, sat down opposite me, and set his eyes toward the table. "No colleague of mine will ever catch me crying."

"What the heck happened, Jonathan?"

My husband's upper lip curled. "I don't know why these interns can't figure out how to suck it up. After we lost the overdose, I turned and asked that shrinking violet to check on the chest pain in bay eight, and it was like a dam had burst—the whole nine yards. That pathetic piece of shit deteriorated into a sniveling red-faced baby. I don't let my emotions run wild like that, and I don't expect to see it in others. I will never cry over anything in the ER."

My mind spun, trying to sort out which was the saddest: Jonathan's absence of understanding for the intern, his dehumanizing reference to his patients as the overdose and the chest pain, or his emotional shutdown. I knew the high rate of depression and burnout among emergency medicine residents and feared Jonathan might become one of those statistics if he continued to close himself off.

"Why is a colleague crying this disturbing for you?"

He heaved a sigh and gave me an icy stare.

"Oh my God! Stop with the psychobabble. Maybe you think you mean well, but it pisses me off."

Asking more questions would ignite a full-blown anger storm, so I did nothing. My instincts told me I had hit a nerve, but to heal one so raw meant Jonathan must give himself compassion. I believed I had enough love to support Jonathan—that is, providing he admitted he needed my help.

Shaking his head, Jonathan got up, walked into the bedroom, and slammed the door shut.

* * *

Jonathan's indecision about his future after his residency added to his pressures during the early months of our marriage. He ruminated for weeks over the what-ifs between working in emergency medicine or pursuing a subspecialty or other fellowship. I coaxed him to clarify what was important to him and always came up short—he couldn't or wouldn't find the answer.

Jonathan's frustration came to a head in early May during one of our lengthy career discussions. "You're all wrapped up in that North Star bullshit and finding a calling in life. I don't know what the hell that means," he said. "What is there beyond status and money?"

In a sense of defeat, I suggested in jest that flipping a coin might settle his dilemma.

Jonathan gave me a dirty smile, poured himself a bourbon, and fell on the couch beside me. "Okay! This is it, Bunny. This is the night I make my decision." He downed the whiskey in one gulp, took out a quarter, flipped it, and looked up at me with a stony stare. "The winner is a hospital position!"

I didn't know whether I should give him a hug to celebrate his decision or cry about how he had made the choice. He never told me why my challenge pushed him to the edge of taking a frivolous action in making such a consequential choice, and I never asked.

* * *

Before we married, the local Columbus scene—dinner at fancy restaurants, dancing at nightspots, attending OSU sports events—made up Jonathan's spare time with me. Like the stop of an unwound clock, these outings abruptly ended a few weeks after our wedding.

Jonathan had never mentioned his passion for golf and belonging to the university golf club. So I was surprised when he used most of his limited free time during the summer and early fall to play the popular OSU Gray and Scarlet courses with his pals. I offered to learn the sport and join him, but Jonathan insisted this was the "selfing" time he needed to unwind with like-minded colleagues and blow off steam.

When the golf season ended, we had more opportunities to be together. OSU football games were a favorite pastime we enjoyed, where we mingled with friends at raucous tailgate parties and shouted, cheered, and acted like overgrown teens at the face-offs with OSU challengers. Post-game, the gang continued with dinner at local nightspots and afterward moved the celebration to neighborhood bars, dance venues, or the house of a member of our group. Jonathan and I found our way home in the early morning hours and melted into each other's arms in passionate lovemaking.

My husband showcased some of his best and worst characteristics during these events. We'd arrive at the OSU games in the Mustang beast, Jonathan decked out in a black T-shirt, an unstructured jacket, and sockless loafers. He put his humor, playful behaviors, and suave look on display. Guzzling beers with the guys, he relived earlier games and argued over predictions for the upcoming one. Even in these social situations, Jonathan used his body language—slapping his friend's backs, initiating eye contact, planting his hands on his hips—to prove he was the group's alpha male.

That was the beguiling Jonathan, but as the afternoon wore on, Jonathan's mean streak took a bow with patronizing remarks toward our women friends. "Hello, baby girl," he'd say as he inched up to Mel's side. She would cringe and hand him a rebuttal. "Are you blind, Jonathan?" Or sometimes it would be, "I'm a woman, not a baby," or "Reserve that talk for a four-month-old."

He cranked up his charm into overdrive with single women, openly flirting and lavishing compliments on them. Mel and Ellen threw glances and frowns at each other as they stared at Jonathan's behavior.

In those moments, I was humiliated, and my inner critic added to my confusion. *Oh, Suzanna! Stop being jealous. Jonathan is just having fun. After all, you're the one he married. You're the one he sleeps with.*

Jonathan, however, didn't give me the same concessions. When another man glanced my way, he'd remark, "Flirting again, huh?" At first, it was strangers who raised Jonathan's jealousy. Over time it escalated, and he started labeling my behavior with our male friends as provocative and inviting.

"What the hell were you doing tonight with Carl?" he asked as we got into the car after a dinner party with our friends.

My eyes blinked. "What do you mean?"

"Oh, come on, Bunny. The way you teased him and fluttered your eyelashes. If I didn't know better, I'd say you were trying to get laid. I don't think we should go out anymore with Carl and Jackie."

The hairs on my neck rose, and I imagined the blood rushing to my face.

"But you *do* know better, Jonathan."

"Do I?" he asked.

In the glow of the parking lot lights, I caught sight of Jonathan's pout as he turned the ignition key. He revved the engine and made the Mustang squeal out to the street. The drive home was a horrifying display of male testosterone and Jonathan's cold shoulder.

* * *

Other than OSU football games, Jonathan begged off most social events with my family and friends. "Go on your own, Bunny," he told me. When I took him up on his offer, he showed his true feelings and stomped off to his study in the basement. In the beginning, I ignored his childish behavior, and I came alone to family dinners or celebrations. I kept engagements with Mel and Bill or Ellen and her current flame, but being the third or fifth wheel made me uncomfortable, not to mention my uneasiness contriving reasons for Jonathan's absence.

"What's with Jonathan? Working again tonight?" someone might ask. As my single appearance became more of a routine, Mel joked, "Should we set you up with a blind date, Suzanna?" I made excuses for Jonathan—he is tired, works double shifts, or needs time with his buddies to release his stress. As much as I tried, there was no fooling my longtime gal pal.

In the ladies' room during one of my solo dinners with my friends, Mel took me aside.

"Suzanna, what's going on? Jonathan is never with you."

I shrugged and told her the truth. "I don't know."

"Honey, I'm here for you if you need to talk."

Although Mel wanted to help me, I did not see unloading my problems as an option. Some things should not be shared with friends. Beyond the privacy concern, the truth was I didn't want to admit I had made a mistake. And, for sure, I wasn't open to opinions or advice.

As the holidays approached, Jonathan started pushing me to turn down all social invitations. He would sneak up from behind and surround me with his arms, land kisses on my neck, and whisper, "We're just married, Bunny. We need time for ourselves. I want more time with you."

Half of me thought Jonathan was manipulative, but the other half believed he was sincere. It wasn't difficult for me to capitulate to his requests. Making excuses that were untrue about his absences wore me out and humiliated me. Incrementally, Jonathan separated me from my support pipeline, which began my divorce from my true self.

The previous year's holiday tumult ticked at my subconscious, and I expected a hassle over family holiday gatherings once more. What I couldn't guess was the surreal way it would turn out. Instead of spending Christmas with one or the other of our families, my husband insisted we spend it together and alone. I was mortified to be in the same town as my parents on Christmas Eve and day and not celebrate with them. To cover my shame, I told Lillian and Robert that Jonathan and I had planned the holiday in Chicago with Bud and Marianne. Then, I said the opposite to Jonathan's parents. The instant I lied to my family, I betrayed my values. Once I agreed to be isolated from them, I cinched my role as Jonathan's enabler and prey. It was soon after that my panic attacks started.

* * *

Besides detaching me from my family, Jonathan's undermining of my self-esteem intensified after our marriage. He escalated patronizing phrases, dismissive body language, and sarcasm. At first, he used these tactics when alone with me—it was always you, you, you. "*You* shouldn't have done it that way," or "What were *you* thinking?" or

"Where did *you* ever get that idea?" Later, he wielded these in front of others but softened the blow: "Aw, Bunny, I know you're trying to do this, but you're doing it wrong," or "Suzanna tries hard, but organization is not her bag." At times, my husband muttered the blistering insults under his breath and cut to the bone. "Geez, how can she be that stupid?" or "How did she ever make it through grad school?" Their impact shredded my self-esteem in a meat grinder and conned me into self-doubt about my worth.

Jonathan had a fondness for keeping track of my comings and goings. He'd couch his concern with "Where have *you* been?" or "I thought *you'd* be home earlier," or "I don't remember *you* telling me you were going." I was a stickler for letting Jonathan know my plans ahead of time (Lillian had trained me well), and in the beginning, I wrote off his questions as absent-mindedness.

Later, I realized he used these interrogations to force me to verify my whereabouts. Any deviation would prove I was lying. The more this happened, the more concerned I became. After returning home from shopping with my mother on Black Friday evening, Jonathan started with, "What have *you* been doing? Did *you* tell me where you were going?" I might have ignored his probing had it not been for something new he lobbed. "*You* don't have many packages. Are you sure *you* went shopping with your *mother*?"

This wasn't a lack of attention. It was an accusation.

I gave Jonathan a kiss on the cheek to lower the emotional temperature. "I'll make us a Tom and Jerry, and I'll tell you all about it," I said.

Later, sipping our drinks together in the living room, I told Jonathan the details of my annual shopping spree with Lillian: the stores we visited, what we bought, and where we ate. "The reason I don't have a lot of packages is that we had the store gift wrap them. Lillian took most of the presents with her to put under the family tree."

My explanation quieted Jonathan, but it didn't answer my question about his distrust. This time, I wasn't going to ignore the behavior.

"Jonathan, why do you always ask me where I've been? You have the recall of an elephant. Help me understand why it is important to keep reconfirming where I am at."

Jonathan took me unawares when he didn't throw back the psychobabble label at me. Unmasking himself may have been due to the alcohol, and it was one of the few times Jonathan allowed me to glimpse his tortured psyche.

"You're right. I need to confirm where you've gone. I guess I'm crazy to second-guess your whereabouts. It's needy. After I do it, I feel as if I'm some kind of warden. I feel empty."

I gave him and myself space. He had acknowledged the problem, but I vacillated whether I should press him on why he acted this way and why it was essential for him to change. I opted for the easier and quicker choice of next steps which, in retrospect, didn't provide the needed long-term remedy.

"What will make this better for both of us?"

He took a gulp of the hot toddy and laughed. "To start, it would be better if I didn't ask the damn questions."

"That would be a great beginning."

"Now you're going to ask me what's behind all this asking, asking, asking?"

He surprised me by broaching one of the why questions. I said nothing. I gave him more space.

My husband smiled back, swaying his head back and forth, and threw me a compliment. "You're good. Damn good, counselor." He sighed and cast his eyes to the floor.

"This distrust thing. It's a cycle that never fucking ends. It starts with doubt. It moves to suspicion. It ends up in distrust. A long time ago, someone I trusted began the cycle. I can't stop it."

"What do you want . . ."

"I tried counseling. It didn't work." He leaned over and kissed me on the cheek. "I love you. Let's leave it at that for now," he said.

We never got to why changing his behavior was important—failure to do that meant things would remain the same.

* * *

Afterward, Jonathan's questioning had its ups and downs like a carousel horse. But the day before our first anniversary, his behavior moved from concerning to frightening and whipped up my brother's anger to a point I never thought was possible.

It was Sunday, March 18. Jonathan had worked the night shift the previous evening, and in the mid-afternoon, he was still sleeping as I prepared to visit Jack and Lorna. As I was gathering my purse and keys to leave, Jonathan strolled from the bedroom.

"Hey, honey. Glad you're up," I said and planted a long kiss on Jonathan's lips. "I was just leaving to see Jack's new Boston terrier puppy. Want to come?"

"Hell, no! You know I hate dogs, except for the one I had as a kid. Anyway, that's kind of sudden, isn't it? I mean, *you* didn't mention earlier you were going to Jack's, did *you*? Why do *you* have to go now? Can't *you* sit here and talk with me?"

"I promised Jack I'd be at his place by now. He's excited to show off the latest addition to the family, and . . . you know how much I love Bostons. I'll be back before dinner."

I leaned in to kiss him again. This time, he brushed me away with his arm and tossed me his disappointed look, a combination of a smug smile, a raised eyebrow, and an arrogant glare. His practiced look denigrated his target and emphasized his superiority. I squeezed my eyes shut, confused. Should I sass back, bargain, or submit to him? I opened my eyes, and Jonathan had left the room—unknowingly, he had decided for me. I walked to the front door and left.

When I arrived at Jack's, I was surprised Jonathan's car was parked in the driveway with him standing next to it. I decided he must have gotten over his hissy fit and decided to join me, regardless of his so-called hatred of dogs.

I grabbed my parcels, stepped out from the car, and skipped like a four-year-old to Jonathan. In place of the happy face I expected, he met me with a clenched jaw and narrowed eyes. "Where the hell have *you* been? *You* should have been here thirty minutes ago. I've been waiting for *you* all that time."

My heart flew to my throat. I nodded toward the packages in my arms. "I stopped at the pet store and got some puppy gifts."

"Oh yeah. And that took you thirty damn minutes. I bet you had these in the car all the time. Who is *he*, Suzanna? One of those dopey assistant professors you work with, I suppose?"

Jack appeared at the front door, brows drawing together. Tears welled in my eyes, but my goal was to keep calm. Defuse the situation; don't attack or defend; clarify what's happening, I told myself.

"Help me understand what's bothering you, Jonathan. When you ask what took me so long to get here, I'm unsure what the concern is. We've talked about this."

Jonathan moved in close, grabbed, squeezed, and twisted my upper arm. "Look, Suzanna, don't insult my intelligence. I know what you are doing. Stop with the psychobabble. The thing I'm worried about is that you are sneaking around and meeting someone on the side."

I winced as he tightened his hand around my arm. My mouth opened, but nothing came out. From my peripheral vision, I saw Jack approaching. I couldn't catch my breath. The world started to revolve in circles.

Jonathan's eyes latched on to Jack. He let go of me and then swiveled his gaze back on me. "Don't stand there like an innocent. You know you flirt with other guys." My husband turned his head, his eyes straying to my brother, sending a warning shot not to interfere.

My body started to shake.

Making sure Jack could hear, Jonathan spewed more vitriol. "You and I know, Suzanna, you *have* a history. A past you hid from Jack and your family. Little Miss Flower Girl, my ass."

Jack's eyes widened. I blinked, and my former football player brother was standing eye-to-eye with Jonathan.

My husband's shoulders slumped. His fists loosened.

"No one speaks like that to any guest of mine and certainly not to my sister. If you want to bully someone, Jonathan, try me, and see how far you get."

The two hyped-up men stood facing each other like bull m.
ready to lock antlers. It was as if Jack's pent-up animosity towa
Jonathan and Jonathan's jealousy of Jack were ready to explode.

"If I ever see or hear of any physical or verbal abuse to Suzanna again,
you'll find out what it is like to have your head spin."

Jonathan laughed. "Is that a threat, Jack?"

"No, Jonathan, a damn promise."

I turned and walked away, with my husband's words boomeranging
in my head. My stomach knotted. The wave of nausea overpowered
me. Memories and voices of my hidden past shook me like an earth-
quake. I leaned on the side of my car. I hugged my arms around my
belly, bent over, and vomited. Wobbling, I opened the door to my little
Civic and crumpled onto the driver's seat.

As Jonathan's car screeched out of the driveway, Jack slipped into the
seat next to me and took my hand. "What's this all about?"

Rivers of tears streamed down my face. My mind was reliving a horrifying event I had told no one other than Jonathan. Now, my husband
had used that trust against me.

"What's this about, Suzanna?" my brother asked again, breaking the
silence.

"I don't want to involve the family, Jack. Please don't tell anyone
what you've seen."

Jack wrapped his arm around my shoulder, his voice steady. "I worry
about your safety when I see that kind of display. His behavior is not
okay. Where do you want to go for help?"

My brother paused.

"Oh, Jack!" I lowered my head and rested it on top of my hands on
the steering wheel.

Jack let me cry. His hand stroked my back as if I were a child who
had lost a coveted toy. It took a few minutes before I caught my breath.

I sat up and stared aimlessly through the windshield. "I'm a counselor, for God's sake, Jack! I should be able to help Jonathan. I know
he has emotional bruises. I've tried to get him to open up. It doesn't
help to broach the subject of his misplaced anger, doubt, and sarcasm.
He flies off the handle and accuses me of psychobabble."

anna, attorneys don't represent family members
son. It's not that we don't care about our family;
Making an impartial assessment is impossible
..ve a personal relationship with the party involved. And
uoctors and counselors don't treat themselves or their families for the
same reason."

I rubbed my temples. "You're right, Jack. You're right."

* * *

The event that precipitated Jonathan's erratic behavior between Dr.
Jekyll and Mr. Hyde happened two months earlier, on January 11. It
was a Wednesday, and I came home dragging from a day at work laden
with emotion. The mother of a female advisee of mine phoned that
morning and told me the tragic story of her daughter's sexual assault
that took place the previous weekend during an off-campus party. As
she described the incident, my breathing became fast and shallow. My
fingers tingled as if a thousand needles were pressing into my flesh.
A knot in my stomach rose into my throat, and saliva started to fill
my mouth. I cradled my abdomen with my hand, knowing what was
coming.

I clenched my empty hand and bit down on my lower lip. I tried to
stay calm. I listened to the mother's words—a mother who I knew was
inconsolable. I told her how courageous her daughter was to report the
abuse to authorities. I told her how important she was to her daughter.
I told her how her daughter trusted and needed her. I struggled to
suppress my tears and trembling voice and thought the two-minute
phone call would never end.

After the call finished, I hurried from my office into the building
lobby. I hoped I could hold back the retching until I reached the ladies'
room at the end of the hallway. In my mind, a broken record replayed,
"You can't forget what he did! You can't forget what he said! You can't
forget."

I made it to the bathroom, raced to the farthest stall, entered it, and
slammed the door shut. I bent over the toilet bowl, and my stomach

emptied its contents. Afterward, I sat on the floor, my cheeks wet and on fire. Like an earworm, the words wouldn't quit looping in my head: "You can't forget what he did! You can't forget what he said! You can't forget." I wanted it to stop; I didn't want to remember it.

* * *

The specific date of the assault hides somewhere in the spaces of my subconscious. I am clear, though, it took place in September 1980, three months after I had received my bachelor's degree. Most other students majoring in education continued for an added year of study to qualify for teacher certification. Unlike them, I pursued a graduate degree in educational counseling, hoping to become an academic counselor. My deepest desire was to help students find their purpose and avoid being rudderless like I had been.

When I began my graduate studies, I landed a part-time job having nothing to do with my future career. My goal was to have a steady income stream with regular hours, so I took the first position I was offered —a receptionist for a manufacturer of construction products. Besides the firm's onsite administrative offices, there was a massive warehouse for storing the company's materials and a separate section for a construction group that installed the merchandise the business produced and sold.

After three weeks on the job, the division director recognized my skills surpassed receptionist duties, and he promoted me to administrative assistant to the order desk manager. My boss, Dave, was a former schoolteacher, and we had an immediate connection. His love for instruction had never died, and he coached me through the ropes of learning my job. He taught me about the company's products and how to process orders for materials. I learned how to check inventory in the warehouse, track railway boxcars that moved company products across the nation, figure out expected product arrival dates at construction sites, and identify and communicate delays in shipment arrivals. For the most part, I enjoyed my duties except when transportation issues held up a prime customer's delivery. Boxcars had continual mechanical problems, and the words "bad ordered car" elevated our stress and more often caused panic, knowing we would have to deal with late shipments and angry buyers.

I had my own desk and worked alongside Dave in a small office behind the other administrative offices. A door connected to the warehouse on one side of our space; the other side opened to a room used by the sales personnel. Due to its location, company warehousemen and semi-truck drivers often used our office as a passageway to access other building areas. It was the warehouse foreman, though, who spent time in our office. Fred would chat with Dave about shipment issues, sports, local news, or family events. Once in a while, Fred acknowledged me in passing, and when Dave wasn't around, Fred stopped for a few minutes and visited with me. It was always general small talk between us —news about his daughters about my age, OSU football, our governor Jim Rhodes, or the Ohio energy crisis. It seemed to me Fred had a grasp of state and local politics. And, of course, anyone who could recite from memory OSU's football scores over the past decade was a friend of mine.

Every September, company employees attended an offsite meeting except for two staff who remained on the premises: the warehouse supervisor, overseeing shipments, and a clerical employee, functioning as a receptionist. Since I was on the lowest ladder rung of office staff, I got the choice assignment to answer phones and track the messages ticking on the teletype while everyone else attended the planning session.

Late in the day, a lull in activity guilted me into a job I disliked. The odious stack of purchase orders was waiting to be filed and cried out to me. I hated the claustrophobic, musty-smelling archival room. It was creepy, tucked away from the other offices, and the wall-to-wall colorless cabinets made it dark and dingy. Get it over with, I told myself. I gathered up the offending paperwork and headed to the "crypt."

Sorting through the hodgepodge of paperwork in front of an open cabinet drawer, I heard it—walking cleats on the cement floor behind me. *Cla-clunk, cla-clunk, cla-clunk.* The cadence of funeral steps. A chill coursed through me—no one was supposed to be in the office.

I whipped my head to the side, but the intruder was faster. A blow hit my back, crushing my chest against the steel cabinet. The drawer slammed shut—metal banged against metal—my cheekbone crashed across the rigid handle, and papers flew to the floor.

What is happening to me?

I heard malignant muttering. I smelled Old Spice!

Oh God, the weight is squashing me . . .

"Fred, what are you doing?"

His sexually explicit words shocked me. His grunting and undulating unmasked my utmost fear.

I screamed to myself, *Turn around. Turn around! You can fight him off better.*

I struggled, strained, thrashed. I turned. His face was an inch from mine. His breath—a hot, vile vapor—cascaded across my cheek and down my neck. He was a madman, his eyes saucers of rage, his lips parted, his teeth locked. His wrestler's arm pressed mine in place over my head. A hardened hand crawled up my thigh and pushed my dress above my waist. His spit sprayed me. His vulgarities riddled me. His sulfureous sweat choked me.

My legs crumbled. My heart stopped.

My brain went into survival mode. How can I match two hundred pounds? How can I get away?

"Fred! Think of your daughters. You have daughters just like me. They're the same age as me. How can you do this to me?"

My pleading fueled his fire—he pressed harder against me. His weight squeezed my ribs.

I couldn't breathe. I closed my eyes. My mind went blank . . .

It may have been minutes, or it may have been seconds before he released my arms.

I grimaced, eyes still shut, and pushed my hands against his hardened pecs.

He was unmovable.

He shifted his face. His putrid breath faded.

What's next? I raise my eyelids.

He stepped back and stood motionless. He said nothing. His eyes were dead. His breath bellowed and broke the silence. He was done with me.

I raced from the revolting room into the empty hallway, past vacant offices. The wretched words and abhorrent assault started to slip away. My cracking voice chanted, "You can't forget what he did! You can't forget what he said! You can't forget!"

I stormed into the restroom. I tasted my tears. Was I safe?

I ran into the stall at the end of the room and locked the door. I retched and vomited over and over and over until I was played out and my soul had left me. I turned my back to the wall, and my legs crumbled. I felt dirty. I sat on the cold cement floor, hugged my knees to my chest, and rocked from front to back. I couldn't stop trembling. Tears flowed over my cheeks. My mind separated, shielding me from the horror. I sobbed while the memory of the horrifying attack and words slid out of reach . . . but I couldn't deny the wetness on my thigh.

I grabbed the toilet tissue and wiped my leg—back and forth and back and forth—punishing my skin until it was bright red and raw. I was angry at myself for closing my eyes, forgetting my attacker's debasing words, and scraping the proof off my leg.

I told no one. What evidence did I have? The stain was gone; the words had fled me. Who would believe me? Fred had more allies in the company than I did. If someone did trust my account, what would be the remedy?

I didn't say anything to my family—they were powerless like me. Who would believe them? What could they do? I didn't want my family to bear that burden. And Robert and Jack! How could I tell them when I feared their only choice to defend me was violence? I didn't want those horrible consequences.

I did the only thing I thought I could do—I left and never returned.

* * *

The images of my sexual assault were unstoppable and rose like a rising tide after the phone call from my advisee's mother. Jonathan had picked up takeout from our favorite restaurant, and the fireplace glowed with crackling flames by the time I arrived home. My husband greeted me at the door, and I put my arms around him, holding him tight while we kissed.

"Ah, you are making me horny," he whispered in my ear as he snuggled me. "I'm not sure I want to wait until after dinner."

My eyes registered romance was not a top priority.

Jonathan creased his forehead. "What's up, Bunny? No roll in the hay tonight?"

I punched Jonathan playfully in the arm to tiptoe around his sarcasm and the tension that brewed. "I had a rough day, Jonathan. I need a little breathing space now."

I took off my parka and hung it on the hall coat rack. "I can hear the fire crackling. Let's have some wine and just sit together for a while."

Jonathan gave my rear a hard pinch. "I'll uncork a bottle and bring you a glass, Bunny."

I flopped on the sofa. How do I move forward? How can I get free of this hurt? Should I confide in Jonathan? I reached for my North Star pendant, but it wasn't there. I groaned, still clutching my neck. I pressed myself. How do I forgive myself for not remembering? For not standing up? For not acting against my attacker?

"You look worried, Bunny," Jonathan said, handing me a glass of wine. "Come on, it can't be that bad. After all, you don't handle life and death issues like I do every day."

I waved my hand. "You're right. I don't make decisions about life or death, but I *do* make them about people's lives. The actions I take and words I say to students do impact their lives."

Jonathan stared at me. "Bunny, how could anything you say hurt someone for life? I mean, if you make a mistake in recommending a class, it's not like it's going to kill a student. You're always blowing your work out of proportion."

Although exhausted, I refused to overlook his put-down. "I address more than academic issues. Some, the like one today, involve personal issues with potentially far-reaching emotional or physical ramifications."

Jonathan scooted closer, lounged back, and put his arm around me. "What was the big deal that happened today?"

I took a swallow of my wine. I was undecided: Should I tell him or blow it off?

"Okay. I was right. It wasn't anything in the grand scheme of things," he said.

His remark pushed a button. "No, you weren't right. It was something, Jonathan. I received a phone call from the mother of one of my advisees. The girl was sexually assaulted Saturday night."

Jonathan sipped his drink and held his remarks. He moved forward and gave me a gentle kiss on my cheek. "Well, that *is* a bad thing, Suzanna. It is a sad thing for the student involved. For your own well-being, you must put things like that behind you. You can't take them to heart. After all, it didn't happen to you."

Goosebumps ran down my arms. I understood my husband's perspective that bringing emotions to bear with every misfortune was unhealthy. What I couldn't accept, though, was his lack of compassion. A view of every man for himself—if it doesn't affect you, then why care?

"And what if that did happen to me, Jonathan? Would that make a difference to you? Would you care?"

Jonathan removed his arm from around my shoulder and fixed his eyes on me. "What the hell are you saying?"

I cast my eyes down.

"When did this happen, Suzanna?"

I had crossed the line. There was no turning back. Over refilled wine glasses, I told Jonathan my story. I hoped he would understand. I yearned to bury the burden I had borne by myself for so long. Throughout the next fifteen minutes, my husband offered no opinion. Jonathan shook his head from side to side when I finished, and his disappointed look appeared.

He shrugged. "Guess no sex for me tonight," he said. He got up, turned, and added, "I'm not surprised it happened to you. You're so flirty. I'm sure you led the guy on."

Jonathan's Mustang peeled out down the street, and I knew he would not return that night. I sat alone with the unfinished wine, a table full of food, and a heartache. I cocooned myself in a coverlet on the couch, staring ahead at the flames licking the sides of the fireplace. Pumpkin scratched at the sliding glass door, asking to come in. I wanted nothing. I wanted no one. I wanted to disappear. My inner critic had a party in my head. *You are such a wimp. Why would Fred attack you if he didn't think you wanted it? You would have fought harder if you didn't want it. Why did you close your eyes? Did it even happen? You can't even remember his words.*

Chapter 11

SOUL-SEARCHING

I have a lot of soul-searching to do after Jonathan's blowup at Jack's. When I arrive home, Jonathan has pulled another of his disappearing acts. After each such outburst, my husband vanishes. He never says where he goes— I suppose it is either to a motel or to the hospital to find an on-call room to sleep. As I step into the foyer of my home, the irony of his actions occurs to me. Ordinarily, I would be frantic, and my judging voice would be running wild with all sorts of recriminations. What did you do to make him angry? Why did you insist on going to Jack's? Why didn't you stay home with Jonathan —all he wanted was to be with you. What's wrong with you that you can't help your husband? What a piss-poor counselor you are! But I say, "Stop!" to these nagging thoughts casting doubt on my behavior. I give the inner critic a one-way ticket to the moon, and I step back, reflect, and seek the truth about my situation.

* * *

The afternoon's event at Jack's shook my worldview. It opened my eyes, changed my perspective, and forced me to admit the problem was not Jonathan—it was my actions enabling his continuing abusive behavior. My distorted self-doubt grew exponentially as, over time, Jonathan's bullying wore me down. The more Jonathan emotionally and verbally abused me, the more I excused him—I sanitized his conduct and crept around it. From our first meeting in my office, he intrigued me. Before long, my fascination turned into my mission—I wanted to be this handsome doctor's savior.

I sat staring out the window to the backyard, and Jack's words earlier in the afternoon sunk in. *Lawyers don't take on cases involving themselves or their families.* I could not control or cure Jonathan. Thinking my background could help him was stupid, if not arrogant. Jack brought me to a new understanding. I knew Jonathan's behavior was possessive, controlling, and manipulative, and I conceded I could not help or fix him. A person with no emotional attachment to Jonathan must assume that role.

I pussyfooted for too long around the issue of professional help and cajoled Jonathan into seeking it, but I never insisted he secure proper treatment. I used the fallbacks of an abused victim to de-escalate the bullying behavior. I pleaded with, acquiesced to, and forgave my manipulator repeatedly. I never gave Jonathan the intervention he needed —straight talk that I would not tolerate his behavior. Now had his abuse escalated to the level where I might be in physical danger? Was it too late for an intervention?

* * *

The next day, the customary script of our abusive relationship played out. Early in the afternoon, Cheryl came into my office, holding a bouquet of Juliet and Campanella roses.

"I believe these are for you, dear," she said and placed them on my desk. "Jonathan loves this arrangement, doesn't he? Will you be going out to dinner tonight?"

I smiled and nodded. "I suppose so." After all, it was our anniversary.

I reached over, took out the card attached to the bouquet, and read it as Cheryl left the room.

> *For my precious Bunny. Forgive me for being a jerk. You will always be my true love. There is no other woman for me, no one better. I want to hold you close and never let you go. I love you. Jonathan.*

I threw the note into the wastebasket under my desk. "Damn him," I said under my breath. I cradled my head in my hands and rubbed the pain from my forehead. My eyes filled with tears.

What was I going to do?

I raised my head and pulled out the drawer underneath my desktop. Reaching in the back of it, I found the soft pink cloth pouch and wrapped my hand around it—my North Star.

* * *

The breeze blew off the Olentangy River as I walked along its bank. In the pocket of my jacket, I clutched the pendant Craig had given me. I sat down on a bench, remembering the afternoon Craig and I had spent here after his PTSD episode. I took in a breath, shut my eyes, and let my mind drift. In so many words, Jack told me I needed to get professional help. And what would Craig say to me if he were here?

I listened to the sounds around me. The gentle lapping of the water on the bank drowned out the drone of cars in the distance and allowed Craig's voice to reach me. "To feel better, you need to know who you are and where you're headed. Begin with the basics—give yourself some space and peace. Change isn't a single event. Change is a process of many steps."

The silence and breeze whisked away my brain fog. I focused. I called on my psychology training and figured out my situation. What stage of change was I in? Was I stuck in the first stage, acknowledging a problem exists but unwilling to do more? No, I was beyond that—I was ready to face the storm. But what was my plan?

As I held my North Star, something else Craig had said reminded me about my strength of kindness. "Suzanna, before you can have compassion for others, you must have it for yourself. Before you can forgive someone, you need to forgive yourself. Before you can live your truth, you must be true to yourself."

I returned to my office, determined to make changes. The first step was to free myself from the dark cloud of anger. "Anger robs a person of their autonomy, their freedom," Robert often told Jack and me. Giving in to anger meant giving Jonathan power over me; it meant assuming Jonathan's problems. I retrieved my freedom by pulling Jonathan's card from the wastebasket and replacing it back on the bouquet. I reread

Jonathan's note from a position of insight rather than anger. This was manipulation. This was control. Action, not anger, is what would get me out of this.

I had seen my primary care physician about my increasing panic attacks, but I didn't think taking the antidepressant she prescribed would change the cause of my attacks—it was a bandaid on a symptom. I needed a professional who could help me acknowledge the problem and find the confidence to take steps to change it. I phoned the employee health center and made an appointment for the following day with Dr. Hall, a physician who had helped several of my colleagues through difficult spots. I knew he was down-to-earth and empathetic. After replacing the phone receiver, a load lifted from my shoulders. I was set to take the next step—an intervention with Jonathan.

* * *

That evening, Jonathan and I celebrated our first anniversary. I was not angry—I had compassion for myself and empathy for my husband. It wasn't about blaming myself or Jonathan; it was about finding a path forward. After we toasted our year of marriage over dinner at the old inn in Worthington, I reached for my husband's hand.

"Jonathan, if we are going to make this marriage work and celebrate another year together, we both need to get professional help. I love you, but that love won't grow and thrive if we doubt each other. Yesterday when you accused me of having an affair, that made me believe you don't trust me. When you said I had a secret life, that made me feel hurt and sad. That behavior, Jonathan, is destructive to our relationship. I will not accept it any longer."

I half expected Jonathan to throw down his glass of champagne and stomp out of the restaurant. But he didn't.

"I'm sorry, Bunny. I truly am. I have demons that make me rebel against people who love me. I'm not sure I am worthy of being loved. My feelings of worthlessness keep me in a cauldron of emotional pain. I am comfortable in that pain. It's an addiction, and if someone tries to stop the pain, I lash out at them."

I wasn't going to play the counselor role that night to figure out Jonathan's pathology. Instead, I used a modified version of Jack's words. "Jonathan, there's a reason physicians don't treat their family members or themselves—they are too emotionally close to the situation. I can't help us, Jonathan. But there are professionals who can. I'm willing to give it a try if you are."

We ended the evening hopeful, starry-eyed, and with Jonathan promising to seek help. The sad part, though, is he never kept his promise.

Chapter 12

SMALL STEPS

Tuesday, June 12, 1984. It is almost midnight. I am driving like a mad person, out of control, to the emergency room closest to my home. My anxiety overrides common sense, and speed limits and red lights aren't obstacles. Until now, the expression "jumping out of my skin" had no meaning to me. Now, I understand. The tingling is like a thousand needles digging into every part of me. It starts in my groin, moves to my torso, and afterward down my arms and into my legs. My hands cramp in excruciating pain. Every heartbeat is like a brick crashing on the interior of my chest, trying to cut loose from my body. Black dots develop before my eyes and join into a dark blanket, almost blinding me. That's when I cry out, "I can't die this way."

* * *

I drove to the hospital in a mental mist, parked the car in an open space, turned off the engine, opened the door, and exited my little red Civic. I teetered toward my target—an entry backlit with white signage and red letters that screamed, "Emergency." A doctor, taking a break and resting against the building's outside wall, rushed toward me. He reached out, and I fell into his arms. Muscle contractions clamped my jaw, and carpopedal spasms stiffened my fingers. Despite my debilitated state, I was thankful this wasn't where my husband practiced medicine.

The doctor's eyes locked with mine. "What drug did you take?"

I grunted through clenched teeth, "I don't do drugs."

The doctor's deadpan stare drilled into me as he repeated his question. Garbling my words, I denied taking any drugs. The physician's strong arms reached out to steady me and leaning against him, I shuffled through the bay doors and into the hallway.

"I need help here," the doctor shouted, and a crew dressed in blue scrubs rushed up and led me to an emergency room bed.

Now spasms rolled in endless waves through my body, cramping muscles from the top of my head through my torso, arms, legs, and feet. It was impossible to distinguish which was worse—the tingling needles or the spasmodic pain. I was a mess. I couldn't breathe. I wanted to vomit.

The physician who rescued me examined me and ordered laboratory tests. He still didn't believe the withering patient before him had not ingested some legal or illegal substance that precipitated this attack. I knew enough about emergency medicine to understand a physician's fear of giving a medication that might interfere with other drugs the patient had taken. As one of my husband's colleagues said, "I want to be sure the fourteenth medication I prescribe for a patient isn't going to kill her." At last, the doctor took my word, and the medication the staff administered, along with the brown paper bag they gave me to breathe into, took their planned effect, and my mind and body started to chill out.

Five hours later, the hospital discharged me. The doctor's instructions were clear as he handed me medication prescriptions to calm my nerves and keep my heart palpitations in check. "I was worried about you in there for a while. Follow up with your regular physician today." His eyes were empathetic, but his well-intended concern added to my amped-up and anxious state.

I hobbled from the ER, found my car, got into it, and fumbled for the keys in my purse. I was always protective of myself, and it surprised me I hadn't locked the vehicle's door the night before. Neglecting this security precaution told me how dazed I had been. I sat still in the passenger's seat for a few minutes, shaking my head.

How did it all come to this?

The silence opened a space for my inner critic to wander in and screech at me. *You amaze me! What the heck is wrong with you? This mess is your fault. Why can't you hold up like other people? You should have gone along and sucked it up.*

The should-haves and could-haves were a waterfall of tumbling tumult. Closing my eyes and taking another deep breath, I fended off my faultfinder's voice. "Shut up," I said. Afterward, the thought I was speaking to an imaginary voice left me wondering. *Am I losing it?*

Starting the car, I comforted myself that I had the strength to straighten things out and find my freedom.

Driving home, I mouthed silently—*It's five twenty in the morning. Five simple steps are five successes already today. Toast yourself.*

Chapter 13

LOOSENING KNOTS

A fear of thirteen—it even has its own name, triskaidekaphobia. Perhaps the numeral thirteen causes apprehension since it is the odd number out. By a whisker, it misses being part of the zodiac, counted as a month in the year, or included among the gods of Olympus. How unlucky could a number get?

But there is another way of looking at thirteen—how lucky thirteen was to carve out a niche of its own! Like the number thirteen, how lucky am I that I dared to face the storm and create my own opportunities? How lucky am I that I bucked the belief that self-sacrifice to keep someone else happy is a good thing?

There's a quote about making choices that has stuck with me since first reading it. It says, "What defines a person is not one's financial or physical attributes or beliefs. Instead, it's the choices one makes in surmounting life's challenges." Like the number thirteen, I chose to be lucky on June 13—I decided to stand up to my fear.

* * *

Considering the respiratory alkalosis I had suffered, it was surprising I made it home without incurring an accident. Unlike my trip to the emergency room six hours earlier, I didn't run red lights or break other traffic laws. Even so, my emotions fought each other—thankful one moment, fearful the next. The trickle of moisture on my cheeks became a torrent by the time I reached home, parked the car, and turned off the ignition key. Crying over the past twelve months had become a central part of my life. Despite the tears, I was grateful for having gotten through the night and back home safe.

Jonathan would be ending his shift at the hospital in about an hour. As a rule, it would be comforting to confide the details of a medical incident with one's spouse, especially if he were a physician. But this was not the situation. My earlier minor anxiety attacks elicited rants from Jonathan and left me feeling dehumanized.

"Suzanna, you know the world doesn't like a crybaby."

"Suzanna, you know this makes you look ridiculous."

"Suzanna, why can't you get your shit together?"

"You sound like a panting dog. Stop hyperventilating. Take a paper bag and breathe into it."

If Jonathan discovered what had happened the previous evening, I knew he would foist his disappointed look on me, along with vicious sarcasm and criticism about my failures. Most of the time, when Jonathan walked through our front door after a night shift, I would be sitting in the kitchen, finishing up my morning cup of coffee. As he entered, he'd shout out, "Suzanna, I'm home," or "Hello," or nothing, and looking straight ahead, he would proceed to the bedroom and fall onto the bed.

I rationalized my husband's behavior, asking myself, How would you act after a twelve-hour shift? Despite excusing his conduct, the custom made me feel small—as if it were a royal show, my husband being king and me his subject. As much as I loathed the ritual, I was eager for it to continue this morning. If Jonathan suspected my sickly state, he'd sling fresh suffering onto my emotional snarl.

I sat in the car as if I had been on an alcoholic bender and smarting from a super hangover. Describing my condition is perplexing. Edgy, unreal, and disassociated are words that come to mind. Even the combination of these can't define the aftermath of my attack. I was wobbly, but I willed myself to pull it together, and I reached for the door handle.

I entered the house and dropped my purse in the entry. I reached out to the wall to steady myself and forced my limp legs to lead me to the bathroom. I grasped the shower spigot and turned it to the topmost tolerable temperature. The hot elixir created a cloud of steam as murky as my brain and filled the room. I shed my clothes, dropped them to the floor, stepped into the stall, and let the vapor consume me like a London fog.

The jet spray streamed across my back and shoulders and cleansed me like spring rain. I lifted my face into the cascade, and the curative water caressed my aching muscles and cleared my cluttered mind. I responded to the showerhead's grasping fingers and considered doing the unthinkable—making it into the office. My body revolted with other plans when I started shaking uncontrollably once more. I realized going to work was a nonstarter.

I needed sleep to cure my emotional and physical ailments. If I had a loving marriage, my husband would tuck me into bed, slide in next to me, and would soothe my suffering with his warm embrace. I knew this was a daydream.

I dried off, wrapped myself in a terry cloth housecoat, and sat on the edge of our bed. What were my alternatives?

Where could I bury myself for the rest of the day and night? Jack's or Mel's wouldn't do. I needed privacy and quiet, not one hundred questions from well-meaning buddies or family. But . . . there was an inn in that small college town that would be ideal . . . a place to put my body and soul together.

I needed a plan and a reason not to be home for dinner or, for that matter, overnight. The challenge was whether I had the physical and emotional stamina to pull this off.

* * *

I was ready when Jonathan returned home. Ten minutes of expert use of a blower and large rounded brush transformed my limp hair into a trendy Princess Di coif. Heavier than usual makeup masked my blotchy skin and dark-circled eyes. A dark blue pants suit, crisp white blouse, and black pumps presented a confident, professional demeanor. I looked in the mirror and studied my face. Gone was the healthy all-American girl with a broad smile, rosy cheeks, and sparkling green eyes.

The necklace Jonathan had given me with the white torpedo pearl and three blue sapphires hung around my neck. I stared at it and laughed to myself. This was a status symbol for Jonathan; it was never a gift for me.

Although muddled, I had the presence not to call in sick. In the past, Jonathan often phoned my office, keeping tabs on me even if I were on-site. When I went on a recruitment trip, he tested the truthfulness of my whereabouts with my secretary. Calling the office, he applied his charm and chatted up Cheryl with compliments. "How's the best secretary at OSU?" he might say. Other times it would be, "I sure wish we could steal you away and have you work for us."

Cheryl detested Jonathan. The fifty-eight-year-old divorcee was no fool. She could spot a con artist a mile away. Cheryl's husband had left her and their four children after his lover became pregnant. Forgiveness and mercy weren't Cheryl's highest strengths when it came to deceitful or abusive men.

Jonathan first alienated Cheryl during a career day held one Saturday afternoon in May, two months after he and I had married. As one of the school's academic counselors, I put my organizational skills to the test in planning the event for over three hundred people. I was thrilled when Dr. Williams, the dean, told me he was blown away by the outcome. At the end of the day, I caught a glimpse of Jonathan studying the exhibits as I spoke with a small group of potential students and their parents. His unannounced appearance surprised me, but this was early in our marriage when I denied signs of his escalating possessiveness.

Most of the participants had left, and I was basking in the high-fives from Cheryl and a professor colleague when Jonathan strolled up and flabbergasted us.

"Wow, Suzanna, this looks way too organized for you to have put together by yourself. Who *is* he?" Jonathan said, staring at the male professor. The flush on my cheeks must have turned cherry red as I dissolved into a vapor. From that day, Cheryl bristled whenever Jonathan's name came up.

Knowing Jonathan's suspicious mind, I left a message on Cheryl's answering machine a little before seven o'clock, saying I'd be out of the office on business. Since I kept my own calendar, Cheryl wouldn't question my absence. In truth, this wasn't a lie. There was a stash of recruitment brochures in my car, and I planned to distribute these to high school guidance offices in the area where I would be staying. To cover my bases if I left before Jonathan arrived home, I penned a note saying I would be on an overnight recruitment trip and placed it on the bedroom dresser. I sat at the breakfast table in my usual spot, sipping my coffee, and waited for Jonathan. The plan was set, and my packed overnight case was beside me. Still, I fretted–my heartbeats joined the *tick, tick, tick* of the wall clock, and I worried—*Will I have the fortitude to carry it out?*

* * *

"Suzanna, I'm home," Jonathan said when he walked through the front door. *God, please make him go straight to bed so I can slip out unnoticed.* My plea floated into the atmosphere unanswered and Jonathan, deviating from his routine, popped his head around the kitchen doorway. He eyed me as a predator appraises its prey.

"You look like crap. What the hell happened to you?"

"Nice talk for a doctor," I said. My smile, I hoped, would signal nothing was out of the ordinary. I might have been happy he detected something was wrong, but his lack of empathy was callous. This time, I didn't let his remark pass without a defense of myself, no matter how pitiful it might be.

"I was up most of the night barfing my brains out." I was truthful but lied by omission.

He gave me another up-and-down scan. The silence was terrifying.

Would his physician's instinct discover the truth that this is more than the common stomach upset?

I got a reprieve when his eyes rested on the necklace I wore. He looked up with a self-satisfied smile on his face.

"Well, don't come near me. I don't want whatever you've picked up."

As Jonathan turned to go, his hawk eyes landed on the small suit-case beside me. The bag was the usual navy blue Samsonite I took on overnight trips. He nodded upward and toward the overnighter. It was clear he wanted an explanation.

"I'm going on a recruiting trip. I won't be home until tomorrow. So I promise I won't infect you."

"Hmm," he muttered, biting his lower lip. "There isn't a trip listed on your calendar."

An electric shock jolted me. He had been snooping through my pocket calendar in my purse! How long had this been going on?

His eyes shifted.

"Of course you didn't see it, Jonathan. I don't show you my calendar," I said.

No one was going to outgun my husband.

"If I didn't know better, I'd think these little overnight trips you take, Suzanna, were covering up an affair. Should I be concerned?"

In two sentences, Jonathan belittled, intimidated, and accused me of being unfaithful.

A choice of alternatives to respond flew through my mind. Engaging in a battle of words was what he liked and thrived on. Verbal assaults were his preferred method of control and humiliation. Through years of practice, he was an expert at this game, always getting the upper hand. If I replied, it would leave me drained and thwarted but give Jonathan the power he wanted.

Submitting by ignoring his outlandish and hurtful remark indulged his behavior and acknowledged his power. In the past, my acquiescence betrayed my helplessness in the face of his bullying, confirming his control over me. My ER misadventure proved the devastating impact of the sustained stress of his victimization.

Then, Jonathan shot a bullseye. "But I know better, don't I? You'd never dare to try something like that on me." He stood to his full height, jutted out his chin, and smirked. "Just remember what happened to Kate Morgan."

My lips trembled. My husband had stepped over the boundary from bullying to threatening me. I remembered Mel's words. "I think he's dangerous." If I valued my life, I had to make this stop.

This time, the confident Suzanna stepped forward. The prey turned on its captor. I clutched my cup and shot Jonathan a steely stare. He shrank back. A calm, controlled voice flowed from my throat, and I delivered the needed intervention.

"That is a serious accusation *and* a threat. For you to make an unfounded allegation like that about me is not okay. For you to threaten me with physical harm is not okay. That behavior is manipulative and cruel."

He stood wide-eyed, his fists clenched and jaw set.

I exploited his silence. "I have to go."

I retrieved the overnighter and pushed past him—no kisses, no hugs, no sweet talk. I grabbed my purse in the hallway and walked out the front door. This is the moment I chose to call a halt to Jonathan's abuse. Getting into my car, I whispered, "It's over."

* * *

I drove my Civic on Olentangy River Road, across to Riverside Drive, and headed south alongside the Scioto River. I loved this two-hundred-mile slow-going snake of a river that slices its way through the flat Columbus city landscape and the countryside beyond toward the mighty Ohio River. In school, they said "Scioto" meant "deer" in a Native American language. As a young girl, I imagined the four-legged creatures blanketing the river's side, some lying on the slopes, others nosing the water, and more scouting the shrubbery along the banks. Scioto means "peace" to me, and I call it my Pondering Place. That morning, I sought solace at its edge.

I pulled into the paved drive of the long, narrow city park that bordered the river. Finding a parking space among a cluster of trees on a grassy knoll overlooking the languid waterway, I claimed the spot. I turned off the ignition and closed my eyes in silent relief. My inner cheerleader shouted. *I did it! I stood up to Jonathan. This time he was the one left speechless, not me. Seven victories for the day, and it is just eight o'clock!*

Except for a few people jogging, the parkland was mine. The heat of the day was climbing, and I lowered the car windows and let the scent of riverbank dampness flow over me. With each deep breath, my rib cage expanded and welcomed the healing blanket of morning freshness covering me.

I jettisoned worrisome thoughts and pulled myself into the here and now, letting the sounds around me magnify. Cars humming in the distance, birds fluttering and chirping in the trees, and runners hitting the blacktopped pathway in rhythmic steps sounded like a symphony in my ears. I didn't judge these as good or bad. Instead, I opened my curiosity like a window.

Who are the people in the cars? Where are they going? What species of birds are keeping me company? What are my feathered friends saying to each other?

My breath became a loving companion. It was steady and firm, as if the honorable Wyandotte Chieftain Leatherlips, whose gravesite was not far away, was sitting beside me and sharing his courage with me.

Tears streamed down my cheeks, not from fear but from gratitude for new beginnings. Earlier that morning, I had pondered, *How did it all come to this?* My life was a tangled ball of yarn. But I chose not to live like that anymore. It was time to loosen the knots and put myself back together in the right way. My life was worth saving by unsnarling the mess.

Chapter 14

FACING THE STORM

The historic inn stands on the main street in Granville, a New England lookalike village in peaceful farming and hill terrain. In medieval times, fugitives sought protection from harm and a reprieve from punishment for their crimes in churches. Though I have committed no crime, I must still seek safety from injury and retribution. This is to be my sanctuary—a historic inn in a picture-book small town.

* * *

The drive wasn't difficult, nor was it far from Columbus. After the Civic entered the highway and was in fourth gear, the little car seemed to drive itself to its serene destination. Jonathan hated my small, stick-shift vehicle, so unlike his Mustang, a muscle car that proclaimed manliness. "How can you drive such a commonplace and cheap car?" he'd ask.

Jonathan didn't get it. Driving a status symbol wasn't my thing. Transportation with a bit of personality, not something that screamed power or position, fulfilled my needs. I thought my car was sassy and spiffy. It was my little Chipmunk, and at different times, its pet name was the Chip, Alvin, or more affectionately, the Rascal. Jonathan hated assigning an animal characteristic to an inanimate object, and I was careful to avoid attaching these to the Civic whenever he was around. I thought it ironic that my husband drove a car with a built-in zoomorphism, but I never made an effort to point out the contradiction to him.

It was midweek, and even at the early morning hour, the inn had a vacancy. The clerk asked if an out-of-the-way room at the back of the building on the second floor would do, and my smile was all the confirmation she needed.

The treads creaked as I climbed the flight of old steps. The floral papered wall hugging the staircase induced a peaceful presence in *this* Flower Girl. I turned to the left when I came to the second floor, walked to the end of the narrow hallway, and inserted an old-fashioned skeleton key into the door of my room. I entered, and antique furniture in rich brown oak, maple floorboards, and floral-printed curtains greeted me. The space was warm and cozy, and a sense of comfort fluttered over me. If the room's walls could talk, there is no doubt they would give up stories of romance and intrigue dating back to the inn's establishment in 1812. I stood motionless. *The energy is here. I have faith there is a ghost or two hanging out.*

It was ten o'clock, and before collapsing on the bed, I needed to do three things. I phoned Cheryl, let her know where I was staying, and told her what I would be doing on behalf of the university. Cheryl didn't question me when I called; it was as if she suspected I was on the lam.

"Keep safe, dear. And please don't overdo it," she said.

It seemed an eternity since the ER physician gave me instructions to call my personal physician, but I decided against following those orders. Dr. Nash treated my complaints as verging on needy when I went to her office in January. Her remedy was a prescription for antidepressants. I wasn't convinced drugs were all I needed. In March, seeking an alternative to pills to quell my nervousness, I attended a support group for anxiety attack sufferers. The meeting shocked me to see otherwise capable and resourceful people leveled into depression and despair because of anxiety brought on by stress. Most of those in the group were professionals who had held responsible work positions. Their stories were heartbreaking. Each reported a descent into a morass of tension and worry, resulting in lost employment and income and sometimes estrangement from their family. Many of them were on medication to alleviate their torment, and some had become addicted to the drugs supposed to help them. Restraining my tears during the session was difficult when several of these sufferers told their experience of going into dependency recovery facilities because of their addiction to these drugs. I left stunned and determined to follow another path.

Due to those experiences, I called Dr. Hall at the employee clinic to make a follow-up appointment instead of contacting my primary doctor. After arranging for my visit, the third call was to my brother Jack.

"How can I help you?" Jack asked after listening to my story.

"I need sleep and peace for twenty-four hours, Jack."

"Flower Girl, I'd like to come and get you. Does Jonathan know where you are?"

Hearing my pet name, I lingered on the sound of my big brother's soothing voice before responding. "Jonathan thinks I'm traveling on business. I didn't tell him where I would be staying, but I bet he will call my office."

"I want you to be safe. I can provide that for you. I don't trust Jonathan," Jack said.

I heard the edge in Jack's voice. "I'm fine here. I don't want to parachute in and disrupt your family. Besides, I'd like to keep this confidential for now."

"All right," he said, but his lowered voice told me his approval was reluctant.

"What I need, Jack, is your legal advice and emotional support. I want a divorce. I know this will be difficult. Can you meet me tomorrow morning?"

* * *

With the phone calls completed, I removed the clothes I had intentionally put on a few hours earlier and placed each piece on a silk-padded hanger from the antique armoire. Being purposeful forced me to put past setbacks out of my mind and avoid headaches about the future. It gave me the calm and continuity I cried out for.

After slipping on a T-shirt and a pair of sweatpants, I crawled between the crisp, white cotton sheets and cuddled under the fluffy chintz comforter. I took easy breaths, stretched my legs, wiggled my toes, and sucked in the sensation of serenity. I rested on my back and closed my eyes. I imagined a healing white light entering at the top of my body, roaming through my head, finding and flushing out the black soot that had eaten away my energy. Afterward, at a protracted pace, I guided the glow into my heart, lungs, arms, and legs to extract every remnant of the infiltrating black dust that had snuffed out my optimism and happiness.

I'm safe. Nothing can harm me here.

* * *

Aromatic smells of dinner preparations from the inn's kitchen woke me from a sound and satisfying sleep. It was late afternoon. The setting sun spread its rays through the lace curtain and cavorted across the comforter. My fingers followed the flickering patterns on the dusky pink bedcover, outlining the intricate designs that pranced across it. I was thankful for the moment, thankful for the peace.

My stomach growled. I hadn't eaten since dinner the previous evening. Even the thought of dining in a quaint onsite restaurant couldn't overcome my listlessness—I needed solitude more. I phoned the front desk about room service, and to my delight, the little inn could accommodate this luxury. I ordered the homemade chicken curry soup, a Caesar salad with shrimp, and a pot of hot chamomile tea.

My comfy chamber overlooked the inn's gardens, and when my dinner arrived, the server placed it on the table by the window. I sat and savored the meal while surveying the beauty of the inn's back garden of summer flowers. How had I missed seeing that when I checked in?

It was early June, but there still was a choice of blooms in the garden. The inn had taken care to create a potpourri of plantings, and I had a clear view of the kitchen garden, which was close by the building and filled with herbs. The lavender grabbed my attention at once, and I made a mental note to steal myself a sprig before going to bed for the night.

Farther on, a compact vegetable plot overflowed its boundaries. No doubt, the melt-in-your-mouth tender greens that made up my salad came from that patch. And a little farther, the sweetest love knot flower garden teemed with bouquets of pink, yellow, fuchsia, and blue blossoms. My flower girl spiritedness surfaced, and nothing could hold me back from collecting a bud or two for my room. I laughed for myself; the flowers' energy started to untangle the knots in the yarn of my life.

Although after-chills from my panic attack still roamed my body, I ventured outside after dinner for a walk through the little village's quiet streets. Fresh country air swirled around me and lifted my spirits. The small retail stores, vintage shops, and galleries had closed for the evening, but I was content to dillydally and marvel at the eclectic collections through their windows. While I stood admiring the artwork in a gallery storefront, an intuitive awareness flowed over me. I seesawed my head and tried sweeping it away. Instead, the window's reflection of the signage behind me caught my eye: Reader's Garden. *How intriguing! A garden not of flowers but of books.* The symbolism was enough to make me cross the street and enter the yellow brick building.

The smell—a blend of burnt coffee, chocolate, and decaying pages of old books—enticed me to step farther into the cramped shop. In a hypnotic state, I strolled among the stacks, my eyes scanning book titles, when something summoned me to the back wall. I stood, locked in position, and gazed at the shelves stuffed from floor to ceiling with books, journals, and registers.

I frowned. Why was I here looking at these old things? I passed my hand over the aged tomes, trying to answer my question, when a cranberry-colored book with a torn spine captured my interest. I pulled it out and read the title: *A Latin Reader 1879*. My curiosity climbed as I thumbed through the pages, wondering who the student was who had toiled over these passages. How many nights had she literally burned the midnight oil completing the language exercises? Then my heart turned in my chest—written in a beautiful script on the front page, I read: Susannah Simpson. I gave the book a hug. I imagined the spirit of that Susannah from one hundred years ago was reaching out to me for some unknown reason.

I ran my fingers over the row of books, and a small robin's-egg blue volume decorated in delicate garlands of white flowers with golden stems attracted my attention. I reached for the thin hardcover. A smile grew across my face: *Souvenirs de Charité* par Le Comte de Falloux. I hadn't thought about my French classes for such a long time. Had it been only seven years since I found my Mon Ange? I read the preface to the work.

Les biographies dont se compse ce volume ont ete imprimees . . .

The biographies of which this volume is composed are inspired by the charity of people of good works . . .

I turned the fragile pages one after another, inspecting the text, most of it a mystery to me. "My French hasn't improved over the years," I said to myself and chuckled. *The charity of people of good works!* I lowered my eyelids and pondered the meaning. Craig's counsel, years earlier, crystallized. "Love begins within you," he had said. "If you don't love yourself, you won't have anything to give to others." Mon Ange was right! My ego, not love, drove me to attempt to remake Jonathan. And his ego, not love, caused him to try to control me.

I clutched the volume and turned to go when something tumbled from a shelf above and just missed hitting me squarely on the head. I looked down at the floor in front of me. An old book with a heavy brown cardboard cover and a wooly mammoth imprint—*The Mammoth Exercise Book*—lay at my feet. I bent over and picked it up. I opened the journal and blinked. Inscribed inside was the name Susannah Simpson 1884. Could it be the same person? What a quirk. I flipped through the ruled pages and thumbed through the first diary entries. I smiled. This Susannah wasn't a student; she was a college teacher like me!

With my treasures in hand, I went to the checkout counter.

"I found these two books belonging to a Susannah Simpson. You wouldn't know who she was, would you?" I asked the salesclerk.

The elderly woman took the books and flicked through the pages. "Hmm . . . interesting. Appears she was a teacher. I bet it was at the women's school here—but that place doesn't exist anymore. They combined it with Denison University decades back. Sorry, but I don't know her," she said.

I left the store disappointed the clerk couldn't provide me with any information about the owner of the books I bought. My inquisitiveness about this other Susannah—who she was and what happened to her— haunted me like a shadow resting on my shoulder until I veered from the commercial to the residential area and became distracted by the architecture. The historic Greek Revival and Victorian homes with trimmed landscapes and picturesque gardens along the shady tree-lined streets took me back in time, and my interest rose. *Who were the earliest settlers of this storybook village? What brought them here? What historical events happened here? How could I grow up so close to this sweet haven and yet know little about it?* Wandering through the village, more rainbow arrays of flowers and fresh scents of newly mowed lawns tickled my senses. *How many simple things do we miss when we're stressed by the past or absorbed by the future?*

I snuck into the garden when I returned to the inn. My childhood skill of flower pinching was still impeccable, and unnoticed, I stole several flower buds and a sprig of lavender. Painstaking in my pilfer- ing, I scrutinized each species, examining the intricacy of the stamens, petals, and sepals. The most difficult decision was deciding which yel- low, orange, purple, pink, rose, red, or white blossoms I should seize. Unable to choose one or two, I swiped a specimen of each and shaped a dazzling petite bouquet.

By seven thirty, I was under the covers in my comfy bed, a lavender sprig beneath my pillow and a stunning spray of blossoms arranged in a water glass on the side table next to the bed. Surrounded by the abundance of floral scents, I entered a gentle sleep, grateful for the successes I secured that day.

* * *

The shrill ring of the phone next to my bed jolted me awake. My eyes opened and closed, trying to remember where I was. It was dark out- side, not pitch black but the dimness of early evening.

Fire alarm? No! Frigging phone!

Groggy, I picked up the receiver and whispered, "Hello?"

"Suzanna, is that you?" asked a familiar voice. My eyes shot open, and I sat up. I began shaking, the anxiety attack chills revisiting me. My mind played out the score of events that had taken place as if it were performing a musical piece.

Oh no, I said to myself. I tried to deny the undeniable. Jonathan would verify with Cheryl my overnight accommodations when I went out of town, but he never phoned me. Tonight, though, he was reverifying my whereabouts. This was a dangerous escalation of his jealousy, his paranoia.

The tranquilizers given to me in the ER had worn off and couldn't ward off the wave of anxiety building. *What will happen if I have another attack? Where is the closest hospital? Where can I go?*

I rubbed the top of my shoulder to release the mounting pressure in my muscles, and I found my voice. "Yes, Jonathan, I'm here. What's happened? Is someone hurt?"

I inhaled and held it. *What will he say next?*

"No, nothing is wrong . . . at least I don't think there is. I thought it was strange, though, you'd stay overnight so close to home. I worry about you, Flower Girl, running off like this."

Jonathan had a habit of using my family's pet name as the preface to launching a vicious verbal attack on me. It was his strategy of belittling his prey, exercising his power, and disparaging Robert's and Jack's love for me. This heavy-handed behavior I ignored in the past, afraid of engaging in conflict. My choice after he abused the term of endearment this time was different and, I rocketed from frightened to pissed off.

"Why would you worry, Jonathan?"

I let the silence hang in the air. He didn't answer.

"Can I come up?" he asked.

My stomach sank. "Come up from where?"

"I'm in the lobby calling on the house phone. They won't give me your damn room number. For Christ's sake, my own wife, and they wouldn't, they won't . . . "

His agitation made his words fall over each other. I envisioned the spittle shooting from his mouth. He wanted—hugs, kisses, and forgiveness. I wasn't falling for his load of rubbish this time.

"Aren't you covering the ER tonight?" I asked.

"Bunny, I'm worried about you. You looked like crap this morning. I thought you might honestly be sick."

Bullshit! I knew Jonathan's temper flares too well. Except for the incident at Jack's, his verbal put-downs never turned into physical violence aimed at me, although he had used his fists to attack pillows, doors, and walls. His clenched hands and set jaw in the kitchen that morning, plus his innuendo about Kate Morgan, were dangerous signs. *If he isn't going to work, what's his plan?* In my heart, I knew the answer —he would use my body as a punching bag.

"I'm fine, Jonathan. Now that you know I'm okay, shouldn't you get a move on to get to the ER on time?"

I envisioned my husband's tortured face, deciding his next step. I waited for his response.

I couldn't risk him coming up to the room. If he did, I was trapped. I promised myself to stand up to him.

"I'll be right down and meet you in the lobby," I said and hung up the phone.

Jonathan greeted me with his disappointed look—the familiar smug smile, raised eyebrow, and arrogant glare. I had made the right choice to meet him in a public place.

"What's up, Bunny?" he asked as I walked toward him. "You left in such a flurry this morning. The more I thought about it, the more concerned I became. I called Cheryl, but she's so damn evasive—wouldn't tell me what you were doing here. I thought you were hiding something from me—you know, like you *were* sick, something had happened at work, or . . . there's someone else up there in your room."

What a con artist!

My blood boiled at his remark about Cheryl and threatening accusation against me. My secretary's evasiveness and an extramarital affair by me existed only in Jonathan's mind. I knew the game my husband played. He didn't believe I was seeing anyone. If he had, he never

would have driven to the inn. Jonathan wouldn't risk a physical altercation with a man his own size. He was a bully; bullies are cowards, and
they don't put themselves in jeopardy. No, Jonathan wanted to convince *me* that he believed I was having an affair. If I fell for his ploy, he
would emotionally control me and savor seeing me squirm and plead
with him to accept my denials.

I had to temper my emotions; otherwise, Jonathan would get the
upper hand. What was coming next was a high stakes conversation.

I steeled myself with courage: *Fun fact, Jonathan, I am not your victim
this time.*

I stepped into a new persona—from a bully's victim to a crisis medi-
ator. "Let's sit down over here, Jonathan," I said and led him to a quiet
alcove. As I walked, I ran the script through my mind.

*I must condemn Jonathan's behavior but not him. I must make clear the
impact his actions have on me. I must not equivocate, send mixed messages,
associate my vulnerability with his conduct, or label his behavior as bad.
Shit! This is a tall order.*

We sat down in chairs positioned opposite each other, and for a few
moments, neither of us said a word. I took the offensive.

"You are right, Jonathan. I am hiding something from you."

My husband looked gut-punched. His mouth dropped, and his eyes
bulged. He started to speak, and I raised my hand and cut him off.

"Jonathan, this morning, when you accused me of cheating on you,
I felt belittled. When you said I didn't have the guts to cheat on you,
I felt threatened. You are right. I was hiding something from you—I
was hiding my feelings."

Jonathan turned his head. He clenched his hand into a fist and
pulled it up to his chest. He turned toward me. "You piss me off,
Suzanna. It is always about you—your feelings. That's so much horseshit."

I sat straight, increased my height, summoned my courage not to
retreat into the victim's cave. I stared into darkened eyes.

"Just now, Jonathan, when you said that my feelings were horseshit,
it made me feel insignificant."

"Can you stop with the psychobabble? It makes me crazy."

"I understand that speaking my truth is difficult for you to hear."

"You won't shut up, will you?" he said through clenched teeth.

I met my husband's scowl. "You're right, Jonathan. I won't stop. I won't stop standing up for myself."

With those words, my stomach and shoulder muscles relaxed. I sat back, relieved—I had sprung the predator's trap. I fixed my eyes on Jonathan and had compassion for my spouse, whose lack of self-worth compelled him to have the upper hand, no matter the cost. I let go of anger and resentment, but I did not excuse his behavior. I moved from victim to survivor and made myself free. I rose and stood next to my husband's side, a metaphor for standing up against his abuse. "I have a lot of work to do tomorrow, Jonathan. We'll discuss the next steps at dinner tomorrow evening."

He glared at me, jaw tightened. "What the hell are you talking about?"

I raised both of my hands in front of my chest. "Tomorrow, we will talk about this."

I turned and walked to the stairs. A storm approached, and I was ready for it.

Chapter 15

CHOICE

I thrash all night. Even the beautiful blooms I picked earlier don't relieve my indecision. I'm stymied about what comes after meeting Jonathan at the inn tonight. I made appointments to see Dr. Hall and Jack. Beyond this, I'm unsure what to do next. Do I go home? Leave home? Do I get an apartment? Does Jonathan move? How does this work?

* * *

Before dawn the following morning, I left a message on Cheryl's voice mail, saying I was taking a personal day off from work. I was grateful my administrative and salaried position allowed me the flexibility to do this. Afterward, I packed my few things and drove to Columbus to meet Jack at a small eatery on High Street near the OSU campus.

I entered the old diner, famous for its gut-filling and inexpensive breakfasts, and felt I was meeting an old friend. Worn wooden floorboards and the smell of burnt toast, fried eggs, potatoes, onions, and coffee transported me into the carefree hours I spent here with college friends and, for a moment, lightened my heavy load. I saw Jack sitting in one of the cozy booths, and when I took the seat across from him, he reached for my hand and held it in his.

"Flower Girl, I'm here for you. Whatever I can do, I will."

I nodded, squeezed my eyelids together, and clamped down on the tears beginning to form.

"Let's order and get some food into you. Then we'll talk," Jack said.

We could recite the menu by heart, but we read each item to collect our thoughts to tackle the weighty conversation that was in front of us. Jack ordered a concoction of bacon, ham, hash browns, and fried eggs topped with sausage gravy. I asked for wheat toast with an egg over medium and a pot of hot tea.

"That's it, Suzanna?"

I unconsciously hugged my stomach. "My insides are jackknifed. Maybe this will settle them down," I said.

"I'm sorry you are going through this. How can I help you?"

I told my story, and I saw the comingling of pain and sadness in Jack's eyes grow. I started with my emergency room visit and the previous day's morning and evening conversations with Jonathan. I told him how my ego outweighed prudence and my need to free myself from Jonathan.

There were no accusations or "I warned you about him." Instead, my brother listened and helped me clarify what I wanted. What else would I expect of Jack?

"What is most important to you now?"

I didn't hesitate. "I want to live my truth."

Jack peered at me with lawyer eyes. "What does that mean, Suzanna? What is living your truth?"

Putting the concept into words was difficult. What was the Emerson quote Craig had shared with me? I stared into my cup of tea, thinking of Mon Ange and our times together. I willed his voice to tell me what I should be able to recall. *To be yourself in a world that won't stop trying to make you something else is the greatest accomplishment.*

"It means I can be myself, not something someone wants me to be. It means staying true to myself—knowing my values and my strengths and using them to follow my dreams, my North Star."

Jack lounged back in the booth and rapped his fingers on the table. "Hmm. What's the real challenge for you? What's holding you back from living your truth?"

Truth! I wanted to say Jonathan was holding me back and put the blame on him. He was the challenge. I bit my lip, and tears trickled down my cheeks. But that wasn't the truth. Damn it, if I wanted to live my truth, I must speak it.

Jack said nothing.

I mindlessly stirred some sugar into my tea. I looked up into my brother's eyes. "I'm the challenge, Jack. I'm the greatest challenge."

"You are? How so?"

My shoulders slumped. "I'm the challenge because of the choices I made."

"So that's the challenge? Living with the consequences of your choices?"

"No, Jack. The challenge is to stop making the same choice over and over and over again.

"And what's that choice?"

"The choice of giving up my freedom, of being another person's ideal."

"Someone else's ideal? What ideal?"

"Sacrificing *all* of myself for others—being a saint."

"How do you meet the challenge to be your own ideal?"

I stared in the distance at the diner's counter, filled with groggy-eyed students hungover from pulling all-nighters or suffering from the aftermath of alcohol or maybe weed. I rubbed my index finger over the top of my lips.

"I understand this is hard. Love and kindness are your strengths. The hard truth is you can't give those gifts to others until you give them to yourself," Jack said.

Who told me something similar before? Craig did. Craig said I needed compassion for myself before I could give it to others. I need love and compassion for myself.

"Hard or not, I must face the situation. I must choose to change. I must live my life, not someone else's picture-perfect stereotype. *And* I must stop trying to make Jonathan into something he's not." I looked down, concentrated on my half-filled cup of tea, and recalled something from months earlier.

"What are you thinking, Suzanna?"

"I remembered what Lillian asked me after she first met Jonathan. She wanted to know if he was the right fit for me—if he complemented me. I didn't have the guts to admit what was true. But I do now. He doesn't balance me. He drains me. He controls me. I want to leave him."

Jack took a refill on his coffee. He added cream and stirred packets of sugar into his mug as he waited for me to speak.

"What's next, Jack? I have no idea what to do."

He cleared his throat, and his legal eyes focused on me. "You need professional and legal assistance from someone not emotionally tied to you. I can help from the legal side. I can call a colleague of mine who specializes in family law, arrange for him to see you this morning. He can tell you the process of beginning a separation or divorce."

I nodded.

"And you need a professional counselor—to help you clarify what you want and need."

I swallowed hard. My eyes wandered the diner walls before turning to Jack. "I remember one of my professors saying, 'It's a wise counselor who realizes she needs a counselor.'"

Jack squeezed my hand and added something else. "The ball is in your court. It always is. Your future is determined by the choices you make."

* * *

I thought my morning toast and egg would land in my lap when reality blew up in my face, and I was unable to answer the attorney's first question.

"Do you have a plan?"

"Plan? What kind of plan?"

"A financial plan."

I stared at him and shook my head.

"Let's get started," he said. "Who handles the finances?

"Jonathan handles all the money—pays the bills, balances the checkbook."

"Is the apartment lease in both of your names?"

"The apartment? After we married, Jonathan moved into my place. The apartment's lease is still in my name."

"That could be either a plus or a minus," the lawyer said. "Do you have your own bank account?"

"No. Why would I do that? I closed my personal account and opened a joint account when I got married."

The lawyer grunted and continued to throw more questions my way. "Is there a separate bank account in your husband's name?"

"Yes, Jonathan has an account for himself."

I spaced out, remembering what Jonathan had said. "Bunny, I need a separate account because of my school loans and other obligations. I don't want to comingle those finances with yours." His explanation sounded reasonable at the time, but now I wasn't so sure.

"I'm sorry. What did you ask?" I said, refocusing.

"What is your husband's income? Do you see his pay stubs?"

"I've never seen Jonathan's paycheck—I see deposits he makes in the checkbook."

"That proves nothing. He could be stashing money somewhere else. Do you check your income tax reports against the checkbook deposits?"

My stomach flipped. "No."

"Have you established credit in your name?"

"How would I do that?"

"For starters, do you have your own credit card?"

"Yes, I do. It's one I had before my marriage, and I kept it active."

"That's a plus. And who pays that credit card?"

"That would be Jonathan, from our joint account."

"Do you have a place to go if you move out?"

"No, I have no clue."

Shit! I'm as stupid as Jonathan thinks I am. Only two pluses in the entire conversation.

The fog of panic dissipated as a strategy surfaced. Step by step, each question was one more insight. I steadied my stomach, squashed the sensation of upchucking breakfast, and opted for finding a way out of the mess. I made myself move from fearing the unknown to embracing it. Why the hell didn't they teach all this stuff to women before they marry?

I left the attorney's office with a ten-page draft divorce agreement and a checklist of financial actions I needed to take—the first being to open my own bank account. I left the bank holding my new checkbook and realized the legal and financial aspects of divorce would be more manageable than the emotional part.

In the bank parking lot, I sat in my car repeating the question I had asked myself almost forty-eight hours earlier outside the emergency room: *How did it all come to this?* I thought about what my brother had said to me that morning.

Choices. My courage started to waver. *Is divorce the right choice? Am I selfish? Have I been fair to Jonathan? Have I tried my hardest to make this relationship work?* My mind ran in circles, an unending loop of uncertainty. I was drowning. How would I swim out of this swamp?

* * *

After leaving the bank, I headed to my appointment with Dr. Hall.

"You were in a serious situation the other evening. Tell me in your words what happened," the silver-haired physician said. He listened to what I said and asked questions. He didn't dismiss my concerns or think the situation was trivial. His eyes filled with compassion as I told him my story.

He mirrored the old-time empathetic family doctor who made house calls. Based on what I had seen in the support group, I shared my fears of not recovering. "I don't want to reclaim my self-esteem and autonomy at the expense of becoming dependent on or addicted to drugs," I said.

My hopes soared when he told me he liked to find the root cause of a problem before prescribing a treatment.

"There are usually options. We won't jump to conclusions now."

He asked more questions—about my relationships, work, exercise, sleep, and nutrition. "I suspect the cause of your anxiety may be stress overload. I'll want to verify this preliminary diagnosis through doing a complete physical exam and perhaps adding a specialist, a counselor, to our team," he said.

"Now, you need rest, Suzanna. Go home, take the medicine I prescribe, and get some sleep," he said and handed me a medication order. Then he wrote something else on a second sheet and gave it to me. "Make an appointment with this counselor for tomorrow. She will help you with the emotional side of moving on with your life. I will tell her you'll be calling. And, with your permission, I will contact Jonathan and talk with him; he must give you his full support for you to heal."

I gasped. "You know Jonathan?"

"Not well, but enough to understand what is happening here. Our paths have crossed a few times. Be assured he will listen to me."

I nodded my consent, relieved knowing Dr. Hall would advocate for me, but I did not want to know more about his relationship with my husband.

Before leaving the exam room, Dr. Hall patted my hand. "This will work out, Suzanna. I have confidence you will make the best choice. You have already taken the first steps toward making a positive change in your life."

I left the clinic and strolled through the park-like green space to my office building, letting the small patch of nature smooth my rough nerves. I smiled at the sprinkling of blooms bowing to me as I walked past. *Flowers! My forever friends.* I stopped and bowed to them in gratitude.

* * *

"Holy cow, Suzanna! You look really sick, honey," Cheryl said when I walked into the reception area outside my office.

I shrugged. "Well, at least you'll see I'm not faking it when I tell you I'm taking the rest of the week off as sick time."

"What can I do to help you?" she asked.

"I'm not infectious, so how about a hug?"

Cheryl got up and gave me a motherly embrace, and I squeezed her back.

"I think I've figured out what's going on. Jonathan called yesterday—several times, in fact, giving me the third degree. Stay true to yourself, Suzanna. I'll take care of the paperwork for sick time."

To myself, I wondered, *What third degree? What does she know? Is this so obvious to everyone?*

"What do you mean, Cheryl? What questions did Jonathan ask?"

Cheryl shuffled papers on her desk. "The usual, for him. Where is Suzanna? What is she doing? Who is she seeing? Who did she go out to lunch with? When will she be back? What school is she visiting? Yesterday, I had it with him and told him to stuff it and grow up."

I laughed out loud, imagining Jonathan's snarl when he was told to stuff it. *No wonder he was snitty last night when he mentioned Cheryl.*

"Well done, Cheryl," I said but walking to my office, my body shook with a combination of fear, humiliation, and anger.

There were two things I still needed to do before I left. The first was to make an appointment the next day with the counselor Dr. Hall had recommended. The second was to retrieve a packet of letters from my desk drawer and read them.

August 25, 1978

Dearest Suzanna,

I'm settled in my new home—my cabin is finished! It sits on the side of a forested hill overlooking a little valley and Slate Creek beyond. I hope to get electricity and phone lines strung up to the house before winter. Currently, appliances are fueled on propane gas (gas refrigerator, gas water tank), and lights run on a massive bank of car batteries. My water supply comes from a spring behind the house that gravity feeds to the bathroom and kitchen. Yep, a little rustic! I'm making a wood dining room table with benches and am getting in some secondhand furniture, although my bed is new—that's one item I won't cut corners on.

The wildlife is phenomenal—deer, groundhogs, birds, and now and again a black bear or two. The other night, I thought an old woman was screaming in the forest, and then I recognized the sound—a screeching cougar. Hah! What a joke on me!

Oh, and dear Flower Girl, the flora is spectacular! I took a hike last week in the back beyond the woods and came across a hidden meadow. I couldn't name many of the flowers, but the ones I knew were white and red baneberry, wild sarsaparilla, and tea berries. I promise you will never need to poach anyone's garden here for a beautiful bouquet.

I wish you were with me to share the beauty of this place. I'd make you a swing hanging from a branch of the massive tree in front of the cabin so you could fly free with the breeze. I'd push you higher and higher just to hear your giggles and to meld with your free spirit. Suzanna, the place is mystic —If you were here, you could hear the ghosts wandering through these hills.

I am finding peace. My flashbacks aren't as bad or as often now. Perhaps it's because I'm on the path following my North Star or because I don't need to prove anything to anybody. Or it's because I can love and forgive myself.

My heart is full of gratitude for that lucky day in September when we met. I miss our coffees together, I miss teasing you, I miss hearing your voice, I miss your smile. Tonight, I will go to bed missing you, sad because my demons will always keep us apart, but I will sleep well on the bed of happy memories of our times together.

Your Mon Ange,

Craig

I read the handful of letters—they lifted my spirits and gave me hope for the future.

* * *

I never found out the content of the conversation between Dr. Hall and my husband, but whatever it consisted of toned down Jonathan's rhetoric and demeanor from the previous evening.

"I'm sorry, Bunny," he said while smothering me in his arms when I walked through the front door at home. "I just talked with Dr. Hall, and I'm really sorry. I'm sorry about everything. I've called in and won't be taking my shift tonight. It's more important I be with you."

On the one hand, I was relieved to have Jonathan home with me. The thought of living through another attack by myself—tingling needles in my hands, seeing black dots comingle into a black blanket in front of my eyes, the spasms throughout my body—made me fearful. On the other hand, I wanted to be alone. Given Jonathan's reception, I hoped for the best and reached my arms around his neck, whispering, "Thank you," and went into the bedroom to sleep.

During the night, I roused, and the warmth of Jonathan's body next to me and his steady breath floating across my face soothed me. I turned to my side and snuggled into him.

If only this peace would go on forever.

I awoke midmorning, and my nose tickled from the scent of a profusion of fresh flowers. The bounty of bouquets Jonathan had bought could compete with the cache in any floral shop. The arrangements mirrored an English country garden—natural rustic baskets filled with snapdragons, alstroemeria, carnations, asters, roses, hydrangea, and lilies. The cornucopia of colors and the delicate displays raised my spirits.

That morning, Jonathan and I didn't talk much—he was abiding by Dr. Hall's advice to give me space and support, and I wasn't ready to share anything beyond the clinical aspects of my anxiety attack. I thought it best not to divulge my meeting with Jack or the attorney until I clarified what I wanted and had a plan in place.

In the early afternoon, I left for my appointment with the counselor. "I'm going out, Jonathan, to see the counselor Dr. Hall recommended. I should be back in a couple of hours."

"What—" Jonathan stopped himself. He bit his lip, struggling not to say more. "Okay, Bunny. Whatever the doc thinks is best."

Like the lawyer, the therapist listened to my story. Her first questions explored my self-esteem and fears before tackling what I believed success looked like in my future life.

"When did you start believing your self-worth relied on you being a giver?"

"Are you overusing your strengths of love and kindness? Is that turning *you* into a controller?

"What are you concerned about?"

"What's most important to you? What do you want?"

"What do you know?"

"If you had no fear, what would you do?"

"What will you do?"

"If you divorce, what will the future look like?"

"What are the consequences of your choice?"

"What would happen if you did nothing?"

"If you were telling yourself what you got out of this session, what would that be?"

* * *

What did I get from my counseling session? I asked myself that question, sitting beside my beloved Scioto at my Pondering Place. It was late afternoon, and the soothing river, sodded slope, and wooded refuge of sycamores and silver maples summoned me into the present. They were comforting companions, giving me the ability to focus and be curious, nonjudging, and compassionate to myself.

The vista was breathtaking. It double delighted me with a mirror image of itself. Was it a mirage that the verdant velarium of trees, the berry-blue sky, and swirling clouds cleverly cloned themselves on the calm water? I smiled—*my calming companions must appreciate something I have not yet discerned.*

From nowhere, Craig's voice floated through the rustling leaves. He startled me. "To feel better, I had to reestablish a relationship with myself. I needed to find myself, know who I was and where I wanted to go. I thought the best place to start was to give myself space and peace and let nature help me free my tangled heart."

I allowed Craig's words to dangle in the air. Then I heard him again. "To find my way, my desire to change had to be greater than my desire to stay the same." Isn't this what Jack and Lillian and Dr. Hall said too? Isn't this what the psychologist said? They were singing me a chorus. I smiled—the answer had been here all the time!

I thought about the actions that took me on an off-ramp and led me to such a dark and unhappy place. I looked inward and saw I was springing a trap! A plight of my making, not Jonathan's, constructed of ego where I lost myself, believing I could be everyone's savior.

I allowed my zeal to help others become an obsession, a mission to reform Jonathan. Through this transformation, my life focused on changing Jonathan's behavior, and by doing so, I made my self-esteem and well-being contingent upon that success. Shovelful after shovelful, I buried myself—I submerged living my truth. I abused myself. My choice was to nurture my happiness—have positive emotions and relationships, embrace life, and see the boundaries of my mission as offering an opportunity to help people flourish but not to change them. My choice was to assume responsibility for my happiness.

A sense of freedom flowed over me. *I cannot make over Jonathan; I cannot be his savior.* I smiled—my desire to change was more than my desire to stay the same. My desire to fulfill my potential was more than my desire to control Jonathan. I looked outward to the river, and there it was—my image smiling back at me. With a deep inhale of courage, I exhaled and unshackled myself from Jonathan.

Chapter 16

THE MERRY-GO-ROUND

I am preparing a plan, made ready by meetings with my counselor and lawyer. I'm plucking up my courage, taking a leap of faith, and plunging into my future. It's the Sunday after my ER visit, and Jonathan and I are taking time to be together and alone. I suggest we drive to Mohican State Park and talk about our next steps. "This is the end?" Jonathan asks. I say, "Yes, it is." Jonathan nods without offering criticism, a cold shoulder, or displaying his disappointed look. What leverage does Dr. Hall hold over the subordinate third-year resident?

* * *

I often came to Mohican State Park with my family, Gary, or other friends. Such a simple pleasure had escaped Jonathan and me, and this Sunday afternoon was the first time I shared my love of the park's beauty with my husband. The temperature was ninety degrees, and there was a cloud-sprinkled sky, a perfect day for a ride in Jonathan's Mustang for the hour-long drive from Columbus. I had prepared a picnic of gourmet salads and sandwiches and tossed in a bottle of wine and flowers. I thought nature's glorious landscape of rolling hills, meadows, forests, and streams would be a neutral backdrop for a crucial conversation about our futures. The muscle car snaked along narrow and winding roads beneath a canopy of tree branches that screened the sun rays and made them dance on the macadam. The meandering drive set a peaceful stage for us to lower our emotional gauges.

We stopped at the Clear Fork Gorge overlook and marveled at the expansive vista of forest. Who knew Ohio kept such a secret! Later, I held on for dear life to the red, rusty-looking steel handrails as we joined other visitors trudging up eight flights of wooden steps to the top of the Old Fire Tower. The view was infinite across the forested hills framed by an endless royal blue sky—it seemed there was no end to the world.

Jonathan's eyes scanned the horizon. "God, Suzanna. Why haven't we taken the time to come here before this? I have missed a lot. I have messed up a bunch too."

How do I answer that? My chest was heavy with sadness.

"Let the past rest, Jonathan. Enjoy this moment. After all, it's all we have."

Reminiscent of our early days, Jonathan put his arm around me and cuddled my neck, but I understood the end of our world together was coming.

* * *

It turned out to be a day of tears, apologies, regrets, revelations, and promises as we considered our future. We sat away from the other tourists under a grove of trees on the edge of a quiet meadow. We had laid our picnic on the soft blanket of grass and, sitting close to each other with intentional looks, sipped our wine and spoke in whispered voices. If an artist painted us, she would assume her watercolor captured a portrait of lovers.

Our eyes welled. Mine from compassion as Jonathan revealed his vulnerability and confessed his skepticism of women. My husband's tears overflowed from his emotional pain and feeling of loss. He told a tale of family tension, mental illness, adultery, and the uncertainty of his parentage.

"My earliest memories are of my father and mother fighting. At first, I didn't understand the reasons for the arguments. Their fights terrified me. As I got older, I understood more. Both made accusations about affairs with other people. My father accused my mother of betrayal.

My mother said she needed love and affection. It was a constant firing circle."

This friction alone would devastate a child. But it was the other secrets that showed a degree of household dysfunction I never imagined.

"Although she covered it up in public, my mother was often depressed. I was in sixth grade when I came home from school to find out she was hospitalized. Not until I was a teenager did I find out she had attempted suicide. Although my father tried to keep his feelings buried, I always felt I was never his biological son."

Who wouldn't have trust and self-esteem issues after this? I understood now that Bud and Marianne put up a perfect public pretense, but beneath the veneer lay codependent behaviors, betrayal, and abuse. As their protégé, and through their role modeling, Jonathan continued the cycle of dysfunction. My heart crumbled as Jonathan shared his story, but he required more than what I could offer to break the toxic cycle. He had to choose to seek professional help to overcome his fears. Another darker thought went through my mind: *How much of what he told me is true?*

I apologized for allowing my ego to supersede the truth—the most fundamental value I held dear. Through my arrogance, I confessed I had wanted to prove I could be Jonathan's savior. If I loved him, I had to abandon that desire.

Jonathan expressed his regrets for his excessive needs for control and attention and the emotional abuse they caused me. He often said he was sorry during our conversation, but I recognized his pathology prevented the phrase from progressing beyond spoken words. Fear was the primary motivator. Jonathan knew his control over his Bunny was lost, and I was leaving him.

We ended with promises. My solicitation of one from Jonathan was for his well-being. I hoped he could find his purpose and happy life. Jonathan conceded he needed professional support to fight his devils, and he pledged to seek help. My husband had moved from denying a problem existed to acknowledging it, but he had a steep hill to climb before he would take meaningful action to change his behaviors.

Above all else, though, Jonathan wanted to pry out a different guarantee from me. "Do you promise to forgive me?" he asked.

"That depends on your definition of forgiveness," I said. "How do you see forgiveness? I have to know what you are requesting before I can give you my word."

The silence was thick. A pain as sharp as a knife stabbed me as Jonathan struggled to slice through the blather he had a habit of serving up.

"Well, I guess I mean not blaming me and not trying to get even with me." His clouded eyes filled with apprehension.

My heart fell with my eyes. How little he knew me!

Mentally, I reached out and embraced him in compassion.

"Forgiveness isn't about justifying a transgression, Jonathan, or overlooking the hurt it caused. And it isn't about reconciliation or forgetting something harmful occurred. Forgiveness is understanding the pain of the person who caused you harm. It's stepping into that person's shoes and seeing things from a different perspective. It's called having empathy for another person, and in the end, it means choosing to be released from anger and resentment."

"Does this mean you won't try to get even? You won't bad-mouth me or ruin my reputation?"

There it was! His greatest fear. He hadn't understood a word I said.

"Jonathan, forgiveness means I choose not to be a victim of anger toward you or try to get back at you. I'm not seeking retribution, but I'm also not overlooking or forgetting the hurt you caused or justifying your behavior."

"But you won't bad-mouth me?" he asked again.

"I will not tell lies about you," I said.

His eyes narrowed. "But will you bad-mouth me? Like what you did with Dr. Hall."

I swallowed hard. Had I made a dangerous mistake coming here with Jonathan? How did I keep myself safe? I thought of the definition of bad-mouth: *to criticize unfairly.*

"I won't bad-mouth you."

Jonathan's eyes lightened. For now, he had gotten what was most important to him.

We discussed divorce arrangements. I quoted from memory from the details the attorney had reviewed with me. Jonathan's low-key behavior surprised me, though. The disparaging and threatening words did not appear, nor did the familiar disappointed look.

We agreed Jonathan would move out of our current residence. I would continue to pay for the lease until its end in August. Jonathan had never liked the Bluffs anyway—not trendy enough for him.

It wasn't difficult to secure Jonathan's agreement on the rest since there was no financial loss for him. We'd be responsible for our own debts before our marriage, split the payment of our joint bills, divide the funds in our joint account equally, and keep our own cars and bank and retirement accounts. All this made Jonathan happy! I had no idea what amount was in his separate bank account or the amount of his salary. Jonathan would take the household items he had brought to the marriage, and I would do the same.

The drive back to Columbus was surreal. Jonathan cranked up the cassette player and blared out Van Halen, Huey Lewis and the News, and Bruce Springsteen. He spoke nonstop about the new position he planned to assume in July, his vacation plans after finishing his residency, and the ideal apartment he wanted in his preferred neighborhood of German Village. It felt like I was returning home from a date with no strings attached. It was as if we had never been married. *How can you live with a person for over a year and have it end with so much emptiness?* My inner voice sent out warning signals. *This is an act. Underneath, he is seething. He can't afford to show his vulnerability or lack of control. He is on the edge of emotionally breaking up.*

We returned home, and Jonathan grabbed a few things before leaving. "I'll be back in a couple of days for those divorce papers, and I'll arrange for movers to come and pick up my stuff."

Without looking back, Jonathan revved his muscle car and drove out of the driveway. This was his way of punishing me—leaving me like an abandoned puppy on the stoop of our home, watching him drive off. I wondered where he was going and would be spending the night.

I shook my head. So many mysteries. I turned and walked into the house. I didn't think it would be easy to be free of Jonathan.

* * *

Perseverance was a strength Jonathan had. No matter the degree of risk or the obstacles in his path, he finished what he started and got his prize. Where others weighed or restrained their course of action with prudence, that virtue was not in Jonathan's repertoire.

Two days later, Jonathan kept his promise and returned. But it wasn't for the divorce papers. Instead, he appeared with a bouquet, imploring me to let him return. The pleadings were familiar—ones he employed all too often.

"I've been such a fool, Suzanna."

"I need you."

"No one can replace you in my heart."

"I promise I will get help. I promise to go to a couple's counselor."

I listened and thought about the promise I had made to myself. *Choose to nurture my happiness—have positive emotions and relationships, embrace life, and see the boundaries of my mission. Help people flourish, not change them. Be responsible for my happiness.*

I handed the draft divorce papers to Jonathan.

His eyes turned cold, and his face reddened. "Why can't we get a separation? Why the divorce? Why so fast?"

I sucked on my lips and inhaled. "It's not possible."

His disappointed look reappeared. "Oh! I was right the night I came to the inn. There is another guy, isn't there? Who is he? Is it that fucking hillbilly—the idiot who follows North Stars?"

My chest tightened. My hands tingled. I lost it. "No, Jonathan, it isn't the hillbilly. There *is* no one."

"If you think you are going to divorce *me*, you're nuts. I'm the one who is leaving you. Got it? I'm leaving you because you screwed around on me. You'll be talking with my attorney." He turned, went to the front door, and looked back at me over his shoulder.

"See, Suzanna. I'm leaving you." He slammed the door as he left.

It ended as it started. In his mind, he was back in control.

* * *

Drama filled the following two weeks. Jonathan wanted a fault-based divorce founded on my alleged adultery, and I sought a no-fault one owing to our incompatibility. There was no way I would agree to his made-up charges of my unfaithfulness.

"I'm not incompatible. You're the problem," he argued in messages left every day on my work and home answering machines. However, the tug-of-war between us was short-lived when Jonathan's rope, to his surprise, unraveled.

It started with a phone call to Mel the weekend after Jonathan and I separated. I called to tell her about the impasse with the divorce and Jonathan's accusations of my adultery.

"I'm driving over right now, and we're having a chat." For Mel, this meant a two-hour drive from Cincinnati to Worthington.

"Mel, that's crazy. We can talk on the phone."

"No, we can't, dear! I'll be there in a couple. Plan on me staying overnight too."

That evening, my childhood girlfriend and I drank wine, ordered take-out pizza, and talked into the wee hours of the morning. Unlike our girlhood days, the stakes of our conversation were higher than when we comforted each other over the loss of our puppy loves.

"Jonathan is a bully. He's projecting his bad behavior on you," Mel said.

I took a long sip of my wine, giving my friend an empty stare, not sure whether I wished to hear more. "Projecting? What do you mean, Mel?"

Mel averted her eyes from mine. *Poor Mel. You're damned if you do and damned if you don't tell me.* I reached over and hugged her hand.

Mel and Bill golfed at the OSU courses, and she told me they had seen Jonathan on several occasions golfing, not with a group of friends but solo with a younger woman. "The SOB would always wave and shout hello as if daring us to tell you he was with someone else," Mel said.

I wondered how many times these sightings had happened. I feared from the way Mel's eyes strayed from mine there were more than the golf outings.

"Don't blame yourself, Mel, for not telling me. I already knew— I mean, I might have buried my radar, but it was still pinging, still vibrating. The day we had lunch right after I got engaged, you wanted to tell me something, but I brushed you off. I'm paying attention now. I *do* need to know it all."

Mel cleared her throat. "When the two of you were dating, Bill and I saw Jonathan on two occasions with another woman—and they were, ah . . . pretty romantic. Since you weren't married, I didn't want to say anything. I didn't know what your arrangements were with him."

I shook my head from side to side. *I've been such a fool.*

"Go on."

"One Sunday evening early this past March, Bill and I were at El Torito, and who shows up? Jonathan and this younger woman—his lady golfing pal. Jonathan didn't see us, but we got enough of an eyeful to know the dinner wasn't of a business nature. I hate to say it, but they were all over each other."

I reeled my memory back. A lump formed in my stomach. "That must have been when Jonathan blew up at Jack's house. One of the times he accused me of seeing another man. That evening Jonathan pulled one of his disappearing acts."

Mel and I sat immobile. My heart and breath quickened. I stared into space and clenched my jaw. I tried to hold back my sadness, embarrassment, and shame and sum up my courage to be truthful to myself. Then I figuratively threw Jonathan's destructive behavior into the trash bin—Mel had given me all I needed to stop Jonathan's nonsense about seeking a divorce on his grounds.

"Mel, I'm not going to obsess over all the shouldas or couldas. As Lillian would say, 'Don't cry over spilled milk—do something!' I must believe in myself and have the courage and perseverance to move forward. No more crying over the damn spilled milk. I'm doing something to get back the self-esteem and freedom I allowed to be taken from me."

"Dreams of freedom without action remain dreams. Your choices determine your future, Suzanna," my wise friend said.

The following Monday morning, I called my attorney and told him about my husband's extracurricular activities. Jonathan's golfing days involved more than golfing, and his disappearing acts had little to do with sleeping his anger off in an on-call room at the hospital—he had another bunny in his hutch.

Within forty-eight hours, Jonathan agreed to all my stipulations and a no-fault dissolution. We signed all required documents, and on July 2, my attorney delivered them to the court. The ending of our marriage would become final within thirty to ninety days. I was stepping off the merry-go-round.

Part II

Chapter 17

FRESH START

Thursday, August 1, 1985. The lease is up on my rental, and I am packed, waiting for the moving van to arrive. I look around and wonder whether energy from the past two years has left a permanent imprint on this house. I hope for the sake of the new renters that just the better stuff hangs around. A few tears are forming. With so many memories, saying goodbye is rough. I am reliving the thrill of moving out of my parents' home and affording my first apartment. There are fun memories too—first nights here with Jonathan. The sexual tension and our passionate lovemaking leave me with butterflies. But I am also thinking about my shattered hopes and the lessons learned.

* * *

Fourteen months before, I thought I had stepped off the merry-go-round. The truth be told, I had gotten off the jumping horse, not the ride itself. Jonathan was relentless in pursuing a reconciliation even after our marriage had been legally dissolved. As his fling with the fourth-year medical student went sour, he professed he had "learned some hard lessons" and was seeking professional help.

At first, he made frequent phone calls to my office and was bold enough to show up unannounced, wanting to plead his case. When it became clear these strategies wouldn't give him access to me—Cheryl was a great right guard—he started phoning and cruising past my home. I screened the phone calls, but I had no control over his nocturnal drive-bys, short of getting a restraining order. Since June, though, his stalking had ceased, and I hoped his therapy sessions were working.

On New Year's, a skylight of hope opened without warning in the form of a letter from Craig. I guess the saying when a door closes, a window opens might be true.

December 26, 1984

Dearest Suzanna,

All yesterday, Christmas, I thought of you—as I chopped wood for the Woodburner, snowshoed to the meadow and back, filled the bird feeders, and sat with a cup of coffee, looking through my dining room window to an icy Slate Creek.

How my heart froze, Suzanna, when I received your Christmas card. You don't say much, except that you and Jonathan are divorced. I know there is more to tell, and I am here to listen when you are ready.

I can't imagine the emotional and physical trauma you have been through. I want you to know you are resourceful and capable of making the right choices. You can follow your North Star.

I wish we could be together like the old days in the Union —me giving you the Craig silence and you rolling your eyes when I do. I'm smiling now at the memories we created. I'm missing your sincerity, selflessness, sweetness, and most of all, spunk.

Every day I keep the graduation gift you gave to me close. I can touch it when I'm ill at ease and the happy memories flood in. Isn't it crazy we gave each other such similar gifts—for you, a necklace with a North Star, and for me, a keychain with a compass.

I laugh to myself at how wide your eyes got when you found out how I could fiddle and sing—and your sweet, flirty smile when I sidled up to you, playing "Soldier's Joy."

I'm also thinking about the day we sat on the banks of the Olentangy after that PTSD episode (that's the fancy name they are calling flashbacks now). You gave me the best therapy—you listened and listened and listened.

I'm sending you the biggest hug, and I'm listening.

Your Mon Ange

My daydreams dissipated when the moving van arrived. I was grateful and excited because the next day, I was figuratively and literally taking an on-ramp back to the highway of my life and following my North Star. I was about to make a fresh start, leaving my beloved Columbus, but there was an edge of fear too—the kind I got before hopping on the rollercoaster at Cedar Point. But once on the ride, my senses tingle, and I am proud I dared to take the leap.

Chapter 18

ME AND A DOG NAMED SAM

I watch the dawn light wander through the window shades of my girl-
hood room. My top sheet is wadded, evidence of my tossing and turning
all night to check and recheck the time on my bedside clock. I'm eager but
anxious about my big moving day. The unknown intrigues and entices me.
Come, it says, see what lies ahead and around the corner. I finger my North
Star pendant that is around my neck again. I feel its energy thrusting me
into a new chapter of my story. Be open and curious, it tells me. Notice and
appreciate every day. Use your kindness and love in creating positive rela-
tionships. Be creative, experiment, and relish new ways and things.

* * *

Sam Adams, the new man in my life, lay at my side. The Boston terrier entered my world a few weeks after my separation from Jonathan.
Thinking Sam and I might benefit from mutual companionship, Jack
told me about the juvenile Boston made an orphan after his master
died. When the two of us met, there was no hesitation on either of our
parts about having a long-term relationship—it was love at first sight.

I mused about the path ahead as I scratched my companion's ears and
gazed at the memorabilia remaining in my old room—books, stuffed
animals, posters, and knickknacks. So many memories! I had dis-
mantled the collage made from the cards Jack sent to me when he was
in college—those would go with me, and I would reassemble them in
my new digs in western New York. The teddy bear Gary had given

me would come along for the ride, as well as the collection of Nancy Drew books to remind me of happy girlhood sleepovers with Mel and Ellen. All the items I acquired during my "Jonathan Years" would not be making the trip. Everything, even household items—dishes, silverware, glassware—found new homes. This wasn't a do-over. It was a fresh start.

The previous evening, Lillian and Robert threw a going-away barbeque party for me. Jack and Lorna, Mel and Bill, Ellen and her current beau, and Cheryl were among the well-wishers of aunts, uncles, cousins, colleagues, and neighbors. In my family, when there is barbeque, there must be beer. In honor of my puppy and my new favorite lager, several cases of Sam Adams chilled in a tub of ice.

Lillian outdid her usual decorating for the festivities, which says a lot. The patio transformed into a dance floor with strings of twinkling white lights hanging overhead. Bales of hay delivered for the occasion were placed strategically among picnic tables covered with red and white gingham cloth. Since nothing was too good for Jack's Flower Girl, my brother arranged for a live country music band. Living up to the theme of barbeque, booze, and bad dance moves, the crowd of partygoers revved it up. While my relatives and friends wished me well and showered me with hugs and kisses, they celebrated more than my move and a new job. They cheered my regained freedom.

As I backed out of my parent's driveway the following morning, Lillian, Robert, Jack, and Lorna waved their goodbyes and threw me kisses. Sam and I were filled with the sumptuous breakfast Lillian prepared for us—blueberry pancakes and sausage for me and cooked chicken breast for Sam. A red cooler was next to me in the passenger's seat, stocked with enough drinks and food for a road trip double the distance I intended to drive. The essentials Sam and I needed before we settled into a new house jam-packed the trunk and half the back seat of my red Civic. I had no clue what kind of home I would get, but I had confidence that a friendly real estate agent named Ray would help me find the perfect spot.

Heading north on the interstate toward Akron, I pushed the accelerator down on the overpacked and underpowered Civic, struggling to get up some speed. I calculated the trip would take about seven to eight hours with stops for gas and puppy and snack breaks. "If we're lucky, we'll be in Alfred by four o'clock," I said to Sam as we headed past Westerville, but he was already settled in his bed in the seat behind me and was sound asleep.

I cranked up the volume on my cassette player and sang along to Lobo, substituting "Sam" for "Boo" and "woman" for "man" in the chorus: "Me and you and a dog named Sam." Each time the lyrics rounded, I sang out extra loud, "How I love being a free wo-man."

Halfway into our trip, I pulled into the rest area at Mentor for a snack and potty breaks for Sam and me—our last stop before leaving my treasured Ohio. Homesickness and nostalgia struck me. I turned to my furry companion. "This will be the first time living outside Ohio. Look at me, twenty-seven years old, acting like a five-year-old on her first day of school! But I have you, Sam; we're in this together, bud!"

Sam wanted to scout, sniff, and mark new territory, but after ten minutes, I called a halt to his exploration and cracked the cooler. While we satisfied our appetites under a stand of shade trees, I watched the traffic coming into and out of the rest area. Children piled from vehicles and hurried to the restrooms, excited to be rid of the confines of their cars. A few families like us took a break for a picnic. Where were all these people coming from, and where were they going? Many acted tired, hurried, or stressed. Others, mostly older couples, took in the park's grassy beauty and appeared contented and relaxed. I was thankful I was in the latter group. I held Sam Adams on my lap and gave the pooch a kiss on his head. I closed my eyes and reached to touch the North Star around my neck. *I am grateful to be free.*

Following our break, we were back in the car and on the road. After we passed through a small section of Pennsylvania, I veered off the interstate at the state line and onto the Southern Tier Expressway heading toward Jamestown. The countryside was as gorgeous as I remembered seeing a few weeks earlier when I came for my interview at the university. I had read the Allegheny foothills were New York State's best-kept secret. I had no concept before my first visit, though, how the luxuriant forests turned rolling hills into a velvet carpet or how expansive valleys cradled rushing rivers and placid streams. I didn't know storybook villages dotting the landscape could compete with those in fairytales. Nor could I have imagined such mind-altering psychedelic-blue skies, accompanied by unending parades of ponderous white clouds, could exist. Observing the potpourri, I thought of Craig as I drove and mused about the quirk of fate that brought me to western New York and its photographic countryside.

After the New Year, Craig and I started up our coffee dates from a distance—while I drank my morning coffee, I'd write him a letter and afterward pop it into the mail before going to work, and he would do the same. Our letters were on parallel tracks. Going in either direction, the trains passed each other and stopped on schedule at Worthington, Ohio, and Canisteo, New York. I rushed to my mailbox when I got home from work, knowing Craig's letter waited for me. Before opening it, I got the fireplace going and poured myself a glass of wine. The anticipation of reading what was inside the envelope was like chocolate frosting on a cake, making what was within sweeter. Sundays were miserable, but Mondays gave double the pleasure.

At first, I wrote about my struggles in rediscovering myself and silencing a contrary inner voice that, on the one hand, scolded me for my missteps and vanity and, on the other, chastised me for lack of compassion and refusing Jonathan a second chance.

Wednesday, January 2, 1985

My dear Mon Ange,

This is a letter I never wanted to write—it is hard for me to admit my mistakes and defeat. Perhaps the virtue of perspective is not my best strength. I lost myself, Craig, in a valley of ego and have paid a high physical, emotional, and spiritual price. More than anything else, what saddens me is that my ego has caused others pain too—my family and even Jonathan.

In June, I had a physical and emotional breakdown of sorts, and I realized my marriage wasn't working for Jonathan or me. As of last November, we dissolved the marriage. Jonathan was emotionally abusive, and the more he would abuse, the more I enabled his behaviors. I knew his faults before I married him. But I thought I could change him. People don't change because another wants it—people change because they want to become better. My arrogance was not that I believed Jonathan would change with love and support. It was that I thought I would make him change.

I remember you saying, "Egotism is a thief that steals your soul piece by piece until there nothing is left." I knew better, Craig, but my vanity prevailed. Why did I not see this? Why was I so willful? I'm mad with myself. I am ashamed and empty. Is it too late? Has the thief stolen every piece of my soul away?

In a deep bow of gratitude to you for being my Mon Ange,

Suzanna

Craig's letters flooded me with optimism that my North Star's light would burn bright. His response to my first letter gave me faith I could give myself the most important gift of all—forgiveness.

Sunday, January 6, 1985

Dearest Suzanna,

I know there is more of your story to tell, and I am here to listen. How could I be your Mon Ange and not listen?

Trust me, your inner light still shines. Those who have nothing left of themselves know no guilt, sorrow, or grief —that is not you! Feeling disappointed for not measuring up to your values is the reaction of an honest person—bad people don't give a shit about those things.

Hey, it's okay to ask yourself, "Why did I not see this?" or "Why was I so willful?" That's self-awareness—can't make meaningful changes in our life without it. Go for it! Sort out those answers and learn more about yourself.

Yep, shame and guilt are traps that keep us stuck—at least that's what I found. I told myself those false stories, hoping to absolve myself from doing the hard work to be better. Ha! That didn't work out well as I smoked and drank months down the drain with my two best friends—wacky tobacky and booze.

To do better, we must have compassion for ourselves and forgive ourselves. If we don't, can we ever have peace of mind? If we're always looking backward, how can we change? For what's it's worth—just my two cents, I don't think so—it'll be the same old shit, only in a different toilet. (Yikes, a whole lot of shit going on here!)

I'm no $100 an hour counselor, but for a nickel, I say, absolve yourself for not living up to your values. Forgive yourself if you have injured someone, make amends, and then get the hell to town and start living a better version of yourself.

Sending you love and hugs,

Your Mon Ange

I folded Craig's note and slipped it into my wallet. When my inner voice made my mind a blender of shame, I reread Craig's words. *Shame and guilt are traps that keep us stuck.* They're false stories we tell ourselves and others, hoping to absolve ourselves from doing the hard work to be better.

In his following letters, Craig tossed me reflections, making me think beyond the trivial. Many times, his correspondence consisted of only a probing question in a sentence or two. Who would have thought the Craig silence was possible through letters?

Monday, January 21, 1985

Dearest Suzanna,

Today, the real challenge for me is looking at the world in ways that are different than my own. When my students think about leaving home, leaving this poor county, and going to college to make themselves better, their parents are fearful. What is their perspective? What is their fear?

Today, Suzanna, what is the real challenge? What is the fear that keeps you from following your North Star?

Your Mon Ange

Sometimes, his letters included a short verse of poetry or a quotation that pushed me to confront myself.

Monday, February 4, 1985

"Before a path is made, you must walk on it,"—Zhuang Zhou

Your path summons you, my fearless path maker.

Your Mon Ange

Like our cafeteria talks, some of his letters mixed philosophy with questions.

Tuesday, February 5, 1985

Dearest Suzanna,

What do you make of this?

Little fears eat away your heart, bite by bite until there is nothing more.

What fears are eating your heart?

What fears are barring your heart from gratitude and hope?

Your Mon Ange

Craig's prose turned the embers in my heart into small fires. *Can our relationship now go beyond friendship?* As much as I wished to be safe in Craig's arms, I didn't want to fall into another trap of my own making, where my ego and kindness went into overdrive. I was not, could not, be anyone's savior other than my own.

Unlike Jonathan, Craig understood himself, acknowledged his flaws, and was honest about what he believed was possible. If I loved him and cherished the caring friendship we had, I would respect his boundaries. It was his birthday letter, though, with a drawing he painted that gave me hope for a shared life, if not in this world, then in some distant time, in some different place and dimension.

> Thursday, March 21, 1985
>
> Dearest Suzanna,
>
> An extraordinary day, for sure! My smile spreads, and my heart spills over, surging in gratitude, celebrating the day you were born. The first time we met, an aura of sunshine surrounded you—sunny yellows, snappy reds, and soothing greens stirred in a stunning sunflower garden—and my North Star steered me toward you. Surreptitiously, while the professor's lecture blended into low-frequency tones, I snuck side-glances so I could ingest your glow. Your strength, sweetness, sincerity, spiritedness, and selflessness bathed me in the serenity my soul craved.
>
> Today, I share the secret of your sunshine aura and honor your birthday with this humble drawing so you can see the light you brought to my world, Flower Girl.
>
> Your Mon Ange

There is always hope—a belief in possibilities. At a time when you least expect it, something comes into your life and hands you an opportunity to change your life—if you are willing to take a risk.

Tuesday, April 9, 1985

Dearest Suzanna,

I was bowling Friday evening with some buddies who work at the state college not far from where I live. One of them teaches in the school of allied health technologies there! I mentioned I had a close friend who worked in student affairs in allied health at OSU. I was afraid the dude was going to hug me to death when I told him. Guess they've been looking for a director of student affairs for some time but just haven't found the right match. I got a copy of the position description and am enclosing it. Don't need to tell you that I would have selfish motives to have my best coffee buddy living near me.

Anyway, for real, look and see if this aligns with your North Star.

Your Mon Ange

I read Craig's letter and yelled out a "Yes!" and startled Sam Adams out of his nap. "Hey, Mr. Adams! What do you think about western New York?"

The following day, I made a phone call to the dean of Allied Health at the university and got the ball rolling.

* * *

I sped along on the four-lane highway, happy in the tumble of these reflections. Except for my little red compact, the road was empty of other cars. I switched my cassette player to Springsteen and spun my car up and down the Allegheny hills. The rugged richness of the countryside shrouded me in satisfying peace, and I thought of the native peoples of this area, the Seneca. They called themselves the Keepers of the Western Door and gave thanksgiving for the abundance the land provided. The spirit of Leatherlips in my Pondering Place on the banks of the Scioto had helped me. Here, the spirits of the native peoples filled me with hope. For the rest of the way, I drove with a smile slapped across my face.

* * *

I glanced over at the dashboard clock, and it said four o'clock. "We've made it!" I called out to Sam when I pulled into the Squirrel's Nest Motel parking lot. Tucked in the forest off State Highway 244, the lodgings were mid-century, with about twenty guest rooms off one central hallway. While its name might make a tourist wary that fluffy rodents could be overnight companions, the rooms were adequate, clean, and free of critters. Most importantly, though, the manager had no aversion to accommodating Sam. A fresh mountain breeze and a chorus of birds rippled through the room's open window as I unloaded my suitcase and stashed the ice chest and Sam's eating bowls in the bathroom.

"I'm sure glad I have you," I said as I flopped on the bed on my back, with Sam jumping up and making himself comfortable at my side. His soulful eyes scanned my face. "Guess you're happy I'm here, too, aren't you, buddy!"

I rested my head on the pillow, thinking of the calendar of events I had for the next day. An early meet and greet at eight o'clock with the dean of the School of Allied Health—a brief orientation and introduction to some of the faculty, I suspected. After that, it would be the usual check-in with human relations—picture taking for an employee badge, picking up the keys to the school building and my office, and signing five thousand documents for salary, direct deposit, retirement, and health insurance.

I stroked Sam's back and wondered at my actions over the past three months. *What a leap of faith!*

* * *

"I don't think Jonathan will ever stop pestering me," I said to Jack over lunch at our favorite High Street diner one Saturday in early May. "It's been over six months since our divorce, and he's still doing those crazy drive-bys in front of my house. It's like he's in high school, acting out, revving his engine as he passes the house."

"You could see about getting a protection order," my brother said. "Jonathan hasn't threatened you, but he *is* harassing you." Then he frowned. "Guess I could take him behind the shed and beat the holy crap out of him."

"Don't you think that might be kind of messy, not to mention smelly?"

My brother choked on his coffee and embarrassingly coughed brown droplets across the tabletop. "Never joke with me when my mouth is full, Flower Girl."

We laughed, and I let Jack clean up his mess before I tossed a shock-wave his way.

"Jack, I don't think Columbus is big enough for Jonathan and me."

"What the hell does that mean? You want to kill him?"

"Not that extreme, Jack! No, I'm thinking about moving to another city . . . to another state."

"Holy shit. What's this all about?"

"There's a job opening at a state university in New York."

Jack's head jerked back.

"It would be a promotion. I'd be the director of student affairs for an allied health school . . ." *He's not buying it.*

"Yeah, I'm still listening."

"Jack, I've never lived outside Columbus—never went away to school. I could leave bad memories here. This would be a fresh start—a change of scenery, a do-over."

Jack looked down. Diner sounds supplied background music for his dominating silence. When he looked back at me, he wore his lawyer face. I waited for a prosecutor's cross-examination.

"Are you running away from something, Flower Girl? Or are you running toward something?"

Jack's razor-edged questions cut me in half. The sound of silverware crashing as the bus staff loaded their bins was a blade cutting across my nerves. I tried to sort out the truth. *Am I running away? Running away out of fear? Running away from Jonathan?*

Jack's eyes knifed through me. "Running from a tiger out of fear with no destination in mind . . . what's the benefit? In the end, the tiger gets you. Tiger and fear always win, Flower Girl."

My mind rolled. *What's the motivation? What's the destination? What's the benefit? I can never outrun Jonathan.*

"You said you wanted a fresh start, a do-over. Which is it? Fresh start or do-over?"

"Is there a difference?" I asked.

"You tell me, Flower Girl."

We finished our coffees. My brother had learned well from Robert. A refrain of my father's surfaced: "Offer a thought-provoking question when you want to help someone. Questions deepen a person's awareness. Questions empower people to make choices and act. That's how I get to the truth—by asking questions."

After lunch, I went to my Scioto Pondering Place for a long think. The soothing waters this time didn't relieve my restlessness. Instead, my mind meandered. It was tricky maneuvering my way out of the maze of questions. *What is my motivation? Do I have more than fear? What about my North Star? Is that all talk? What's the difference between a do-over and a fresh start?*

Barricades in my mind's maze blocked me, but I persisted. *Turn around! Try a different direction! Find the exit! What does the Scioto teach me?* I paused and gazed at the flowing water. *The river knows itself. It has no fear. It sees its destination, cuts its channel, and flows forward. There are no do-overs.*

I reached out and hugged Craig's words, "To make the path, you must walk it first."

This was not a do-over! It was a fresh start. I saw my destination. I was not running out of fear. I was making my path walking toward my North Star.

* * *

We made my interview trip in early June a family affair. Robert always spoke of the beauty of western New York and the Finger Lakes region, and after I had secured an interview date, he, Lillian, Jack, and Lorna wanted to come on the jaunt.

"Let's make this a little family getaway," Robert suggested at the family Memorial Day picnic.

I wagged my index finger at my father. "You didn't raise a dummy. You say this is a family vacation, but I know better! It's called reconnaissance and support."

"Hey, Flower Girl, even if you bomb the interview, which you won't, it will be a great road trip," Jack said. Lorna gave Jack a swat, and I stuck out my tongue and gave my brother a dirty look. The antics between us had started. *This is going to be fun!*

"Road trip! No way!" Lillian cried. "I'd have to kill all four of you if I were cooped up for seven hours with you. No, we'll fly to Rochester and rent a car to go the rest of the way."

Since none of us wanted to die or see Lillian locked up in prison for life, we agreed to her transportation mode. "First class, of course, Mom," Jack said.

Lillian stared at my brother, smiled, and straightened to her full height. "Of course, Jack. Thanks for offering."

I laughed to myself. *Jack should know better than to smart-mouth with Lillian.*

Lillian, Lorna, Robert, and I all smiled because we'd be flying first class.

* * *

Monday, June 10, we boarded a flight to Rochester—first class, on Jack's dime. The van we rented at the airport was tight for the five of us and our luggage, but we managed without any murders or other untoward events. It was a two-hour drive from the airport to our destination, a cottage Lillian had lined up on Lake Demons about thirty minutes from the state university. We followed a meandering two-lane state highway that, to Robert's delight, hugged Conesus Lake, the westernmost of the eleven Finger Lakes, and delivered us into the arms of the Allegheny foothills. When we arrived at the lake (the locals, we discovered, called it Demons Pond), we found the cabin was more bunkhouse than a quaint cottage, but we all agreed it was perfect. Fitting its rustic style, the owners had outfitted it with a humongous woodburning stove, minimalist furnishings, and a collection of books a librarian would kill for. That evening, we grilled burgers and roasted ears of corn, drank beer, and afterward melted marshmallows around an outside pit under a sparkling sky. "This is heaven," Robert said to me, and I agreed.

The next day, we piled into the van and drove into Alfred, a village tucked between two valleys with a late 1800s picture-postcard main street. The one-stoplight town beguiled us. At the intersection of North Main and Pine, the town's sole beacon separated the entrances of two colleges, one public, the other private. Although it was summer break, the tiny village couldn't shake off its pulsating scholastic cloak. Funky little shops and eating places with names like the Kampus Kave and the Collegiate kept the college vibe alive.

I spent the day interviewing with the school's dean, the department chairs, and faculty members while my family scouted the downtown and surrounding neighborhoods. The dean rolled out the red carpet, hosting a few of the faculty and me for lunch at the Collegiate, the best (and some might argue the only) eating establishment in the small downtown. I must have made an outstanding impression because, at four o'clock in the afternoon, I left the dean's office with an offer for the position of director of student affairs, which I had accepted on the spot.

The following four days proved to be the family holiday we hoped for—barbeque every evening, flapjacks, eggs, and bacon for breakfast, and Scrabble and euchre challenges in the evenings. The two "boys" even tried fishing (unsuccessfully) from a canoe.

A highlight was including Craig in our extended family and festivities. After Robert and Jack's unfruitful fishing day, Craig showed the two of them the secrets of lake angling and afterward how to clean and fry up their catch.

One day, Craig took us to Watkins Glen. There, our jaws dropped as we oohed and aahed spellbound by the two-hundred-foot cliffs, the tiered waterfalls, and the path that tunneled and wound through the steep gorge. In the evening, Craig accompanied us with his guitar in a group sing-along around the firepit at our cabin as we stuffed ourselves with s'mores. He ended with "Franklin County Woman," to the whoops and hollers of my family. Craig often teased me and said he was jealous that I was on a first-name basis with the song's author since, in his day job, Cowboy Bob worked as a medical illustrator down the hall from my office at OSU. That evening was no different, as Craig tried to wheedle an introduction to the Ohio celebrity from me.

After Craig left for home, my father and I sat alone while the embers of the fire died down.

"A fine man . . . a very fine man," Robert said. "He's been through a lot, Suzanna. I know what it's like from the battle fatigue I suffered. The difference between Craig and me is I've dealt with it better and approximated the life I had before the war. Craig hasn't been that lucky."

I opened up with my father. I told him about Craig's flashback I had seen almost a decade earlier and stories of similar events Craig had shared with me. "We have a friendship, Dad. Craig told me long ago his burdens were enough for him to handle without being ridden with guilt by placing them on someone else."

"Like I said, Suzanna, a fine man."

* * *

I let those happy memories from a few weeks earlier drift away as I rested on my bed at the Squirrel's Nest. Now, it was just a dog named Sam and me who were cutting a path toward my North Star. I was empowered. But with the freedom, a bit of loneliness and fear came along for the hike.

A pair of brown pleading eyes stared at me. "All righty, let's go and scare up some grub," I said to Sam.

It wasn't a long drive to the nearest eatery, more like a hop, skip, and a jump to the diner up the road from the Squirrel's Nest. I got out of the car and left Sam Adams on guard with a few doggie appetizers. I eyed the restaurant sign—Stern's Little Red Hen.

Do they name everything around here after animals?

Chapter 19

HONEY BEAR

I'm on a quest today with Sam, looking for our new home. My realtor, Ray, is a full-time professor who dabbles part-time as a realtor. High energy and impulsive, I don't think Ray can organize himself out of a paper bag. I get into the front seat of his car, and I'm fending off real estate listings scattered everywhere. It's a surprise he has made tenure in the School of Business at the state college. I rethink that judgment. He does have all the characteristics of a full-on absentminded professor. Putting aside his disorganization, he comes recommended by my new dean and has no issue with Sam Adams joining us in the backseat as we scout the area for a promising prospect.

* * *

"You sure you want to rent, Suzanna?" Ray asked as we left the parking lot of the Squirrel's Nest. "Makes folks around here think you're a short-timer." He shook his head from side to side and looked me up and down. "Don't think you fit with the rental crowd either. You know what I mean?"

I had no idea what Ray was getting at but before long, I understood. Renting in the small village where the student population outnumbered the locals by two to one meant occupying a small one-bedroom apartment in an old home that was sliced and diced into multiple apartments and filled with predictably rowdy university students. Even when I was college age, such a housing arrangement didn't appeal to me. After a tour of three different properties, I shrugged. "All righty, Ray, you hit the nail on the head. Apartment living here won't make it for me. What can you show me for sale that has character?"

Ray took us on an all-day house hunting trek from Alfred to Almond, Hornell, Canisteo, and back to Alfred. Late in the afternoon, Ray and I finished a deferred lunch at the Collegiate, tired and discouraged that we had not found anything that turned me on. Some homes were too mid-century, others too musty or needed too many repairs, a few too far from the university, and many in tidy neighborhoods made me feel closed in.

"I need a house that represents the area, Ray. Something open and welcoming, something that sets me free. A place where I can hear the spirits sing."

Ray stared at me. "Well, if you want to hear spirits singing, I recommend you go to church." Then he laughed and afterward said, "Just joking with you."

Lowering his eyes and absentmindedly swirling the fries on his plate, he flipped a ketchup-drenched one to the side. He snapped his fingers and peered at me.

"Hey, I've got it! There's a long shot up on Hartsville Hill. Kind of out of the way, but could be the character you're looking for . . . but again maybe not."

"What's wrong with it?"

"Finish up, and you can be the judge," he said.

"Go now?"

"Yeah, the place is empty. Folks skedaddled a couple of weeks ago. Gone down to Pennsylvania." He turned and gave me a grin. "Something about spirits, I think, drove them away."

"I'm ignoring that last remark," I said and, before leaving, gathered up the extra burger patty intended for Sam.

Ray drove us two miles to Tinkertown, this side of Alfred Station, and then made a turn across State Route 21. The car chugged past the Old Mill tavern and up Hartsville Hill, and then the wilderness set in. It wasn't the backwoods that threw me off since nature recaptured anything outside a few blocks from the village. What awed me was the steep road in front of us.

Ray caught my look. "No worries. Just a thirty-degree incline."

With my back pinned to the seat, we climbed the hill, but it felt more like a ninety-degree than thirty-degree slope. "How do people handle the snow going up this road in the winter?"

Ray shrugged. "Very carefully going up, but more carefully coming down."

I took in a deep breath as Ray gunned his car.

A mile farther, we reached the hilltop where the forest cleared into pastures dotted with grazing cattle. I could not deny the beauty of the landscape. The cotton ball clouds above us were floating so close I wanted to reach out and pluck one from the sky. "Holy Toledo, Ray! We're at the top of the world here!"

Ray stopped the car and pointed to the panorama of thickly forested hills with valleys in between. "Guess that view to the left is five miles or a little more. Yep, this is one of the higher hills in these parts."

The paved road curved and continued down the other side of the hill, but we veered off on a gravel side road that followed the hill's ridge. Ray pushed the accelerator down and drove like a male teenager with heightened testosterone, swerving side to side to skirt the potholes and leaving a cloud of dust behind us. My realtor's mad maneuvering didn't faze him or impede his motormouth.

"Wild up here, but it sure is nature's beauty. Be a pretty and peaceful spot for you. Nobody to pester you up here . . . well, at least nothing two-legged." He took his eyes off the road and turned to me, frowning. "By any chance, do you own a rifle?"

I furrowed my brows. "A rifle? Why would I need one?"

"Don't *need* one. Simply curious is all. Like I said, nothing out here to bother you . . . saving the big bad wolf."

"There are wolves up here?"

"Nah. Just funning with you. The timberwolves are long gone. Catch you a coyote from time to time, but they're skittish . . . except you don't want Mr. Sam Adams there roaming these parts on his own. A few weeks ago, one of the farmers up here lost a couple of dogs to something having big claws."

Wonderful! I started to squirm and was about to suggest we turn back. Maybe this wasn't the place for me. But when I gazed to my left at the expansive tapestry of green hues that covered the hills juxtaposed with a crystal sky, my anxieties quieted, and serenity blanketed me. To hell with Ray's scary stories!

We turned onto a long dirt driveway that wandered through the woods, and Ray dropped the nature lesson and swung into a salesman pitch. "Place is called Honey Bear House. Can't tell you why. A story about a woman who used to live here a million years ago who had beehives. That explains the honey but not the bear."

I laughed to myself. I bet he used that line many times with prospective buyers.

Ray continued chattering in clipped sentences, and my interest grew as to what I would see at the end of the drive. "This place comes with thirty acres *and* a spectacular five-acre pond. No other ponds around here near the size. Spring-fed and always clear water. Most of the land is forest. That's an asset. Can cut your own wood. You're going to need at least a couple cords for winter. Has a real sweet meadow too. One of the prettiest places up here on the hill."

"I'm assuming there is a house too?"

Ray cleared his throat and overlooked my joke. "Oh, of course! Of course. Charming cottage. An authentic log cabin. Well, not the whole house. The original part was built about a hundred years ago. Been added to over the years. All modern now."

"No outdoor toilets?" I asked.

Ray once more missed my friendly sarcasm. "All indoor plumbing, no privies . . . won't freeze your bum off in winter. Has electricity, and phone, and septic, and well too. Don't need to go out and hand pump your own water."

I gasped when we rounded the corner of the drive. My eyes became a camera shutter in wide-range view. Nestled in the woodlands stood a bucolic log and wood home with a full-length front porch. The front door, set off in a reddish-brown stain, contrasted with the sienna exterior, and on either side across the width of the house were double-hung windows. Metal sheets with a worn look covered what appeared to be a sunporch and added a rustic texture against the wood shingles covering the rest of the roof. The natural garden bordering the porch made my flower girl heart race. Outlined with a fieldstone border, countless wildflower varieties in creamy hues accentuated several low-growing evergreens. Fronting all this was a sunlit grassy area, and within eyeshot stood the pond whose water mirrored the brilliant blue sky overhead.

We drove farther, and as I got a better view of the home, my spirit somersaulted and a chill rippled across my shoulders. The comfy charm captivated me. But beyond that, the house was familiar in a curious way. *Had I been here before? Were those the spirits singing?*

Ray stopped the car, and I turned toward him. "All righty, Ray, I don't need to see anymore. This is the place I want."

* * *

My house hunting complete, I arrived back at the motel, wanting to sing and dance in the hallway. I couldn't wait to call Craig to tell him the good news about my find.

"Takin' you to dinner tonight at the fanciest place around," Craig said. "I'll come up and take a look at the house and property tomorrow and check with my buddies to see if they know anythin' about it."

As I changed from my jeans and T-shirt into a summer dress, grasshoppers had a reunion in my stomach. In June, when Craig and I were together with my family, we had little privacy to talk about our lives over the past eight years. I chuckled to myself, thinking of my anxiousness. Craig would say I was having a bout of the "allovers."

Goosebumps covered my arms when I saw Craig's broad smile as he pulled up to the Squirrel's Nest. *How I have missed that handsome face.*

Craig jumped from his pickup and came over and gave me the warmest bear hug I had had in years. Unlike in June, where we were on display, I was comfortable nestling in his arms, relaxed and secure. I closed my eyes, wanting never to leave. On his leash, Sam Adams sat with question marks in his eyes.

Craig pulled back and ran his eyes over me. "Oh God, Suzanna. It's been a damn king's age since we've been on our own together."

A tear trickled down my cheek.

Tears?" he asked. He gave me another hug and held me close.

"Ones of happiness," I whispered.

* * *

My eyes scanned the Tudor-style building we parked in front of—the Big Elms Restaurant in Hornell.

"Different for the area, huh?" Craig said as he helped me out of the truck. "Don't worry. No sucklin' pig or wild boar medieval fare, just down-home food here."

If nothing else, the restaurant had décor. White linen skirts with green tablecloths covered the tables, and white cloth napkins standing in a stiff crown fold in the middle of white china place settings completed the presentation. The floral wallpaper, pictures, memorabilia, and hushed conversational tones of the filled dining room swept me into a Victorian yesteryear ambiance. We sat at a small table for two on the side of the room—I was happy there was no fireplace in sight—and fell into a familiar conversation as if our eight-year separation never existed.

Craig's eyes sparkled more now. Instead of sharing his aspirations like he did on our coffee dates, he was living them as a high school mathematics teacher.

"I *am* the math department!" he said, the pride written on his face. "The school has two hundred students, give or take, grades kindergarten through twelve. Poor high schoolers, no gettin' away from me for math, no matter if it is algebra, geometry, or trig."

I pounded Craig with questions about his life, career, and ambitions. I listened to his answers, my eyes glued to him. I could tell he was settled and at peace with himself more than in our OSU days. Although he said the flashbacks still hounded him, they were not as bad.

"What's it like to be living your calling?"

"Every night, I go to bed and can't wait to get up the followin' mornin' and get to school. Hell, when the students see me walkin' down the hall, they say, 'Here comes smiley face!'"

"What are your students like? What are their biggest challenges?"

"The kids are fabulous—energetic, inquisitive, smart. The biggest challenge around here . . . well, it depends on who you're talkin' with —lack of jobs, poor wages, lack of opportunity."

But his eyes danced when he talked about his students, how he had helped many secure college scholarships, get into trade schools, join the military, or find their passion in carrying on with family businesses or farming.

"Each of their successes, Suzanna, are my successes. At last, I feel fulfilled."

"Tell me about your cabin and the meadow with all the flowers . . ."

His features softened, and a smile fluttered across his face when he described his hillside log home. "The place is rustic, Suzanna. I'll give it that. I got a lot of pleasure designin' and helpin' build it. All self-sustainable. I never did get those electrical lines pulled. They call it livin' off the grid now. Who knew I'd be such a trendsetter?"

He regaled me with stories of the wildlife—deer, bobcat, woodchuck, raccoon, and the occasional black bear—and about the flock of sheep that shared his land.

"I can't wait for you to see my place, Suzanna. I have one hundred acres, and down my drive toward the dirt road is a pasture I rent out to a lady named Eleanor for her sheep. She lives up the road a bit and keeps a barn for the sheep when winter comes. Those buggers bleat and drive me plum crazy, but they don't complain when I play my guitar and sing to them. Kind of a draw, so to speak. And then there's Shep, the Australian sheepdog who keeps his eyes on the flock and safe from predators."

I wanted the conversation to be all about Craig, but my dinner date wanted it to be about me. Craig pummeled me with questions, listened, and often gave me the familiar silence that made me dig deeper within myself. The toughest question he asked, "What's the boldest thing you'd like to do?" had my mind spinning.

"Hmm . . . the boldest? Buy a house called the Honey Bear and start raising bees?"

"Are you tradin' in Flower Girl for Bee Girl?"

"Why can't I be both?"

We talked, joked, laughed, and teased each other. Older now, I saw Craig and our relationship through different and more mature eyes. I was an eighteen-year-old girl with little life experience when we met at OSU. Sheltered and living at home with my parents, I was unaware of my strengths and drives, much less my calling. Seven years had passed, and both of us had begun to cut our paths to fulfilled lives. I better understood my motivations and knew that what is important in life extends beyond titles, money, or status—the joy of life comes from taking advantage of the present and contributing to something bigger than ourselves. I had Craig to thank for a lot of that introspection.

* * *

We returned to the Squirrel's Nest, and Craig and I shared the high and low points of our lives during our "absent years," as Craig called them. Craig's demons from his combat experiences still plagued him, but he was getting professional help.

"In the old days, they called this shell shock and later battle fatigue. Now it's PTSD. They know more about this condition than when I got out of the service. I'm still broken, I still have the dreams and flashbacks, but I'm mendin'. I'm hopeful for the future."

When Craig asked me about my story, my words rushed like water through a broken dam. Except for my counselor, I had not divulged the extent of Jonathan's emotional and Fred's physical abuse. The wounds in my heart still burned as I tried to talk through the darkness. Craig hugged my hand and comforted me, understanding that I was suffering from my own form of PTSD. After that night, Jonathan and Fred would never have a hold on me. Craig called it "talkin' therapy." But he gave me more. When I confessed I had allowed my ego to override my common sense, Craig put it another way.

"May I give you another perspective?" he asked.

I nodded, but I was uncertain how a different opinion would relieve me of my shame.

"Suzanna, I see your actions as a misuse of your love and kindness, not an ego run wild. Egotism is inflated self-importance. It's an excessive focus on yourself. I doubt either of these applies to you and your desire to help Jonathan."

The familiar Craig silence surfaced. I gazed downward to let his words sink in, trying to make sense of them. "How can you misuse something good? Aren't love and kindness good? How does that turn into something bad?"

Craig winced. "Ouch, that hurts! The word *bad* gives me the heebie-jeebies. It makes me think of somethin' evil, corrupt, and blameful. Let's replace *bad* with malfunction," he said and added a wink to lighten things up.

"All righty," I said.

"How many times have you misused salt in a recipe?"

My eyes vacuumed the carpet, and my lips turned up to match the simplicity of Craig's example. *What a comparison.* "Got me! More than once or twice . . . What you're saying is balance is the key. Harmonizing your wants, passions, and strengths is what matters?"

"Yeah, pretty much. When things are out of balance, they don't function to their best; they go haywire. If you use too much salt in a dish, it doesn't taste right. And if you use too little salt, the same result. Either extreme causes the system to malfunction."

"So too little or too much love and giving make a relationship malfunction."

"Yep. That's what I'm sayin'. And gettin' to the sweet spot can be tough because balance is never identical in each situation. Just like a recipe—one takes a teaspoon of salt, and another uses a half teaspoon. It's a damn predicament."

I rolled my head and heaved a sigh. "All righty, smarty-pants, how do you figure this predicament out?"

Craig laughed and looked down to his lap. "I always thought I had smart-lookin' pants."

We were reverting to our OSU days. It felt comfortable.

"Cut it out!" I said and gave him a punch in the arm.

"I think it boils down to self-awareness and experience. Look at the Jonathan situation—when did things start malfunctionin'?"

Oh, tricky question! "Counseling suits you—answering a question by asking another one," I said.

"I'm a hell of a learner. Been in enough counselin'. I should know how it's done. So . . ."

"When did it malfunction with Jonathan . . . It started when my love and kindness weren't authentic, and I pushed too hard. I wanted him to change, but that's not what he could or wanted to do. The key to when things went haywire began when I hurt myself. It's when I lost myself and my freedom. When I stopped living my truth."

I drew my eyes down, sorting the pieces as I would a jigsaw puzzle. As I placed them together one, after another, after another, the picture became clear. "Is that my measure?

"I'd say that's a mighty good place to start."

* * *

Craig and I figured out our new relationship—who we were now and what we wanted to be to each other in the future. I wasn't the starry-eyed teenager I was when I met Craig, wondering what it would be like to have him be my first *it* moment. In the intervening years, I had had many of those. They all lacked the qualities that make a healthy, intimate relationship—a bond filled with mutual trust, emotional connection, and a sense of safety and respect. Deep love can manifest in many forms, not all of them romantic. My relationship with Jack, my parents, and Mel proved that.

"We're not the same people we were almost a decade ago, Suzanna. We're better people. We're stronger. We know our truth and the path toward it."

"We do, don't we? But I wonder . . ."

"Wonder what?"

"How different our paths might have been if we had not met. If we had not stayed in touch."

"The "how" is unanswerable. In some way, we are all interconnected. Our lives crisscross with others seen and unseen, and the consequences may be significant or insignificant. Some paths go beyond a brief intersection—some intertwine, and those are the ones we notice more."

There was silence, and I found his hand around mine.

"You, my Franklin County woman, *will always* be the aura that brings light to my world."

"And you will always be Mon Ange—my champion and guide."

Before Craig left, we embraced, celebrating that we were two people who understood, completed, and enriched each other's spirit as we walked toward living our truth and cut our paths that intertwined.

Chapter 20

THE START OF SOMETHING GOOD

*I*t's Wednesday. Sam and I have been here less than a week, and I'm closing the deal on my "forever" home. Like the old inn near Worthington
Square, this patch of property has stories to tell. The house, the pond, the
woods, and the meadow create a restful rhythm linked by history I don't
know yet. Their interconnectedness pulsates and attracts me. I join them in
kinship as I walk through the forest, skip through the open spaces, and sit
beside the spring fed waterhole that is my new Pondering Place. I am like
them—I met a challenge and came away steady and strong.

* * *

Inside, the house matched the cozy welcome of its exterior. The common areas opened to each other and fit with the home's log cabin ori-
gins. The living area extended into an ample dining space separated
from the galley kitchen by a rustic bar. I swished my foot back and
forth across the floor. How many generations had walked these wide
pine planks? How many fathers and mothers? Sisters and brothers?

But it was the fieldstone fireplace, covering one wall from the floor
to the ceiling, that held authority, gathering the pieces of the home in
harmony. The aesthetic arrangement and variety of stones—large, tiny,
rough, smooth, dark, light—was captivating, comforting, and alluring.
I ran my hand over their curvatures, stunned by how flawlessly they

surrounded and snuggled together. Who was the clever craftsman who created such charm?

I smiled at Craig's remarks when he first examined the hearth: "There's no lack of stones in these parts—stub your toe in the field, and you'll kick up a rock. I bet each of these grew here on the property," he said. My heart leaped with his observation—there it was again, the interconnectedness among the parts of my new world. What stories could this house reveal?

Next to the dining and living areas was a sunroom. I already imagined myself resting in a cushy rocking chair in the homey space and reading a book with sunrays crossing my lap and a chorus of birds outside serenading me. Best of all, there was a view of the pond, meadow, and forested spaces from every room in the house. Two bedrooms downstairs and two baths made up the remainder of the first floor. The master suite was situated on the south side of the house—I envisioned awakening to sunshine each morning and dreaming peacefully as moonbeams danced across the room at night. An open staircase in the living area led to a tranquil loft, perfect for a studio of some sort. I joked with Craig that I might get myself a loom and learn to weave using wool from the sheep who grazed in his pasture.

As I waited for Ray to arrive with the papers I had to sign for homeownership, I explored my land with Sam. The sun warmed the meadow, the trees in the forest stood still as statues, and jays flitted here and there and conversed with each other. I collected a basket of summer blooms from the meadow to make bouquets for my home. Orange touch-me-nots produced a stunning contrast with the royal purple vervain, but many others—white, pink, blue—I couldn't identify packed the area. I wanted to jump in and start cataloging, welcoming the hours I would spend searching and naming the flora on my thirty acres. I scanned the pond, imagining the troupe of characters I might see parade along its shore and swim in its waters.

But the shadows of my past snuck in and distorted the present beauty of these images. Remnants of my severe panic attack over a year ago were persistent companions. Repeated stress trained my nervous system to react to any tense situation by releasing too much adrenaline.

This imbalance caused the unwanted side effects of the fight-or-flight hormone I experienced in the ER to engage—rapid heartbeat, hyperventilation, tingling, dizziness.

I took in a deep breath and slowly let it out, tamping down my excitement and telling my body to slow down. I stood still and let an imaginary white light course through me at a slow pace, moving from head to toe and bringing me a sense of calmness. The distressing symptoms subsided, and I decided to explore more.

I walked down the gravel road and saw a neighbor repairing an old stone wall that bordered his front yard.

"That's beautiful," I called out to him. "It reminds me of pictures of stone fences in New England. Must have taken a long time to build."

The man looked up at me and had the bluest eyes I've ever seen—they were electric.

He stopped his work, walked over, and extended his hand to me. "Hi, there! I'm Barry Callahan."

He told me he was from Buffalo and that since he was a boy, his family had owned the A-frame cottage behind him.

"Yep, for over thirty years, my folks used this place and our twenty acres as a vacation retreat. Since my parents are older, they don't often make it down here. Lots of happy memories, though."

My new friend entertained me with stories about the wildlife—deer, raccoon, and woodchuck—and about the neighbors too. A professor lived a few hundred feet farther down the road—his home hid in the forest, and I couldn't see it. There was an old, eccentric farmer who lived at the intersection of the gravel and paved roads . . .

"I'm jealous of that pond you have up there," Barry said. "Around Labor Day, the place will be filled with Canadian geese on their way south. It's quite a sight."

"Well, don't be a stranger, Barry. You're welcome to come up anytime to visit," I said.

I turned with a smile and walked back to my new home. Today I made my first friend in the neighborhood.

When I first caught sight of the Honey Bear, I had had a pleasant déjà vu, a sense of being there before. In that snapshot moment, I had taken in everything—the house, the woods, the meadow, and the pond. I felt a connection. It was as if I were coming home.

I rounded the corner of the roadway and came to the entrance of my driveway. I stopped and took in the setting and remembered what Gary told me long ago: *Noticing and appreciating nature is the groundwork for knowing and respecting yourself.*

Nature surrounded me, and it was the start of something good.

Chapter 21

TENDERFOOT

The first months in my home are a welcome whirlwind of new experiences because I am a homeowner for the first time and a rural tenderfoot. Beyond the novelty of these undertakings is my personal growth—being more present, more curious, and more compassionate to myself. I've deepened my relationship with Craig, made new friendships, and am happy. My joy comes from having peace in my life, awe in my surroundings, purpose in my work, companionship with friends, and accomplishment in my career.

Craig and I have resumed our coffee dates. This time, though, rather than donuts and coffee at the OSU Student Union, we commandeer a booth at the "Slick Chick," Craig's nickname for the Little Red Hen. We meet on Saturday mornings for a hearty breakfast of comfort food—eggs, ham, hash browns, and biscuits—that completes a caring and compassionate relationship. It reminds me of the old days but a hundred times better. We accept each other for who we are. We're not trying to change one another. Instead, we cheerlead and coach each other to be our best selves and achieve a fulfilled life.

* * *

Like first responders, Craig and I were ready to lend each other a helping hand in our renewed relationship, although Craig seemed to do this more for me than I did for him. Craig offered his muscle power at the very beginning to help me settle into my new house. What a chaotic and fun time we had when my furniture and household items arrived. At first, it was difficult for me to decide where to place the bigger pieces—I wanted to maximize the views. Should the sofa face the fireplace or go cattywampus to catch the outdoor view? The kitchen table I had brought from Ohio was all wrong for the rustic décor and didn't look right at any angle.

"If I have to rearrange and move another item of furniture, I'm loadin' it in my truck and takin' it home," Craig said with a wink.

I held out his favorite—a Bud brew. "Well, will this make up for all your work?"

The entire day went like that. We teased back and forth and forth and back. After I unpacked the record player, we plugged it in, and Craig whipped out "Franklin County Woman," wheeling me around the living area in a country two-step. Even the moving haulers got into the spirit—they had the lyrics down pat before they finished unloading the van.

My job began on Monday, August 19, and I had one week to organize everything at home in tip-top shape after my household things arrived. Over breakfast at the Slick Chick, Craig and I made out a list of must-haves. Luckily, he either knew where to obtain the items or services I needed or helped by doing the work himself.

"We got to find you a chimney sweep. Can't be havin' a chimney fire in the middle of the winter."

"A chimney sweep? Doesn't that just happen in Mary Poppins?"

Craig laughed and signaled the waitress for more coffee. "You're gettin' what I call a rural education, Suzanna. Let's add a couple of cords of wood to the list. Always want enough on hand in case the electric goes out—which I guarantee will happen, many times."

"Ray said I can cut the wood from my forest."

Another chuckle from my friend. "You got a chainsaw, by any chance?"

"No. But I can buy one."

"I'll come up and cut wood and show you how to split. Still, you'll have to buy. No way to cut enough before the snow flies."

"Put down a plow guy on your list. That driveway is a long, long way to the road."

"Got to make sure the furnace is in workin' order. Want me to check around for someone to come up for a look at it?"

The items on my paper kept growing, but when Craig mentioned my little Civic, I worried he might suffer from a disorder like Jonathan's when it came to cars.

"You don't like my car?"

"Oh no! I love that little thing. It's cute, like you," he said, adding a grin.

I pointed my finger at him, like on our old coffee dates. "You're trying to butter me up. I caught you looking at Alvin. What's wrong with it?"

He gave me the Craig silence. "Well, nothin' is wrong with the car. The problem is the vehicle is wrong for here."

I furrowed my brow. "How is the Chipmunk wrong for here?"

"Well, it's that darn steep hill! Think the Chipmunk is going to be able to climb up and down that monster in the winter plus navigate that long driveway?"

I tightened my lips. "They *do* have snowplows here."

"Yes, my Franklin County Woman, they got plows here, but this ain't Columbus, Ohio! You're livin' in rural northern America. Plows come through in the mornin' before the school bus picks up the kids and in the afternoon before the bus drops them back home. When there is no school bus, well . . ."

I caught Craig's drift and recalled what Ray said about a snowy Hartsville Hill. The tenderfoot was learning. "You're saying no school bus, no plow. No school bus on weekends, no plow on weekends?" I asked.

"Yep, that's right. And if it snows between the afternoon plow and when you come home at night, well . . . the snow can get mighty deep. You'll want to consider gettin' a four-wheel-drive."

"How can I do that? There is emotional and sentimental capital invested in the Chipmunk. Trading it in would be the same as dumping a friend. It practically drove itself, taking me to the ER. It took me to my Pondering Place, brought me to my new home. It's the one symbol I have to remind me I stood my ground in the face of Jonathan's criticism."

Craig reached across the table and took my hand. "It doesn't need to be door number one or door number two. Think door number three."

"Door number three?"

"Yeah, what's behind door number three?"

Silence. I tapped my fingers on the table and stared beyond Craig at the waitress serving the next table.

"Door number three!" Craig announced. "How about a brother or sister for the Chipmunk?"

A big smile crossed my face. "Brilliant! I don't need to give up my car."

"That's right! You can wrangle a deal on a reliable used vehicle that can tackle that mean ol' hill."

In the end, I'm thankful to Craig for reminding me to think beyond a choice of two options.

"Too often folks get caught up in an *either this or that* trap. There's always at least a third choice waitin' to be found," he said.

With Craig's coaching on boosting my haggling skills, I bought Jay-bird, a snappy midnight-blue Jeep CJ to tear up and down that mean old Hartville Hill and to keep Chipmunk company in my garage.

* * *

My new position had invigorated me and skyrocketed my personal growth. At OSU, I was an assistant director of student affairs, advising current students and recruiting new ones. Now, as a director working with a dean who had the energy and vision equal to a NASA scientist, my focus was strategic. What services could we offer to help students flourish and be their best? How could student services be reimagined?

The faculty called Bob, my dean, "the Grants Man" because he se-cured millions of dollars to support novel projects in the school. It blew me away when I saw allied health students learning anatomy, medical terminology, and other subjects using a computer lab devel-oped a decade earlier, in the mid-1970s—we didn't have it that good at OSU. But it was the buses that transported our nursing students to their clinical affiliation in Rochester that astonished me. The vehicles looked like cabins on modern commercial planes and were fitted with televisions that delivered prerecorded lectures. "Why waste two hours of travel going and coming from Rochester when we can deliver lectures via television?" Bob asked me. The solution for Bob was to always do better.

During my first week on the job, I wasn't surprised when Bob challenged me to broaden my perspective. "Getting a grant isn't about money, Suzanna. It's writing the grant that offers benefits. Putting together the application for funding stirs up your imagination. It makes you consider possibilities. It forces you to think outside the box. Get to it, Suzanna. Set your imagination free."

I took up the challenge to run the gauntlet, and each week the dean and I discussed the progress I was making to meet my goal of submitting a grant. To "free my imagination," I met individually and in groups with undergraduates, faculty, and staff, asking them what they envisioned, what they wanted, and what they needed in student affairs services. I listened to their input and asked questions that challenged them further. "What are the benefits of doing that?" "What are the consequences? What's the boldest thing we could do?"

My chats opened avenues to meet people I never imagined. I formed relationships with dozens of professors and staff. Ron, the anatomy professor, was rough-and-tumble, a hunter and fisherman, but whose soft side showed through his passion for helping students be their best. There was no foolishness in Ron's classes—if he caught a student nodding off, he slammed down his anatomy text on the sleepyhead's desk. He walked up and down the aisles during his presentations with his eyes on every scholar—can't hide from Professor Ron, the students told me. Like many teachers and other personnel, Ron was knee-deep into community service—a certified EMT for the volunteer fire department and a local school board member.

When I talked with students, they spoke with pride in taking a class with "Professor Ron."

"Oh, we love him," one of them said. "Hard as nails, but we know he's got our backs."

And there were more like Ron—Barb and Carole in nursing, Frank in medical technology, Art in pharmacy technology, Earl and Bill in biological sciences, Marie in continuing education, Marty in medical assisting, and Fritz in chemistry. These were people who lived life dedicated to their students, community, and families. They were committed to making the most of every day.

Another was Betty, my secretary, a woman almost sixty years old, born and raised in Alfred. "I'm one of the original pieces of work around here," she liked to say.

She became "distance friends" with Cheryl. The first day I started my new position, Betty came into my office and asked, "Suzanna, who is the best secretary you've ever had?"

My eyes must have turned into saucers. *What kind of question is that?* "I guess, Betty, it would be Cheryl, my secretary at OSU."

"Super. I need to talk with Cheryl, because I want to be her equal."

From that day, Betty phoned Cheryl every week. At first, they spoke about my likes and dislikes. "Oh, she likes a tidy space," Cheryl said. "Be ready for that dry sense of humor of hers. And you'll need to put up with her saying 'All righty' a lot of the time."

As the weeks progressed, the two secretaries discovered they had similar backgrounds and mutual interests that superseded me. Like Cheryl, Betty was single and had several grown children. They both were avid readers and quilters. The two of them formed such a warm relationship they planned a summer quilting rendezvous together.

Betty was a mother hen, and when she found out I had bought the Honey Bear on Hartsville Hill, she had a list of to-dos that equaled Craig's.

"Oh, that hill is a real bugger in winter. You got to get yourself a four-wheel-drive."

"As I recall, the Honey Bear driveway is a long one. Going to need someone to plow."

"Have you thought about a generator if the electric goes off?"

"I know someone you can call for a couple of cords of wood."

One of her statements, though, stood out and perplexed me. "Oh, the Honey Bear. It does have a history."

"What do you mean?" I asked.

"You know that place goes back about a hundred years. First owned by a woman who had beehives."

"Yes, Ray told me about that. Said the name accounted for the honey, but he didn't know anything about the bear."

"Well, there's that mystery and more, I'm sure," Betty said. Then she turned and left my office, not giving me a chance to probe further.

* * *

In early fall, the trees in western New York start to show their mettle in competition with those in New England. The hills are a variegated scene exploding in vibrant reds, oranges, and yellows that make the most delicious eye candy. It was the last Saturday in September when I met Elliott Taylor. I was walking with Sam through a color wheel of enchantment in my woods. My eyes danced, and my lips smiled while I twirled round and round, one with the opulent extravaganza. Sam and I had our heads down, scouring the forest floor to inspect and collect the best specimens of leaves for designing collages to make into bookmarks.

"It looks like the two of you are having yourselves a ball."

My heart leaped into my throat. Sam started barking. I turned and looked up, and a figure who appeared like he had walked out of a 1960s western stood above me.

"Sorry to creep up on you. I'm Elliott," said the six-foot-three man wearing a cowboy hat and boots and a shy smile. "You must be Suzanna. And who is this little fella here?" he asked as he stooped down and, with caution, extended his hand to Sam.

"This is Sam Adams, and yes, I'm Suzanna."

"Pleased to meet both of you in person," he said as he scratched Sam behind his ears.

I checked him out: wholesome appeal and easy on the eyes. Betty and Bob had recommended Elliott without reservations. "Was told you're looking for a dependable person to do plowing for you. Got the right man. Name's Elliott Taylor," Betty told me and handed me his phone number.

"Oh yes. Elliott is head of campus security. You'll be happy with him," Bob confirmed.

I chatted with my soon-to-be plowman, and it was clear Elliott didn't miss much.

"See a CJ in the drive. Smart to have a vehicle like that up here. With that Jeep, you'll be able to make it out okay with less than half a foot on the ground. More than that will get tricky. When it snows more than a flurry, I'll be by in the morning before seven o'clock. Then I'll check on everything again after five in the afternoon."

"And the charge?"

He waved his hand. "Ah, don't worry about it. Happy to give Bob's new staff member a helping hand," he said. "Besides, it's neighborly. I just live up the road a piece. I'll catch you on my way to and from work."

"Well, all righty," I said.

His shy smile reappeared, and his earth-toned eyes sharpened. "Hmm. *All righty.* Haven't heard that for an age."

He tipped his hat, turned, and walked back in the same direction he had come.

* * *

"Storm" is different in western New York than in Central Ohio. I chuckled when I found out the locals called three to five inches of snowfall a flurry and one to three feet a storm. After a snowstorm, the powerful plows push through, and drivers still struggle to steer their cars and grimace at the sound of their vehicle undercarriages scraping the top of the plow leftovers.

I got my first dose of a western New York snowstorm on Sunday, December 15. Appropriate for the date, it was a fifteen-inch drop of fluffy flakes. I knew snow in Columbus but nothing as gorgeous as this. The evergreens bowed, bundled in white, and fragile snowflakes clung to the barren branches of the beeches and maples. The sunrays cut through the clouds, landed on the ground, and created a glistening garment that rivaled a starlit night.

Poor Sam Adams couldn't cut a trail through the icy barricade to do his outdoor business. As I strained to shovel a path for Sam, I shook my head. *Craig and Elliott were right! There is no way I could dig myself out or plow my Jeep down a two-hundred-foot driveway through this amount of snow.*

The storm subsided in the late afternoon, and like a knight in shining armor, Elliott's silver four-wheel-drive truck with a plow on the front came chugging up my lane. I loved that Elliott named his vehicle too —Old Smokey, he called it.

Through the living room windows, Sam and I followed Elliott as he drove forward, backward, forward, and backward, clearing section by section of the drive. For twenty minutes, he plowed until he reached my front door. Before he could turn his truck around and leave, I stepped out on the porch, waved to him, and hollered, "Why don't you come in? Have a cup of coffee or hot chocolate with Sam and me." It was the least I could do since I wasn't paying him anything.

"Hot chocolate sounds good," he said, dipping his head. He had the same shy smile I remembered seeing when I first met him. I liked it.

He stepped out of the silver pickup and walked toward the house in long, casual, confident strides. But there was more to this enigmatic man who appeared as well-worn as the boots he wore—decency, honesty, integrity. *I wonder what the points of his North Star could be?*

Walking into the house, Elliott took off his hat, his eyes doing a slow-motion sweep of the downstairs area. "Always was interested in seeing the inside of this place," he said. Turning to the wall next to us, he ran his hand over the wood, inspecting the log. "Appears to be a lot of the original cabin in this area. Looks to be in decent shape."

Elliott made himself at home, sitting on one of the stools across the kitchen bar from me, while I heated the milk and made hot chocolate with marshmallow topping. His relaxed posture and composure dispersed calming vibrations that embraced me. I didn't have to impress him or be anything but myself in his company.

As we made small talk, more about him caught my attention than when we first met. His eyes were unusual, a fusion of brown, hazel, and green that drilled through me without making me anxious. He had a weathered complexion that was attractive, and crinkles appeared at the side of his eyes when he smiled—which was often. With a bit of a wave, his hair was the texture and color of burnt wheat. His hands were rough and callused, a testimony, no doubt, to a lifetime of hard physical work. Again, his speech was purposeful, delivered in a low and steady voice with simple sentences that lacked unnecessary adjectives —definitely a man who appreciated facts to hyperbole.

Like Betty, Elliott was an Allegheny County native. He said he graduated from the private university in town, a history major who enrolled in the ROTC program and afterward served in the army. I asked about his military role. He alluded to working in military intelligence and then guided the conversation in a different direction as we took our warm drinks to the living room and sat down.

"Did you know this place is called the Honey Bear?" he asked.

"Yes, I did. My realtor told me, but he didn't have much information beyond that. Do you know anything more?"

He sat back on the sofa, relaxed, and crossed his legs. His rugged country look was a natural fit with my home's rustic walls and floors.

"I guess it was in the 1880s, a woman purchased the place. She was single and a teacher, like you. The story goes that one day, a big old black bear came and started to dig out the honeycomb from a hive in one of the trees not far from her house. The legend is she became a kind of a bee whisperer."

"Do you know what happened to her? Did she marry?"

"I don't know how long she stayed. As for being married, the rumor mill of the day whispered she was running away from something or someone."

I dropped my mug of hot chocolate, spilling it on the floor. Before I could blink, Elliott bent over, picked up the cup, and had it in his hand. His eyes met mine.

"Hope you don't think I'm clumsy like this all the time, Elliott." I grabbed the utensil from him and dashed to get some paper towels in the kitchen.

He shrugged. "I'm surprised it was you and not me. As a kid, I was always the one who knocked over my milk. Still do, as a matter of fact."

Either a good guest or detective, I thought.

Afterward, I shot him a barrage of questions about the wildlife, my new home, and his life, trying to cover my embarrassment at being a klutz.

"Speaking of bears, do you see many here?"

"Up here on the hill, I've seen one or two a year. Nothing to worry about. They stay clear of folks."

"What about bobcats? My friend says he's seen them at his place along Slate Creek."

"Yep. They're around. Won't bother you. Except don't leave Sam out by himself."

But when I asked more about him, he became circumspect again. His response about being married—"No, no children. No, not married now,"—sent my antenna up. *Another man with secrets.*

While he was putting on his overcoat and hat to leave, I wanted to settle a nagging question. "Elliott, by any chance, do you know the woman's name, the bee whisperer's name?"

He glanced down and turned the handle on the front door, and when he looked my way, his eyes revealed more than he was willing to say. "Well, that's a long time back, Suzanna. I'm not sure I could give you a name and be one hundred percent sure it was correct. Being in the business of security, I always like to give folks the correct information."

He tipped the brim of his hat and gave me a boyish smile. "Thanks for the conversation and hospitality. With this almost officially winter, I'll be seeing you soon, I'm sure. But call me if you ever need any help. Just a few minutes away."

I closed the door after him, and through the window, my eyes followed him as he walked to Old Smokey. He looked as if he needed a regular haircut and shave; the entire package of Elliott Taylor's scruffy appearance, craggy face, and tanned complexion made him ruggedly handsome and alluring. He was a man whose eyes spoke more than his mouth, and I liked that. I knew only sketchy details about his past, but I sensed life had thrown him several curveballs and handed him some strong knocks. *What's his real story?*

Chapter 22

STORM CLOUDS

*People are packing the Honey Bear for my first ever New Year's Eve bash.
The fun begins early at seven o'clock in the evening for those who are
party hopping or want to come and go early, I wrote on the invitation to my
new group of friends.*

*Besides Craig, Elliott, and Betty, many of the faculty I work with and
their spouses are here, including Ray and Bob and their wives. Even my
neighbor Barry Callahan and his brother Joe and his wife have dropped by.*

*People are helping with the food and are turning my kitchen bar into
an eclectic smorgasbord of favorite dishes complemented by soft, hard, cold,
and hot drinks. Lillian taught me well—the Honey Bear sparkles. Two
Christmas trees and an assortment of holiday greenery and decorations be-
deck the house from floor to ceiling, the fireplace crackles in the background,
and twinkling lights make it appear Santa's elves are eavesdropping.*

*Thanks to Elliot and Craig moving my furniture, the living area is a
dance floor and a seating gallery for those who want to sit out the toe tapping.
Courtesy of Craig and his two band members, the revelers listen and dance
to live music, a mixture of country and rock with a few old swing favorites
thrown in for those over the half-century age.*

*"What a party!" Craig says as he sidles up to me while taking a break
from playing and gulps down a brew.*

* * *

"Well, here comes Elliott in his Old Smokey," Craig said, looking out
the front windows as he helped me rearrange the furniture and put up
more New Year's decorations.

"You know Elliott?"

"We see each other at the VFW hall. Been in the service like me. Tried to get him to join my band but couldn't snag him. He's a piano player—classical for the most part," Craig said as he hauled off my coffee table into the spare bedroom.

"Really? He never mentioned that to me," I said, trailing behind Craig. "He holds his cards pretty close to the vest. Do you know any more of his story?"

"Not much. Like most things, you have to dig for the truth," he said, bending over and putting down the table. He stood up and turned his head my way. "But once in a while, when you dig, you uncover dark things you'd rather not find out."

I surmised the forbidding things Craig referenced had to do with Elliott's military service. Older and wiser than in my teens, I knew better than to ask more. I would be an indifferent friend if I tried to force the unearthing of damaging memories.

"Hey, get your butt in here, Elliott, and give us a hand," Craig hollered from the front porch.

Elliott lumbered out of his truck and walked toward the house, the two men giving each other a knowing glance. From some fifth sense—maybe from their smiles that didn't quite smile or the weariness in their eyes—a deep sadness rolled through me as I grasped the significance of the war experiences linking them.

* * *

Before the clock struck midnight, Craig announced to the funmakers he was dedicating a song and the 1986 New Year to me and struck up the band, playing my theme song, "Franklin County Woman." Elliott, who hadn't danced all evening, stepped out of character, grabbed me by the waist, and whirled me around the living room impromptu dance floor. "Can't have the main attraction sitting out her own dance, can we?" he said.

I was growing accustomed to his shy smile. "You are a man of many surprises and talents."

"I would agree," he said.

The man of surprises revealed something else that evening. About thirty minutes before midnight, Elliott and I were chatting with Dr. Golden, an emeritus professor from the state university. Golden was a dear old soul—kind and committed to helping younger professors hone their craft and calling.

"Oh, I didn't realize you lived in Susannah's home until Elliott brought me up here tonight," he said.

Elliott frowned at his friend. "No, Walter. You know this *is* Suzanna. This *is* Suzanna's home," Elliott said.

"Yes, Elliott. This is Suzanna Jordan's house now, but it used to be Susannah Simpson's home."

"Another Suzanna lived here?" I asked.

"Oh, yes. Except she spelled her name S-u-s-a-n-n-a-h."

My heart raced out of my chest. "Dr. Golden, did you know her?"

The charming man with a shock of silver hair chuckled. "My dear, I got age on me, but I'm not *that* old. Susannah Simpson had left these parts by the time I was born in 1906. My mother knew her, though, even came up here and got honey from time to time, or so she told me."

"What happened to her? Elliott says she was a teacher at the private university."

"Ah yes, that she was . . ." He dropped his eyes, and a void of silence filled the space.

"I've heard there are rumors about her. My secretary said she had problems at the Honey Bear."

"Yes, there are always rumors, aren't there? But we don't want to spoil ringing in the New Year with those, do we? A story for another time," the senior professor said.

The festivities overtook me on one level: laughing, dancing, joking, and enjoying the present moment with Craig, Elliott, and the host of new friends. Underneath the evening gaiety, I had an unsettling premonition when it came to my home's history. It was akin to ignoring the *drip*, *drip*, *drip* of a faucet that leads to catastrophe.

* * *

With holidays over, my work schedule resumed the following Monday, and as I hugged Sam Adams goodbye for the day, the familiar feelings of guilt surfaced when I looked into his big brown eyes. Many workdays, I had time during lunch to scoot up Hartsville Hill and make it home to let Sam out for a potty break, but today wasn't one of those.

"You're going to have to hold it until tonight, Sam," I said.

The campus bustled with students and faculty walking between buildings, bundled up against the cold when I arrived. The western New York winter was living up to its reputation and then some.

I had five meetings on my calendar to prepare for the onslaught of students after the holiday break. I slipped into my office, shed my down winter coat, changed from my heavy snow boots into a pair of flats, and was on my way to my first meeting before Betty had arrived at eight o'clock.

"Morning Suzanna, or is it afternoon now?" Betty asked when I returned.

I checked my watch: twelve ten. "Looks like it's afternoon. Just came in to check my phone calls before going to a luncheon meeting," I said as I flipped through the pink message sheets on the edge of Betty's desk.

"Nothing that can't wait till later. Before you go rushing off again, you should check on the surprise in your office."

Surprise? My adrenaline rushed as if I were a five-year-old. *From whom? Jack, Craig, Mel, Robert, Lillian? What could it be?*

I opened my office door and walked in.

"Gorgeous, aren't they?" Betty said.

The room turned cold, my stomach rose to my throat, and the surge of adrenaline turned into a torrent of torment.

"What's wrong?" Betty asked. "Are you okay? You look like you've seen a ghost."

"I think I might have, Betty."

A magnificent flower arrangement overpowered my desk. My eyes blurred as I pulled out the small envelope embedded in the blooms and removed the gift card in it. Chills iced my veins as I read the greeting. "They had no Campanella roses. Still loving you. Happy New Year."

A statue couldn't have had a tighter jaw or more frozen stare. I turned to my secretary. "Please take these, Betty, and before I get back, get them out of here and arrange to give them to the hospital or the nursing home, to a patient who needs them. Thanks for doing this for me."

* * *

If a day could be described as a wasteland—black, barren, and bleak—this one hit the mark. I careened back and forth from the pounding misery of a headache and the anger of a boiling geyser. My anxious mind churned like water in rapids throughout the afternoon. I couldn't wait to finish up the list of meetings and get home. How the hell had he found me? How dare he come after me? What did he want? Where was he?

When I arrived back at my office, the flowers were gone. Bless Betty! I wondered what she must have thought, then reconsidered. *Knowing Betty, she called Cheryl about my strange behavior.* I put on my snow boots and heavy coat, hoping to leave my unhappy memories and worries in the wastebasket. *The flowers are gone. Throw out the fricking worries with them.*

The drive home was later than usual, which meant the lag between the plow and my Jeep traveling the road was a good four hours. Several inches of snow had fallen during that time, and to commandeer the steep Hartsville hill, I needed a running start after crossing the state highway. The school of hard knocks taught me I would slide sideways down the incline if I didn't build up momentum before reaching the Old Mill Tavern. Tonight, my fury fueled my four-wheeler as much as the gasoline in its tank, and the new snowfall could not deter me from reaching my destination.

When I walked through the front door, Sam Adams ran like a bullet toward me, barking, jumping, waving his paws, and circling me several times before taking off in a tear running through the house.

"What's up, boy? What's the matter?" I asked, crouching down to extend my hand to pet him.

He walked over to me, but his panting told me his agitation was far from over.

I took his harness down from the peg by the door and got him ready for a quick walk. After all, I was over an hour late. I'd be going nuts, too, if I had to hold it all day. We stepped out into the frigid night, our breaths creating white clouds against the pitch-dark backdrop.

"No moonbeams coming through the windows tonight, Sam," I said, scanning the star-studded sky and the tiny sliver of moonlight overhead. My boots pressed through the newly fallen snow and crunched the icy surface below. "We're not going far tonight. Too cold, too dark, and too late, Sam."

But my companion was persistent, extending the leash to its length and straining, still panting. After fifteen minutes, we found ourselves at the end of the darkened drive and down the gravel road as far as the Callahan vacation cottage. I looked at the vacant home and recalled the New Year's Eve party when Barry and his brother regaled me with stories of their childhood summers here and unveiled a secret or two about Elliott.

"Oh yes! Elliott was a real badass in the sixties," Barry had said. "Now, look at him."

"Real upstanding dude," Joe had added.

I had turned to Elliott. "Badass? Is this a cautionary tale? Should I be afraid of you?"

Elliott's shy smile crept over his face. "Well, it all comes down to what you consider a badass, I guess."

The Callahan brothers had shaken their heads and rolled their eyes, leaving me wondering what *badass* meant.

"Time to go, Sam," I said, bringing my thoughts back to the present and realizing there had been a dramatic temperature drop and that I was chilled.

We doubled back, and Sam had settled down into his usual walking stride—stopping here and there to smell and "pick up the mail" left by other critters. But when we reached the driveway to the Honey Bear, the Boston terrier stopped and refused to budge.

"What *is* the problem, Sam?" I asked.

He answered me with mournful eyes as if I were making him do something unpleasant. Frustrated, I picked up my twenty-five-pound fur bundle and slogged up the drive with him in my arms. When I got into the house and put Sam down, I was relieved—he seemed like himself, begging now for his evening meal.

* * *

Later, the crackling fire's comfort, together with the Maker's Mark in my glass, soothed my unhinged nerves from earlier. I sat on the couch, bundled in a woolen blanket with Sam snuggled to my side, and I stared into the fireplace flames. *Dammit! I promised myself I wouldn't think about Jonathan. The more I give his antics freedom to roam around in my head, the more I become his victim, his prey. But bullies don't let up unless someone makes them stop. He's going to be back.*

I took more sips of my bourbon, but the alcohol didn't stamp out my worries. If Jonathan knew where I worked, did he know where I lived too? My pulse and heart galloped. Should I call Mel? What could she do? Should I call Craig? And tell him what? Should I call Jack?

A wave of chilly air interrupted my thoughts. I snatched a glance over my shoulder and was sure I had seen a shadow. Sam raised his head and looked in the same direction. His eyes roamed an empty space, and a gurgle rose from his throat.

"Sam, what's up?"

My furry companion leaped off the couch, stood frozen on the floor, eyes riveted forward into nowhere. The hairs on his back jutted up in a straight line and made him look like a mini ridgeback hound. Almost as fast, he stopped his gaze, turned, and joined me back on the sofa, circling and circling until he positioned the cushions to his liking and flopped down with a heavy sigh.

Jonathan's antics refueled my anxiety tank and started to make me question my sanity. Had Sam and I really seen a ghost?

Chapter 23

BUNNY HUTCH

The rest of the week, I'm burying myself in work—work at work and at home. Yet, even in the best circumstances, the beginning of an academic semester is an unending schedule of meetings with students and helping them find, add, and drop classes. In addition, grade appeals from the previous semester are frequent. These are usually paper formalities; sometimes, though, students must appear in person at committee appeals. As a result, the range and intensity of student emotions at the start of a new term, no matter the circumstance, are as broad and deep as the sea—frustration, anger, fear, sadness, depression, anxiety, elation, happiness, gratefulness.

To indulge in self-worry, self-pity, or any other kind of "self" is out of the question. Students are preeminent. Meeting their needs and consoling, reassuring, guiding, and advising them on their journeys to better selves must be my goals.

* * *

After Monday's incident, Betty didn't mention the arrival or disposal of the flowers. Except for Craig, no one in the area was aware of my past personal life, and I wanted to keep it that way. My nerves were too raw and my self-esteem too wobbly to face probing questions or meet raised eyebrows about a failed marriage. What did you do wrong? Didn't you see that coming? Can we trust you not to make bad choices again?

Though not a constant companion, my negative inner voice found wiggling space into my psyche and tried to pile on shame and humiliation. Fending off the crafty intruder took psychological resolve and chipped away at my emotional reserves. I expected many miles of unforgiving mountains lay ahead before a rolling landscape might appear.

The first time seeing the Honey Bear, I felt positive energy and heard the spirits singing. Those lighthearted celestial souls were quiet now, replaced by out-of-focus, dusky flickers appearing in my peripheral vision. I might have ignored these, but I believed Sam saw them too.

The initial encounter with the shadow spooked me. Since our first brush with these unexplained phenomena, Sam appeared undecided whether he should bark, growl, pounce, or flee. Often, he sat rooted to the floor for several minutes, ears alert, while his eyes swept an empty wall.

The evening after the flowers arrived, an alarm buzzed like a broken record: *If he knows where I work, he knows where I live.* My eyes walked the walls as I sat in the living room—not a curtain on any window. I was surprised at the paucity of window coverings when I moved in, but the locals pooh-poohed my concerns.

"No one out here puts curtains up. Spoils the view," Ray had said.

Craig confirmed my realtor's assertion. "The worst of who's goin' to be lookin' in is a couple of deer or raccoon."

After I settled into the home, I had to agree with them. During the day, nature and the Honey Bear became one. I looked out the windows and could shake hands with the tree limbs, share winks with the birds, and go nose-to-nose with the deer. In the evenings, the woods, meadow, and pond created alluring landscapes spotlighted by vacillating moonbeams. Now, though, I feared other critters besides deer and raccoons might want to peer through my windows. The weekend after the apparitions surfaced, I got to work sewing curtains for the Honey Bear.

* * *

Should I mention the flower arrival to Craig? *What can he do?* The question played again and again in my head throughout the week. I thought about Jonathan's behavior soon after our divorce—the flowers, phone calls, and cruising by my home—and realized I needed a support system. I had no doubt Craig would stand with me, and in the end, my better judgment ruled.

"Well, the son of a bitch," Craig said while stirring his coffee during our Saturday breakfast date at the Slick Chick. "So he sent flowers last Monday. What's the dude's next move?"

"I wish I had a crystal ball. But I want to be prepared for anything. One thing I've learned is not to be caught off guard."

"Good start. What's the objective?"

"Never to hear from him again in any form—no phone calls, no gifts, no person-to-person meetings."

I knew Craig's silence precipitated a question that would make me search for the truth. "Why is that important to you—to not have contact with him?"

I looked down and stirred the food on my plate, waiting for the honest answer to materialize. *I could say Jonathan is a bastard. But that's name-calling; it has no substance. I could say he's insincere; I don't want to deal with hypocritical people. But deceit is his behavior; I don't own his dishonesty. Changing him is out of my control.*

I scrutinized Craig. His eyes talked to me, encouraging me to find my truth. "It's important to me because I want my freedom—freedom from being swept into a narcissistic spiral."

"You have the objective and the reason. What are you goin' to do?"

"Don't engage. Don't reply. Don't let Jonathan set up home in my mind."

* * *

I knew responding to Jonathan would power up his mean side. He was a man who took his thirst for attention and conflict to the highest levels. He demanded both. The intervening time without contact from him was probably due to him finding another victim, another bunny. Perhaps that woman had rejected him, too, and sent him on his way. Like a tiger, he was on the prowl again. Jonathan had an enormous ego, craved control, and denied defeat. He was pursuing me to put me back into his bunny hutch.

Chapter 24

PERFECT

Deep winter is stunning in western New York. Growing up in the Midwest is not an adequate preparation for the gifts and challenges my new home serves me. "Cream puffs," Craig calls the two of us. "No doubt about it," I agree, after experiencing the first weeks of the Siberian season.

Here, winter storms shower feet, not inches of snow, and chilling temperatures push thermometers to zero degrees and below. Blizzards, whiteouts, thundersnows, and freezing fog are the smorgasbord wintertime here dishes out. The locals warn me to stock blankets, food, water, votive candles, and matches as part of my winter survival kit in my car. "Candles? Like the little ones in church?" The tenderfoot in me questions whether the candles are enough to stave off frostbite, but I'm not going to take any chances. I pack a dozen in my Jeep with the other items to survive if I get stuck in a storm.

* * *

I compiled a diary of morning temperatures that greeted Sam and me on our walks. It provided proof of bragging rights to family and friends in Ohio that I had transformed from pampered city girl to hearty pioneer who, among other things, chopped her own wood to heat her home.

January 13, 1986: 5°: Crunchy snow and breezy

January 14, 1986: -2°: Crunchy snow, a slight breeze

January 15, 1986: -12°: Over a foot of snow, the slightest breeze is bone-chilling today.

January 16, 1986: A heatwave of +6°: Crunchy snow, clear skies

The temperatures were the cuts of a prism that accentuated winter's faces: the diamond tapestry of snow, the checkerboard of woody brown limbs, the lucidity of a lapis sky. I was taken to a higher plane of consciousness, vibration, and healing energy when I walked within the prism. I now understood what Barry Callahan told me when he came by to see the geese on my pond last Labor Day.

"I am never alone here in the woods. It's as if the forests have retained the energy and whispers of phantoms of generations past," he said.

I chuckled under my breath. "What a coincidence. The day I first came to the Honey Bear, I believe I heard the spirits sing."

Barry's face gathered a frown, and he shook his head as if he were trying to whisk a memory away. "Do you believe in coincidences? Things preordained?"

I faced the opposite direction and viewed the pond. *Coincidences? Such a simple word, but what a complicated concept. Was it a coincidence I met Craig? Was it preordained that I met Jonathan? Was it planned that I encountered Barry?*

I turned back and faced my neighbor. "I don't hold much in predetermined events, in fatalism. If I did, I'd have to abandon the notion of choice. But I do believe random acts can occur at the same time, and together they can form something curious."

Barry's eyes turned cloudy. "A long time ago, a woman I knew believed that too."

No one had to tell me a bundle of heartbreak bubbled from his memory. *Who was she? Men and their inner demons—Craig, Elliott, and now Barry.*

* * *

In the evenings, a crackling fire kept Sam and me cozy. There was no cable, and television reception from Buffalo was limited to four channels on clear days (down to one or two on cloudy ones). I ditched planning on watching regular TV shows and instead buried myself reading fiction and accounts of local pioneers and started a new hobby—weaving.

In the autumn, I had met Craig's "sheep lady," who raised a flock and had their wool sheared, processed, and dyed.

"I don't do much with the crafts these days except for a bit of knitting," she told me when I went on a tour of what she called her studio. It consisted of one sizable room, which I surmised had been the original dining room in her Civil War-era farmhouse.

I stood in awe of the wall of yarn across one side of the room. It was a kaleidoscope of exploding color—daisy, daffodil, dandelion, marigold, rose, periwinkle, iris, shamrock, and shades in between. Unable to contain myself, I reached out and ran my hand across the organized rows, delighting in touching the textures of the fibers—soft, prickly, bumpy, fluffy, smooth. I removed some skeins, squeezed them between my fingers, and rubbed my thumbs over their warmth as if they were stuffed animals. The ambrosia hooked me, and Eleanor insisted I leave with her small rigid heddle loom and a stash of yarn that would supply me with projects for weeks.

"Get to know the feel of the yarn with your fingertips. Allow its fidelity to flow through you. Be at one with the animals and the earth that have given you this gift. A happy weaver makes a happy cloth," Eleanor said.

With the fire popping and warming my face in the evenings, I warped the loom, loaded the shuttle, and weaved to a methodical rhythm of opening the shed, beating the yarn, closing the shed, and repeating the process over and over again. The cadence—one, two, and three—centered me in the moment and chased away the inner critic, fending off burdens of the past and fears of the future. I was not an expert, but I mastered a simple pattern for a daffodil-colored scarf that kept me comfy on my walks with Sam.

Weaving wasn't my only new hobby. Craig showed me how to tramp through the wooded wonderlands and sparkling meadows with snowshoes. We traded breakfast on Sundays at the Slick Chick for hearty brunches at either Craig's cabin or my home (mostly Craig's). Getting to Craig's bare-bones place was a challenge. Taking the shortcut meant traveling as the crow flies on narrow, rutty lanes across two hills almost as high as Hartsville Hill. Even in the best of weather, driving on these was tricky; in winter, it was treacherous. I chose to go the long way, following the paved streets through Hornell and Canisteo until I got to the gravel road that paralleled Slate Creek and led to Craig's driveway. The challenge didn't end there—traversing Craig's uphill lane for several hundred feet demanded the skill of a balance beam gymnast.

Whenever I visited, I was at ease in the cozy house. The cabin's simplicity was calming and unpretentious, just like its owner. A kettle of water would be simmering on the black iron wood-burning stove—a natural source of humidity, Craig had informed me. We ate on the wooden table and sat on the benches Craig had made. I loved running my hand over the golden tabletop's smooth, shining surface. Each time my fingers traced the grain, I paused and pondered about this gorgeous specimen. *What things had this tree seen? Where did it come from?* Craig said the tree's life did not end; instead, it suspended itself in time to keep us company. I chose to agree with him—I felt the wood's warmth talking to me, loving me.

We stuffed down fresh sourdough bread, baked earlier in the morning from Craig's starter, and filled up on egg scrambles with ham and cheese over hash browns. Not the ideal meal for weight loss but a necessary one for our snowshoeing adventures.

The land was hilly, and we got a workout trudging up the steep incline to a clearing for another top-of-the-world experience. Sam Adams joined us, dressed in his argyle sweater, but the Boston's short legs were no match for the snow's depth. So he sat in a sled Craig pulled, surrounded by comfy blankets. On each trek, I reminded Craig snowshoeing would be better on the Honey Bear's flatter ground. He'd laugh and call me a loafer, and I agreed.

Craig and I settled into a routine, filling the rest of Sunday afternoons and early evenings piecing together jigsaw puzzles or playing Scrabble or with Craig trying to teach me how to master the guitar. Craig repeated his moniker of us from our OSU days, "Beauty and the Old Fart." We found the sweet spot for a satisfying and fulfilling relationship filled with respect, love, and understanding.

MERIDA JOHNS

* * *

Entertainment choices at nighttime for a young, single woman were slim unless you were a college student. Because bowling leagues and small bar scenes were not my style, I improvised and turned the Honey Bear into an entertainment venue every second and fourth Friday evening. January 24 was the kickoff. Although I was too young to have taken part in the 1960s coffeehouses and hootenannies, I challenged myself to create a laid-back music venue on Friday evenings. I wanted a place where people could drop by, kick back, and enjoy good food, conversation, music, and brew. At seven o'clock, the party began. People brought a dish to pass, a voice to sing, and, if inclined, an instrument to play. The Honey Bear's first event brought together an even dozen celebrators. The next time, fifteen showed up, and by the middle of February, a crowd of twenty-five packed into the living area.

"You keep this up, and you goin' to need to be puttin' on an addition to this place," Craig said.

As Robert would say, my life was running on octane. My work was fulfilling as I cut a path toward my North Star. My strengths of love and kindness overflowed with supportive friends and colleagues and a trusting relationship with Craig. My home and the splendor of western New York powered my appreciation of beauty. And new hobbies and music, music, music on Friday evenings nourished my soul. It was perfect until . . .

Chapter 25

A BAD PENNY

There is an adage: A bad penny always turns up. Last evening, like a clipped and ragged coin from the Middle Ages, the bad penny slithered its way back into my perfect life. Choices have consequences. If you choose well, the outcome falls somewhere on the plus side of the continuum above zero to infinity. If you choose poorly, you land in the opposite direction. Over the years, when Robert was practicing law and defending a client, he often mused during our family dinnertime conversations that people can't calculate the good or harm of their choices if they fail to balance emotion and reason.

Seldom do we make up the distance we lose from our poor choices. Three years ago, my choices landed me on the minus side of the equation—with grit, guile, and guts, I'm dead set on making it to the positive side.

* * *

I stayed up late, making sure the Honey Bear was in tip-top shape for the next day's Valentine's Day music extravaganza—vacuuming, dusting, rearranging furniture, setting out dishes, cutlery, and condiments on the kitchen bar, and devising decorations for the event. Since it was a sweetheart holiday, I expected a few more couples than the regular mix of twenty or so people; I wanted the house ready for a bigger than usual crowd.

I juggled these activities with baking and frosting heart-shaped cookies to take to work the following day. If anyone was peering through my windows, I'm sure I looked like a madwoman, running between shoving cookie sheets in and out of the oven and doing the other chores.

At eleven o'clock, I called it quits and crawled into bed with Sam Adams beside me. My little Boston never ceased to amaze me with his sleeping habits. To anyone else, his snoring would drive them nuts. To me, the rhythmic, low to high crescendos were the same as a rocking chair sending me off to dreamland. Before falling asleep, I looked outside my window, and the forest was dark—the tiny sliver of moon wasn't sufficient to pierce the canopy of limbs that shook hands with each other. The night creatures didn't stir—no raccoons making a ruckus circling the house or bobcats screeching like old women. The in and out of my breath and Sam's snores accompanied me into never-never land.

* * *

February 14, 1986. Today, during a slip and slide down Hartsville Hill to work, my mind traveled back to another Valentine's Day and the night of my engagement. It had been three years, but it felt like a lifetime!

I long ago had rid myself of the yellow diamond engagement ring, the pavé setting diamond wedding band, and the Tiffany pearl and sapphires—these were easy to discard. I hoped the physical objects would bring someone happiness, and the money I got for them and donated to the nonprofit women's shelter would supply items of comfort and need.

I drove past Tinkertown, and my mind turned cartwheels, trying to untangle the web of emotions making my heart heavy. Forgive and forget—it's an enduring sentiment, but I'm confident most people don't succeed at either. Forgiveness requires the abused to acknowledge an offense, not condone or excuse behavior or reconcile with the offender. When there is no justice and no commitment by the wrongdoer to apologize and change, can there be forgiveness? Whether lacking these or not, to enshrine hate, to seek revenge and retribution, is a burden that kills the soul. Is that what forgiveness is—releasing the hurt and moving forward? But forgetting is a different story. Harm sears an indelible mark in the mind and on the body. Memories of emotional and physical injury brand a person, the same as a red-hot flat iron stamps a cattleman's mark.

I shook off the cooties, left those heavy thoughts in my Jeep, and tried to move my energy in a positive direction. "Morning, Ms. Jordan," one of the students said as he held the door open for me and I entered the building foyer. I was Ms. Jordan to everyone here—I took back my maiden name after my divorce, resolved never to lose my identity in someone else's surname again.

"What's up today, Chuck?" I asked.

My advisee ignored my question. His eyes focused instead on the brown grocery bags I carried. He gave me a sidewise smile accompanied by bright eyes. "Are those for us, Ms. Jordan?"

The students knew I filled my office with yummy treats like a kitchen pantry. They were also shrewd and knew they would find something extra waiting for them on holidays. Today was no different. Besides the five dozen cookies I baked last evening, I placed four bowls of an abundant assortment of chocolates around the office suite for the sweetheart day.

"You shouldn't spoil them like this," Betty said as I put out the cookies.

"I'm not spoiling them, Betty. I'm keeping an eye on them. Each time a student comes in to grab a goody, it lets me get the scoops about what is going on."

She gave me a crooked smile and nodded her head. "Yeah, Cheryl told me there was more to you than meets the eye."

At five o'clock, I considered the day a success when I saw the bottoms of the cookie platters and candy bowls. Chuck and his classmates left with smiles on their faces.

* * *

Sam flew by me like the house was on fire when I arrived home and opened the front door. My eyes followed him as he zigzagged from side to side, running down my lane.

I dropped my purse and keys and charged after him. "Sam! Sam! Come!"

When he left the driveway and jumped into the thick of the forest, my frantic button engaged. It was a fortunate turn since the snow was deeper in the woods than on the plowed lane. Sam ended up doing the equivalent of a belly flop after he cleared the snowbank created by Elliott's plow.

The only visible parts of his body were the top of his head and ears, and I took advantage of his immobile predicament. I dashed over, picked up my pooch, and, as I held him in my arms, I could feel his heart galloping under my fingertips. I walked back to the house thinking, *What the hell happened?* I shook off a chill, wondering if this was a repeat of the night a few weeks ago—I didn't want a return of the shadows, but I couldn't fend off the premonition.

* * *

The Honey Bear pulsed. Voices belted out the choruses to Pete Seeger tunes, and feet tapped to their beat. Sam Adams had calmed down and was cozy, curled up in his doggie bed, snoring in time with the music. The fireplace put on a spectacular show; its flames swirled around and swept through the wood as frantic as a flamingo dancer and cracked and popped in time to the songs' refrains. Craig and his small band were the principal musicians. Ray and his wife, Eleanor, and my coworkers from allied health—Marty, Bob, Barb, Carole, Earl, Bill, Art, and Ron—and their spouses or current squeezes came, and some new faces showed up too.

The crowd clapped their hands, swayed their bodies, tapped their feet, and laughed when the band played "My Get Up and Go Has Got Up and Went." But we all turned pensive, wondering where all the flowers had gone, and couples held hands and snuggled as they sang the chorus to the love song "Kisses Sweeter than Wine." Our emotions went on a roller-coaster ride—we sailed up and down, up and down, and up and down, dizzy on the rhythms. Somebody called, "Break!" and the ride stopped so the guests could scatter to the food bar, the keg, the wine, and good conversation.

It happened when I was standing with Craig and Elliott in the sunroom. The three of us were guzzling beer and finishing off a shared bag of popcorn, and from time to time, playing catch with Sam and cheer-leading him when he jumped to grab the popped kernels we threw to him. Sam's average would make even the best catcher envious.

Craig frowned. "Sam, you missed that one," he said.

Sam's four paws stood their ground as he turned his head and let out a rumbling growl.

The hairs on the back of my neck sprung out ninety degrees, and I took a deep breath. It couldn't be! I turned, and my mouth dropped when I saw him—the flirty grin, the same posture. He leaned against my sunroom doorway with arms folded across his chest. How long had he been here watching me?

"Who is that?" Craig and Elliott whispered in unison.

"A bad penny," I said.

Chapter 26

PREMONITION

A premonition can be unconscious anticipation of something good. But it has a decent chance of being a forewarning too. I held the former close to my heart, hoping to ward off the latter. After all, I did hear the spirits sing when I first laid eyes on the Honey Bear. But then, the shadows came. I needed to believe the singing spirits would win in the end.

* * *

I walked over toward Jonathan, and the muscles in my shoulders and jaw drew as taut as stretched rubber bands. I eyed him, curious whether there were any changes since the last time I saw him eighteen months earlier. He still had that handsome suaveness—the self-assured slouch, sharp clothing, stylishly shaggy sandy-blond hair, cool-gray eyes, and a shit-eating grin. But his presence was out of step with the others congregated in my home. Where they were genuine, he was as phony as an eye-catching celebrity touched up picture-perfect and posed on a make-believe landscape. How could I have been so hoodwinked?

The last thing I wanted was for him to stay. On the other hand, I didn't want a verbal altercation in front of my friends. A no-win situation—his customary play. Twisting me into this conundrum would be his downfall tonight.

He grew out of his slouch, uncrossed his arms, and held them out, looking for a hug as I approached. My arms stayed glued to my sides.

"Looking foxy, Bunny," he murmured, his eyes moving over my body. "There is so much I need to tell you. There is so much I am sorry for."

I stood beyond his reach, my thoughts clear. *It's always about you, Jonathan. You do have a lot to be sorry for, but I'm betting the lack of an apology isn't part of it.*

"You're not welcome here. You must leave."

He half-smiled, and his eyes roamed across the room of partygoers, oblivious to his presence.

"Maybe I shouldn't have shown up like this. But I was anxious. I wanted to be sure you were okay. Every week, I've sent flowers and heard nothing from you."

A tornado stormed through my head, dredging up and discharging debris indiscriminately. *How did he find me? Here—at my home? Why isn't he in Columbus? So he had sent more flowers!*

"I can't leave until I explain. I got a fellowship in Buffalo, and I live there now. I'm seeing a counselor," he said.

His sentences hit me like buckshot. *Buffalo! He lives in freaking Buffalo?* I buried emotion under my face.

"It's good you landed a job you wanted and are consulting a therapist. But you must go."

"I don't want to go. I want to be with you." His smile reappeared. "This seems like such a cool place and party. It would be horrible to ruin it."

I stared him down. "Those men I was talking with, if I ask them, they will make sure you leave. I don't want to do that, but I will."

Jonathan peered over my shoulder, sizing up Craig and Elliott standing behind in the sun room. Jonathan was buffed like a magazine cover model but could not compete with the brawn of either of them. Both had seen war and had fought for their lives. My former husband was a milquetoast compared with them. A bully knows when the opposition outmatches him.

The smile on Jonathan's face sank, and a strained silence smothered the air. His disparaging look that had crushed me in earlier days appeared. "You've hardened Suzanna, and it doesn't suit you."

He turned, walked across the living room and out of the house, slamming the door behind him.

It was déjà vu! Same bullshit, just a different pasture.

* * *

I had been so focused I didn't notice Sam was standing guard next to me.

"I thought Mr. Sam Adams, here, would tear that dude's leg off," Craig said after he came to my side. "But if the guy hadn't skedaddled, I would have joined Sam and ripped off his other one. It *is* him, isn't it?"

I squeezed my lips and nodded. From the corner of my eye, I saw Elliott leaving the house through the sunroom door. My eyebrows shot up, and I looked at Craig.

"Does he know?" I asked.

"Security is Elliott's job, Suzanna. He can spot a bad situation. He's gone to make sure Jonathan has left."

Craig took my hand and squeezed it. "About time to get the music started again, don't you think?"

I smiled, but my mind rewound. *What could Elliott be doing?*

* * *

Craig knew how to return me to a lighthearted mood. "In honor of our hostess, the quintessential Flower Girl, we're startin' the next set with 'The Garden Song.' C'mon, Suzanna, get on up here with me. We're doin' a duet."

His strategy worked its magic. His rich baritone voice and his strumming beat resurrected vibrations that evicted the darkness that had slinked in as we sang together. The metaphor I needed materialized. *Little by little, I'm making my garden grow.*

The songfest of humorous, poignant, and romantic tunes continued. Elliott slipped back into the house, and only Craig and I were the wiser he had left for a while. The group wound up the evening with the usual "Franklin County Woman." Elliott whirled me around my living room floor, but my hand on his shoulder couldn't help detect his muscles were tighter tonight, and his arms around me felt as if he would never let me go.

Another supporter had slipped into my life—this one I called *Mon Guardian*.

* * *

Eleanor, Betty, Craig, and Elliott stayed behind the rest of the crowd to help clean and straighten up my digs. Elliott tended to the fire, Craig replaced the furniture, and Eleanor, Betty, and I pulled the kitchen into shape. In my heart, I was happy to have them stay. I had a premonition: *Jonathan always must win. He will be back.*

My gut told me Betty's and Eleanor's sharp eyes didn't miss Jonathan's entrance and exit.

"That was the flower man, wasn't it?" Betty asked as the five of us stood, gathered around the fireplace.

Elliott and Eleanor gave me a stare that said, *Want to explain?*

I was torn between telling my story and keeping it secret. I rationalized. I didn't want to burden anyone. I didn't want to put anyone in an uncomfortable position.

I caught Craig's eye, his silence challenging me. *The truth, Suzanna, is you don't want to admit the truth. You don't want to open yourself to criticism. You don't want to take the chance people might judge you or think less of you.*

"Take the chance," my inner voice said.

"Why don't we all sit down, and I'll tell you about the flower man."

* * *

I took the risk, and I added to my cheerleading team. There were no reproaches or retorts. They offered no opinions or advice. They listened. They asked, "What can we do to help? What do you want to do?"

After Betty and Eleanor had put on their heavy coats and prepared to leave, we gave hugs all around. I stood on the front porch, waving to my lady friends.

"See you Monday," Betty called out as she and Eleanor returned my wave and got in their cars.

I turned around, expecting to see Craig and Elliott right behind them, but the two were hanging back, standing hunched together beside the fireplace, talking in muted tones.

"What's up?" I asked.

They turned to me with deadpan faces.

Elliott stood with his weight shifted on his right leg, the fingers of his right hand on his hip with his thumb tucked behind his waist. Craig had the Craig silence. Elliott had the "Elliott stance."

I didn't have to be a telepath to decipher what was on their minds.

"I followed Jonathan after he left," Elliott said.

My heart went into overdrive. Was there an altercation? Elliott looked okay. No visible injuries. "What happened?"

"His car went down your lane and turned toward Tinkertown. I had a funny feeling—call it a premonition. I stood in the drive and listened. And then his revved-up car motor quit, and I figured he was close by."

I lowered my head, closed my eyes, and rubbed my thumping forehead. I didn't know if I should scream, cry, or do both. *Damn the son of a bitch. Will I never be free from him?*

"I walked to the end of the driveway, and sure enough, his Mustang was parked a couple hundred feet away on the side of the road."

"And? Is he still there?" I asked.

"I called one of my sheriff buddies, and he took care of the matter. Did a casual drive-by, stopped, and asked the guy if he needed any help. He said he didn't and left. The sheriff is going to do a few more drive-bys tonight to be sure he doesn't come back."

My insides churned, and my body replayed the evening of June 13. Tingling began in my chest, followed by needles digging into every surface of my body. My breaths quickened. Everything started to blend —Jonathan and Fred—and I wanted to vomit. I sat down on the couch, and Sam jumped into my lap, coaxing me to relax.

Craig sat next to me and took my hands. "I don't think you should stay here on your own tonight. How about Elliott and me bunkin' in to make sure everything is okay."

I looked over to Elliott.

"No worries. I'll stay," Elliott said.

An hour later, a car pulled into my lane, drove up to the house, turned, and left. By the sound of the motor, it wasn't the sheriff as I had hoped.

I should have known better. Predators don't easily let their prey get away.

Part III

Chapter 27

A GOOD PLACE TO START

*C*oincidence. *"I don't hold much in predetermined events, in fatalism. If I did, I'd have to abandon the notion of choice. But I do believe random acts can occur at the same time, and together they can form something curious." I had said that to my neighbor Barry Callahan on Labor Day.*

Jonathan's reappearance a month ago has challenged my thoughts about coincidence. I'm not willing to accept fatalism and reject my belief in choice. I'm inclined, though, to meet the coincidence believer halfway. Coincidences may happen, but alternatives exist within these quirks of fate. What we choose to do is up to us.

* * *

"Suzanna, are you going to open the box of books stashed in here?" Betty asked toward the end of the workday on Friday, March 14.

I had stowed the medium-sized, beat-up box in the supply closet during my first week on the job. I gazed at it now. *How pathetic.* A vestige of my move, I had forgotten about it.

"Been sitting here almost seven months; it can't be important. Want me to toss it?"

I knew a threat when I heard one. "Not a chance, Betty. I'm hauling it into my office now."

"Humph! I suppose it will stay there for another six months?" Betty threw me a smile coupled with a raised right brow, her take on humor mixed with sarcasm. I called it Betty's "humorcasm," and she loved the label. Humor or sarcasm, I knew Betty meant business.

My secretary and I had a healthy mother-daughter thing going. Depending upon the situation, she excelled at listening, protecting, coaching, prodding, accepting, helping, and communicating. Today she used her prodding skill.

When we were growing up, my father reminded Jack and me that "subordinates" often saved their bosses' bacon. Indeed, when working in the law firm together, Robert and Lillian had such a relationship, and my parents never lacked examples of Dad's truism. Over the past months, Betty had saved my bacon many times—getting the correct forms completed on time, prioritizing phone calls, editing memos, suggesting the best person to contact. Today, I didn't mind her nudging. I grabbed the box and threw it into a corner behind my desk.

It was past five o'clock by the time I was ready to go home, and I was running late. I had a ton to do before guests arrived for hootenanny night at the Honey Bear. As I reached to turn off my office lights, I saw the offending box in the corner. *Betty will kill me if I don't get this sucker out of here. What's the deal? Why did I forget this box?*

On the ride home, I ruminated. Jonathan had not turned up again since Valentine's Day. Or if he had, I didn't know about it. Our wedding anniversary was in a few days, followed by my birthday on March 21. Valentine's Day. Wedding anniversary. Birthday. All prime targets for Jonathan to wiggle back into my life. I didn't know whether he had persisted in sending flowers since his Valentine's Day intrusion. After his first bouquet, I asked the florist to deliver any orders from him to the local nursing home as an anonymous gift, and I didn't inquire whether the orders had kept arriving.

There was more weighing on my mind, though. Since Jonathan's unexpected appearance, the shadows came more often—in fact, every day. I kept these "visitations" to myself. If I said anything, I believed people would consider me a candidate for a psychiatric ward. At times, the shapes were dark and hovered close, giving me the heebie-jeebies. Other times, they floated like gossamer cloth, making me warm and comforted. But the heavy footsteps pacing back and forth—clomp, clomp, clomp—in the loft awoke me and made the hair on my arms rise. Who were these phantoms? Why were they here?

* * *

"That's right! Sam Adams was playing with a ghost, an apparition, or a spirit. Call it what you want," I told Craig over fried eggs, ham, and hash browns at the Slick Chick the morning after the Honey Bear mini music fest. I got the Craig silence in response.

My breakfast partner waived over the waitress for a coffee refill. "Tell me once more."

I sighed. Did I have to go through this again? "All righty. Last evening before the hootenanny, Sam went to the staircase. He stood on his back legs, looked up to the loft, waved his front paws, and whined."

Craig stirred cream in his refilled coffee. "And?"

"Sam kept this up for two minutes. He was happy. Like what he does with you and me when he wants to play."

"Well, maybe Sam has an eyesight problem. Or a light created a shadow on the ceilin' or wall. Or Sam spotted a spider steppin' across a beam. Perhaps Sam smoked some wacky tobaccy or ate some mushrooms."

"Okay, you can cross out the tobaccy, mushrooms, and spiders. There's none of that at the Honey Bear. And Sam does not have eye issues."

"How do you know? Have you had his eyes checked recently?"

I was getting nowhere with this nonbeliever. "If you're going to be that way, I'm not telling you the rest."

Craig eyed me over the top of his cup as he took a gulp of coffee. "Okay. I always like a fairy tale."

My brows tightened. "It's crazy, Craig. Ever since I got those damn flowers from Jonathan, strange stuff has been happening at the house."

I told him about Sam's lightning dashes I wrote off at first as cabin fever. I explained how Sam growled while he scanned an empty wall and described the creepy pacing across the loft floor in the middle of the night.

Craig's boyish smile vanished by the time I finished. "I don't believe in goblins and vampires. That said, I know you, Suzanna. You don't exaggerate. I believe you when you say somethin' is goin' on."

My shoulders relaxed. I cast my eyes aside and sucked in my lower lip.

Craig read me like a book. "What's botherin' you? What else is there?"

"One thing is scarier." I felt my chest rise and fall faster than usual. "I think I'm going crazy."

"I doubt that. What's happened?"

"The last two Sundays when Sam and I have come home from your cabin, I swear Jonathan's been in the house. I smell his odor when I go to bed and put my head on my pillow—his cologne mingled with his body scent."

"I think I should come up to your place today. Maybe stay the night."

"I'm fine, Craig. I just *smell* Jonathan on Sunday nights. And besides, Elliott might come by and plow this afternoon. I always invite him in for hot chocolate. He'll be there to check things out."

"It's mid-March, Suzanna. I doubt we'll be havin' a blizzard. But speakin' of Elliott, what's goin' on with the two of you? You both look good dancin' to 'Franklin County Woman.' Kind of made for each other."

My eyes wanted to pop out of their sockets. Talk about a switch in topic! "What's going on? Nothing except that he plows my lane and drinks my hot chocolate."

Craig gave me a sheepish smile.

"You know something I don't?" I asked.

"Just that Elliott asked me what you and I had goin' on."

"And what's that supposed to mean?"

"Well, Flower Girl, once he found out that I'm just your Mon Ange, he sort of asked my permission to like, um, date you . . . It made me feel like your grandpa."

"And what did Grandpa Craig tell him?"

"Go for it, man!"

As I drove up Hartsville Hill, I shook my head. *Going to have to settle this with Mr. Elliott Taylor.*

* * *

It was four o'clock when I heard Old Smokey coming up my drive. Craig was right that no big snowstorm was brewing, but a fair amount of snow still covered my long lane. I chided myself. I should have seen this coming! I never gave Elliott's extra plowing a thought; I believed he was just helping a tenderfoot. Did I lead him on, inviting him into the house? Offering him hot chocolate? Dancing with him at the songfests?

Our conversations were short—small talk about local politics and university gossip. Elliott and I avoided straying into our personal lives. Even sharing our professional backgrounds, we were cautious. He told me he had been in the military, but when I tried to probe further, I got his customary line, "If I told you, I'd have to kill you."

Craig hinted Elliott's work involved intelligence. I flippantly asked Craig one time whether Elliott might be like James Bond. "To be honest, I think he was better," Craig said.

My plowman shared little about his family besides mentioning two brothers, one living in Rochester and one in Buffalo. I had no idea whether his parents, both deceased, had been farmers or townspeople or had blue- or white-collar jobs. He said he was a bachelor and lived about two miles from me in an old farmhouse. There was a quality about him, a sadness I caught in his eyes when he mentioned his bachelorhood. It led me to believe he was grieving a loss. Was it a loss of a partner? A wife? A young love?

Elliott was older than Jack and Craig, but his mannerisms—how he sized up and responded to circumstances and people—made me think he was seasoned in more than years. Challenges that Jack or even Craig had never braved tempered Elliott's face. I noticed this the first time I met him in the woods. His eyes were a whirlpool of observation, appraisal, and calculation, taking the measure of me and my surroundings. Furrows ran across his forehead, and frown lines marked the space between his brows. The crinkles below his temples balanced these—remnants of years of shy smiles, I imagined. There was more to this book than its cover. His eyes—those rich caramel-colored eyes—told that story. What was it?

I stood on my front porch watching Elliott approach in Old Smokey. I clutched my arms around my body, fending off the cold. His shy smile greeted me when I signaled for him to come in for his usual hot chocolate.

* * *

Just like Elliott—needing to be useful. He was adding more fuel to the fireplace as soon as he had hung his deerskin-colored leather jacket on one of the pegs at the front door entrance. While he fiddled with the logs, his back toward me, I stirred hot chocolate in cups on the kitchen bar. I never paid attention to his physical build, other than noting his six-foot-three height dwarfed me. Now my eyes took another look. Broad shoulders and muscular back well proportioned and tapering into a tight waist. He stood up, rubbing his hands back and forth, examining his work. His jeans fit tight around his hips and athletic legs. *Am I just awakening to this man's charms?*

He turned around and strolled over to me. "Catch you daydreaming there, Suzanna?"

My cheeks started burning. "You could say that."

"Hope it wasn't anything bad."

"Well, I'll let you determine," I said, handing him a mug and walking to the living room. I made myself comfortable on the couch, and he took the old craftsman rocker to my left. I stared into the fire. *Fireplaces! Will they bring me the same warmth I had before Jonathan? Has Jonathan spoiled even this one pleasure for me?*

"I'm listening," he said, breaking the silence.

I shook my head. "I'm sorry. I was far, far away."

I looked at Elliott. *There are those eyes—observing, assessing, calculating. Take a chance!*

"Yeah, I used to like fireplaces a lot. I mean really a lot. But Jonathan ruined them for me."

He cradled his mug with both hands, scooted to the front of his rocker, and leaned toward me. "If we give up control and allow people to take things from us that are not theirs, we lose everything."

I watched the orange and yellow flames twisting and jettisoning themselves up the chimney. "You're right. This is my fireplace. This is my moment." Then I turned and smiled into his eyes. "This is my time with a friend."

Still cupping his chocolate, he sat back in his chair. "What were you daydreaming about over there?" he asked, nodding toward the kitchen.

I turned his phrase on him. "If I told you, I'd have to kill you."

He chuckled. "What goes around comes around, they say."

The floor creaked under the weight of the rocker while he sipped his drink. Was silence a learned behavior of military vets? If so, Craig and Elliott did it well.

"Since murder won't be on your hands tonight, how about some pizza and beer? I bet you haven't tried one of the area's best-kept epicurean secrets."

I waited to catch my breath. *That sure came out of nowhere!* "If I agree, this isn't a date," I said.

He leaned toward me, hand on his knee. "Craig been talking with you?"

"I talk with Craig a lot."

He nodded. "I suppose he mentioned that, aah . . ."

My nerves wouldn't allow me to enjoy his torture. "Yes, he said you wanted to see me socially. And let me be clear, Elliott, I'm not into dates with anyone now. I just got out of a . . ."

He cut me off. "You don't owe me an explanation. Let's not make it a date."

I set my jaw and studied him.

"I'm hungry, and hot chocolate doesn't go far. It's dinnertime, and I could enjoy a bit of company," he said.

"I'm hungry, and I could use the company too."

* * *

Faithful to Elliott's word—it wasn't a date. No teasing, no innuendos, no passes from him. No goosebumps on my arms, no casual touching of hands, and no flirting either. Just companionship. He wasn't asking for me to prove anything. I was able to be me in his company.

The epicurean delight was a dive—a small wood-clapped building beside the train tracks outside Hornell. The atmosphere was not
four-star, but the pizza, thick-crusted and gooey with cheese and
plastered with pepperoni, peppers, sausage, and mushrooms, was the
comfort food I liked. The Saturday night crowd packed the place
tighter than sardines in a can—table abutting table and plates snuggling against each other. Everyone seemed to know my escort as we
entered. "Howdy, El," one man said. "Hey, big guy, what's happening," asked another. "What's up, El?" barked one. We slithered like
serpents between the tables until we squeezed into an empty spot.

"El?" I asked. "What's that about?"

He shrugged. "Known these folks all my life. I'm El to them."

"Do you prefer El or Elliott?"

He took a breath and focused his eyes on me. "I like Elliott. That's
the name my folks gave me. What they called me. Yeah, I prefer
Elliott."

"I lean toward Elliott too," I said.

We quibbled about the toppings on the pizza but not on the pitcher
of brew—no light beer! The raucous atmosphere—people bellowing,
laughing, and joking—spilled over and stuffed me like happy pie.

"Be about twenty minutes," the waiter said after we ordered a loaded
pizza.

Elliott and I stared at each other. *Now what?* "Are we going to sit
here and look at each other until the food arrives?" I asked.

He smiled. "We could do that . . . but that's not keeping company,
is it?"

I laughed and then got the conversation rolling. "I like to know the
company I'm keeping, but am I going to have to check yearbooks to
find out how old you are?"

Elliott Benjamin Taylor was born in 1944, fourteen years before me.
His paternal grandparents were farmers, Seventh Day Baptists, and
descendants of the original Alfred settlers who traced the family history
to the Revolutionary War. Several of his relatives had fought in that
war and the one in 1812 too.

Like Robert, his father had served in World War II in Europe and, when he returned home, got a job with the Erie Railroad, working up to the position of conductor on the passenger lines. His mother, like Lillian, was a stay-at-home wife and mother to her three sons. I dug for more information about his high school and college years. A football team member, I knew, but high school valedictorian wasn't what I had expected.

I asked about his badass reputation the Callahan brothers had alluded he had. Elliott smiled.

"Well, like beauty, badass is in the eye of the beholder. If you want to call drag racing on these country dirt roads badass, then I guess I was one."

Details, though, between his college years and his current job were off-limits. "I don't talk about what I did in the army—partly because I can't and partly because I don't want to."

I waited.

"It's related to what I told you earlier this evening—giving up control to others over your life. I'm not sacrificing my present life to my past life in the army . . . What matters is living each day in the here and now. Like being here with you, enjoying your company."

My lips crept upward. "That's enough for me."

* * *

Elliott took the narrow, weaving Crosby Creek Road on the drive home. As fast as the curves he navigated and potholes he swerved to miss, my thoughts bounced between *Should I?* and *Should I not?*

I took the risk. "Elliott, can you come in for a while?"

From the illumination of the car's dashboard, I saw his shy smile. "Aah! Going to tell me about those daydreams?"

"I don't know whether I should smack you for your wisecrack or thank you for your interest."

"I prefer the second. And . . . you're welcome."

* * *

We took Sam out for his evening constitutional. The leftover snow from dozens of storms crackled underfoot as we walked toward the woods. Smoky scents, floating in the air from fireplaces miles around, triggered nostalgic feelings of childhood days in Ohio—when Mel, Ellen, and I camped out as Girl Scouts and when Gary and I tramped the autumn woods. These were strong enough memories to blot out my Jonathan Years.

Afterward, Elliott, Sam, and I settled ourselves in front of the dying embers of the fireplace.

"What's on your mind, Suzanna?"

"You *do* get to the point, don't you?"

"In most situations, it's a good place to start."

Getting to the point miraculously erased my trepidations—*What will he think? What will people think? Am I crazy?* Elliott extended me a magic wand, and I accepted his invitation to lay bare my fears. I was unencumbered, unabashed, unapologetic.

For the next hour, Elliott listened, interrupting now and again to clarify. I told the story about hearing spirits sing when I first saw the Honey Bear, about the good and bad shadows, about the pacing footsteps in the loft at night, about Jonathan's scent on my pillow on Sunday evenings.

When I finished, an occasional crack from the fire and Sam's snoring were the sounds breaking the silence. Elliott sat still in the rocker, his chin resting on his folded hand, his eyes sweeping the floor. *He's analyzing. He's trying to figure out an answer. I have faith in him.*

He raised his head, his features softened. "I don't discount the sixth sense. Whether it's called intuition or a hunch, a premonition, a ghost, or a spirit. It's not silly. I never discount it."

My eyes asked for an explanation.

"My sixth sense has saved mine and other's lives . . . many times. There's more to us than our bodies. Discounting our intuition strips us of being total."

My fingers traveled up and down my temples. I gazed at the fading light in the fireplace, seeking help. "Being total?"

"Systems theory. The whole is greater than the sum of its parts. Everything is related. When we subtract one part, it can adversely affect all the rest. You have a lot of beautiful parts, Suzanna. Best not to deny any of them."

Elliott had made the complicated simple. How much had I subtracted?

"Well, I better get along," Elliott said, rising and walking toward the entryway.

He put on his leather jacket, grasped the front door handle, and turned to me. "The spirits don't concern me. Sensing Jonathan's presence does. Be sure your doors are locked at all times."

The taillights of Old Smokey disappeared down the drive, and I latched the door. *What a wise, kind, and ruggedly handsome man inside and out.*

* * *

It was eight o'clock when Elliott left. It felt off-kilter. Except for Craig, there would have been cuddling, drawn-out kisses, and perhaps more with any other man. Elliott was different. Romance's biological trappings—racing heart, damp palms, goosebumps—were absent, but my sixth sense told me there was more. I didn't know what I had just experienced. But I did realize it was special—it would take time to break the surface. For now, I was satisfied keeping the seedling in a dark and nurturing space.

I went to the kitchen and was making a cup of tea when it hit me. That damn box from work was still there in my bedroom! Should I open it or have it bug me the rest of the night?

I placed my cup on the coffee table and hauled the ragged thing from where I had left it the evening before. "What's in you?" I said as if I were talking to a person. I set the box down next to my tea, broke open the top flaps, and peered inside. Well, not much there! Lots of old stuff. My high school algebra and geometry books, a college world history text, and one of my French college books, *Le Moulin à Paroles*.

I took time and leafed through each one, laughing out loud at the slips of paper I discovered tucked away and covered with doodles. It's no wonder I wasn't a math whiz! Pages of drawings of palm trees and people's faces, lines scribbled with Gary's and my name—must have been a super dull class. A sales receipt for ninety-three cents, a university course drop card—Had I really dropped the course? A graded French exam tucked away on page 193. I didn't recall a C grade in French. There were a bunch of office items—paper clips, scissors, letter opener, stapler, ruler—the usual junk drawer items.

Then I saw them, on the bottom of the box. The books I found in the bookstore in Granville: *A Latin Reader, Souvenirs de Charité,* and *The Mammoth Exercise Book*!

My mind replayed June 13, 1984. My stomach somersaulted. My heart skipped beats. I held and studied the books. Now I recalled! These belonged to another Susannah—Who was she? I thumbed through the brittle pages, rubbing my fingers across them and remembering. That's right—they are Susannah Simpson's books. She was a teacher like me.

I flipped through the Latin reader and French book, hoping to find snatches of notes or paper that would give me a picture of the woman who owned them. No luck. Apparently, that Susannah was more studious than me!

I opened the exercise book and started to read the first entry. This was her journal—Susannah's journal!

> Friday, June 13, 1884
>
> It is a lovely day here in Elmira, New York. But it is a more appealing day for me. I've wanted to capture my thoughts and feelings for a long time. Now, I am free to do it.
>
> Some may say my narrative is inconsequential, fanciful, or seethes in self-justification. It's unnecessary to argue or disavow these opinions. I do not intend this as an autobiography subject to such criticisms. And who else but I should read my ramblings? I mean this to serve as a chronicle for me, for my satisfaction, so I can learn from my advancement, development, and improvement that I expectantly believe will lead to the rekindling of my spirit—Susannah Simpson.

I thumbed through the pages, allowing the writer's script to message me—the ordinary life of a young woman, I thought. I stopped cold. My eyes blinked, trying to deny the unbelievable.

Monday, August 11, 1884, Alfred, NY

I arrived at Alfred Station at 7:30 o'clock this evening on the Erie. A carriage met those of us at the station for the ride into Alfred. I was the only teacher in the group. All the others were students coming to attend the university. Arrived at my prearranged boarding house, the Burdick Hotel, at 8 o'clock. A hot kettle of tea, biscuits, and honey were awaiting me, for which I was grateful. My first impressions of the town are favorable. The three-story buildings in the Burdick and Green block on the main street are sturdy, constructed in red brick. I can't wait to explore! Unfortunately, no gaslights illuminate the roads here, but in the approaching evening dusk, the residential area looks filled with pretty and well-maintained homes.

But to my delight, the university dominates the small town, and it is the reason I come here. Oh, how I yearn to be among townspeople who value women's rights and equality for all! My heart races with the expectation of attending the lectures of luminaries such as Frederick Douglass, Julia Ward Howe, Elizabeth Cady Stanton. No more subjugation and criticism of my mind and no more fear of peril to my body by a man who is more a master than a husband. My spirit is being set free, and I feel safe. This is a good place to start.

I got up from the couch, chills spiraling like corkscrews through me. *Coincidence?* I went to the fireplace, stirred the embers, and added two more logs. I gazed at the fireflies flowing up the chimney. Holding a journal written by another Susannah who lived in Alfred a hundred years earlier was quirky enough. But another coincidence stood out too—the mention of Frederick Douglass, the great abolitionist and founder of *The North Star* newspaper. I had forgotten about the news-paper—somewhere in the background of my memory—that paid trib-ute to the slaves who used the North Star to guide them to freedom. I reached to clutch my necklace, my own guiding light. As Susannah and Elliott told me tonight, *This is a good place to start.*

It was going to be a long night.

Chapter 28

SUSANNAH SIMPSON ROTH

The two logs I add make the fire roar as if it were a voice that has found freedom. Its cracking and warmth spread over me like the words of a prophet's sermon. Sam is snuggling beside me while I reread the August 11 entry. My heart pounds harder. My eyes have not deceived me. Susannah Simpson Roth is talking about Alfred—the Alfred where I now live. I cannot believe this!

I'm on a rumbling Ferris wheel as I read her meticulous script—up and down, my emotions go wild, are out of control. Who is this man who was master more than a husband? What were his criticisms? What did she fear?

I jump to the beginning of the journal and stare at the first entry. How could I have missed that June 13 date? I pinch myself. Am I dreaming? I read the last sentence aloud: I intend this as a chronicle for me, for my own satisfaction, so I can learn from my advancement, development, and improvement that I expectantly believe will lead to the rekindling of my spirit.

I need more than tea. I go to the kitchen, pour myself a glass of wine, bring the bottle back with me, and don't stop reading until I reach the last page of Susannah's story.

* * *

We sat across from each other at Craig's kitchen table, finishing our usual Sunday brunch, neither believing what we had read.

"It's quite a story, Suzanna . . . or I should say, Susannah Simpson," Craig said after reading the diary entries.

"What do you think?"

"It's weird. Damn weird!"

"That's it?" I asked, my eyes widening.

"No. That's not all." He closed his eyes and took a deep breath. It was the Craig silence on steroids.

I waited. I knew what came next would be earnest. He stalled, got up for the coffeepot, refilled our cups, and sat back down.

"It's strange but not trivial. It's a movin' story of courage, persistence, and adherence to one's values and self-belief. Susannah Simpson was a remarkable person."

I noticed Craig addressed Susannah by her maiden name, not Roth. Susannah's boldness, challenging norms, and exercising her autonomy gave me courage. Didn't I reject keeping my married name too and go by Suzanna Jordan after my divorce?

"What should I make of the similarities between the two of us? For goodness' sake, I'm living in her house!"

Craig shook his head, and a wave of hair fell across his forehead. He pushed it back in place with his strong hand and looked up at me. "I can't explain the similarity. That isn't close to the right word—I can't explain how your paths have crisscrossed. A parallel universe, time warp, reincarnation? Heck, I don't know. Is the explanation important? Is it necessary to ask how our paths—yours and mine—crossed? Divine intervention, predestination? Does that matter?"

I rocked in my seat, allowing the rhythmic motion to open a window to my understanding. "You're right. What do we gain by trying to figure out the how of it? How did it happen? It's more essential to understand the why—what we can learn from it," I said.

I squinted my eyes shut. Time stopped. Perhaps it was a split second, maybe a couple of minutes. Whatever! The first diary entries rumbled through my second self.

Saturday, June 14, 1884

My body has stopped its constant trembling and tingling. I took the laudanum, and it helped. I went to Mother today. I told her I had to leave Johannes, that I had made up my mind. She says I must go back to him. Is there no choice? How can I live with a man who disrespects me, who criticizes all I do? I am never good enough. And when he drinks, he pushes himself on me, or he hits me. He hates my readings of women's rights—he says women have no rights, and this includes me. He says he gives me everything I need—that I should not want for more except to make him happy. I am not a slave—I must not succumb to him as my master.

Sunday, June 15, 1884

Johannes's words break my heart. "You're as dumb as a mule," he says. Since my attack, his criticisms are harsher . . . then he says he is sorry. He says he does not deserve me. He asks me to forgive him. I say I do. What other choice do I have? If I don't forgive, he lays the switch, his hand, or his belt on me.

Monday, June 23, 1884

I am fearful of writing lest my husband finds my journal. But I must write. I cannot give up this small freedom. If I do not confide in my dear diary, I will lose myself. I have spoken with my brother. I am worried this was a mistake. George now has hate in his heart for Johannes. I have pleaded with George to let well enough alone. Johannes brings me flowers tonight, ashamed of threatening me with the switch. I go through the motions to accept them. It is what I must do to survive.

Monday, June 30, 1884

George promised to help me. For now, he says he will not go after Johannes. George mailed my post. I am holding my heart to get a response soon. Today I walked along the river to my special place. Here I am, alone. My cares are relieved when I am here. I listen to the sweet songs the birds sing to me. I smile. I pretend to fly like them—fly away from the nightmare I find myself in. I think about school and graduation and receiving the gold pin and my degree, equal to any man's. Oh, how happy I was! I loved learning, I loved the music, I loved the literature. Then a handsome man turned my head with promises I believed. There is no fault here, except my own. But I should not be harsh with myself unless I continue with this charade. I must fly away like the songbirds.

Wednesday, July 16, 1884

There is still no word from my post.

Monday, July 21, 1884

I have received good news that George delivered to me to-day from the post. The plan is ready. George is helping me. I am grateful for such a brother. He is my savior. He says he will stop Johannes from following me. I'm not so sure —George does not know Johannes like I do.

Saturday, August 9, 1884

I am fortunate to have many who believe in me. My brother, George, and a former sympathetic teacher who knows my situation are willing to help me. The recommendation of "Susannah Simpson" to be an assistant in French at the university overwhelms me. That is the name on my graduation certificate since I was not married yet. I'm gathering my belongings while Johannes is at work. George is to keep them for safekeeping until I leave on the train on Monday. My nerves are on a razor edge, afraid Johannes will find me out before I can leave. Can I act naturally? Tonight, we go to the opera house—that will occupy my mind. Tomorrow, I will busy myself with church activities.

Afternoon, Monday, August 11, 1884

I'm on the train passing through Corning. My stomach was in knots all day, thinking Johannes might come home early from work at the Institute and I would not be able to slip away. Oh, but that was not the case.

I left him a note and lied. I told him I went west to Chicago. He will believe I was untruthful and think I went east and not west. His disbelief, I hope, takes him off my trail. Two people know where I've gone—George and my former teacher. My heart breaks that I could not tell my mother or my dear friends beforehand. But I could not put them in that position. George purchased my rail ticket to Alfred Station, and I paid for one to New York City. George and I figure Johannes will bully the ticket clerk and get him to confess that I bought passage to New York. I am no longer Susannah Roth. I'm starting back to where I'm supposed to be—to the Susannah Simpson I thought I had lost forever. Oh, this is a lonely journey.

Craig's eyes focused on me. "Are you okay, Suzanna?"

"Yeah . . . yeah, I think so. It hits close to home, thinking about what I read. Everything comes rushing back. It's like I'm reliving my life."

"Then, let's wash away those demons," Craig said and nodded toward the door.

As we left the cabin, Craig stopped and looked back.

"Something wrong?" I asked.

"Nah. Just the damn roof. I need to get up there and patch the thing. It's started a leak into the loft."

"How can you get up there and fix it with all the snow and ice on it?"

"Very carefully," he said as he put his arm around me, and we started on our walk.

* * *

It was mid-March, but snow still packed the path in places. On our walk to the meadow, Sam made us laugh with his antics. Now, he wasn't confined to a sled but was a crazy dog, rushing into the snow-banks, barking, snorting at suspicious channels marking the snow, and digging tunnels following the scent of a critter. From time to time, when the snow got caught between his paw pads, he acted like a jumping jack, dancing and shaking until the icy stuff fell to the ground.

With Sam's escapades and the snowball fight between Craig and me, laughter cleared my head from its darkness. The Allegheny arctic-blue sky and bulbous clouds further lightened my spirits on the drive home. Climbing up and going down the hillsides and winding through the valleys, my thoughts turned to how Susannah Simpson flew away like a bird from her nightmare. In retrospect, her journal was comforting—I had found a kindred soul. Like the curving roads I traveled, my mind wandered, trying to discover what messages Susannah was sending. Craig was correct. *It is not important to know how the meeting between Susannah and me came about. What's important is to learn from it. But what are the learning lessons?*

As dusk turned into evening, I curled up on the couch with a glass of wind and flipped through the diary, anxious to find these lessons. Many of the entries were about everyday routines and shed little light on my new friend's feelings or thoughts. Those I skipped over. Her more soulful and passionate writings unearthed her emotions—tears, anxieties, fears, and convictions—but others seemed a mystery, almost as if she were writing in code.

Saturday, September 13, 1884

I am here but a month, and already I am attached to this place. My work begins at the university. Oh, how fulfilled I am! To be treated as an equal, respected for my knowledge, and asked for my opinion brings life into my soul. I am just an assistant, but how the village people look at me for my worth. I am happy to be here. It brings tears to my eyes.

Sunday, September 14, 1884

I believe I would like to move from my boarding place and have my own home. I went riding today and found a sweet pond surrounded by a meadow and a small log home close by. I fell in love immediately with the situation of it. The house did not look occupied. When I returned, I inquired with the hotel owner about the property, and he told me it was for sale! But he discourages me from buying it. He says it is too far out for a single woman to live. I wonder at his discouragement since he will lose a boarder!

Monday, September 22, 1884

Oh, I receive a post from George. He says Johannes is angry, calls me such bad names but still wants me back. George has told Mother and the others I am safe. He says they understand they must keep my location secret for now. Johannes tells our friends and his colleagues I have gone to New York to continue my studies. He puts on a good front. As George and I thought, Johannes does not believe I went west. I am relieved because he is not on my trail. George and I are careful with the post. I put a fake name on mine, and he addresses his to S. Simpson and does not mail from Elmira. We cannot be too careful. I fear for my life should Johannes find me.

Saturday, October 4, 1884

Tonight, I am cozy in my own little house. How freeing this is! I have a comfortable sitting room, kitchen, bedroom, and a loft overhead. My furnishings are meager, but they will do. I have the most beautiful fieldstone fireplace to keep me company. I also have a wood burner to keep warm on cold days. There is a dear farmer at the four corners who has helped me out with wood. My dear brother advanced me the funds to buy this piece of tranquility. Here I can write, read, and work on my lectures. I have a sweet old nag named Rosie who gets me to and from the university—her name matches her color, a rosy brown with a white blaze. She is smart and gentle, and we are the best of friends. There is a small barn for her and for the two cats I have gotten. When the weather gets too bad, I can stay at the hotel and board my horse at the stables there. This makes the proprietor happy. Because of the change of seasons, I expect to stay in town when the New Year begins.

Friday, November 7, 1984

The post I received from George today distressed me; it brings me to tears tonight. My insides tremble, and I think I may need the laudanum again. George says Johannes has hired detectives to find me! George says Johannes suspects him now of helping me. George has confronted Johannes and tells him to leave me alone—he says to call off his dogs. Johannes said the day that happens, he will be dead. Johannes believes I'm in Chicago like I told him in the note when I left. I am worried now that I should have changed my name from Simpson, but how could I do that and secure my position? It is an impossible situation I find myself in. I cry tonight.

Saturday, November 15, 1884

I have put Johannes out of my mind. I refuse to give up my life to laudanum. I refuse to give up my life to such a hard-hearted man. I have such wonderful new friends here—they know me as a single woman of character and merit. I have proven myself as a capable assistant in French, and all the faculty and students love me, and I love them. Mr. Brown, the librarian, and I have become friends and have attended lectures together. He is a single man. My situation troubles me. I cannot marry since I am already married. I cannot lie to an upstanding man like Mr. Brown, so I half-lied and said to him I am promised to someone else. This is a complication I had not imagined.

Sunday, November 16, 1884

I cannot get my plight out of my mind! I am angry Johannes can take my freedom from me, and there is *no* recourse. My life is nothing with Johannes—he berates and beats me—and I cannot divorce him. New York does not allow it, except for adultery or desertion. Perhaps Johannes will divorce me for desertion. Oh, how I pray he does, but he is a vengeful man who wants his way, and he will never let me go until one of us dies.

Christmas Day, 1884

I enjoy the holiday at the Burdick. I have had to relocate earlier than I had thought because of the bad weather. The ride up and down the hill for Rosie and me was too much. Rosie is in the stables here, and the farmer at the four corners has taken the cats. All are comfortable, including me. George and Mother sent me a pair of black gloves and a pretty hair comb with pearls. I cannot believe such extravagance, but George says he has but one sister. George still has not shared where I live with anyone—he says he dare not tell Mother lest she let slip my location. George tells her I am safe and has impressed on her what an evil man Johannes is—she now believes he beat me. But I am sad she believes George but dismissed me before. Alex (Mr. Brown) gave me a gift—Ishmael by Mary Elizabeth Braddon. Oh, how could he know why this novel stirs my soul —this favorite author, who rejects the patriarchal society and the imbalance of power among the genders. I think there is a connection between Alex and me more than we understand. I have said nothing to him about my circumstance, yet I believe he knows. How else can he give me a gift so connected to my own life? I told him I could not accept such a fine present, but he said to take it on loan. Therefore I have accepted it with that condition. On this

Christmas Day, I am thankful for having my freedom and being at peace with myself—being happy in my choice to leave Johannes even though I do not know what the future brings.

Saturday, March 14, 1885

I am so excited! I am back in my cozy home. The weather has broken, and Rosie and I can travel to and from the university. Oh my, but what cleaning I must do. Mr. Chaplaine (the farmer at four corners) has supplied hay and oats for Rosie. I can tell she is happy about the exercise; it has been a long winter for her at the stables. I collected my cats and got a sweet puppy from Mr. Chaplaine to keep me company. He is beautiful—part sheepdog, black and white. I will call him Sampson because he has such thick fur. Mr. Chaplaine says I should have a dog for my protection. I ask him, "Protection from what?" and he says, "You never know." I have sufficient wood left over from the fall to heat for several weeks. Mr. Brown has brought up supplies for my pantry, and I have invited him to stay for dinner this evening.

Tuesday, March 17, 1885

I am much distressed today. I heard from Mr. Brown there are detectives in town looking for a Susannah Roth. They have been around to the hotel and dry goods store and have come to the university. I expect the president to call me to his office. What shall I do? I am Susannah Simpson, not Roth. My references prove this! My brother can confirm this!

Wednesday, March 18, 1885

I am relieved. The president called me to see him today. He said detectives were inquiring after a Susannah Roth. He asked me one question: What is your name? I replied, Susannah Simpson. He said, "As I thought." And that was the end of it.

Saturday, March 21, 1885

I was sitting at my writing desk and looked up when Sampson barked. I was horrified. Two men on horseback were approaching my house. I did not answer their knock. I let Sampson bark and warn them off. When Mr. Chaplaine said I needed protection, had these men already been to his home? I think now he was giving me a warning of their presence here. I believe they are the detectives Johannes has sent after me.

Sunday, March 22, 1885

Alex came for supper with me today. I told him about the two men on horseback yesterday and described them. He said these are the detectives. He told me the entire university knows of my story, but everyone wants to protect me. He says, "We all know you are Susannah Simpson and deny we know a Susannah Roth." I can't hold back—my insides tremble, and the tears break away from my eyes. Alex held me. "What am I to do?" I ask. "Stand your ground," Alex said. "No person, man or woman, is a slave to any man."

Saturday, April 18, 1885

I am so happy! There has been nothing of Johannes or his detectives. Spring is coming! I yearn to plant flower, herb, and vegetable gardens. I am making a plan for all of them. For the flower garden, I like blooms that will invite bees and butterflies—black-eyed Susans, moonbeams, red yarrow, purple royal candles, and white echinacea. For the herbs, I like mint, lavender, parsley, sage. For the vegetables, beans, potatoes, cabbage, radish, spinach, lettuce, cauliflower, celery, beets, turnips. I would like to grow fruit trees if that is possible. Sampson and I have marked out places for the gardens. He is such a companion to me. Mr. Chaplaine's son will do the spading for me, and Alex has offered his help. The ground is too thick, and I do not have the strength for it.

Friday, April 24, 1885

Johannes has found me! Now I know those men on horseback were his spies. I received a letter from him yesterday addressed to Susannah Simpson. He says he loves me and wants me back. He wants to come and get me and take me back with him. Throughout his letter, there is no apology from him. He never has said he is sorry for beating me or berating me. I know going back to him will be no different. In fact, it may be worse. I sent a post today to George and told him Johannes has discovered where I am at. I told George I would not go back to that man. I would rather die. I am worried about my reputation and position at the university. I need to think of a way to get myself away from Johannes forever.

Monday, April 27, 1885

My situation has shattered my nerves like broken eggs. I was fearful Johannes might show up at my home. What would I do? I know Johannes's character—he likes to be the center of the wheel, is happy when people accede and comply with his demands. His position in society is vital to him. He is prideful. I will use this weakness against him and get him to let me go.

I read on, and I found Susannah Simpson's plan! What had I said to Craig earlier? "What do we gain by trying to figure out the how of it?

How did it happen? It's more important to understand the why—what we can learn from it."

Bless Susannah Simpson, she gave me a lesson—Would I have the wisdom to learn from it? Would I have the fortitude to follow my guiding North Star?

Chapter 29

OLD DOG, OLD TRICKS

I put down Susannah's diary, and the fury in the fire's flames is gone. Soft embers blink at me like a view of city lights from the height of thirty-five thousand feet. I frown and close my eyes, and the muscles in my jaw tighten. My thoughts go haywire planning my strategy, stymied by what if this or what if that. A web of contingencies develops. I'm not learning Susannah's lesson—the battle plan must be pinpoint perfect. I mentally throw out the eventualities and zero in on making the perfect plan. Successful war plans, I remind myself, focus on the opponent's vulnerabilities; I nod and smile as my plan comes together. It isn't hard; Susannah gave me the step-by-step map.

I open my eyes and wonder whether I will find Jonathan's Sunday evening scent on my pillow. But something else is happening, and Sam notices it too. His ears are at attention, his eyes are roving the living room. His growls are rumbling and mean. Now, I see the Dark Shadow dancing across the wall.

"Damn you, Johannes Roth. Get the hell out of my home," I scream.

I hear a grotesque voice raging through clenched teeth. "Susannah's plan worked for her, but it won't for you. I'm already damned, you silly woman!"

The Voice's squinted eyes pierce through me like an electric drill, and a mocking smile ripples across his face, allowing his mouth to open larger and larger as if it will consume me. He releases a bloodcurdling Dracula laugh that echoes off the walls and freezes Sam and me in place as he lunges at us.

He is gone as fast as he appears. Did I fall asleep? Have I dreamt this? This can't be real! I look at my wine glass. It's empty. The bottle next to it is empty too.

"This was a nightmare," I say to Sam. My dog's eyes, as gigantic as beach balls, are staring at me.

"That's right, you don't drink," I say.

The good news is that when I go to bed, there is no whiff of Jonathan's scent on my pillow. But the grotesque laugher I heard earlier doesn't leave my ears.

* * *

The following two days were humdrum, but my intuition told me to brace myself for one of Jonathan's old tricks on my wedding anniversary. Midway through Wednesday morning on March nineteenth, Betty remarked, "Goodness, Suzanna! You're as jumpy as a cat on a hot tin roof."

My secretary was correct. Each time the phone rang or the door opened to our suite, my reflexes jerked. *What might he do? What could he do? Will he do a repeat of visiting my office? He could do anything!*

I left work after six o'clock, held up by student counseling sessions. I rushed to my Jeep, knowing Sam would be anxious to get out for his evening run when I returned home, and I needed a walk and some fresh air to clear my head. Besides worries over Jonathan, it had been a rough day— conducting a student grievance committee meeting and fielding an investigation into student plagiarism. I hated these confrontations, not because I disliked facing conflict, but because the parties involved could have avoided the face-offs without much effort. Often a student complaint escalated due to poor communication between instructor and student, and plagiarism resulted more often from a student's lack of understanding than outright cheating. It was tricky repairing bruised egos and patching up relationships after these accusations. The ones today climaxed and left the students defeated. There was the option for an appeal, and if I thought there was an advantage for the student, I'd recommend it. Today, I didn't believe that was a choice in either case. In unhappy circumstances like these, I tried my best to counsel the student—What are your options? What's the obvious thing to do? What do you want to do? What's the truth in what you're saying?

As I drove home and neared my lane, I slammed on my brakes so hard to stop, my Jeep skidded sideways on the dirt road. My heart pounded in my throat. *Sam! What the hell!* I rolled down the driver's window and hollered out into the evening. "Sam, come over here!"

My little rascal, standing in my headlights, turned his head, stared at me for two seconds, and darted into the forest opposite my driveway and down the hillside. I pulled into the lane, grabbed my flashlight from the glove compartment, and got out of the Jeep to search for Sam. My brain whirled in a state of cognitive dissonance. *How did Sam get out of the house? That was Sam, wasn't it?* A stream of worries rushed over me: *What if he doesn't come? What will happen to him out here?*

My blood pooled in my head, and visions of my pooch being torn apart by vicious critters—raccoons, bobcats, groundhogs, or bears—sprang up. My flashlight scanned the woods, my voice trembled, and I yelled out for Sam as I stumbled down the steep hillside. Out of nowhere, he ambushed me, running circles around me. I was between angry and grateful. I bent down, picked Sam up, and nuzzled him.

"Sam, you bugger. What are you doing out here? How the heck did you get out?" I asked as I struggled back up the hill and carried him to the car.

Sam started barking and scratching at the passenger window when we arrived at the house. I reached over. "Hey—hey, boy," I said, petting him until he calmed down. I turned off the ignition and sat staring at my home. Nothing I could see in the dark seemed unusual—no cars in the driveway, the living room light on a timer was on, and the front door closed. *Should I call Elliott or Craig? And tell them what? I found Sam outside of the house, and I'm freaked out?*

My pulse raced, and dampness formed in my armpits. *Get a grip, Suzanna. There's a reasonable explanation.* I grabbed Sam, got out of the car, and walked over to the house. I tried the front door. It was locked. It didn't appear jimmied. Still holding Sam, I maneuvered pretzel-like, put my key in the lock, turned it, and opened the door. Once inside, I put Sam down, flipped on the entry lights, hung my coat on the peg, and flung my purse in the corner.

Sam walked away, nose to the floor, snorting and sniffing. *Well, he's not barking; that's good. How did you get out?*

I turned and checked the living room. My stomach flew to my throat. I squeezed my arms around my waist to quell the pain. "Oh no!"

My shriek stopped Sam in his tracks.

"You bastard," I said under my breath as I walked toward the coffee table.

I grabbed the vase, pulled out the Campanella roses, and threw them across the room into the fireplace. I tossed kindling on the flowers, made a funeral pyre, and lit a match. I was beyond tears. A bomb went off inside my chest, and my blood boiled a river that raced through my body as I watched the inferno consume the bouquet.

After the blaze died down, I swallowed hard, picked up the poker, turned away, and scanned the room. Was Jonathan there? Was he watching me? I'd kill him.

I looked down. Sam was on guard by my side, eyes wide and ears up. I thought we were safe but didn't want to assume anything. I kneeled down and petted Sam. "Good boy. We're searching the house."

Our search found nothing. It wasn't that Jonathan found where I lived that worried me as much as wondering how he got inside. I re-examined the doors and windows. No one had broken the locks, and there were no signs of tampering. Even so, I wasn't safe. I phoned Elliott.

* * *

I paced the floor until the roar of Old Smokey blew up my lane like a hurricane. Elliott stopped his truck in front of my house, and I looked for him through the front room windows. Like a magician, he already stood at my front door.

Adrenaline drove me, and now it was dissipating. I opened the door and fell into Elliott's arms, almost to my knees. He raised me up and guided me to the couch, all the while doing a sweep of the surroundings. Shattered glass from the flower vase lay across the floor. I didn't remember doing that. The fire poker lay in the middle of the living room. I didn't remember throwing it there. The smell of vomit permeated the room. Was that Sam or me? I didn't remember getting sick.

After Elliott cleaned up the putrid mess and made a pot of tea, quieted now and in command of my senses, I told him what I found when I arrived home—Sam in the road, door locked, the vase of flowers on the coffee table.

Elliott made the rounds, examining all doors and windows. "Doesn't look like anyone has tampered with these. Someone got a spare key to the place, or the door lock was picked. Whichever, this place is not secure."

I didn't need much urging by Elliot to call the sheriff's office and file a report. After the deputy left, Elliott and I sat in our usual seating arrangement in front of the fireplace—Sam and me on the sofa and Elliott in the Mission-style rocker.

"What *is* the story about Jonathan? What's his profile?"

I had opened the door to Elliott's questioning by asking for his help. To be honest, I was relieved to give him the details. Elliott was a good listener and a questioner.

"What concerns you most about Jonathan?"

"Other than what happened today, what has he done that frightens you the most?"

"What is his usual mode of operation?"

"What do you expect he might do next?"

I answered his questions and filled in the blanks on what he already knew about my former husband.

"You should have been a counselor," I said after answering his last question.

"Well, in my business, being half detective and half counselor has its advantages," he said.

After running through Elliott's questions, my insides were empty, and my hands trembled at thinking of my vulnerability. "By breaking into my home, I'm angry with Jonathan, but his violation, his selfishness, his bullying supersedes that. I'm not safe. He is victimizing me all over again."

Elliott repositioned himself in his chair, reached over, and held my anxious hands. "I understand. I agree with you. I don't think it is safe here for you and Mr. Sam tonight. Okay with you, if I stay over?"

"I appreciate that, Elliott. The spare room is always ready for expected and unexpected company."

His eyes tightened. "It would be better if I did this like a stakeout."

I tilted my head. "Stakeout?"

"Inside, I'm at a disadvantage. Outside, I have a drop on anyone who approaches."

"You are the security guy! But the least I can do is make you a thermos of hot coffee."

"Make it hot chocolate, instead?" he asked with his shy smile.

For a split second, I surveyed him—a boyish bashfulness in a man's rugged body. *There's more to his story. In many ways, I know he's as vulnerable as I am.*

* * *

The remainder of the night was uneventful, that is, if I excluded the footsteps I heard pacing overhead in my loft. Now, they did not frighten Sam or me. This evening, the steps were light-footed—a woman's—walking in full-note beat from one end of the loft to the other. Their timing and spacing, slow and short, were contemplative, not anxious, strides. I fell asleep to the perfect rhythm of Susannah Simpson planning her escape from Johannes.

* * *

I was up early the following morning, anxious to get to my two top priorities—contacting a home security company and leaving a message at work I was taking the day off. After thumbing through the phone book searching for security companies, I went to the front windows to see whether I could spot Old Smokey. *Of course not! Elliott will hide somewhere. So much for asking him in for breakfast.* Ten minutes later, I heard the silver beast's familiar sound and went out to meet Elliott.

"I want a full reconnaissance report," I said, waving my finger at him.

Elliott laughed. "It won't take up much time, just about a cup of coffee's worth."

The two of us sat at my dining table, and my friend gave me the lowdown while we drank our coffees.

"Your right. Jonathan fits the profile you gave me. A real piece of nasty work."

I stared at Elliott, my lips separated. "What do you mean? How do you know?" I asked.

"Dudes like him like don't like to be left in the dark. What gets them off is seeing the results of their bullying. He was waiting."

My mouth dropped full open. "Where? Where did you see him?"

"After I left, I got to thinking like a bully—Where would he hang out until it was late, like around eleven o'clock, before showing up here again?"

My eyes must have looked like gigantic question marks to Elliott. "And? . . ."

"I drove down to the Old Mill Tavern and bingo! There was the Mustang."

My emotions swirled in a whirlwind. Blood rushed to my face from anger, and my stomach churned with nausea from fear. But my heart filled with gratitude for Elliott. "What happened?" I whispered.

"I radioed Steve, the deputy who had come out here before, and we set up a plan. I went in, spotted Jonathan, and sat at the bar about five stools away from him but keeping him in my line of vision. Steve came in on cue two minutes later."

"And then what?"

Elliott related the drama from a few hours earlier as if he were reading a play script.

"Hey, Steve! What are you doing out here? Come over and sit down," I said loud enough for Jonathan to hear.

Steve, dressed in his uniform, nodded to me and took a seat to my side. I noticed Jonathan had turned toward us. We had hooked him, as we planned.

"Up here patrolling, El. Had to check on a break-in up on the hill. Some predator is stalking his ex," Steve said just above a conversational tone.

I had Jonathan in my sight and saw an angry face studying us. I lowered my eyes and flashed them back up, letting Steve know that we had an eavesdropper.

"What kind of dude does that? Must be a real insecure son of a bitch," I said.

"Usually, they are El. Usually, they are. We'll be keeping a patrol on the place. Nothing I hate more than goddamn bullies and stalkers."

The bang of a beer glass on the bar counter made Steve turn around toward Jonathan and me to look up and stare at him.

"Something wrong?" Steve said to Jonathan.

"Nothing that a long drive to Buffalo won't cure," Jonathan said through clenched teeth as he threw a twenty on the bar.

Our eyes followed him as he got up, sauntered out of the tavern, revved up that Mustang, and headed down to the State highway.

I sat in stunned silence. *Oh, I bet hearing that exchange made Jonathan pissed.* I could see my ex-husband's lip curl and his fists clench. Jonathan hated being caught off guard, being out of control.

"What do you think?" I asked.

"What do you think? You know him better than I do."

I lowered my head and fought back the tears. "He's not done yet."

"What I figured too. We'd better get that security system in place today, and I'll ask the sheriff to keep a patrol on your place for a few weeks."

* * *

Friday, March 21, 1986. My twenty-eighth birthday. I met the day with excitement and couldn't keep my eyes off my wall clock, counting the hours until my birthday party.

"It'll be a shindig," Craig told me the evening before. "Invitin' the whole county. Bring on your happy face, best voice, and tappin' toes. It's about time you get goin' to town with your life."

"I love you, Craig Fitzgerald," I said before hanging up the phone.

"Well, you know I love you too," he said.

My hands rubbed the anxiety from my neck and shoulder muscles as I watched the clock tick the minutes away. Concern over Jonathan's next move overshadowed my joy as I sat alone in my office. I checked off the precautions I had taken. *The security system is working, Sam is safe. There will be no more surprises waiting for me inside my house. I'll be secure at night. But hell, what a way to live!*

There was another darkness intruding in my life I couldn't shake— the one that wouldn't be deterred by installing an alarm system. I sat at my desk, and my thoughts turned from Jonathan to the reappearance of the Dark Shadow—the one that made Sam sit alert, stare into the wall, and bark. The one that made me feel stalked and uncomfortable. Was the Dark Shadow Johannes's miserable spirit wandering my house? Like Jonathan, did Johannes persist in trying to control, bully, and subdue?

The previous evening, Sam's eyes had darted across the wall, the fur on his back stood straight up, and his growls became more guttural as the evening progressed. Messing with me was one thing, but making my dog anxious elevated my maternal instincts. I'd had it with the Dark Shadow, and I decided to apply some twentieth-century psychology to rid myself of its presence.

"Johannes, I know you're here. I acknowledge you, but I'm not your Susannah. That Susannah left long ago. You know that. Why do you punish yourself? By returning here, you harass yourself, not Susannah. You victimize yourself, not Susannah, when you come back."

I waited, my shoulders tense. Had I done the right thing?

Sam stopped growling, sighed, turned around, laid down on the rug in front of the fireplace, and went to sleep. The Dark Shadow, for the time being, was gone.

I went to bed and waited for the rhythmic, light strides I had heard the night before. But they did not return.

"Did Johannes frighten you away, Susannah?" I asked. "Or perhaps your absence is a decoy, enticing him from the house?"

I missed Susannah's comforting steps, but I did not forget their message. She urged me to take one small step and then another to garner the courage to purge Jonathan from my life.

* * *

A weird sense of someone watching me interrupted my thoughts of the Dark Shadow and my mentor's footsteps. I glanced up from my desk, and the familiar flirty smile from a man leaning against my open office door, arms folded across his chest, met my eyes. His ogling froze me to my chair and left me speechless. How long had he been there? How did he get in here? Betty? She wasn't here. She was helping Craig prepare for my birthday party. I was alone. So this was Jonathan's next step.

"I'm here to wish you a happy birthday, Bunny," he said, walking into my office and offering himself a seat across the desk from me. I stifled a scream while my eyes glanced across my desktop to my phone.

Jonathan glared. "You're not going to call the police, the sheriff, or whoever is the law in this backwater place, are you? After all, you don't want to let everyone know about all your personal problems, do you? Do they even know you are Suzanna Spencer?"

"A threat, Jonathan, is not what I'd call a birthday wish."

"I'm disappointed in you, Bunny. I went up to your house today to leave you a surprise. And what was I greeted with? A bunch of house security signs! Really, Bunny! You think those can keep me away from my true love? You gave me no choice but to come here where you work."

"You had other options, Jonathan. But you chose this one. Why did you come?"

His eyes settled on my neck, and his jaw tightened.

"You're wearing that thing again. That's why you came here. Came here to be near the Ohio hillbilly."

I breathed in the strength of my North Star—its points, my strengths, gave me courage. I was not his victim. I rose from my chair. "Leave, Jonathan. You're not welcome here. If you come back, the police, or sheriff or whoever the law in this backwater place will come and drag you out."

His weapons—the smirk across his face and the hate in his eyes— were impotent. He was not wise to my plan. This time, I had the advantage.

Jonathan got up, shook his head, turned sideways, and threw metaphorical darts at me before he left, hoping they hit deadeye.

My nerves were on a butcher's block. I locked the outer door to the office suite after he had gone and returned and sat at my desk, wishing I had a bottle of bourbon hidden in a drawer, like in the movies. I shook my head. What was I thinking? My office should be open to my students. He's gone for today.

I got up and unlocked and opened the door, and a student, needing my love and kindness, was waiting for me.

I smiled. "Come on in, Denise," I said.

* * *

Craig scheduled my official birthday party to start at eight o'clock, but he had insisted on hosting an earlier, more intimate dinner and gathering with only close friends.

"Be here by six," he said. "Goin' to fix you the best barbeque. And bring a little overnight bag. You and Sam Adams plan on staying over —that way, you can let loose and have all the beer your heart desires."

I got home by five o'clock, took a quick stroll with Sam for his predinner constitutional, and was back in the house thirty minutes later. Sam was eating his supper, and I was throwing together a few things for my sleepover—toothbrush and paste, makeup, change of underwear, clean flannel shirt—when I heard Old Smokey roaring up the drive. What the heck? What was Elliott doing here? My heart fell to my knees. *There's just one reason Elliott would be tearing up my lane. Jonathan must be hanging around to ruin my birthday party. Damn him.*

I came out of my bedroom, threw my overnight satchel on the couch, and rushed to the front door. I walked out on the porch and stopped. *Eleanor? Betty? Why are they here? They're supposed to be getting the dinner ready with Craig.*

My friends' faces came into focus: jaws set, skin flushed, eyes narrowed. Right off, I knew this was bad.

"What's wrong?" I asked as they approached.

They stopped. Three pairs of eyes cast down.

Eleanor and Betty hung back a few steps, and Elliott walked up to me and stood close. The color had left his eyes; there was no shy smile. He laid his hand on my shoulder.

"There's been a bad accident, Suzanna."

"Jonathan?"

"Um . . . no. It's Craig."

My eyes shut. Pressure filled my head, and I thought it would explode.

"What did Jonathan do to him?"

Elliott's voice was low and calm. "No, no. It has nothing to do with Jonathan."

I took in a deep breath, and I heard a trembling exhale. I looked at Elliott, my eyes asking the question I didn't want him to answer.

"Eleanor and Betty found Craig when they went over to his place about four o'clock. It looks like he fell from the roof of his cabin."

The roof. That damn roof. I knew in my gut last Sunday . . . I knew it! Why did I not say something?

I bit down hard on my lip, and the taste of blood flooded my mouth. "And?"

"He's being transported up to Rochester. I'm sorry, Suzanna. It's critical. We came by to let you know and to be with you . . . and to drive you up to Rochester if you want."

My heart pounded like a jackhammer and tried to escape from my chest. I turned away, walked to the edge of the porch, and leaned over.

My stomach flipped inside out, and nausea crept up my throat. *Hold it together. He'll be okay. He'll be okay. He's in the best hands. Hold it together. Did the world stop? How long have I been standing here like this? A second? Minutes? More?*

I turned and faced Elliott. "Let me grab my things and get Sam. I need to be alone. I'll drive my car and follow you, Elliott."

Our little caravan weaved its way down my lane. It was six o'clock. *My birthday party!*

I cried until I had no more tears throughout the hour-and-a-half drive to Rochester.

Chapter 30

REQUIEM

I sat in the pew, surrounded by two hundred mourners, but I was alone within myself. I listened to the tributes about his good life—courage, compassion, kindness, and love. But no one gave testimony to his hard life—that was a mental conflict too intense for a liturgy that celebrates a just God.

The priest grasped the censer, spewing a screen of scented smoke that seeped out of the sanctuary and suffocated me. Watching the cleric, costumed in a coal-black chasuble, sent waves of medieval darkness through me. It was as if Lucifer had come to officiate in my soul.

The celebrant circled the casket, swinging the metal vessel in hypnotic beats. One, two, three, the censer's gold chains clanked against each other over and over and over the pall-draped coffin. I closed my eyes to erase the image, but my ears heard. To the beating chains, the priest sang, *"Requiem aeternam dona eis Domini"*—Eternal rest grant unto him O Lord—over and over and over. The choir chanted the "Dies Irae" in Gregorian rhyme and rhythm, and my hands clenched, my blood boiled, and I screamed silently: *Screw Judgment Day!*

I willed myself into never-never land, away from the sickening sight. I spurned the supposition of a sympathetic Father, and instead, I searched for Craig's star: his handsome face, comforting voice, and gentle touch. I waited . . . for his last words, "I love you too."

Mon Ange, I see nothing. I hear nothing. I am nothing.

Silent rivers of tears streaked my face.

Mon Ange, how will I be anything but nothing now?

Chapter 31

TANGLED HEART

I walk to the front window of my home and gaze outside. It's been a month since Craig left me. I squeeze my hand, and I bite hard on my right index finger. I am hollow. I am punishing myself. The virginal blue sky begs me to dispel my depression, catch the breeze, and pull myself from grief's doldrum. My eyes meet my sweet Sam. Through mournful dark saucers, he tells me he has lost his bearings. He mimics me—he does not eat, does not sleep, does not cry, and does not feel joy. I know I'm not doing what is right for my faithful friend or for myself. Despite this, I fear the agony of untangling my heart is greater than the pain of staying in knots.

I touch my neck, and my fingers reach for my North Star. I clasp my hand so hard around it that the sharp points cut into my palm. I close my eyes and remember what Craig said long ago:

"Deep inside, though, I knew actin' out wasn't goin' to make me happy. To get on track, to feel better, I needed to know who I was and where I wanted to go. I ended up thinkin' the best place to start was to go back to the basics—give myself space and peace and let nature help me free my tangled heart."

My reservoir of tears is empty, but an ember still burns in my soul. "It's time, Craig. It's time for me to free my tangled heart."

* * *

The weeks after Craig's death passed at a snail's pace and in disbelief that he was gone.

There were no more Saturday breakfasts at the Slick Chick or Sunday brunches at his home.

No more easy conversations where we celebrated our successes.

No more friendly arguments about philosophies of life.

No more cheerleading and offering support in the challenges we face.

No more Friday evening hootenannies filled with frivolity, friendship, and affirmation.

Now, only "no mores" filled my world.

At times, I hated Craig for leaving me. *Why did you climb up on that damn roof? Why on that day? Why on my birthday?*

I listened, and if I waited long enough, I heard a smart-aleck reply. "So I'd always be in your heart, Suzanna."

Often I hated God. Merciful, my ass! Why did God allow bad things to happen to good people? Why did God allow such a waste of potential?

Other times, I hated myself. Why didn't I follow my intuition and warn Craig it was too dangerous to go up there? Why didn't I say no to such a big f'ing deal birthday party? Why wasn't I there with him?

Hate devoured my days until evenings turned into nights. Then I took comfort in Craig's voice as he tucked me into my bed. I lay on my side, looking out into the forest lit by the sparkling stars and shining moon. I replayed our last words to each other. I yearned for the scent of Craig's breath. I reached for the warmth of his arms around me.

I was grateful that in our last rushed phone call, I said, "I love you, Craig Fitzgerald," and he said, "I love you too." I wanted my words to travel with him into his deep sleep. I whispered them every night like a mantra until I fell into a shallow sleep, and, reawakening, I'd utter the chant over and over until the light of day appeared.

* * *

The shadows, pacing footsteps, and Jonathan gave me a month's reprieve. Even for these intruders, grief's shell was too thick to penetrate. Then on Monday, April 21, they broke their silence and pounced on me like ferocious beasts who haunt a stinking swamp.

"Suzanna, the dean wants to talk to you," Betty said to me on the intercom.

The red light on the phone console blinked, and I lifted the receiver and pushed down the button.

"Good morning, Bob. What can I help you with?"

"Got a few minutes?" he asked.

"Sure, I'll be right down."

"Nah. I'll come to your office."

I hung up the phone. *That's odd.* My dean's habit was for faculty to go to his office.

Bob walked into my office a few minutes later, but furrows between his brows had replaced his customary sparkling eyes and smile.

"I don't need to be a clairvoyant to see you're a bearer of some bad news," I said. "What's up?"

Bob sat down in the chair across from my desk. "Well, I'll be straight with you," he said. "The university president received an anonymous complaint that needs to be investigated."

The words used together—anonymous, complaint, investigation—raised my curiosity to its highest level.

"Complaint? What kind of complaint?"

"To be blunt, some creep, jerk, or whatever you want to call the person said you lied on your resume. Falsified your credentials, exaggerated your presentations, and accused you of plagiarizing articles."

My face went limp. *How far will that SOB go? I guess I've gotten the answer.*

"I don't believe a word of it, Suzanna. None of us do. It isn't the first time a jealous colleague, ticked-off student, rejected lover, or general nut case has done something like this to make life difficult or attempt to destroy a reputation."

I looked away. Was this real? My inner critic exploited the crack and went into high gear.

"It's my fault, Bob. All of it."

My boss jolted and sat up in his chair. "You can't mean these accusations are true?"

I cleared my throat, uncertain about how much I should reveal. Jonathan's abuse had escalated. It wouldn't be long until he hurt me physically.

"No, no. It's not what you are thinking, Bob. What I am responsible for is the choice I made in marrying such an unprincipled man. I'm ashamed to cause the university these problems. I believe my former husband is doing this."

Silence, except for the pounding of my heart, depleted the oxygen from the room.

"Tell me more about this ex of yours. Threatened you before? Threatened you here?"

I refrained from personal details and gave Bob the facts of Jonathan's continued obsession—flowers showing up at work, the break-in at my home, and Jonathan's surprise visit to my office on my birthday.

My boss frowned. "These are significant additions to the case, Suzanna. Our principal concern when we receive an allegation is to verify or disprove it. We don't investigate who sent it or why. On the other hand, if you believe the person lobbing these charges is someone who has come on campus and harassed you, that changes how we handle the situation. Such a person potentially puts the entire university community in harm's way. We might be able to expand the investigation."

"What does that mean?"

"We have resources here, investigators on retainer, and we can coordinate with law enforcement. They can look at things like postmarks, dates, evaluation of handwriting or typewriters, computer printers, copy machines . . . a whole range of tools. I'll give Elliott a call, and he'll get the process started."

I sat motionless, unsmiling, staring into space. I wanted to run from the room, fade into the background. "I am so ashamed and humiliated."

"Suzanna, you are not answerable for your former spouse's actions. Shame is a dangerous and greedy emotion that always wants more. There is no shame here, certainly not yours. Shame should not hold power over your life."

I looked away with knitted brows. Bob was correct; there was no shame here. I made a bad choice, but that didn't make me a bad person. This was Jonathan's shame and humiliation, not mine.

After Bob left, I took a deep breath and considered my options. *I'm accountable for what I do. Self-flagellate and assume Jonathan's blame, then I excuse his behavior. In a way, I become his accomplice.*

* * *

Elliott was standing in my office within an hour after my conversation with Bob.

"I guess you heard the news," I said.

"Yep."

"What happens now?" I asked.

Elliott lifted the chair from the other side of my desk, set it down next to and facing me, and hunched forward. It was a position I had seen him in many times in the rocker in my living room—a position of intent, concern, and support.

"Have you seen the letter? The accusations?" Elliott asked.

"No. I was floored when Bob told me, and I didn't think to ask about it."

"I need to make clear my role. My department doesn't assess the veracity of the accusations. That's the job of different departments on campus. We investigate who wrote and sent the letter to help protect campus safety. Does that make sense to you?"

I nodded.

"I have the letter, but before I show it to you, I want to hear how you are doing with all this."

"I'm not sure. I am defenseless. There is no way to confront Jonathan. With no evidence, he'd laugh in my face, call me nuts, hysterical, delusional. How can I get justice?"

"Having false stuff hurled at you face-to-face or in private is one thing . . . But having it made anonymously . . . Well, that's another thing. It's bullying, and either way, you are traumatized . . . But having it done in public . . . Well, I think it is much worse."

There was no shy smile. Here was the Elliott precise phrasing and the Elliott tone—confidential, careful, comforting. My lips curled upwards.

"Aah . . . What are you thinking?" he asked.

"I think you should be the counselor."

"I think someone told me that before and . . . that is debatable." He chuckled and let the sentence hang in the air and waited for me.

"Two years ago, I made a promise—I was going to free myself from my abuser's snare because my life and following my purpose were worth the fight. Let me see the letter, so I can finish off this fight."

* * *

The letter was typed on fine linen stationery. I recognized the paper.

> April 11, 1984
>
> Dear President McCullough,
>
> It's come to my attention that Suzanna Jordan has taken a position as the director of student affairs in the School of Allied Medicine. I have known Ms. Jordan for many years and throughout this time I have been familiar with Ms. Jordan's previous employment, education, and professional activities. I hold an academic position and have viewed her resume. I want to alert you to review Ms. Jordan's resume for any falsified information on her employment documents. This includes exaggerating her professional activities, such as holding elected offices with community and professional groups, and misconstruing the topics and dates of her professional presentations. In some cases, you may want to check if she plagiarized the works of others, and published these as her own.
>
> I hope that the above information is useful to you in your review of Ms. Jordan's qualifications.
>
> Yours truely,
>
> A concerned colleague

I lifted my eyes, looked at Elliott, and nodded. "It's his. It is Jonathan's."

"How do you know that?"

"First, it's the paper."

"The paper?"

"Jonathan used this type of paper when he applied for jobs after his residency. I know because I bought each of us a small box of it. In fact, you can check the resume I submitted for this job, and it will be on the same paper as this one."

"You said first. Is there something else?"

"Yes, it's those stupid punctuation errors."

"Which ones do you mean?"

"Jonathan could never distinguish independent from dependent clauses. I'd always have to correct his grammar before he submitted a paper. He'd neglect to put in a comma between independent clauses like here," I said, pointing to the mistake. "See. There should be a comma after the words 'many years' before the 'and.' Over here, in this sentence, he inserts a comma after the word 'groups' where there shouldn't be one. And after the word 'others,' there's another misplaced comma."

Elliott's shy smile crossed his face. "Smart detective work. It's not definitive, but they're clues."

"Oh, and one more thing. Jonathan could never spell 'truly' correctly."

"Makes sense that a man who isn't true can't spell truly."

* * *

Elliott offered to come up to the Honey Bear after work, and I took him up on it. I had been a hermit since Craig's death increasing my grief and punishing myself in a world of hate. Now I had a choice of going deeper, losing, and giving up on myself, or I could climb out of my self-imposed misery. Jonathan wasn't going to win. At least not without a fight.

"Come for dinner. I'll make you more than coffee," I promised.

The short trip home gave me time to unwind from Jonathan's latest bullying efforts. Driving through the quiet village, passing by the charming, wood-clad, white 1840s Greek Revival homes, and traveling up Hartsville Hill framed by dense forests felt like receiving a shot of Valium. This evening, I refused to allow Jonathan's dirty work to ruin this small comfort.

The roadside snowbanks had shrunk from their eight-foot glory in February to a measly one-foot height. Birds had arrived from points south and were chirping and cavorting in love dances. The local flora was starting to awaken, a snippet of green foliage here and there. Longtime residents told me not to expect Easter flowers, customary in Ohio, to peek through the earth until May, but I was still curious about what might pop up on the Honey Bear grounds.

As my Jeep climbed the steepest part of the hill, I thought about the garden plots Susannah Simpson described in her journal. *I wonder where she placed them?* I smiled, thinking of Craig. His eyes had lit up like fireworks when we found a folded piece of paper tucked in the back of the journal that laid out the plots.

"Wow, Suzanna. You have everything you need to replicate her garden. How cool is that? I'll come up and plow the land and help you plant."

"Yeah, and I'll do all the care, hoeing, and harvesting, and you'll be doing all the eating?"

"There's a reason they call you the Flower Girl."

"Yeah, Flower Girl, not Vegetable Girl," I said.

Now, none of that was possible to share with Craig. What the hell was life about anyway? What trickster set this all up, goading us with feelings of happiness and then stealing it all away? Was life just a junior high student's one big, failed science experiment?

* * *

It turned out to be a cathartic evening for Elliott and for me—secrets revealed, emotions displayed, and confidences shared. I knew Elliott wasn't a wine man—so I put his preferred beverage, beer, in the freezer for quick cooling after I arrived home. When I opened the case of brew in my pantry, my thoughts turned to the folk music Fridays at the Honey Bear. I looked at and fingered the cans of Bud as I removed them from their box. Craig's preferred brand, not my fancy Sam Adams brew. *When did I buy these? Yeah, it must have been right before March 14—the last party I had here.*

"It's not a fancy dinner—meatloaf, mashed potatoes with mushroom gravy, vegetables, and salad," I told Elliott when he arrived.

"It sounds like gourmet fixings to me," he said.

Fixings! I winced. It was as if a nail scratched across a blackboard. *No longer will I hear fixin's, doin's, comin', goin', thinkin'* . . .

"Did I say something wrong?"

"No, nothing at all," I said and moved on.

"What are your thoughts on this whole letter thing?" I asked, handing Elliott a can of beer as we sat down at the dining room table.

"Crazy shit. There's not much to go on other than what you provided. It was postmarked from a place in Illinois."

I choked. Half of my beer flew out of my mouth across the room. "Sorry for the mess, but that hits a chord."

"Really?" Elliott asked as he got up to collect a few paper towels in the kitchen.

"Thanks, Elliott," I said, and I took the towels and mopped up my mess. "Yeah, Jonathan grew up in northern Illinois. You don't recall the postmark, do you?"

"I think it was Crystal something."

"Crystal Lake?"

"That would be it. Still, it's not enough to prove anything. Wouldn't have anything around here with Jonathan's fingerprints? It would be a longshot to identify them since so many people have handled the letter now."

"I don't. But there's a diary that gives a rather good prescription to end Jonathan's harassment."

"What do you mean?"

"Eat up. Elliott. I'll tell you the plan over dinner."

* * *

Elliott turned page after page of Susannah's diary while we ate dinner, grunting at some entries and reading others aloud. His interest was intense and surprised me.

"I thought you were a man who liked facts and data. I never saw you as a person who would get into snooping and enjoying the personal musings of a woman who lived a hundred years ago."

"Aren't stories filled with facts and data? Sometimes you must dig deep to find the facts. Diaries and letters, on the other hand, can give you facts plus real insights into people. This journal here answers a lot of questions."

Elliott closed the diary and looked at the floor as if he were a guilty three-year-old. "I have a little apology to make to you."

My head jerked back. "Really?"

"Yeah . . ."

Silence circled us. "I promise not to shoot you or anything if you tell," I said.

His shy smile slipped across his face. "Mighty relieved . . . Do you remember our conversation with Dr. Golden at the party on New Year's Eve?"

I thought back. Why hadn't I connected the dots?

"Oh my gosh, Elliott. I had forgotten. Yes! Dr. Golden talked about Susannah. He mentioned there were rumors about her that weren't good. What could those be? From her diary, it looks like people were sympathetic to her cause."

Elliott tapped his empty Bud can in a nervous rhythm on the table. I got up and got both of us a second brew.

"What do you know that isn't in this diary?" I asked.

"Well, you know rumors. Best not to put too much weight on them."

"C'mon, tell me. What have you heard?"

He rubbed his fingers across his chin and gently fixed his eyes on mine. "Folks around here said she had disappeared under mysterious circumstances. Some thought her husband might have . . . you know, done away with her and her lover, that librarian fellow. Others thought she died in a tragic accident on her way to Ohio. I think the journal refutes the rumors. Which is a good thing."

I took in a deep breath. "Yeah, I think those rumors can be put to rest. The tragic accident part sounds more like something Johannes and his detectives manufactured. Like Jonathan, Johannes was all about saving face." I said.

"Tell me, what's this plan you think the diary lays out?"

"In one of my last conversations with Craig, he said not to concentrate on the similarities between Susannah Simpson and me, but instead look for what I could learn from her."

"And what has she taught you?"

"She taught me to use Jonathan's weaknesses to my advantage."

I outlined my plan step-by-step. Elliott added his know-how, and he updated Susannah's steps using some modern technology. When we finished, I grinned—I was going to lead my abuser into his own snare.

* * *

After dinner, we sat in our usual places in front of the fireplace, and for the first time in several years, I felt a blanket of ease fall over me. Jonathan bullied, blamed, accused, and threatened me. I had lost control of my life and my freedom. Craig loved and cherished me, but there was sadness mixed in—the barrier of his emotional scars was too strong to allow us the complete intimacy we deserved.

With Elliott, my hormones released a sweet elixir when we danced to "Franklin County Woman," but I had quashed wanting more of his touch. Now, an ocean wave rolled into our relationship I couldn't categorize, but the words *rising tide* popped into my head.

While we finished off our beers, Elliott asked me questions that peeled away my outer layers one after another until he reached my core.

"What kind of kid were you?"

"Joyful."

"And what does that mean?"

And I explained—my days of flower pilfering and ecstatic times with Jack, Mel, Ellen, Gary, and all the rest.

"What was your biggest desire growing up?"

"That's easy. To be a Rockette."

"Why a Rockette?"

And I explained—Christmas time in New York, the dazzling costumes, the intricate dance steps, and all the rest.

"What influenced you the most when you were a teenager?"

"I'm not sure. I think I was pretty rudderless until I met Craig."

"How *did* you and Craig become friends?"

"In my first class at OSU."

"That's how you met—how did you become friends?"

"Donuts and coffee. Lots of them." And I explained—the make-believe forest hike, the points of my North Star, the PTSD flashback, and all the rest.

"What was the tipping point with Jonathan?"

I gazed down. "It was when . . ."

"What about your North Star? What's the dream you're reaching for?"

"To flourish—be happy, have meaning in my life, be engaged in what I do, have good friends, and to live a joyful life again."

By ten o'clock, Elliott knew dancing and singing lit my fire and the reasons why my family lovingly called me Flower Girl. He learned Mel and Ellen were my childhood friends, Gary was my teenage love, and Craig and I were soulmates, each the other's unrequited love, the vestiges of Vietnam holding us apart. Elliott understood Jonathan was a shiny lure, who I fell for hook, line, and sinker. I told him when the tipping point with Jonathan occurred. The day when I should have expected a husband's support and love—the day Jonathan said I deserved to be raped.

"No one, Suzanna, deserves abuse. No one," Elliott said.

He put his hand out for me to clasp, and I reached for it. "Thank you for that, Elliott. Deep inside, I know that is true. Why is it shame, anxiety, and blame keep coming back?"

"Your brain remembers abuse, physical and emotional. It keeps a record, a tally of the hurts. I don't know how to erase the ledger of abuse, but we should never stop trying," Elliott said.

The evening conversation, though, wasn't all about me.

"You've asked me a slew of questions. Now it's my turn," I said.

"Well, I'm an open book . . . sort of." His smile didn't cover the fact that pulling secrets from him would be difficult.

* * *

Elliott Taylor allowed me to undo many of his riddles, and they revealed the man's truth. Some wear their hearts on the sleeves; Elliott wasn't one of them. There was more to the man than that. When I met Elliott, I sensed that character etched his face. As he told his story, the flickering light of the fireplace revealed what I already knew to be true.

Elliott's greatest dream was to be a history professor. "I loved history. I was a maniac for it. I wanted to bury myself in history books. Read first-person accounts. Learn from the past. Help others learn from the past . . . so they could do better in the present," he told me. Then he gave me the Elliott chuckle, a combination quiet half laugh and half grunt. "Guess that's why I liked Susannah's diary tonight."

I knew Elliott's philosophy about systems theory—that the whole is greater than the sum of its parts and when we subtract one part, we prevent the other parts from fulfilling their potential. It was also clear to me he didn't worry about things he had little control over. "Leave the past in the past and the future to the future," he had told me. But I didn't know he believed living a decent life is all the reward one deserves or should expect.

"No afterlife?" I asked.

"Don't know. Don't care."

I never knew anyone who had so bluntly challenged the existence of heaven, purgatory, or hell or why people should care about reward or punishment after death.

"Is this thought frightening to you?" he asked.

"Not frightening. Simply different. Something I've never considered," I said.

"I'm not religious. What happens after death isn't a concern for me. The thing that matters is the present and how I conduct myself every day. If I live a moral life, I get all the rewards I need now. If there is something later . . . well, I guess I'd call it a bonus."

"Where does that put God?"

"Beyond my pay grade."

I shook my head. "Easy way out! I take it that means maybe, maybe not?"

"I don't hold much with either scripture or dogma. People often use snippets from such stories and rules like a . . . free pass."

I frowned. "A free pass for what?"

"To reject free will—refuse responsibility for their actions."

"What do you believe? What's your guiding principle?"

Elliott looked down at the Bud can between his palms. "Guess the word for it is humanist. I'm neither here nor there with the existence of a deity. There's some power making this universe turn . . . but who or what doesn't matter to me. I believe people are flawed, but each has worth, free will, moral capacity, and can improve. In the end, we should judge people by the choices they make and actions they take—whether they respected and valued others and made this crazy world a better place."

The dimmed lights, glowing fireplace embers, and silence turned the Honey Bear into a monastery. I sat in a place of reflection, a medieval sanctuary, an asylum safe from the outside world.

"What about people like Jonathan? Like Fred? Like Johannes? Do they have value in your principles?"

"Everyone has value. But value is a funny thing, isn't it?"

"What do you mean?"

"Value can remain constant, increase, or decrease. People can squander their worth. Those fellows . . . they wasted their value, they decreased their value by hurting others."

"What happens to those who waste their value? Who hurt others? Do we forgive them?"

Elliott leaned back in the rocker and lifted his head upward. His eyes stared at the ceiling. "Forgiveness. That's a tough one. Can I ever forgive the man who killed my wife and son?"

Chapter 32

FORGIVENESS AND HOPE

I am the first to admit forgiveness and mercy are not my top strengths. After all, I never forgave red-haired Tommy Braden for biting me on the arm when I was four years old. I never forgave Jack's high school heartthrob, Clare, for trying to take my place in my brother's eyes. For that matter, I never forgave Jack for giving Clare his letterman's sweater. My heart bleeds with darkness in losing the most important person in my life, and I do not forgive God for his role in that. Above all, there is one person who ceaselessly digs a bottomless hole of self-doubt in my heart who has not received my forgiveness. I have not forgiven myself for so many poor choices.

* * *

Elliott's words sucked the air from my lungs, from the room, from the world. Time stopped, and I was not sure it could resume after he revealed the sadness I often caught in his eyes.

"It happened twelve years ago. Twelve years ago . . . I still can't say the date out loud."

My throat tightened. "Elliott, you don't have to go on."

He shook his head, his eyes closed. "No. Silence is death. I've been at war with myself for too long."

"It may be time to end that war," I said.

The thirty seconds of silence before Elliott answered was like suffering through an hour of doubt and uncertainty. Had I done the right thing, opening up a long, festering wound? Was he able to face its rupture? Was I prepared to face its puncture?

Elliott cleared this throat, and afterward, as he began speaking, his voice was difficult to hear above the crackling fire sounds. "I was coming home on leave for a few weeks. I remember sitting in the aisle seat of the plane, thinking I was finished with the service. We were out of Vietnam, but that didn't mean we were out of a war. There's always another war on the heels of the last one. I didn't want to see or take part in death and destruction anymore. I had made up my mind that I'd finish my tour and get back to what I wanted all along . . . being that history professor, being a real husband, being a real father."

The floorboards creaked in sympathy with Elliott's broken heart as the Mission-style rocker crossed the old wooden planks. Elliott's eyes were unmovable, fixed on the fireplace embers.

"What was it like for that young man to have made that decision?" I asked.

He looked my way. His shy smile appeared. "Good. It was freeing." He closed his eyes again. His breath was steady, his facial muscles relaxed, his lips parted. I hoped he was reliving a slice of happiness. He raised his eyelids and looked back to the fireplace.

"When I got off the plane in Rochester, I strutted through the gateway as if I owned the world. I had my duffle bag slung over my shoulder, my heart was racing, my palms were sweaty, and I was humming . . . humming the song from the Hollies about breathing air and loving someone."

He bit down hard on his quivering lips.

"I couldn't wait to get to the waiting room and put my arms around Penny and whisper the lyrics to her. But . . . it didn't happen. Penny and Seth weren't there. They were gone."

Elliott told me that holding back speaking the unspeakable truth about his trauma robbed him of his value, prevented him from being better, and denied him coming to terms with forgiving himself and forgiving the man who killed his family.

Penny was driving with their toddler, Seth, from Hornell to Rochester on the two-lane State Route 256 to meet Elliott at the airport. A delivery truck coming from the opposite direction swerved over the white dividing line into Penny's car. When the medics arrived on the scene, they removed the two occupants in the car—but they were too late. Penny and Seth had already died.

"The accident report quoted the truck driver saying he rounded a curve and there was sun glare. He said he reached for his visor and remembered nothing more before hearing the mangling of metal."

Elliott paused and took in a shaky breath. "There was more . . . He was under the influence. At ten o'clock in the morning, he was drunk."

What do I say? What can I say? I let silence do its work—the pop, pop, pop from the burning wood in the fireplace marked time until Elliot was ready to continue.

"I waited about a half hour at the airport, thinking traffic held them up. When they still hadn't arrived, I got this wrenching punch in my stomach—something was wrong. I called Penny's mother. She told me she and Penny had coffee that morning. Said Penny was bubbly and couldn't wait to see me. Penny left with Seth from her mother's home—an hour earlier than she needed so she'd be on time to meet me."

Eliott halted. The stillness of sorrow weighed down my shoulders, blinded my sight, and pained my heart. I bit my forefinger to stop my urge to sob.

"After the phone call, I waited at the airport, and a trooper came up and asked, 'Are you Captain Taylor?' That's how I found out. Losing that last goodbye crushes me most. Their bodies were so mangled, I was denied even touching them in death."

"I'm sorry, Elliott . . . How can I help you?"

"Help me? Suzanna, you've been helping me from the day I met you out there in the woods with Mr. Sam Adams."

My eyes drifted away, staring at nothing. "I don't understand. *How* have I helped you?"

"By letting me help you."

* * *

Trauma and loss had captured our souls, and Elliott and I were trying to find our way back to ourselves. Could we have normal emotions again? Had life bruised and permanently changed us for the worse? Could we see a path back to our "before" selves, our true selves?

"Silence is death," Elliott repeated. "But grievance against another is death too. When we make grievance our traveling companion, it blocks out light, distorts our perspective, and consumes our hearts until nothing is left. It is a fool's dream to believe that grievance, holding a grudge, getting even, will fill the hole loss has made in us."

"How do you deal with that, Elliott? How do you rip grievance into shreds and throw it away, burn it up?"

"By speaking the truth."

My brain went in circles, looking for an off-ramp to try to make sense of Elliott's remark. *Truth? The truth about what? About how crappy trauma and loss are? About people who perpetrate abuse?*

"What does the truth look like to you, Elliott?"

His smile returned. "Doing your counselor thing, huh?"

"Yeah, you caught me."

He turned silent as if the heartbreak made it too difficult to continue. The seconds seemed like minutes before I heard his voice again.

"I mean the truth in every respect. Accepting the truth about your feelings, your vulnerability. Admitting things will never be what they were. Acknowledging your loss. Recognizing the truth that your abuser is flawed."

"You're saying because Jonathan is warped by a weird Dr. Jekyll and Mr. Hyde thing going on, I should excuse him? Not demand justice for his behavior?"

I visualized the Elliott stance and heard a deep sigh. He scooted the rocker closer to me.

"We are obliged to condemn immoral behavior. We must always seek justice for harm. But those are different than holding a grudge, wanting payback, or pummeling a person. Did I want to beat the living shit out of that truck driver who killed Penny and Seth? You bet I did and more."

"Why didn't you?

"Killing the dude would never bring my wife and child back. The best justice, imperfect justice, was seeing him in court—tried, convicted, and sent to prison. Sending him to jail was better than murdering the guy and getting locked up myself."

"Was it fear that prevented you from killing him?"

"No. Not fear. Telling myself the truth stopped me. I went back and forth. I thought wiping him off the face of the earth would protect others. But ending his life would cause a loss for others—his family, wife, and children. I couldn't be a part of doing to him what he did to me."

"So you didn't excuse his behavior, and you sought and received an imperfect justice. And his flaws? Have you accepted them?"

Elliott got up, went to the fireplace, stirred the embers, and added more wood.

"That's a good question. Have I accepted his flaws?" he whispered, his back toward me. He played with the fire iron, shifting the wood mindlessly. He put the iron back in its holder. As he sat back in the rocker, I could hear the beat of his thoughts, playing like whole notes on a piano.

"I recognize his flaws, but I don't accept or excuse them. He had an addiction problem, and it controlled him. His flaws explain his actions. I think that's what compassion is—understanding people by standing in their shoes. That understanding gives me a semblance of peace. It takes away the grievance. It allows me to get on with my life."

My mind beat like the quarter notes on a keyboard. *Jonathan! His egocentricity. His low self-confidence. He told me something long ago I chose to bury. He was unsure of his parentage. Did he feel unwanted and unloved by one or both of his parents? Was there another betrayal? It happened in college. He said someone had rejected or betrayed him—another woman? He said people liked him for his trappings, his degree, and prestige but not for himself.*

"A nickel for your thoughts?"

I chuckled. "You're going to owe me a lot of money if I give them to you."

Elliott reached in his pocket and laid a dollar's worth of change on the coffee table. "There's enough there for twenty thoughts."

"You said something a while back about forgiving yourself. What is that about?" I asked.

"I guess it means not beating myself up about my past choices. It entails accepting responsibility for my behavior, understanding why I did things at the time, and learning from it. How can I have compassion for others if I don't have it for myself? How can I improve if I don't forgive and have understanding for myself?"

"What was it you had to forgive yourself for, Elliott?"

"Lost time, Suzanna. Lost time is one thing we can never recover. I lost time with Penny and Seth. I was off fighting a war, then re-upping after it was over. I had no choice in the first part—I was paying back my college debt through ROTC. But I didn't have to re-up. That was a choice. My wife and son would be alive today if I didn't make that choice."

"How do you forgive yourself for that?"

"I do better . . . I don't lose what I have now by ruminating, traveling back in time to change things, thinking about the shouldas, couldas, wouldas. I grab on to the moment, and I hope. I hope the moment I have now with you leads to another one. And that one results in another, and another. For each moment I have, I'm grabbing onto it, and I'm living it."

Chapter 33

FRIDAY, JUNE 13, 1986

*F*riday, June 13, 1986. Can it be another June 13? Two years. So short, it was yesterday. So long, it is a lifetime. *The early morning sunrays flicker on the pond's placid waters, and I raise my hand above my eyes to shield the penetrating brightness. I walk along the water's edge, pick up a few pebbles and throw them in, trying to make them skip over the water. Sam Adams barks at the spectacle, but he is not a water dog—no swimming or cavorting in the pond for him. I sit in one of the chairs on my little dock. Elliott made this little floating peninsula for me so that I could surround myself with the therapeutic waters.*

I look across to my gardens, and my flowers show me the endearing pattern of life. Elliott has helped me with these too. They join the pond, the forest, the meadow, and the Honey Bear house as my refuge and healing places. There is a plot for the vegetables, laid out just as Susannah Simpson would have it and another one for my kitchen herbs—basil, rosemary, thyme, lavender, mint, and chamomile.

But it is the flowers that connect me to myself and turn me into a child again. I've made a flower wilderness garden that challenges Monet, filled with pink, orange, yellow, lavender, and blue hues. I've added sunflowers —symbols of good fortune, vitality, and happiness—in a separate patch that will receive sunshine all day. Elliott and Eleanor say these are an oddity for the area, and they are as anxious as I am to see how they grow.

My thoughts move from my gardens to the plan I will execute today. It seems I must free myself from two men. As Jonathan stepped up his ugly tactics, the Dark Shadow has too, visiting me almost every night. I know it is Johannes—he feeds off Jonathan's energy. Today, their harassment ends. Who can deny the power of June 13—after all, it is the date Susannah Simpson and I chose to control our destinies.

"It's time, Craig," I whisper as if he's sitting at my side. "It's time I fulfill my promise. The fight to flee my abuser's snare and follow the guidance of my North Star is worth it."

* * *

The anonymous letter to the university president accusing me of falsifying facts on my resume wasn't enough for Jonathan. No, he had to go further. After the first letter came, two or three letters of the same ilk began appearing in my colleagues' mailboxes each week afterward. Carole and Barb were the first to receive letters from the unnamed sender. Then it was Art, Earl, and Fritz. After a month, all the school's faculty and staff received the letter or were aware of its contents. The situation was dire, and Bob called a school-wide meeting to refute such an unfounded attack on my integrity and ensure my coworkers that the administration was taking proper investigative measures. One of my biggest fears was the falsehoods would reach the students and undermine my credibility to effectively function in my position.

The more Jonathan increased his intrusion into my life, the Dark Shadow's visits to the Honey Bear became more frequent. My peripheral vision caught quick glimpses of a flickering shadow that popped up from nowhere and followed me—in the living room, kitchen, dining area, and bedroom—at any time during the day or night. I'd turn my head in its direction to catch a look—Poof! Gone! Was I going freaking crazy?

Sam's attention, though, seemed to latch on to the Dark Shadow like a fighter plane's radar. The pooch sat frozen in one spot, and for several minutes his eyes scanned what looked to me like an empty wall. Back and forth, his eyeballs trailed the wall. "Sam, you're seeing a ghost, or you've got a neurological issue. My bet is on the medical issue," I'd say to him. I made the flippant comment to comfort myself that there was a rational or scientific explanation for Sam's behavior. I preferred to believe these manifestations resulted from my emotions, negative energy, or anxiety rather than an otherworld psychic phenomenon.

Whatever the explanation, I was determined the swaggering spook would travel on its way along with Jonathan, and I had a team helping me and a cheerleading squad rooting for me. In her diary, Susannah Simpson had shown me how to spring Jonathan's snare. Elliott's shy smile danced across his lips when I told him the sting I had in mind to rid myself of Jonathan.

"You're going to have to have some brawn to help with the heavy lifting. I know just the fellows who can provide that," he said.

* * *

"What's up, Flower Girl?" my brother asked when I phoned him two weeks after I found out about Jonathan's letter mischief-making.

"He what?" Jack asked.

I read a copy of the letter's contents to Jack and explained the school's steps to investigate the allegations and discover the anonymous sender.

"Slippery son of a bitch. He doesn't make a direct accusation. Just says your resume should be reviewed carefully."

"There's more, Jack. Two similar letters have been sent to a couple of my coworkers."

"Has the postal service been contacted?"

"Yes, the university is taking care of that angle."

"If there were a way to determine Jonathan sent these, you could have an attorney prepare a cease and desist order. If he doesn't stop, then a court order. But you can't prove he sent the letters."

"That's why I'm calling you, Jack. To ask your thoughts on a plan that might get him to admit he's the one behind this."

"I'm intrigued. Go on."

* * *

My stomach tossed like a rowboat in an ocean storm during the two-hour drive from my home to Buffalo. I had performed on stage many times during my high school years. I was a counselor for four years at a performing arts summer camp. I knew acting techniques; I had practiced the art and developed the skills. Would such amateur performances be enough preparation for what I was about to try to pull off?

I had visualized and practiced my lines and moves for weeks. I was in control of setting the stage and arranging the props. I knew my part and the script. I understood how to interact and engage with Jonathan. Discarding my victim role, I was ready to exploit Jonathan's greatest weakness—his pride.

I arrived in time for Jonathan's open office hours at the medical school. With me was a private detective who was hired through my attorney's office in Hornell. Elliott's recommendations landed me the two best, no-nonsense backup members for my team who dotted every "I" and crossed every "T." My attorney, Frank, was the way I liked my airline pilots—graying at the temples. Frank's silver streaks assured me he had the knowledge and experience to handle any situation, not to mention his lawyering stereotype was straight out of *Anatomy of a Murder*. Nick, my investigator, was a cross between Rockford and Rambo; his presence screamed, "Don't mess with me."

It was Friday midafternoon. On that day and at that hour, I suspected there wouldn't be a line of students waiting to see Jonathan. Nick had phoned the department administrative assistant earlier in the morning and, impersonating a student, verified Jonathan would be at his desk at two o'clock. "Yeah, make sure he's there," Nick told her. "I've got to go on shift at three o'clock, and I must see him before then."

My nerves were in knots when I got out of the car in the faculty building parking lot. Flashbacks of Jonathan's bullying flared and sparked my stress hormones as if I were addicted to the pain of victimization. My heart raced, my palms turned sweaty, my gut thrashed.

Nick saw my chalk-white face, walked over to me, and took my hand. "You're going to do well, Suzanna. You're going to get the bastard."

I swallowed hard, took a deep breath, and focused on my goal. I reached inside my purse, pulled out a couple of Pepto-Bismol tablets, took them out of their wrappers, and popped them into my mouth.

"You know, Nick, these little pink pills are miracle workers. They got me through a lot of stage fright when I was a teenager. And in every performance, I hit it. I can do this."

* * *

Jonathan's fellowship was in medical education in emergency medicine. His training would prepare him for an academic and administrative role in curriculum design, administration, and education for clerkships and emergency medicine training. So it wasn't unusual he would have his own small office.

Nick and I checked the aluminum-framed staff directory board at the building entry. Jonathan H. Spencer III, MD 209. We looked at each other with reassuring smiles as if we were prepared to pull off a jewelry heist rivaling the one in *To Catch a Thief*.

We took the stairs to the second floor, and when we reached the hallway, it was as silent as a tomb. I went ahead to room 209, and Nick walked a short distance behind me. The click of my shoes echoed off the walls like a rumble of distant thunder and equaled the sound from my chest. Jonathan's office door was open. I stood silent, immobile when I arrived at the room's entrance, watching Jonathan unawares as he had often done to me. My blood boiled thinking of those times, and its heat ignited my determination. There is an old saying—catch a liar by doing and asking the unexpected. I reached into the bulky black purse I carried for the item that was going to free me from my abuser's snare. I felt for the rectangular metal object, and as I ran my hand over it, my courage rose. I pushed a button, heard it click, and walked through the open door.

Jonathan raised his head. His mouth dropped, and his eyes widened. He sat nailed to his seat.

"Suzanna! What are you doing here?"

"I'm here to see you," I said, articulating each word in a slow rhythm.

"Well, I'm busy," he said and averted his eyes, shuffling the papers on his desk.

I brushed aside his comment, walked into his office, and slid into the chair opposite him

He glowered at me, his face turning pink. "Well, you can't stay. I'm expecting a student."

"I won't be long. If someone comes, I'll leave."

He repositioned himself in his chair. His jaw tightened. His eyes narrowed. "What's this visit all about?"

I didn't answer. I figured the silence would make Jonathan lash out, and I was right.

"You refuse my flowers. You kick me out of your office when I come to see you. Really, Suzanna, you expect me to welcome you here, at my place of work, with open arms?"

"No, Jonathan. I don't come with any expectations but one."

He lounged back in his chair. His hallmark seductive grin crossed his face. "Well, I can't imagine what that could be."

Silence crept into the room like a thief.

"Well, damn it, Suzanna. Are we going to play a guessing game here? I'm not telepathic. Why are you here?"

"I'm here about some nasty letters. Letters that make false accusations about me, about my credentials, about supposed falsifications on my resume."

"How intriguing."

"These were mailed to my place of work—to the university president, to a number of my colleagues."

He sat up straight. He lifted his chin, and his eyes looked down on me. "What do these have to do with me?"

"I don't know. What *do* these letters have to do with you?"

His lip curled. "Of course, you'd come here to accuse me. It's always about you, isn't it? You're never to blame for anything. Ever think you've made enemies along the way? Hurt people who might want to get back at you?"

Does he actually think I'm still in his snare?

"Jonathan, I'm not saying you wrote letters that allege I falsified my credentials, plagiarized others, and exaggerated my accomplishments. You don't have the guts or courage to do that. You'd be too afraid of being sued, revealed, and humiliated. You're not a risk-taker. You can't handle direct conflict."

My ex-husband's eyes roved my body as if he were a hawk ready to descend. "You're crazy. I didn't mail any damn letters."

"What do you suppose a man would do who didn't have the intestinal fortitude to write his own letters? What would a man like you do, Jonathan?

I raised the stakes and stared the hawk in the eye. "He'd take the coward's way out—he'd get some clod to do it for him."

The room was a pressure cooker, and the release valve was about to blow.

Jonathan rocketed halfway out of his chair. He slammed his fist on his desk. The arteries in his neck bulged. "You dare to call me a coward? You dare to say I have no guts? You dare to say I lack intestinal fortitude? You don't know the half of it, Bunny!"

I slumped in my chair. I lowered my eyes. I manufactured tears and let them flow down my cheeks. I let the hawk think he would sink his talons into his prey.

"Oh yes, I got people to help me. But I was the brains behind it. I did the planning and the organizing—that's what a smart man does —then he hires out the execution. I paid the damn detectives to hunt you down, Bunny. I hired them to find out where you went, where you lived, who you saw. I had you tracked every day. I came to your house. I laid on your bed."

Fear struck like a knife between my ribs. Worry intruded on my acting, hearing the lengths Jonathan had gone, but it didn't overcome me. I stuck with it—I hung my head lower, I wrung my hands, I bit my lip.

"You think I can't do things on my own? That I must get others to do my thinking? Well, I'm not stupid like you. I didn't have to have anyone write the letters. I got someone to mail them, but I wrote my own damn letters."

I shook my head back and forth, and I tasted the salty tears draining from my eyes.

He got up, walked over, stood behind me, bent down, and put his face next to the side of mine. I felt his hot breath run down my neck and imagined his clenched teeth.

"Bunny, those letters don't accuse you of anything! They don't make any claims! They just suggest human resources do their job! There's no crime here. You should know that. After all, your father and brother are lawyers."

I said nothing. I looked into Jonathan's hollow eyes.

He backed off. His lips quivered.

Like a rabbit, I froze. My aim was to confuse my predator. This bunny was ready to spring the snare.

He stepped back, his eyes frantic. Did he believe he had revealed too much? Did he realize he confessed to something much worse than mailing anonymous letters—breaking and entering my home?

"You can't use anything I've said here against me. It's your word against mine. Believe me, you don't want the trouble I can cause you. Get the hell out of here, Bunny."

He walked back to the other side of his desk, and his eyes flashed up to the hallway. "There's someone here to see me."

I stood up. I walked toward the doorway, stopped, and faced Jonathan. My breath was even. My tears were gone. My head was held high. I reached in my purse and pulled out the rectangular black metal device. I clicked it, clicked it again, and then again. It started to play . . .

"Suzanna! What are you doing here?"

"I'm here to see you."

I stopped the playback and stared at Jonathan.

"Bitch!" he snarled, eyes bulging, nostrils flaring.

He began to move toward me, but he spotted the person in the hall-way. He halted and stood beside his desk.

"It's *your* words, Jonathan, against yourself. A copy of this recording goes to my workplace, another to Jack. The original stays with my attorney."

His brows pulled together. His eyes clouded. "Bunny, you promised you would never bad-mouth me. You lied to me. How can you . . ."

I raised my hand. "Bad-mouth Jonathan? Bad-mouthing is to criticize unfairly. I would never criticize you unfairly."

He cocked his head to the side. His eyes narrowed.

The wall clock ticked the seconds of silence like a heartbeat—one, two, three.

My eyes stayed on him.

"If you ever do anything to me—come after me, hire detectives, write letters, do anything to hurt me—all this harassment will be revealed, will be criticized fairly, including how you perpetrated it all through the federal mail. Using the mail, Jonathan, that *is* a crime. Breaking in and entering into a person's home, Jonathan, that *is* a crime."

He stepped back and swallowed hard—his shoulders slumped, the snarl was gone. In my eyes, his confusion was clearing, and reality was setting in. I had the upper hand, and I used it to my advantage.

"If anything bad happens to me . . . I slip on ice, I fall off a chair or down the stairs, my house catches fire . . . anything bad happens to me, you will be the first person the police visit. Erase me from your memory and your mind forever, Jonathan! . . . Because, believe me, you don't want the trouble I can cause you."

I turned and walked from the room. I passed Nick, standing in the hall opposite the open office door. I gave him a nod. He returned it.

I heard Jonathan say to the waiting stranger, "What can I do for you?"

My heart rate slowed. I walked through the hallway, and my shoes echoed off the walls like a distant rumble of thunder—click, click, click, click.

Chapter 34

A WELL-EXECUTED PLAN

I wait in the car for Nick. I don't want to imagine what is happening in Jonathan's office. I lay my head against the passenger-side window, and the afternoon sun filters through my closed eyes. I roll my head. I deserve an Academy Award! The pressure and the pain behind my eyes are beginning to evaporate. My legs still quiver. I'm somewhere between elation and collapse. Oh God, all I want is a chocolate malt!

* * *

Nick flopped into the driver's seat and closed the car door. "It's done!"

"I would have loved to have been a fly on the wall," I said as Nick started the engine and pulled out from the parking lot.

"He is a nasty piece of work—I'll give him that."

"That's what Elliott said, too. How did he take it?"

"Not well. But he'll abide by it."

I didn't have to coax Nick to reenact the script he and Jonathan played in my drama. His impression of a defensive Jonathan—cocky attitude, snarly voice, squinted eyes, curled lip—hit a home run.

I crushed a smile at Nick's interpretation of himself. His massive six-foot-four, two-hundred-twenty-pound frame, dressed in a casual blue button-down shirt, checked sports jacket, and navy blue trousers, matched his laid-back but no-nonsense presence. Nick's dry humor, off-the-shelf clothing, and masculine self-assurance must have driven Jonathan nuts!

"I walk into his office. He's flustered from his little chat with you. He's doing the power thing—standing behind his desk, shuffling papers, preoccupied. He looks up and says, 'What can I do for you?' Since he can't do anything for me, I don't say a word, and I walk over, fix on his narrowed eyes, and offer him the envelope."

Nick started laughing so hard he snorted, and he infected me, getting me giggling until the tears started flowing.

"Quit it, Nick. You're going to make me pee my pants."

"Well, hell! I don't want that kind of accident in my car."

"Then, get on with it! Did he take the envelope?"

Nick continued, peppering the story with dramatic grunts, snarls, and facial contortions.

"At first, he reflexively put out his hand, then jerked it back. I drop the envelope on the desk. He stares at me, glassy-eyed, and smirks. 'Who the hell are you? My wife's errand boy?' he says."

I held my breath. *A typical Jonathan insult. How did Nick handle that one?*

"I don't do well with put-downs. So I say, 'Nah. More like her hatchet man.'"

My eyes flew open. "I didn't expect that!"

Nick chuckled. "Neither did he!"

"I bet he didn't," I said.

"I love disarming bullies like him with the unexpected—the truth usually works," Nick said.

I gave Nick a sideways glance. "Are you really my hatchet man?"

Nick roared and slapped the steering wheel so hard I thought it might snap. "Only if you want me to be."

"Okay. Seriously, what happened next?"

"I stand there and give him my vacant-eye Rambo look. I don't say a word. Jonathan does a body scan on me. He knows he can't beat me in a physical fight. His only weapons are his smart mouth and swagger, which ain't working on me. He checks out the envelope and frowns. His eagerness gets the best of him. He picks it up, opens the flap, takes out the typed letter, reads that, and gawks at me."

318

I was on the edge of my seat as far as the seatbelt would allow, wondering whether Jonathan stayed in character. *Would he strike back? Would he threaten me?*

"He stands there, trying to use the silent treatment on me, to intimidate me, but the dude has a terrible poker face. Ever see the quiver in his chin? A dead giveaway he thinks he is cornered."

"I never noticed that telltale sign, Nick. Guess that's why you're the hatchet man, not me. Don't keep me in suspense . . ."

"Well, he fashions himself as some type of Sonny Crocket. He tosses the letter on the desk, shows me his snarl, and clenches his teeth. 'This stupid letter, this cease and desist, doesn't mean a damn thing. I'll deny I ever received it,' he says."

Nick gave me a dramatic pause and readjusted himself in his seat before reaching the drama's climax.

"I say to him, 'You should know all about stupid letters! But . . . you're entitled to your opinion . . . even if it is wrong.'"

Nick deserves an Academy Award too!

Nick smacked his lips, and his face said he went in for the kill. "Now, I can't wait for the finale! My eyes bore a hole into him as if they were power drills. I reach into my pocket and take out my recorder and switch it off. Jonathan's mouth hangs open. I shake my head and say, 'Some people never learn.' Then I turn and walk out."

"Wow!" I said, letting the word fulfill its potential to express my amazement and joy.

Nick broke my momentary euphoria. "How did you think up this sting anyway, Suzanna? How did you know he'd fall for it?"

"Oh, I had a good teacher. Her name is Susannah Simpson."

"Don't think I've met her."

"I'd hope not since she lived ninety-nine years ago."

Nick's eyes shot open, and he turned his head toward me. "You've got my attention. Go on."

I gave Nick an abbreviated account of how I had bought Susannah's diary, forgot about it, and how it resurfaced. I explained the parallels between Susannah and myself: we shared the same first name, worked in academia, married abusive men with identical first names who were physicians. We fled our husbands, but they tracked us down, and we lived in the same home outside Alfred Station.

Nick chewed on the inside of his cheek and grunted. I couldn't figure out if he thought I was pulling his leg or not.

"It's as if the other Susannah and I traveled on parallel tracks of time, separated by precisely ninety-nine years."

"You're not going to tell me this other Susannah came in a dream and told you how to put together this scheme, are you?"

"No weird dreams, no seances, or talking with the spirits. Susannah gave me the idea in her diary."

> Saturday, June 13, 1885
>
> Johannes's weaknesses have undone him. I am sure he will not bother me again. I laid the trap using his pride against him and getting him to admit his devious ways in writing. Now, there is a record that he cannot deny. He does not want me to make this public. It would destroy his good name and career. My dear brother, George, was my co-conspirator. George told Johannes he did not believe his lie that I was in New York City. George told Johannes, "You're not smart enough to find my sister." This resulted in a big argument. George said, "If you're so smart, Johannes, write to my sister and tell her what you have done. That you have found her. How you went about locating her. But you're a coward and a bully. You can't do that."
>
> The letter I expected from Johannes has arrived. In it, his arrogance and self-importance are on stage. He writes:
>
> *"Your silly brother says I can't do things on my own, that I couldn't find you. What do he and you know? I have found you! I hired detectives to track you down. I will never leave you alone. You can never run from me. I will kill you before I let you go. You will come back to me, or I will kill you. I am no coward."*

Today, I returned to Corning. My lawyer and I confronted Johannes at his work with the letter. Johannes is undone. My lawyer will use the letter against Johannes if he keeps determined to trace me. My lawyer warned Johannes. He cautioned Johannes that if anything untoward happens to me . . . I slip on ice, I fall off a chair or down the stairs, my house catches fire . . . anything like that happens to me, Johannes will be the first person the police visit. My lawyer told Johannes I can ruin his reputation. "Erase Susannah Simpson from your memory forever, Johannes," my lawyer says.

In sadness, I leave my sweet cottage soon. Even with my lawyer's assurances, I am safer putting as much distance between Johannes and me as possible. But I look to a new life ahead with my dear Mr. Brown. Next week, I go to the bucolic countryside of Granville, Ohio, where I take up a position at the Young Ladies' Institute there, and Mr. Brown takes up an appointment at the college there. I am now free to live a whole life of true happiness.

I leaned the side of my head on the car window, looked out, and joined the clouds in flight. Was it over? Could it ever be over with someone like Jonathan?

Wondering is lost energy. Once we waste it, there's no regaining it. As Nick cranked up the speedometer, the roadway became a metaphor for my life. *This has just been an off-ramp; I have a lot more traveling in front of me. Drive as fast as you can.*

Chapter 35

A LIFE WORTH SAVING AND LIVING

I
t's Saturday. I'm at my Pondering Place, sitting on the edge of the dock,
swishing my bare feet back and forth in the cool, calm waters of my pond.
Sam Adams sprawls out next to me, taking in the late afternoon sun's rays
with no care disturbing his breathing and occasional snore. It's a month, shy
one day since I sprung my abuser's snare. The past four weeks have given me
the peace, time, and space to consider my journey following the guiding light
of my North Star.

* * *

Four weeks after the showdown with Jonathan, I found myself in a psychological and emotional space to reflect and assemble the patchwork quilt of my life into something meaningful. I pondered how pieces came together in a person's life, how bits collided together and changed how the whole became greater than the sum of the parts. I guess that's what Elliott called systems theory. Still, I was confused about how choice fit in.

Some philosophers believe our lives are the sum of our choices. If so, what did that look like on a number line? Did choices consist of only whole numbers? Could they be fractions or decimals? If I measured my life by adding up my choices, what number did I give to the choice of my first coffee date with Craig? What number did I assign to the choice of marrying Jonathan? What number did I give to my choice of being an academic counselor?

Forget the number line—I could segment my life into good and bad choices. Perhaps I could assign weights to each choice within the two categories and see what their sums equaled. Wouldn't that lead me into a schizophrenic world with life a constant battle between regret and joy? Are our lives were more than the sum of our choices?

Jack once said a person's success depends upon their choices and what they learn from them. Learning from my choices and then doing better —wouldn't that be a solid bedrock for conducting and measuring my life?

If Craig were with me, he'd push me to think deeper. "Handy slogan," he'd say. "Isn't there more? Shouldn't there be a *how* in there somewhere? How do you learn from your choices? How do you do better?"

I asked myself those questions as I sat beside my pond. I laughed and shook my head. Either Craig was a good teacher, or I was a good student, or maybe it was both. The how begins in knowing what makes me tick. Knowing my strengths, being clear on my values and purpose, being curious about my behaviors and how I can use these to improve myself and the world around me.

Yes, those were part of it, but not all. I realized there's more to my life than the sum of my choices or knowing my strengths and applying them to live my purpose. It's something Elliott said. *Leave the past in the past and the future to the future—live each day in the present.*

I let the sun's warmth cradle me and the cool pond water splash on my ankles. *All the wise people in my life—Lillian, Robert, Gary, Craig, Elliott, Mel—have given me a map. It is so simple. Why has it taken me this long to understand it? Life is a flow and connection of moments. I can do the* how *by living each day to its fullest, looking for and being curious about new things without judgment, seeing myself in others, having concern for them, and having respect and love for myself.*

I looked toward my gardens. The moment was delicious! Flowers, vegetables, and herbs lived together without conflict. My house was filled with one bouquet after another, and a delightful fragrance saturated every room.

I reached up to touch the flower wreath on my head. I was four years old again! I took a deep breath and sucked in the energy from my sunflower garden. It was a tribute to Craig and the gifts we gave each other in our quests following our North Stars. It reminded me of the qualities Craig saw within me—strength, sweetness, sincerity, spiritedness, selflessness. Seeing the sunflowers growing filled me with pride. I was impatient for the golden spectacular to arrive in a few weeks so I could be the Flower Girl drifting among those gorgeous giants that Craig imagined and drew.

I gazed into the distance. *What now, Craig? I'm listening for your voice in my Pondering Place. What now, Mon Ange?*

I closed my eyes. From nowhere, Craig's breath glided past me, and his voice floated through the rustling leaves.

"Get goin' to town! Live a better version of yourself. Follow your North Star. Get goin' to town and live your life."

It's so simple. Thank you, Mon Ange.

* * *

I heard Old Smokey approaching, and I shook my head to awake from my meditation. I saw the familiar silver truck coming up my lane, and I strolled from my Pondering Place to meet Elliott at my front door. He wore his shy smile, and his eyes followed me as I walked toward him.

He shook his head up and down. "It's lovely."

"Lovely?"

He pointed to my head. "The flower arrangement. The wreath. It suits you."

"That's why I'm Flower Girl."

"Okay, Flower Girl, I have a surprise for you."

"A surprise?"

"Yeah. A little something I made. Belated housewarming gift."

I couldn't imagine what he had concocted. "Well, where is it?"

He nodded toward the truck.

"Okay, what is it?"

"Come over and see," he said.

Elliott and his short sentences!

We gave each other side glances and smiles as we walked to the truck. I was like a child waiting for her birthday gift. I stopped beside Old Smokey, and Elliott made me wait for my gift.

"Do we need a drum roll?" I asked.

"Um . . . Well, you could do that."

I performed my version like I was in a vaudeville show—hitting my hands on my thighs, adding a couple of two steps, waving my arm at the truck, plastering a big smile on my face. Sam got in on the act, barking and running in circles.

Elliott chuckled. "Impressive," he said and went to the bed of the truck, pulled out the surprise, and showed it to me.

"Oh no! Elliott, I love it! You made this?"

Elliott puffed up his chest. "Yeah, I did. Kind of a hobby of mine. Thought it was about time, you know, that the Honey Bear had a sign."

Elliott's eyes sparkled like water flowing over pebbles in a stream. "Welcome to The Honey Bear!" the sign said. I took a deep breath. It was the most beautiful, burned cedar sign I had ever seen.

"You know what's strange? I never did read anything in Susannah's diary about beehives, honey, or bears," I said as I ran my hand over the perfect lettering surrounded by silhouettes of a bear, a beehive, and flowers.

"Guess that's called a mystery still to be solved or a story to be made. Maybe that bear and those bees will decide to show up now," Elliott said. "Come on. I brought my tools. Let me put this thing up for you."

We looked for the best place to hang the sign.

"How about here? Right near the front door?" Elliott asked.

I stepped back and squinted. "Perfect, but a little lower—all my guests aren't over six foot!"

Elliott got to work and put the sign in place, and then we stepped off the porch and admired my friend's handiwork.

"Plowman, artist, carpenter . . . What other talents are you hiding from me, Elliott?

"Me to know . . . and maybe you to find out!"

"Hey, El and Suzanna," someone called to us.

We turned around and saw a man and woman holding hands as they walked up the Honey Bear's lane, laughing and nudging each other. I sure knew two people in love when I saw it.

"I didn't think Barry Callahan had a wife. Elliott, do you know the woman who is with him?"

Elliott's eyes almost fell from their sockets. "Why, I'll be dammed! It couldn't be! But it sure as hell is! It's Luci."

I sized up the woman as she came closer. She looked about the same age as Barry and Elliott, with a gorgeous smile, delicate features, and shoulder-length brown hair. But as she came closer, it was her eyes that were her defining feature—expressive, rich, milk-chocolate eyes. I liked her at first sight.

Elliott opened his arms and smothered Luci in a hug. "I never gave up hope we'd see you again," he said.

Barry did the introduction. "This is my, um . . . my soulmate, Luci," he said. We just finished a picnic lunch in the meadow behind my folks' house. I wanted Luci to see your pond if that's okay."

Soulmates! The word burned through my heart. "You are always welcome at the Honey Bear. Stay as long as you like . . . the moon-beams shimmering on the water are marvelous!"

The couple didn't tarry for small talk, and Elliott and I watched them head toward the pond, hand in hand. Was Luci the heartache I heard in Barry's voice many months ago? Was she the one Barry said dis-counted coincidence like me and believed random acts could coincide and produce something curious?

Before I could ask more about the lovers' story, Elliott broke into my thoughts.

"Um . . . there's something else, Suzanna."

"Something else?"

Elliott got into his Elliott stance.

I squeezed my hands together and waited.

"How about, Suzanna . . . How about dinner and dancing? How about going to town with me tonight?"

My heart skipped a beat. I fixed my eyes on Elliott and swallowed hard. "Is this a date?"

"Yeah . . . Yeah, it's a date."

I tipped my head and grinned.

"All righty! Let's get going to town."

Chapter 36

EPILOGUE

I use the word "progression"—advancement, development, improvement—in describing my journey. These are the stepping-stones that guide me on my self-discovery path. My journey has been slow and arduous, executed through perseverance through which I have gained self-confidence and agency. My goal is to discover, savor, and leverage what's best in me for a flourishing life, a life that was worth saving and is worth living.

I view my continuing journey as an open highway crisscrossing the countryside of my beloved home and adopted states. Like the scenic and undulating Ohio and western New York hill country, there are ups and downs. The challenges are tricky, but their unpredictable nature sustains my interest in seeing what's around the next curve. When it gets too risky, off-ramps take me on interludes where I can explore, discover, frolic, and rest. On these forays, I'm playful and skip and run with open arms as a child. I laugh, and I am as free as the breeze whisking over the Buckeye State prairie grass. When my curiosity is satisfied, on-ramps return me to the highway. There I accelerate to speeds that boost my desire to consume more and more miles of uncharted territory as fast as I can.

My philosophy of life: The road is as long and as thrilling as you make it. Go slow, and the ride is short and boring. But go fast, and the trip is expansive and enthralling. Some may say this is life in the fast lane—I think this is life in the best lane.

Flower Girl

Made in the USA
Monee, IL
12 January 2022